An Unexpected Bo

The Cowboy and

To Listen to Janette's audiobooks for free, subscribe to her audiobook channel on YouTube here:

https://www.youtube.com/channel/UCh0_trjYz3T_Hd72bM0qk_Q

THE WIZARD'S MARK

JANETTE RALLISON

OTHER TITLES BY JANETTE RALLISON/CJ HILL

Adult romantic comedies

An Unexpected Boyfriend for Christmas

The Cowboy and the Girl Next Door: Wyle Away Ranch Book 1

My Fair Lacey & A Perfect Fit

How I Met Your Brother

Covert Kisses

Masquerade

What the Doctor Ordered

Her Ex-Crush Bodyguard

A Longtime (and at One Point Illegal) Crush

A Longtime (and now NFL player) Nemesis

Medieval Fantasy romance & adventure

The Wizard's Mark

YA fiction

Son of War, Daughter of Chaos

The Girl Who Heard Demons

Revenge of the Nerd Goddess

Just One Wish

My Double Life

Life, Love, and the Pursuit of Free Throws

Playing The Field

The Wrong Side of Magic

My Fair Godmother

My Unfair Godmother

My Fairly Dangerous Godmother

All's Fair in Love, War, and High School

Blue Eyes and Other Teenage Hazards

Revenge of the Cheerleaders

Fame, Glory, and Other Things on my To Do List

It's a Mall World After All

How to Take The Ex Out of Ex-boyfriend

Slayers (under pen name CJ Hill)

Slayers: Friends and Traitors (under pen name CJ Hill)

Slayers: Playing With Fire (under pen name CJ Hill)

Slayers: The Dragon Lords (under pen name CJ Hill)

Slayers: Into the Firestorm (under pen name CJ Hill)

Slayers: The Making of a Mentor: A Tor.Com Original (under pen name CJ Hill)

Erasing Time (under pen name CJ Hill)

Echo in Time (under pen name CJ Hill)

If you like audiobooks, try:

Just One Wish audiobook

My Fairly Dangerous Godmother audiobook

How I Met Your Brother audiobook

Erasing Time audiobook (under pen name CJ Hill)

Echo in Time audiobook (under pen name CJ Hill)

Masquerade audiobook

What the Doctor Ordered audiobook

My Double Life audiobook

Her Ex-crush Bodyguard audiobook

Covertly Yours audiobook (novella)

To everyone who loves the Middle Ages. (The historical period, not the time of life—although being middle-aged, I'm finding, has its benefits too.)

Stop raising your eyebrows. Some people live to be one hundred and sixteen. I'm totally in the middle of my life.

Also, special thanks to Cathy Morgan, Marina Gardner, Suzi Janda, and all the ARC readers who took the time to point out typos and grammar mistakes. Without you, my genteel ladies would've been gentile ladies, one character would be wearing breaches, and another's stomach might wretch on the floor. Quite a different story. Thank you so much!

CHAPTER 1

$\mathcal{T}$he most vexing part about being an invisible thief was that if I met my demise during a mission—this mission, for example—my friends would have no way to retrieve my body or even know exactly what had befallen me. The jutting stone wall of Barviel Castle was slippery in places. If I fell while scaling it, no one would notice my broken body heaped on the ground.

I probably thought about ways to die more often than was healthy for a young woman of my station. Most noblewomen concerned themselves with safer things, like embroidery and finding husbands.

But then I, Lady Marcella Thornton, wasn't a real noble-woman, not one born with a title. I owed the renegades for my escape from the lowborn rank of a servant. I repaid them with theft, in this case, a scroll that would reveal the location and number of the king's troops around the border of Marseden. The renegades frequently took refugees from the servant class to that country, and they liked to avoid troops whenever possible.

I moved upward slowly. One hand in front of the other, one

1

foothold, then the next, scrabbling up until I was level with Lord Bettencourt's balcony. I wished I'd brought a hook for the rope in my pack. That would've been the sensible thing to do, but hooks were noisy, and, once something was more than two feet away from my body, it became visible. So, I'd determined to scale Barviel Castle unaided. The climb hadn't appeared that difficult from the ground.

Foolish overconfidence.

I needed to grab the side of the railing. If I missed, if I lost my balance, I'd fall to my death.

Instead of lunging for the balcony, I stayed where I was, clinging to the wall. Death was such an unpleasant thing to consider.

From a place in my mind that I could never completely banish, I heard Ronan's chiding voice telling me that nerves would be my undoing. Back when we were children, he would tease me and make a game of whatever I feared until my fright seemed ridiculous, and I was forced to act just to silence him.

I paused and looked for a bit of humor to distract me. If I fell to my death, at least my sprawled invisible corpse might trip soldiers. Of course, eventually, they'd throw a cloak on top of me, see the outline of a person, and carry my body to Lord Bettencourt's wizard for a disclosing spell. If that was the case, I hoped the soldiers found me before I'd decomposed to some gruesome state. I have many faults; vanity is one of them.

I let go of my hold on the stone and practically flung myself at the balcony. I grabbed the railing and hauled myself over. My landing wasn't as graceful or as silent as I'd planned, and the fear of plunging to my death was immediately overtaken by the fear of discovery.

Had the noise awakened Lord Bettencourt? I crouched, still as a gargoyle, staring at the balcony door and straining to hear any sound from the room.

If I rushed inside and put a dagger into the lord's throat, he wouldn't be able to call his guards. I could take the scroll and flee. If, however, Lord Bettencourt managed to alert his guards, his wizard wouldn't be far behind. A disclosing spell would erase my invisibility and leave me vulnerable.

Besides, I'd never killed a man and didn't fancy taking up the habit tonight. Cook Lindon, who'd been a mother to me after mine had died, told me that when murderers passed out of this life, they were cursed to walk the dark places of the earth, always trudging, never resting.

I'd walked enough dark places already.

No noises came from the room: no bark of a dog, no sound of stirring.

My first piece of luck. My second was that not even the smallest magical protection guarded the balcony door. Lord Bettencourt was either careless or optimistic in supposing the sheer castle wall wouldn't accommodate climbers. Well, perhaps most people wouldn't attempt it, but I'd grown up scaling the walls of Docendum Castle.

I pulled out my unlocking charm, a small wooden horse I wore on a string around my neck. Back when Ronan was thirteen, he'd whittled it while memorizing spells. He didn't think the horse was well-made, and I'd had to rescue the figure from the kindling pile.

I uttered the words of the unlocking spell and tapped the horse against the balcony door. The figure thinned and lengthened, changing into the form of a key. I opened the door and slipped inside.

The coals in the fireplace burned low, but a wizards' orb sat on the table, throwing out just enough light to see by. A large four-poster bed dominated the room, its dark wood carved into elaborate peaks. The curtains, tied back, revealed the bed was empty and the blankets undisturbed.

The lord was quite late in retiring to his chamber. Probably out gambling, drinking, or visiting a mistress. I thanked whatever vices had called him away. Stealing from an empty room was much easier.

Alaric, who was the one who gave me these assignments, had said Lord Bettencourt kept his documents in a small wooden chest with a brass lock. I wouldn't have much luck searching among Lord Bettencourt's belongings in the room's low light. I pulled my finding charm from my pocket, a thumb-long shell bleached white with hints of sunrise orange at its tips. Another of Ronan's gifts.

Sentimentality is another one of my faults.

I held out the shell and whispered the words of the spell to make it glow. "Find a wooden chest with brass fittings."

At once, the tip of the shell turned in my palm, pointing to the door of an adjoining room. I padded there and entered a dressing room. The shell pointed toward the man's wardrobe. It might not be the scroll's hiding place. The wardrobe was also made of wood and had a brass lock. Finding charms had their limitations.

I changed the horse into a key and opened the wardrobe. As I slid the charm back into the neck of my tunic, I wondered what Ronan would think of me using his gifts as wizards' charms. He'd no doubt be angry. But then I suppose that was the point of choosing them. Pettiness is another one of my faults.

Although, in this instance, such pettiness bit me rather than Ronan. Every time I stole something, I thought of him. Wherever he was, he most assuredly wasn't thinking of me.

I pushed aside robes trimmed with the fur of some unfortunate animal and silk tunics so smooth they felt like water running over my fingers. I didn't expect to find more than the court's latest fashions, but there in the back corner was a chest, a stout wooden thing that seemed to be squatting defensively, waiting to snap at my hand.

Not a very secure hiding place for documents, but the choice showed that Lord Bettencourt trusted his chamberlain. His servant must know its location. Lord Bettencourt might blame him when the box went missing.

I picked up the chest, ready to slip it into the pack slung on my back. Then I thought again of the chamberlain whom Lord Bettencourt trusted so much that he left his lockbox amongst his robes. I knew nothing about the chamberlain except he wasn't working with the renegades, but that didn't necessarily make him pro-loyalist.

Some servants were near enough paying off their servant price they didn't want to risk trouble. Others had family to worry about. Some didn't believe change possible. And maybe it wasn't. What could any number of renegades do against the king and lords who not only commanded armies but had wizards at their beck and call? I was either an optimist or a fool to have joined their cause, or perhaps just so angry at wizards that I was bent on my own destruction.

I unlocked the box, rifled through its contents, and found the almost finished list of the provisions Lord Bettencourt would shortly send to the king's troops. A very nice record of where those men were.

I ought to take it and run. The chamberlain wouldn't be accused of opening a locked box. Unless that was, he knew where Lord Bettencourt kept the key. I sighed and trudged back into the lord's bed chamber.

A desk stood against one wall with pens and an inkwell. A stack of parchment, edges curling, sat in the middle. I pulled my wand from my pocket. Unlike most wizards who used polished wood, ivory, or even silver to hold their enchantments, my wand was a knitting needle. Such a thing in my pocket, along with its unmagical companion and a small ball of yarn, raised no suspicion.

I enchanted the pens to copy the words of the scroll. It was an imprudent risk, taking extra time, but at least I wouldn't lay in my bed tonight wondering about the fate of the chamberlain.

And besides, this way Lord Bettencourt wouldn't know the troops' locations had been leaked.

Time plodded on. I'd brought bits of jerky in case I needed to bribe any dogs. I nibbled nervously on a piece. The pens finished their work and dropped dramatically onto the desk like footmen shot by arrows. While the ink dried, I returned the scroll to its chest. Finally, I could leave.

I'd just relocked the wardrobe when I heard a door swing open.

I bit back an oath and whispered the counter spell to extinguish my shell's light. Fortunately, no one could see the light from the bed chamber, but I still had to retrieve the copy of the scroll from the desk.

A man, his voice slurred with drink, tromped into the room. "You ought to be thankful I've chosen you. It's an honor."

The sound of a woman crying followed him. So, he hadn't been with a mistress. At least not a willing one. Lord Bettencourt was the sort who forced himself on the women folk in his castle.

I tiptoed into the bed chamber.

Lord Bettencourt stood by the fireplace. He was a middle-aged man with a graying beard and a stomach that strained against his embroidered tunic. He threw a log onto the fire and jabbed the embers with the poker. "We'll have it warm in here soon enough."

Flames flickered around the wood, lighting the area. A scullery maid, judging from her dingy gray dress, stood trembling in the center of the room, head bowed and weeping. She didn't speak and that somehow made her presence here worse. It was as though she knew pleading wouldn't matter.

And there I was, an unwilling witness to this event. Evidence of my crime lay on Lord Bettencourt's desk, although I imagined he was too drunk to notice such things. I ought to scoop up the parchment and take my leave while he was occupied.

I couldn't risk getting caught. The information on that parchment was worth many lives.

Silently, I hurried to where the parchment lay. It was dry enough not to smear. I tucked it into my boot and trod toward the balcony. With Lord Bettencourt preoccupied, he wouldn't see the door to the balcony opening.

He took hold of the woman's arm and tugged her toward the bed. "Come, come. You've nothing to blubber about."

"Please, my lord…" With her face lifted, I saw how young the woman was, a girl really. Perhaps no more than eighteen. Just a couple of years younger than me.

I couldn't help her. Making my way out of the castle and across the grounds without discovery was already no easy task.

Still, I didn't move. My feet seemed to be planted on the floor of their own accord. How could I leave the girl to her fate? I'd once been a servant in a castle, the sort that nobles thought of as little more than property.

My hand went to the hilt of my dagger. If I killed the lord, the maid would be blamed for his death. She probably wouldn't consider a hanging much of a comfort. Fighting him with less than deadly force, invisible or not, would draw his attention to me. He'd call his guards, the dogs, and worse, his wizard.

But I could at least knock him down and give her the chance to escape. I strode over to him and with one sweep of my foot, he fell, smacking onto the floor. Unfortunately, he pulled the maid down with him.

His grip broke and she edged away from him. Instead of fleeing from the room, she stayed where she was, gaping at the man with wide uncertain eyes.

"Run," I muttered but spoke the word too low for her to hear.

"Clumsy girl!" Lord Bettencourt snapped. "Your insolence caused me to trip."

She got to her feet, keeping a wary distance. "I'm sorry, my lord. Are you injured?"

Saints in heaven. Was she going to stand about exchanging condolences? Did the girl have no sense of preservation?

"Help me up," he demanded.

She gave him her hand. I tried not to grit my teeth at her foolishness. Only two and a half years had passed since I'd been a servant in a castle, but it was already becoming hard to remember how powerless I'd been. If the maid ran away from the lord now, he'd only be more cross with her later. Well, if he was sober enough to recall any of this.

Lord Bettencourt stood, wobbling. "There now. I'll have no more of your hysterics." Or at least that's probably how the sentence ended. The last part was muffled because as soon as he took another step, I swept his foot out from under him again.

His head hit the floor with a satisfying crack. He moaned, rolled over, and rubbed his ankle. It too had fared ill in the fall.

The girl put her hands to her mouth in alarm. "You're unwell, Sir. You should rest." She backed away from him. "I'll fetch your physician."

Before he could respond, she sped from the room.

Finally.

I wanted to kick Lord Bettencourt on my way out, but that would be pushing my luck and it had already stretched as tight as his embroidered tunic.

While the man pulled himself from the ground, still cursing, I slipped out the balcony door.

CHAPTER 2

I rode from Barviel Castle toward The Painted Stallion, the inn where Alaric was staying. He'd rented a small cottage behind the inn's gardens and would be up waiting for me. He was the only one who knew where I'd gone tonight.

Alaric had been a stable hand for Lord Haddock at Carendale, the castle Mage Wolfson sold me to three and a half years ago. One day a few weeks after I arrived, I wasn't as careful as I should've been in my thieving. Alaric's older brother Barnaby, who worked in the kitchen as a pantler, caught me with an apple and a piece of cheese I'd stolen from the larder. Instead of turning me over to the master cook for a whipping, he took me behind the stables to bargain with Alaric.

"I don't know how she keeps getting to them," Barnaby said, presenting me to his brother like I was an exotic animal he'd stumbled upon. "I wouldn't have known she was the thief at all if I hadn't caught her eating the goods myself."

In my defense, undercook Fletcher had given me nothing to eat for days except small portions of gritty porridge and bread so old that even soaked, it tasted like wood. She was starving me, then asking me to carry heavy buckets and trays so she could yell at me for my sloth when I faltered. She either enjoyed torturing new servants or was looking for a reason to dismiss me to the ranks of the scullery maids.

Alaric had seemed quite intimidating at the time. He was twenty-one but looked older because of his height and broad shoulders. He had hair as dark and wild as mine along with serious brown eyes. Handsome yes, but his draw didn't come from that. Plenty of strong, handsome men worked in Lord Haddock's castle. Alaric had a bearing of intelligence and responsibility. Everyone in the stables deferred to him.

He looked me over, but not with disapproval. He was pleased or at least curious about the news of my theft. "How did you do it?" he asked.

I gulped and didn't answer. They wouldn't suspect I had magic. Only men were ever wizards.

"What else can you steal?" Alaric asked.

A dangerous question. "Nothing," I stammered. "I've repented of such wickedness. I only nipped the food because Cook Fletcher has withheld decent meals from me. One can't perform a day's work when one spins from hunger."

Alaric cocked his head. "You don't speak like a kitchen girl. Are you highborn?"

My gaze dropped to the ground. Servants often didn't like other servants who'd been educated beyond their station. I'd not only learned to read and write from Ronan during my time at Docendum Castle, I picked up his vocabulary and the cadence of his speech as well. If I'd had any sense of self-preservation, I would've reverted to speaking in a lowborn manner, and yet I refused to. I'd already lost so much. I couldn't lose my words too. I'd hoped they might one day help save me from my fate in the kitchen.

My gaze stayed on the ground. "I'm lowborn, sir."

"You do a fair imitation of your betters then. One is left to puzzle why."

My eyes flew to Alaric because he'd delivered the sentence like a highborn gentleman.

He laughed at my surprise. "I'm a groomsman. I have to know how to greet Lord Haddock's guests properly. When I was in training, the head groom whacked my knuckles if I got so much as a syllable wrong. What's the story behind your speech?"

My story was that I'd been a pawn in a game of Mage Wolfson's creation. I didn't want to recount it. I kicked at some bits of straw on the ground and held my tongue.

Alaric's voice went low and sympathetic. "You don't need to fear me. I know as well as you how horrible masters can be."

For a moment, impossibly, I thought he spoke of Mage Wolfson, that somehow Alaric knew the wizard had sold me to Lord Haddock in order to be spiteful.

"Fletcher can be a shrew," Alaric continued, "especially to young and pretty girls. It's as if beauty offends her."

Of course, he didn't know about Mage Wolfson. Alaric only meant the undercook.

"Do you want to be well-fed from now on?" Alaric asked.

Such offers came with prices. I'd no friends at Carendale Castle, no one to help or speak up for me. Most of the woman folk seemed to resent me on sight, or if not on sight, then when I spoke in my highborn manner. They thought I supposed myself better than them.

I lifted my chin the way I had at other men at Carendale who'd made leering suggestions. "I have a beau, a wizard's apprentice at Docendum Castle. That's why I was sold here. But Ronan will come for me when he finishes his training." So far, the story had kept the leerers at bay. During brief moments of delusion, I even believed those words. It was the reason I didn't become invisible and leave Carendale.

Alaric's eyebrows raised in amusement. "A wizard beau?" Everyone knew that mages could have their choice of women, and they never picked lowborn kitchen maids.

My cheeks went hot. "I ought to return to my duties. Tell the master cook of my crime, if you must."

Barnaby snorted. "We don't want our way with you, you silly girl. We want to, uh, reward your considerable skill."

"You want me to steal for you," I said flatly. "That way when I get caught with Lady Haddock's jewels, I'll be the one strung up to feed the birds. No, thank you."

I turned to leave. Alaric moved to stand in my way. "You don't strike me as the sort of girl who wants to spend her life pounding bread dough and cleaning pots. If that's the case, and your abilities are as good as my brother claims, certain organizations might wish to employ your talents."

"Organizations meaning whom?"

He lowered his voice. "Just as Fletcher is in the wrong to starve those under her care, lords who buy and sell servants are also in the wrong. We ought to have some say in our wages and a choice of whom to work for. We ought to control our own fate."

That was renegade-speak, traitor-speak, and yet I nodded in agreement. The law stated a master had to pay his bought servants wages. The idea being that after twenty years of service, a person would earn enough to pay off their indentured servitude. I wanted my freedom long before then.

"Those organizations," Alaric went on, "might even buy your freedom, should you prove useful."

He was taking a chance to speak to me like this. I might report him to the steward, although, new and friendless as I was, Alaric was well aware his denial would trump any accusation on my part.

I folded my arms. "How do I know your organization would carry through with such promises?"

"You'll have to trust me." Alaric shrugged. "Or if you'd rather, you can continue to wait for your wizard beau. I'm sure he won't desert you here." Alaric stepped out of my way, allowing me to return to the kitchen if I wished.

I stayed where I was. This wasn't one of the times when I deluded myself that Ronan would come for me. "What do you want me to steal?"

The answer to that, it turned out, was many things. First I just stole from Lord Haddock and his highborn guests. Usually documents. Sometimes other treasures. Once I replaced the ruby in a baroness's necklace with an imitation. After a year, I'd stolen so many secrets from Lord Haddock that King Leofric no longer trusted him. Highborn visitors stopped coming to Carendale.

True to Alaric's word, the renegades arranged to have a highborn woman come to the castle, claim to be my long-lost aunt, and pay off my serving price. Lady Edith Thornton also paid for Alaric to join us as a groomsman. Lord Haddock didn't mind selling him. With fewer guests to entertain, he didn't need all of his stable hands anymore.

Although Lady Edith was technically my adopted mother, it was clear she had little desire to be anyone's parent. She had no children with her late husband, and my arrival at her estate did little to alter her daily schedule. She was busy with the demands of her lands and tenants, and her attentions rarely turned toward me.

Paxworth was rundown, understaffed, and in constant want of repair. The renegades had paid Lady Edith handsomely to adopt me, but I was grateful for her generosity in taking me in, nonetheless. Without letting anyone know, I used growth spells to increase her fields' and orchards' output.

For the last two and a half years, I lived peacefully enough, learning the rather tedious arts of the upper class: needlework, dancing, and playing the dulcimer. The peace was only broken by Alaric stopping by to take me on one mission or another. I always went with him. I owed the renegades my freedom, and they paid me too. Besides, by then Alaric and I were friends. I trusted him.

When I finally reached The Painted Stallion, dawn was just lightening the edges of the sky. I expected Alaric to be waiting for me in the rented cottage. *Waiting* meaning sleeping in a chair with an ear cocked toward the door.

Instead, he sat by a lit fireplace, speaking to a gentleman and a woman. The man was at least two score with thinning brown hair. He wore the sort of wool tunic, hose, and overrobe one saw on men who were wealthy, but not wealthy enough to pay much notice to. The woman was of the same age, plain, stout, and wore a simple maroon gown and linen headdress. Her erect posture more than her clothing marked her as one who was used to giving orders.

It was much too early for social visits, and I could tell from Alaric's pleased expression these were no normal guests.

I stepped into the room, quite visible now. I'd canceled the invisibility spell on the ride into town. It only affected objects smaller than my mass, and the night watch tended to think something was amiss if they saw a riderless horse going down the street.

Alaric stood and waved me over as proudly as if he was my father. "Here is Marcella now. May I present Master Grey and Madame Sutton to you? They're guild leaders."

Part of the renegades. This was unexpected. And important. Alaric had never introduced me to his superiors before or even told me their names lest I be captured and give away information to enemies.

Master Grey and Madame Sutton stood and nodded genially, studying me with hawk eyes. Neither appeared perplexed to find me dressed in leggings and a tunic, indicating they knew where I'd been. Men's clothes were much more practical when it came to scaling walls.

"Pleased to meet you," I murmured.

Without waiting for more pleasantries, Alaric asked, "Do you have the letter?"

I retrieved the parchment and handed it to Alaric. "It's a copy. The original is back in his lockbox. That way no one will know we have it."

"Well done." Alaric read over the list and gave it to Master Grey. "I told you she would retrieve it. The woman can steal anything."

"Yes." Master Grey scanned the document. "So it would seem." He showed the parchment to Madame Sutton before folding it and slipping it into the top of one of his leather boots. He took five silver denarites from his pocket and dropped them in my palm. My usual payment.

The two guests settled back into their chairs. Alaric offered me his, but I sat on the hearthstone to warm myself.

"How were you able to take it?" Madame Sutton asked, demanded, really. She had the familiar look of resentment I'd seen from so many in my gender. I hadn't expected that sort of reaction from this woman. She was obviously important on her own account, and if her title was accurate, married as well. Why did she care whether I was pretty or not?

I smiled politely anyway. "A good thief doesn't reveal her methods." I hoped the two would drop the subject. Instead, their eyes bore into me. I knew the look. They wanted something from me. And since they'd come to speak with me face to face, it was undoubtedly a mission no sane person would attempt.

"My dear," Master Grey said, "so far you've only been biting at the heels of the nobility. It's time to be more than an annoyance. It's time to strike a death blow to the king."

Strong words that, if overheard, would get one killed quickly.

I chastised myself for the thought. It was pointless to worry over words when my deeds were already sufficient to see me hanged a dozen times over. I swept my hair off my back and leaned closer to the fire. "You speak metaphorically of death-blows, I assume. I'm not an assassin."

Many in the servant class believed our troubles came directly from the throne. King Leofric's father and grandfather, after all, had raised the number of years that kept indentured servants tied to their masters from seven to twenty. When King Leofric had taken the throne ten years ago, he'd done nothing to ease the servants' lot. I had no love for the man, but I had no death wish either. The king chose the most powerful wizards in the land for his protection. Not just one. Five. Any single wizard who tried to fight them would lose.

Madame Sutton gave me a patronizing, impatient smile. "No one would accuse you of being an assassin. In fact, we've noticed you've managed to steal from nobles without so much as even killing one of their guards. For that reason, some in our organization wonder about your methods. Some believe that only a person secretly working for the king could avoid capture as completely as you have."

I flinched. Madame Sutton's earlier expression wasn't resentment. It was suspicion. I was so surprised by her accusations that I hardly knew how to defend myself. "Why would I work for the king and steal things for you?"

Madame Sutton laid her hands across her lap. "Money and power are the top reasons for betrayal, but there could be others." Her eyes went over me again, like a shepherd about to shear wool from a flock. "What a pretty girl and yet you've no desire to settle down? Or do you have a secret beau we know nothing of?"

Not only was I under suspicion, an imagined boyfriend was also. I wondered when Madame Sutton thought I'd been courted by this illustrious person. "I find myself too busy in your service for such things."

She made a huffing noise. But my personal life was none of their concern. I wasn't about to tell her I'd stopped trusting men when Ronan sent me away.

I stood from the hearthstone. "If you no longer have confidence in my services, I'll happily retire to Lady Edith's estate and attend to the duties I've neglected there." I'd always imagined the leaders of the renegades to be older versions of Alaric: a mixture of heroes and saints, ready to become martyrs to provide better lives for those who had no voice. Madame Sutton seemed no different than many of the noblewomen I'd met: disdainful and dismissive.

Master Grey held up his hands in a conciliatory manner. "Lady Marcella, we require your services more than ever, but we must be careful whom we trust. So, we'll ask you again: How do you manage to get into noblemen's chambers unseen?"

I'd never told anyone that I could wield magic. Women weren't supposed to have it. Not even Alaric knew how I managed to accomplish the tasks he gave me.

Still, my superiors were waiting and had grown wary of me. I'd trusted the renegade leadership enough to risk my life for their cause, I could give them a vague admission. "I was raised in Docendum Castle." It was the castle where the wizards instructed their apprentices. "I picked up some magic there that helps me steal."

Madame Sutton outright scoffed. "Do you suppose us ignorant of wizardry? Magic can only be taught to those born with it, and unfortunately, only men are ever born with a wizarding mark. Are you saying you're actually a man whose wizard's mark was never discovered? I don't see it on your neck. Have you cast a spell to hide it?"

I pursed my lips. It had been some time since I'd been openly mocked, and anger sparked in my chest, making my cheeks burn with its heat.

With one uttered incantation, I went invisible.

It was foolish to let her goad me into such an action, but when the three of them gaped in speechless astonishment, I felt triumphant anyway. Because what Madame Sutton had said was true. A wizarding mark was no normal trait like hair and eye color that any child could inherit. The mark was in the realm of beards and broad chests, only appearing in men, and even then, the trait was as rare as a unicorn. Usually, only one or two boys a year in all the country could boast of the sign that indicated they could use magic. For a few years, there had been no new boys at all.

Every parent checked their sons for birthmarks on their necks that would, as they grew older, darken and grow into the shape of a crescent moon. To have a son taught at Docendum Castle was not only an honor, it led to riches and power.

I spoke the invisibility counter spell and flashed back into the seen world. Alaric laughed and clapped at my performance. "Bravo, Marcella! But how is it possible? How did you learn magic?"

I couldn't tell him the truth so I just smiled in a mysterious manner. "I'm a thief. I stole it."

This was enough of an explanation for Master Grey. He grinned so wide I could see that one of his back teeth was missing. "Brilliant! We have the perfect agent. No one would ever suspect, let alone believe it—a woman with magic."

Madame Sutton put her hand to her chest, still disbelieving. "How did you disappear? How could you possibly have magic?"

That was not a simple question and even thinking about it dragged me back to Docendum Castle.

There I was, ten years old, gangly and clumsy as a newborn calf, watching from the henhouse as the steward escorted the year's new apprentice across the courtyard. Watching, though I didn't know it, my whole life about to change.

CHAPTER 3

*leven years earlier*

ON THE DAY I saw Ronan Clarke deposited at the courtyard of Docendum Castle, I wasn't comely, but he certainly was. Even at twelve years old, he had a strong jaw and solid cheekbones. His black hair was as shiny as crows' wings and his blue eyes shone like a summer wish. Confidence exuded in every footstep he took toward the castle. He hadn't cried as I'd seen the boys last year do when their parents hugged them goodbye. He followed the steward into the castle, spilling out eager questions.

Over the next few days, I noticed him with the other apprentices—while I delivered food to their table or took dishes away. I liked to linger and watch them practice their tricks. They might make the napkins soar about the room or command the salt cellar to waddle across the table.

The older boys usually put the newcomer in his place before the sunset on his arrival, but as the days wore on, Ronan refused to be intimidated by their threats and pranks. He was better at magic right off than some of the older apprentices, a fact they didn't appreciate. Most impressively, one day Ronan changed two of his tormenters into geese. They flew across the dining hall table, honking and knocking over glasses until Ronan changed them back. Animal transformation was a skill very few wizards ever achieved. He did it within his first weeks at the castle.

After that, Mage Wolfson, the head wizard, watched Ronan with greedy, expectant eyes.

Ronan would've never paid any notice to me if the older boys hadn't been so persistent in their harassment. A month after he came, three of them managed to gag and bind him. From my spot in the kitchen door, I saw them levitate him in the courtyard, upside down and thrashing furiously. They moved him toward the stables where a manure pile sat, clearly planning on dunking him, face first, into the pile. I couldn't stand to see anyone treated so, even if Ronan was a wizard and therefore bound to be arrogant and disagreeable.

Mage Wolfson had a distinctive whistle he used to call his apprentices inside, and I knew how to imitate it. Keeping hidden in the doorway, I let out a shrill whistle.

The boys lowered Ronan, none too gently, and scattered back inside. In their haste to escape, they left him tied on the ground. He twisted to and fro, red-faced and grunting. I couldn't leave him like that. I grabbed a kitchen knife, ran over, and cut through his bands.

He was too furious, too busy hurling curses at the boys to thank me, and in truth, I expected no show of gratitude. Nobles and wizards rarely thanked servants for their service. But the next day when I had to go out in the rain to fetch eggs, an invisible covering hovered over me from the kitchen door to the hen house. Not a drop fell on me. When I turned and gazed back at the castle, Ronan was grinning at me from one of the windows.

I didn't speak to him again until a couple of months later

when I was caught unnecessarily risking my life. Perhaps I wanted to better myself because I felt the vastness of the distance between the apprentices and myself. Perhaps I just had a social climbing nature like some in the kitchen afterward accused me of. Servants weren't supposed to be educated, lest they get ideas.

But I wanted ideas. Most of all, I wanted to learn to read.

Mage Wolfson and his assistant Mage Quintal only taught the apprentices magic. Several professors also lived at Docendum to instruct in reading, history, logic, and mathematics. At times, I caught snatches of their lessons as I performed my duties.

One day, I brought food into a side courtyard where the reading teacher had convened class for Ronan and the two apprentices a year his senior. Instead of leaving after I deposited the tray, I hid behind a tree to watch. It was easy enough to do because no one ever paid attention to the comings and goings of the servants.

I knew Cook Lindon would smack me with her spoon for not returning to the kitchen promptly, but I decided the future welt was worth it. When I couldn't hear the teacher properly, I darted over to a hedgerow and tiptoed along it to get closer. From this spot, I pushed away a few branches to see the words the teacher held up on a wax tablet.

I didn't understand much of what was being said, but what I pieced together of the letters and their sounds made me feel like I'd reached out and caught hold of something as rare as the yellow orioles that came to the castle orchards in the summer.

When the instruction ended, I waited for the four to leave so I could slip away undetected. The teacher and the two older apprentices strolled toward the castle door. I'd lost sight of Ronan. I peered around, searching for him.

His voice came from beside me. "You'd make a terrible spy."

I jumped and put my hand to my throat. I couldn't justify my actions so I sputtered, "How did you catch me?"

He crossed his arms, the smile I'd adored earlier nowhere to be found. "You're so clumsy, the dead themselves would notice you tromping around."

I lifted my chin. "Well, the dead ain't got nothing else to do 'sides watch for people, do they?"

Ronan almost laughed at my response. I could see him fight the impulse and turn cross again. "If you keep spying, you'll soon find out about the habits of the dead. Trying to learn wizarding secrets is treason, Sella."

He knew my name. Or at least the nickname the servants used. I refused to show him how pleased I was about that. I brushed off bits of bark and leaves that had collected on my skirt. "I don't care none about the wizarding stuff. I just want to learn how to read regular words."

He frowned. "And what would you do once you learned to read?" His expression grew sterner. "Don't think of lying to me. I've said an incantation that will make your fingers blister if you don't tell the truth."

My mouth went slack with fear. I could get in so much trouble in a castle with nine boys who knew magic. "I...I might peek at some of the books in the guest library."

A library was a display of wealth, and Docendum had an entire room lined with tomes of history and philosophy, elegant gold lettering decorating their spines. I longed for the thinner books, though, tales of the adventures of knights who fought dragons and, even better, rescued princesses.

"I'd be careful," I added. "Not a soul would even know I'd borrowed one." No one ever read the books there. Neither of the wizards was married or had children, and their visitors didn't stay long enough to finish a book. The guest library was just for show.

Ronan shook his head. "That is an even worse idea than you

skulking around here—borrowing something that costs more than you do."

"I cost more than a book," I insisted, lying before I realized what I was doing.

"Not much more," Ronan said. "So it's still a bad idea."

The truth was the wizards hadn't paid a servant's price to anyone to buy me. My parents died when I was seven, and Cook Lindon, a friend of my mother's, had convinced the wizards to let her take me in. In exchange for a place to live and food to eat, I served in the castle in what little ways I could until I turned twelve and began work in the kitchen.

Ronan must know my parents weren't servants at Docendum and had assumed I'd been sold by villagers who were too poor to take care of their children. It also meant he'd lied to me about the truth incantation. My fingers didn't blister.

I folded my arms. "Wizards can't really force people to tell the truth, can they?"

He blinked at me and raised his brows. "You lied about how much you cost? Hmm. I wouldn't think a kitchen girl would risk blistering her hands over such a small matter."

I didn't want to explain that I'd just been indignant and forgotten about the blisters. "If wizards could force the truth out of folks, there wouldn't be so much intrigue in the kingdom, would there?" I'd learned from serving the wizards' guests that intrigue was a staple of the nobles. Someone was always plotting against someone else.

Ronan nodded, impressed. "You're a bright girl. It takes most apprentices weeks to figure that out."

Apparently, the truth incantation was one of the tricks the older apprentices played on the newer. I wondered how many secrets new boys spilled before figuring out the incantation was a ruse. "How long did it take you?" I asked.

Instead of answering, he cleared his throat and gazed around the hedgerow. "If you really want to learn how to read, I suppose I could teach you—on one condition: You don't pinch any of Quintal's or Wolfson's books."

"Very well," I said because I knew I could lie without my fingers blistering.

That was the start of our friendship. I expected we would always have to keep our meetings a secret. The wizards would never condone one of their own associating with a lowly kitchen maid. Especially not Ronan, their most promising pupil.

When I was twelve years old, Mage Wolfson summoned me to his receiving room. He'd never taken any notice of me before which meant I'd been caught doing something I oughtn't. If the matter had been a complaint about my serving, he would've just told the housekeeper and she'd discipline me.

Something horrible was about to transpire. I just wasn't sure how severely I'd be punished. Cook Lindon—no teller of fantastic tales—had said Mage Wolfson kept a wolf, and he'd magicked the creature to be as large as a lion. If you were a thief, Mage Wolfson turned you into a fawn and let his pet rip you into pieces and devour you.

I took mincing steps into the wizard's receiving room, hands trembling like branches in the wind. I'd never been inside this room before. A two-story stone fireplace spread out against the back wall. The stones around the hearth and mantel had either been carved or magicked into the shapes of prowling wolves. Vicious, snarling creatures. An enormous wooden desk stood in the middle of the room, covered with books, parchments, and small boxes that housed a number of oddities—feathers, branches, things that looked suspiciously like bones.

My gaze stopped on the wizard sitting behind his desk. Mage Wolfson had a hooked nose, dark hair, and an overgrown beard that sharpened into a point. His expression was cold and disapproving. This was his usual countenance so it gave me no clues as to how severe my punishment would be.

He cast me a glance, then his gaze went to the other side of the room where Ronan stood, stock-still and wide-eyed.

Ronan. This was about our friendship.

The wizard got to his feet and ambled around the desk. His black robe swept across the floor like night itself. "You taught her how to read?"

He knew that too? Ronan gulped and pressed his lips together.

The wizard picked up a strip of dried clay from his desk. Ronan and I used clay to pass messages to each other, rewetting it to erase our letters. My writing was on the strip.

Mage Wolfson gripped the clay. "Is this why you've fallen behind on your lessons?"

"No," Ronan stammered. "That isn't it."

"Then why have you turned in so little of late?" Mage Wolfson threw the clay onto his desk where it shattered into skittering pieces.

I winced at the noise and wanted to cry.

"I'm sorry, sir." Ronan's chin dropped in a sign of penitence. "I've had trouble finishing the writing, but that doesn't mean I don't understand the principles." His chin lifted again. "You know I master those well enough."

The wizard put his hands behind his back and rocked on the heels of his pointed shoes. "You haven't mastered nearly enough. You suppose because magic comes easily to you, you've nothing to learn. You think your teachers are relics whose wisdom you can ignore."

Mage Wolfson's eyes snapped to me so suddenly that I drew in a breath and gripped the sides of my skirt. He stared at me, considering me like a cloth to be measured and cut. My fate was in that gaze, my sentence ready to be declared. I was certain I would never see Ronan again.

Mage Wolfson returned his attention to Ronan and his voice calmed. "You have trouble studying with the other apprentices.

Perhaps you need a different sort of study companion." He gestured to me, as though presenting a gift. "You seem to like writing to her. If she can help you finish your lessons, she can take a break from her duties in the kitchen and help you study. If not, she'll go back to scouring pots."

I didn't see Ronan's response to this edict because I was too busy gawking at the wizard in stunned surprise. I'd always thought him a harsh, horrible old man, and yet he'd just plucked me from kitchen drudgery and given me a position so sweet I hadn't even thought to hope for it. I could spend more time with Ronan, more time with books, all with Mage Wolfson's approval.

Had the wizard been the approachable sort, I would've rushed over and kissed his hand. Instead, I turned to Ronan expectantly. Surely, he would approve of such an unexpected boon.

He still stood as straight as a sword, staring at the wizard. Cautious and perhaps a little offended.

"Well," the wizard said, already making his way back to his seat, "take her to your chamber and start on your work. I'll check it nightly." He smiled as he spoke, but still didn't manage to look kindly. Perhaps the stern lines of the wizard's face were incapable of forming a kindly expression. He had little practice at that gesture.

I didn't ponder his motives. I was busy rejoicing in my good fortune.

* * *

RONAN'S CHAMBER was a small room with not much more than a fireplace and a desk to keep his rickety bed company. Several shelves stood over his desk, filled with scrolls, jars of all sizes, and items used for spells. A wizard's clock sat on his desk, a disc with shadows that swept over its face to tell the time.

Only one chair perched by the desk so I sank onto the end of Ronan's bed, feeling as bright and light as a birdsong.

He paced back and forth across the room. "What did Mage Wolfson mean by that edict? Was he trying to insult me by giving me a serving girl as a study partner? Is it punishment for not getting along with the other boys or punishment for teaching you to read?"

My happiness dimmed at Ronan's disapproval. "It might not be a punishment at all. Maybe he just thinks I can help you with your lessons."

Ronan huffed. "The other apprentices will taunt me. Ceaselessly."

I crossed my arms, offended. "Do you want me to go back to the kitchen?"

He stopped his pacing and sighed. "I didn't mean that. I suppose a break from your chores will be nice for you." His gaze traveled over me, taking in my worn and stained clothes. "What do you do with your hands anyway? They always look like you've been trying to cook them along with the vegetables."

I scowled. Perhaps being distant friends was better than being an unwanted companion. "They've grown chapped doing dishes for ungrateful boys." I stood. "If you don't want my help, just tell the wizard so. I imagine that's what he expects you to do. He thinks you'll go back to your own kind." This was the worst insult I could think to throw at him. He considered the other apprentices to be pompous and selfish, already grappling for power.

My statement brought forth another sigh. "Sit down, Sella." He went to his books, pulled one from the bottom of a stack, and flipped through the pages. It was one of his books on magic. I could tell because the title on the spine made no sense. It seemed to be a jumble of letters thrown together, with some upside down and some backward.

People without a wizard's mark couldn't read the spells. Just touching a book on magic would burn your hands. The maids always dusted around them. Still, I peered at the pages longingly. Part of me believed that, mark or not, I must have a tiny spark of magic inside me.

Ronan located whatever incantation he'd been searching for. He mouthed the words as he read, repeating them to place them in his memory. Incantations always sounded like gibberish to me, a crash of vowels and consonants with an occasional click or hiss not found in common language.

Ronan flipped to another page and started working on a second incantation. I watched him quietly for a few minutes. "I'm supposed to help you study. Shouldn't I do something?"

"Shhh."

Fine. I swung my feet back and forth in boredom. Sitting here was still better than turning a spit or washing dishes. Once the other serving girls knew I'd been excused from my duties, they'd be indignant with jealousy. This thought caused a happy moment of revelry followed by several moments of worry. They already thought I was putting on airs and pinched me when I used words they didn't know.

Ronan pulled a small clay jar from the shelf above his desk. He rolled it between his fingers, speaking one incantation and then another.

When he finished, he took off the lid and checked the jar's contents. "Give me your hands."

I held my palms out warily. Anyone would worry about having an apprentice magic something. I'd seen them practice spells on livestock. Once a poor goat burst into smoke.

Ronan spread some grease from the jar onto my hands. It felt as cool and sleek as stream water.

"What is it?" I asked.

"Fourth-year work," he said proudly. "That ought to satisfy Wolfson."

I didn't ask further questions because I both saw and felt the change in my skin. What was red and cracked became soft again. Unblemished. Even my callouses healed—which was not necessarily a good thing.

I gaped at my hands, turning them front to back. "Can wizards cure all wounds?" My mind went to my parents and the sores that sprouted when the pestilence took their lives. I'd had them too, painful seeping boils under my arms and on my thighs. My father sold everything we had and only managed to buy one dose of medicine from the apothecary. He told my mother to take it, but after he died, she gave it to me.

Ronan put the lid back on the pot. "The more severe the wound, the harder it is to cure. Deep wounds require serious magic. Trying to save the dying could cost a wizard his life."

I nodded, my mind still on my parents. Perhaps magic couldn't have helped them, but if they'd been richer, they could have afforded three doses of medicine. I might not ever have a skill that paid well, but I could, given the right fortunate circumstances, marry wealth. Wealth worked its own kind of magic.

Ronan replaced the jar on his shelf with a satisfied thud.

I scooted to the edge of the bed. "Could you make a beauty potion for me?"

"Why would you want that? Beauty is a frivolous thing that isn't worth what it costs."

"You're only saying that because you're a boy, and besides you're already handsome so you don't care."

He plopped down at his desk, angling his chair so he could see me. "And you're only wishing for beauty because you haven't considered what you ask. Do you want every scoundrel in the castle to take note of you? Do you want some lecherous noble buying you from the wizard for twisted reasons? Each time a mage called for you, you'd wonder if they wanted more than your service."

Ronan made a fair point. Still, in my heart, I couldn't wish for plainness. I was not that farsighted.

I sat straighter, weighing his last statement. "Does Mage Wolfson call for young women?" Mage Quintal flirted with the noblewomen who visited the castle to buy things, but I'd never seen Mage Wolfson take an interest in anyone.

"He says he has no time for women." Ronan's tone indicated he thought it more likely Mage Wolfson was too cantankerous to attract women. "He's too busy for a family. He says all powerful wizards are."

I, who'd lost my family, couldn't understand such a thing. "Then I hope you are never a powerful wizard."

I expected Ronan to agree with me. He had a brother and sister he hadn't seen since he'd arrived two years ago. Instead, he said, "You shouldn't gossip about Wolfson. If he hears you, he'll be angry."

How many times, I wondered, had Mage Wolfson been angry with Ronan and what had he done to him? As bad as the kitchen work was, at least I knew Cook Lindon cared for me. Along with her scoldings, she gave me the occasional word of encouragement and more than enough advice. She'd also saved me from the wrath of the head cook a time or two by doing one of my chores when I was dallying someplace.

I tucked my hands in my lap. "How should I help you study?" I didn't want to shirk this important duty.

Ronan shrugged. "I don't see how you can. You haven't read any history or etiquette books, and you don't know mathematics."

"I'll read your assignments and question you."

He took an exceptionally large book from his shelf with the title *The History of Aerador* and laid it on my lap. "This is volume one. I'm on volume two."

"Oh." I opened the book and squinted at the small writing that filled the page. "Your first questions won't be for a while."

"I'm sure Wolfson didn't expect that of you." Ronan paused, choosing his words carefully. "I've been sometimes gloomy of late. I'm sure he just meant for your company to cheer me." His spirits raised as he considered his own words. My presence wasn't necessarily a punishment of any kind. "He gave Stewart his own horse for that reason."

Stewart was seventeen, the second oldest apprentice. I'd seen him ride out on the black charger. A beautiful horse. One fit for a wizard.

"I can help cheer you," I pronounced. "When you finish the day's lessons, we can explore the forest. We'll play chess, and I'll teach you whittling. You'll see, I'll be much better than a horse."

I'm not sure Ronan initially agreed about that. None of the apprentices had chided Stewart about getting a horse. Whenever the apprentices spotted us together, they commented on his lowborn associations and asked whether he helped me gut fish. While I was with Ronan, he bore their taunting as though he didn't hear them. I loved him during those times.

Once, when I brought food to his mathematics class amid a test, Osborn, who was two years Ronan's senior, leaned over and said, "There's your scrawny little studymate. Perhaps she can tell you the answers."

Ronan whispered back, "Perhaps when you earn the wizard's favor, he'll give you your own servant, and then you'll have time enough to study."

I forgave Ronan for that response. I *was* a servant. I hadn't forgotten my place. And besides, when we were alone, he never treated me like I was lowborn. I was his best friend.

I read his books even though I found history dull and etiquette perplexing, all in an effort to help him.

For his part, he did his lessons quickly. In fact, after a few months, he grew so frustrated that memorizing incantations left so little time for our chess games that he sought out all sorts of spells and cobbled together one of his own making—an incantation that let him immediately recall any magical text he read.

His lessons took no time after that, and his chess game improved considerably. He beat me nearly every time.

The next two years passed away in the sort of happiness that comes only to those who don't know how little control over the future they wield. We ought to have been more careful. We ought to have at least paid attention to see what happened to Stewart's horse.

One day it disappeared, and Stewart never spoke of it again.

CHAPTER 4

*W*hen I was almost fifteen and Ronan nearly seventeen, things began to change between us. Ronan shared enough food with me that I'd stopped being thin and knobby long ago, but at that time I underwent a transformation in both figure and feature. The way the other apprentices eyed me, the way they spoke to me, all told of the difference.

Cook Lindon complained to the housekeeper that I was no longer a child and shouldn't be unchaperoned with a young man. I didn't appreciate her efforts to preserve my reputation. I'd no desire to return to scrubbing pots. But the fact that she thought I might tempt Ronan—who would have his pick of powerful noblemen's daughters—was more proof of my alteration.

I knew it had happened. I just didn't know if it was natural. Ronan had given me a few magical presents—a charm that kept my straw mattress free of bugs, a blanket magicked to keep me warm, and socks that always stayed dry. He'd also enchanted my boots so they made no sound when I walked. He and I snuck out of the castle at times, and he insisted I couldn't be quiet otherwise.

He might have given me a beauty potion, and if he had, had he done it to fulfill my earlier desires, or had he done it to silence the other apprentices' tauntings? It would be fitting revenge to make them jealous that the wizard had given him a beautiful girl to be his companion.

One day, after Ronan's instruction with his teachers, I went to his room and found him at his desk writing a letter. Over the years, his shoulders had filled out as broad as a plow hand's, but his features still had a patrician look—strong chin, straight nose, clear skin. His blue eyes were just as striking, and his black hair was tied at the nape of his neck with a leather string. He hadn't decided whether to keep it shorter as was the style of the nobles or to grow it long like many wizards did, so he just kept it tied out of the way.

I sank down at the end of his bed with a thump. "Osborn told me I was fetching, but I wasn't fetching anything." Osborn was now the oldest apprentice, eighteen and nearly ready to take a job with one of the noble families. What puzzled me was that although it seemed like a slur on my servant status, he hadn't said the words like an insult.

Ronan's pen stopped its forward progress, and his eyes lifted to mine. "Did he?"

"What does it mean?"

"Well, I suppose it means that as thick as Osborn is, he still manages to take note of some obvious things."

"Are you going to tell me or not?"

Ronan laughed. He had an easy, open smile that only I ever saw. With the apprentices, he was cautious and reserved. With the other servants, he was imperious. It was part of a wizard's job, after all, to be imperious. "Fetching means pretty. I'm surprised you don't know the word."

Oh. A compliment. Or probably one. With the apprentices,

one could never be quite certain of their intent. "I only spend time with you and Cook Lindon. Evidently, neither of you compliments me as much as you should."

Ronan returned to his letter. "I will endeavor to be better in the future."

The subject brought to mind the question I'd pondered. "Did you give me a beauty potion? Is that why I've become pretty?"

Another laugh. "No. You managed beauty all by yourself. Congratulations, you've proven magic is unnecessary to get what you want."

I was glad my beauty was natural but at the same time, a bit sad Ronan hadn't given it to me as a gift. It meant he didn't care how I looked.

I suspected, even back then, that I was in love with him, but Cook Lindon said a young woman's feelings changed with the seasons, and I supposed mine would eventually change too.

I must have scowled because he said, "I thought you wished to be beautiful." He went back to writing. "Congratulations, you've also proven that it's impossible for a girl to be content with what she wishes for."

What I'd proven was I listened to Ronan's opinion, and he'd warned me of the dangers of beauty. "I'm not discontent. My goal is still to catch the eye of some passing nobleman's son who is both handsome and virtuous. Then we'll fall in love and move to his manor, where I'll happily give birth to five lovely children. But I won't be ready to marry for several years and the wrong sorts of people might notice me first."

"Hmm. We need more noblemen passing through the area. It might take a while to find one who's virtuous."

"I want to be pretty, just not yet."

He shrugged. "You could try mucking out the pigsty more. That always puts me right off your prettiness."

I had chores while Ronan was at classes and was frequently assigned that one. With the exception of Cook Lindon, the other servants resented my elevation in the household and shunned me, but they didn't dare be outright hostile. None wanted to risk Ronan's displeasure—or worse, Mage Wolfson. He, after all, had given me to Ronan and showed no signs of changing the arrangement. Now, when the wizard passed me in the hallways, he looked me over with smug satisfaction.

I traced the lines of Ronan's quilt with my fingers. "You could help me," I said quietly.

"You think I have a spell that delays beauty until wealthy eligible men are around?"

"No, I meant you'll know noblemen's sons soon." The apprentices generally found employment at the end of their eighteenth year, but with Ronan's abilities, he would complete his training earlier. If it weren't for Mage Wolfson's and Mage Quintal's pride, they would've already admitted they had little left to teach him. Ronan had not only mastered the required spells with amazing ease, he also had the enviable ability of being able to take parts of several different incantations and combine them to come up with new ones.

When Ronan left Docendum, powerful lords would compete for his services.

I shifted on the edge of the bed. "You could find a way to introduce me to some eligible men."

One of his dark eyebrows quirked up. "A wizard and a matchmaker. My career possibilities are endless."

"Matchmaking would be more entertaining than casting spells on horses so they run without tiring or magicking roads so they don't wash away. Mage Wolfson must have a love potion spell somewhere."

Ronan paused in his writing to send me a wry smile. "Like beauty, I doubt you'll need a potion to provoke someone into loving you."

A sweet sentiment but considering my station, one that was completely untrue. "Could you at least look for a love spell?"

"Trust me on this matter. If the other apprentices weren't afraid of me, you'd find roses, daily, lining the kitchen."

That didn't mean anything. "Flowers cost wizards nothing—just like their flirtations. If I'm to escape the kitchen, I'll have to find a wealthy husband. Besides, think of the fun you could have with a love potion. You could make the steward fall in love with himself."

"Again, a potion isn't necessary for that."

I laughed and he smiled. That was perhaps my greatest contribution as his companion. I appreciated the wit he showed to no one else.

I picked up his pillow and tossed it at him. "I will die in a kitchen, kneading bread, and you won't care. You'll forget me as soon as you leave."

"Don't be ridiculous," he said with a smirk. "I have a memory spell. I remember everything of importance."

He probably expected me to say some jest of my own. I couldn't. I could only stare at him, suddenly miserable at the thought of him riding away from me in some nobleman's carriage. Everything I'd come to enjoy about life was tied to Ronan.

That was another change that had happened to me. I could go from laughter to tears in the span of a breath.

His smile faded and he got out of his chair and sat beside me on the bed. "It won't be so bad when I leave." He motioned to the books on his desk. I had read all of his school books except for the magic ones. "You know history, etiquette, mathematics, and you speak like a highborn lady. You've far too many skills for Wolfson to keep you in the kitchen."

"Where will he put me then? Will he give me to the next apprentice he's trying to cheer?"

Ronan grew a shade paler. Perhaps I did as well. I'd never considered the possibility of being given to one of the other apprentices until I said the words out loud. It might actually happen. Mage Wolfson clearly didn't care about my virtue. He wouldn't have let me be alone with Ronan every day, unchaperoned, if he had.

I placed my hand on top of Ronan's. "Could you take me with you when you leave?"

He frowned. "I wouldn't have the funds to buy you until I'd worked for a while. And even then, what respectable family would approve of their wizard sending for a beautiful young woman to live with him? The noble households have their own servants and think it their right to choose all who work in their castles."

"You could tell them I cook well," I whispered. "That is, if you don't mind lying." I couldn't say what I really thought, which was that marriage laws allowed servants to marry outside their master's estates if their husband or husband's master paid off the servant's price. Ronan was bound to marry a highborn woman who'd give him connections and prestige. "Will you even think of me when you work for nobility?" The question was asked with no trace of jesting this time.

He dipped his chin to indicate I shouldn't have asked, which I shouldn't have. I had no claim on him. "What do you think, Sella?"

I thought he was avoiding the question. I had no right to press the point. "Could you give me a protection charm to keep me from the grasp of rakes? Invisibility perhaps?"

He shook his head. "To achieve invisibility, an incantation must be spoken each time. You'd need to have a wizard's mark for that."

"Extra strength?" I asked.

"You'd also need a wizard's mark for that."

"How about—"

"Any magic of substance requires a wizard's mark." His eyes were truly regretful. "I want to help you. I'll think on it."

It wasn't enough reassurance. I snapped, "Why can't you just give me a wizard's mark?"

The words hung in the air, petulant and impossible. He stared at me without answering. I'd pushed our friendship too far. I was blaming him for things not his fault.

He leaned forward, elbows on his knees, and gazed at the books on his desk. "I've never thought of whether such a thing might be possible."

"Could it be?" Surely it couldn't. And yet Ronan's thoughtful expression gave me hope.

As though reciting a lesson, he said, "The wizard's mark is a manifestation of his magic. It can't be given. One must be born with it. But then, perhaps wizards just don't try to give it because they've no wish to share power. A group of mages can take a wizard's magic by removing his mark. Who's to say there isn't a way to give a mark?"

Ronan had never mentioned that magic could be taken from a wizard. I supposed it wasn't something wizards wanted people to know.

"The teachers have always said," he went on, "that trying to give someone magic would be like trying to teach a man with no eyes to see, and yet with enough magic, theoretically, I might be able to give a blind man eyes. Why not a wizarding mark?" Ronan leaned back and put his hand over mine. His touch was soft and reassuring. "I'll study it. We have time."

At the most, he had a little over a year left. But the fact that Ronan would do something so grand and illegal for me—it made my affection for him swell and my caution disappear. I breached all manner of etiquette and twisted my hand so it held his. Proper maidens wouldn't be so forward, and as soon as I did it, I worried I'd made a mistake. The last thing I wanted was to make things awkward between us with unmet expectations.

I felt him staring at me, but I looked only at our hands, fingers clasped together.

Mistake, mistake, mistake.

Now he would have to pull his hand away from mine and that would feel like rejection.

"You asked if I would ever forget you," he said softly. "The answer is no, never. Never, Sella."

I didn't trust myself to speak, so I only nodded.

With his free hand, he gently took hold of my chin and turned my face to his. "I won't leave you without protection."

"I wish you didn't have to leave at all." My voice cracked, betraying more emotion than I wanted.

He didn't reply, just leaned forward. I thought he would rest his forehead against mine in a gesture of affection. It would have been enough. I tilted my face to see his expression. His eyes met mine, then his gaze slid to my lips.

My heart beat wildly in my chest like a bird startled into flight. I dared not move for fear it would break his gaze. I had no magic and yet something inside of me was trying to summon that power anyway, to pull Ronan to me.

He lowered his head and kissed me. It was a soft, tentative kiss, the first for both of us. Joy shimmered through me, as warm as sunshine piercing a cloudy sky. I leaned into him, my lips eager and growing reckless. Even as I answered the teasing of his mouth, I was afraid of what would happen when he stopped kissing me and thought better of this.

Finally, he lifted his head and sighed. "Suddenly it's just become harder for me to study."

CHAPTER 5

*A*s I stood before Master Grey and Madame Sutton, Alaric was still beaming at my trick of invisibility. He'd asked me many times over the last year how I accomplished my thievery. I'd always told him I couldn't reveal my methods because, after all, I might someday want to steal from him.

Showing any of my abilities had been impetuous. I'd been goaded into it by Madam Sutton's disdain, accusations, and no doubt, my lack of sleep. I regretted it already.

Master Grey smiled his approval. He seemed even happier than Alaric. Madame Sutton alone retained her air of skepticism. She scanned the area around me. "Was that true magic or just trickery?"

I raised my brows in question. "You don't believe what your eyes have shown you?"

She stepped to my side and sliced her hand through the air, checking for some hidden device. "My father used to pull eggs from behind my ears. That didn't make him a wizard."

I smiled patiently. "You're correct. It was all trickery. And now I'll use the same trickery to find a comfortable place to sleep. If you want to talk further, you can try and find me. Perhaps that will convince you sufficiently."

Before any of them could answer, I disappeared again. With my enchanted boots, my footsteps made no sound as I strode around the group to the door.

They protested, all of them calling my name profusely. I opened and shut the door, giving the impression I'd gone outside. The three went after me, still calling to me in hushed, urgent whispers. When their voices grew softer, I said the incantation to reverse the spell and headed to the bed.

The evening's events had left me weary. I flopped onto the bed and pulled the covers on top of me. Alaric would return eventually, but I hoped he'd come back alone, or if not, I hoped the covers would sufficiently hide me so I got a few hours of shuteye.

I'd both given offense to Madame Sutton and made it clear I wasn't easy to work with. With any luck, these superiors would let things go back to the way they'd been before.

I'd hardly slept before the door swung open again. The group traipsed inside. "The impertinence." Madam Sutton huffed.

"Ah, but the magic," Master Grey said. "I'll take her impertinence as long as we've access to magic."

"She'll come around." That voice was Alaric's. "Marcella cares about the plight of the servants as much as any…"

Their conversation stopped. They'd spotted me.

I silently willed them to go away.

"Shall we let her sleep?" Master Grey whispered.

"She isn't asleep," Alaric answered. "She's too careful for that. She woke up as soon as the door opened."

Alaric knew me too well.

I heard the rustle of skirts marching toward me, then Madame Sutton leaned over me. "Really, Lady Marcella, if we're to work together, you'll have to learn how to take orders without complaint."

I still didn't move. "If we're to work together, you'll have to learn that I don't take orders." Or at least I wasn't today. Upon my arrival here, instead of being thanked for risking my life—again—I'd been interrogated.

Madame Sutton pulled the blanket away from my face. "You're our highest-paid agent. Paid higher than myself, I'll add. We're not beyond our rights to question your methods."

I sat up on my elbows and opened my eyes to glare at her. "Your payments are for the tasks I perform, not for the privilege of my secrets." It wasn't as though I kept the money. I'd used it to pay off Cook Lindon's family's servant prices and make improvements on Paxworth. "I've told you more than anyone else is privy to, and for that, you questioned my integrity." I lay back down and pulled the covers up to show I was finished discussing the matter.

"Do you care nothing for the servants who—" Madame Sutton started, but Master Grey shushed her.

His voice was much more conciliatory. "We didn't mean to indicate any mistrust on our part. We're simply ascertaining how to use your talents. What is the extent of your magical abilities?"

I didn't answer.

He drew his own conclusions from that. "Quite considerable, then. Good. Good." He slid a chair next to the bed and settled into it, addressing me as though I wasn't sprawled under the covers, doing my utmost to ignore him.

"We've never had magic at our disposal before. This changes matters. We've enough support from the lowborn that we've begun to form an army, but we don't know how to best use this force."

I lifted my hand to stop him. "I can't protect an army. And even if I could stand against one wizard, if an army with two wizards opposed me, I'd lose." In Aerador, a country with more than forty wizards, a group of nobles could easily call up more than two. "Our best option is to continue fighting through subterfuge."

Master Grey focused his gray eyes on mine. I wondered mildly if that's where he'd gotten his name from. Certainly, the two leaders wouldn't give me their real names. "We can do more," he insisted. "We *must* do more. But to be effective, we must know your capabilities."

I sighed. I didn't want to tell them more, but I knew the plight of the servants, poor, uneducated, and controlled by the whims of their lords. Hadn't I already committed to help them at any cost? Perhaps my magic could be better put to use now that my leaders knew of it. Still, they needed to understand my limitations. "My invisibility doesn't mean invincibility. Wizards have disclosing spells. Dogs still smell me." I knew a silencing spell to keep them quiet, but it didn't keep them from finding or biting me.

Master Grey nodded, taking in this information. "What other magic can you work?"

I'd never counted how many spells were lodged in my brain, recipes and incantations filed away in my memory. I'd little need of most and was wary of attempting unfamiliar ones lest they go awry.

A large array of incantations required items I didn't have, things like sprigs of wildwood sage grown only in the shade or the spikes of a hedgehog from its first quilling. Other spells I'd never tried because they were hard to perform in secret. Wizards could make a show of performing magic, but I didn't dare reveal myself that way.

"I know many spells," I finally said, "but not all of them." I imagined no one knew them all, especially not when wizards like Ronan came up with new ones that they kept secret. "However, even if I were the best-trained wizard in the land, I couldn't successfully take on several others. I can't lead you to victory that way."

Master Grey grinned, unperturbed, like a kindly monk about to bestow blessings. "The way to victory has various roads."

Some of them, no doubt, involving my untimely death. I propped myself up on my elbows to better regard him. "What specifically are you hoping I can accomplish?"

Madame Sutton had been pacing the length of the room during Master Grey's speech. Without pausing, she said, "The king's death."

Oh, surely not.

The renegades wanted me to kill someone, and not just anyone: King Leofric. I sat up all the way, pushing the covers off. "No. It isn't possible. And I wouldn't do such a thing anyway." If murderers were cursed to walk the dark places of the earth, what was in store for those who committed regicide?

Madame Sutton flicked her hand in my direction. "The people need you. This is no time to be squeamish."

Alaric sat down on the foot of the bed, his eyes pleading. "Hear them out."

There was no point. "King Leofric's death won't put an end to the servant's fee. We'll only trade one tyrant for another."

King Leofric's wife and son had died in a boating accident the previous year, but he had a two-year-old daughter, Princess Alfreda. Should the king die without any male heirs, Baron Mowbray, the former queen's brother and a formidable baron in his own right, would act as a regent king until Alfreda was old enough to take the throne.

From all accounts, Baron Mowbray had a vicious nature which he inflicted on his servants, villagers, and even the nobles who crossed him. He'd done his best to root out the renegades in his lands, meaning he hanged all those he suspected of insurrection in the town square. He suspected quite a few people, most of them no doubt innocent.

Master Grey leaned closer to me. "You haven't heard about the change in regents?" His eyes twinkled like a man who was about to play a winning hand of cards. "The king has changed that position to his sister and brother-in-law."

Several years ago, King Leofric's sister Beatrice had married Lord Clement, one of the grandsons of King Regnault of Marseden. Lord Clement's mother, the eldest daughter of King Regnault, had wed an Aeradorian earl, and Lord Clement had spent his time back and forth between the two countries until he'd married Princess Beatrice. Although Lord Clement still had holdings in Marseden, he'd sworn fealty to King Leofric.

"How does that change things for us?" I asked.

Master Grey steepled his hands together. "Lord Clement and Princess Beatrice would be much better rulers for Aerador. Lord Clement has strong ties to Marseden and its practices, including its views on the length of the indentured servants' price."

Over the last century, the pestilence had taken many more people in Aerador than it had in Marseden. As a result, the Aeradoran kings kept raising the amount of time servants were indentured to their masters, while Marseden had left theirs at seven years.

"Lord Clement believes in giving the lowborn more rights," Master Grey continued, "including lowering the servants' price in both countries. He's publicly encouraged King Leofric to shorten the servants' price to match Marseden's. He thinks the law inequitable."

Could such a nobleman exist? "He cares about the servants?"

"Well," Master Gray admitted, "in the very least, he cares about Marseden's ability to trade their wool, cloth, and tin. Since nobles here pay less for labor, they trade their goods to other countries at a more favorable price. In return, Marseden puts tariffs on any goods from our country. Lord Clement believes Aerador should lower its servant price not only to benefit the servants but also to benefit Marseden's economy. And in return, Marseden would lower its tariffs on our goods."

That sounded more like a nobleman. Self-interest held greater weight than the travails of the lowborn.

Master Gray edged closer in his chair, his gaze continuing to bore into me. "We need to strike before King Leofric changes his mind and makes Baron Mowbray the regent again."

"Why would he do that?" I asked.

"Baron Mowbray is powerful, and many in the country believe Lord Clement is too close to the Marseden throne. They still see him as a foreigner."

With the way the royalty intermarried, it could be said that any of them were foreigners. King Leofric had not long since become engaged to Princess Marita, the daughter of Oderic of Odeway, a kingdom across the sea. Instead of resenting her for being a foreigner, most of Aerador considered the king's wedding a boon for the country, a union that would ally us with a powerful land.

I had to point out the obvious. "You don't know for certain that Lord Clement would lower the servant price to seven years. Assassinating the king in the hopes that the next ruler might be better seems like thin justification for murder."

Madame Sutton waved a dismissive hand. "We've reliable sources that say he would lower it to five years. Lord Clement believes if he did, Aerador's servants would stop fleeing to Marseden and Marseden's servants would begin coming here. With the extra workers, the country would thrive again."

Alaric looked at me with imploring eyes. They were warm brown and so earnest one couldn't help but be swayed by them. "Barnaby has joined the renegade army. They want to fight the king's men. They're tired of waiting for change to come."

My stomach sank. Not Barnaby. Alaric's older brother was

his best friend. "He shouldn't have enlisted. He'll be killed. You need to stop him."

"I'm thinking of joining him." Alaric cut off the protest that sprang to my lips. "Madam Sutton can tell you of your missions as easily as I can. The army needs strong men."

Such talk was madness. "The king has wizards. The renegade army hasn't a chance." I'd grown to depend on Alaric's friendship. I couldn't abide the thought of losing him.

"Perhaps that's true," Alaric said. "And yet I cannot leave my brother to fight alone. If he goes to battle, how can I not be at his side?"

Madame Sutton looked pointedly at me. "A revolution is coming. It will be fought with thousands of deaths or with only one. The choice is yours."

A cold choice.

"We can assure the military leaders," Master Grey added, "we've other plans to reach our goals, and they must stand down for a season. Think of the lives you'll save."

"What would I be required to do?" I hoped for something small—perhaps unlocking a door or levitating weapons over a wall.

Master Grey rubbed his hands together, warming to his explanation. "Next summer when the king marries, a great number of nobles will fill Valistowe castle to celebrate. Every lord will want to hobnob with the king and every highborn mother will bring her daughters in hopes of catching the eye of a wealthy bachelor. For two weeks, they'll busy themselves with feasting, dancing, and clandestine meetings around the castle grounds. You'll accompany Lady Edith there."

"Has she an invitation?" Paxworth was a small estate with a nearly dilapidated manor house. Usually, my adopted mother only interacted with a handful of servants, the tenants in her village, and the merchants who did business there. I assumed her frequent association with the common folk had made her sympathetic to the renegades' cause, but at times I was just as certain she only helped them to get funds to fix Paxworth's manor and grounds.

"She is of the peerage," Madame Sutton answered, at last taking a seat by the fireplace. "And therefore invited. The other nobles will simply think she's trying to regain some status in court and attempting to find a suitable husband for you. Alaric will accompany you there as her groomsman."

"And?" I prompted. I hadn't heard anything that actually resembled a plan yet.

Madame Sutton folded her hands in her lap. "We've knowledge of several secret passageways leading from various places in the courtyard to the king's chambers. They were built to allow him an escape route should the castle ever be under attack and will no doubt be locked. But you've no problem getting through locked doors."

"That depends on the door," I said. Some had more than locks to keep intruders out.

She went on as though I hadn't spoken. "All guests are searched upon arrival, and their weapons taken from them until they leave again. You'll either need to sneak something in or use whatever magic at your disposal to end King Leofric's reign."

I shook my head. They didn't understand what they were asking.

Alaric put his hand on my arm to draw my attention. "I can strike the necessary blow if needed. You'll just clear the way."

I kept shaking my head. "The king has five wizards protecting him."

"Yes," Madame Sutton said, "but our sources report they're rarely by his side. Even if you couldn't access the passageways, only a couple of men-at-arms guard his chambers. With your abilities, you should have little trouble dispatching them."

Madame Sutton's sources were uninformed. I didn't know anything about the king's wizards, but I still knew one essential fact. "The wizards don't need to stay at the king's side to protect him. They've cast a reflecting spell on him."

The group stared at me blankly. I shouldn't have been surprised. Very few besides wizards knew of the spell. I only knew of it because back when I'd lived in Docendum, Ronan had hunted for information about it and had been frustrated when he could find nothing. The spell had been created by King Leofric's father's wizards and, presumably, the secret hadn't left Valistowe Castle or the wizard council there since. This was probably in part because the spell would only protect a king. If one of the wizard council, in an act of avarice, had wanted to sell it, none of the nobility would've cared to buy it.

"A reflecting spell is formidable magic that requires the wizard council to enact and maintain it. The result is that any action taken to kill the king won't affect him but will reflect back on the assassin. If you were to stab King Leofric, he would pull the knife from his chest, unharmed, and watch you bleed to death. If you put poison into his cup, you would drop dead when he took a sip."

"Oh." Madame Sutton winced and placed her hand on her chest. Her voice was tinged with a sudden sadness. "That would explain certain things."

Had they already attempted to assassinate him?

"How do we counteract that magic?" Master Grey asked.

Madame Sutton's jaw grew tight with determination. "We have to kill the wizards, obviously." Really, for someone who looked like she could blend in at a nunnery, the woman had a vicious streak. She stood and began her pacing again.

I pressed my lips together, trying for patience. "Do you realize how difficult it is to kill a wizard?"

"For a normal person," Master Grey said, "I'm positive it's quite hard, but wizards know how to accomplish such things, don't they?"

"They might, but I don't." It was a lie. I knew a few ways to dispatch a wizard, but they were all dangerous. And besides, I'd already told Madame Sutton and Master Grey that I wasn't an assassin, and in response, they kept adding bodies to their requested death count.

Alaric studied me. "Are you sure you don't know of a way?"

We were too well acquainted. He could tell when I was lying.

I thought of the list Ronan had written once on the topic, and it appeared in my mind as though floating before my eyes. I ticked off the ways on my fingers. "You can trick a wizard into taking poison made by his own hand—which is why wizards are careful to destroy any unused poison they make.

"You can overcome their magic with a stronger force of your own. This is the common way to kill a rival, but most wizards don't attempt it without securing help from other wizards, as an opponent's strength might surprise him. I've no allies, and fighting a wizard outright would draw all sorts of unwanted attention to the event—you know, bolts of lightning, tidal waves, sea life flinging by, that type of thing. People would discover my identity, and the wizards would be so outraged by my existence that a pack of them would hunt me down."

Master Grey held up a hand to stop my list. "Is there a safe option?"

Alaric rubbed his chin in mock thought. "I rather like the idea of flying octopi. If I'm discovered as a renegade, I hope a few air-squid are involved."

I ignored Alaric and his ambitions of a martyrdom littered with sea life. "The safe option is to wait for old age to make a wizard careless with his protections, but that won't work when time is of the essence."

I held up another finger, continuing with my list. "Unknown pestilence or deep wounds can prove deadly, but I can't produce a pestilence or in all likelihood manage to overcome a wizard's defenses to strike a blow. Or…" I'd forgotten about the last option until I read the list floating in front of me. "Or one can remove a wizard's mark, rendering him magicless." There would be no need to kill them if I accomplished that task. The wizard council would no longer have the power to protect the king.

Madame Sutton swished to stop. "How is that done?"

Most people didn't know such a thing was even possible, let alone know the answer to that question. Mage Wolfson, who produced as many enemies from his apprentices as allies, certainly didn't teach it. Ronan had said the procedure, on the rare occasion the king ordered it, was performed by a group of wizards acting in concert.

But I knew of another way. I knew it because Ronan had diligently uncovered bits of information about the process and pieced them together while he searched for a way to give me a wizard's mark. Ronan had not only given me magic, he'd unwittingly given me the knowledge of how to take it from others.

The process, like most complicated spells, involved multiple incantations tweaked and strung in a sequence. Ronan was fond of saying that new spells didn't need to be invented to produce new magic, just as new letters weren't needed to form new words. And he was as good at finding ways to form magic to his will as a poet creating a sonnet.

But knowing the incantation and performing it on five of the most powerful wizards in the land was another matter.

"How is it done?" Madame Sutton repeated.

"As you can imagine," I said, "people with magic don't share those details."

She cocked her head, birdlike. "Meaning, you don't know how or you won't tell us?"

My gaze flicked to Alaric. That was a mistake. He could tell I was checking to see how closely he was watching me, checking to see if I could get away with a lie.

He smiled. "She knows." For someone who was supposed to be my friend, he had no compunction betraying the meaning of my gaze flicks. In the future, I wasn't going to be nearly as open with him.

Madame Sutton made a trilling noise—either happiness or accusation. "We've people in noblemen's estate. If they could remove the wizards' marks—"

"They can't," I cut her off. "Only another wizard can."

"And you," she clarified.

And me because I was, for all intents and purposes, a wizard.

"It's perfect," Alaric said. "The wizards will never suspect a woman can do them harm. You won't have to kill them, just neutralize them. Then I'll take care of the king."

I held up my hand. "Let someone else act as the assassin." I didn't want to save Alaric from death in battle just to lose him to the king's guards.

"Very well," Master Gray said. "We'll send a lady's maid with you who is capable of the job. Alaric will go along to help as needed."

Alaric grinned, happy with the arrangement.

There were downsides to working with people who didn't mind being martyrs. None of them seemed to fully understand that it was one thing to work bits of magic to steal jewels and documents; it was another to challenge the king's wizards. The task was too formidable.

And yet how could I refuse to help? I'd been a servant, powerless and at the mercy of those who owned me. Mage Wolfson had cared little about using me or destroying my life. Lessening the servant's time bound to masters was worth the risk. And if I didn't act, Alaric and Barnaby would join the renegades' doomed army.

"I'll do what I can," I said. "It probably won't be enough, and everyone involved will die."

The group took that to mean a hearty consent and an assured victory.

As they made more plans, I thought about the five mages of

the wizard council. In my mind, they all had Mage Wolfson's face.

The sight of that face, even in memory, filled me with fear but also with a growing desire for revenge. If the king's wizards were like him, and of course, they would be, I might enjoy taking their marks and leaving them to live normal, vulnerable —and in their own minds—pitiable lives.

CHAPTER 6

 *our and a half years ago*

ONE DAY, not long before my sixteenth birthday, Ronan finished his classes early and told me he wanted to go to the forest for a picnic. I thought nothing of it until we left the castle grounds and entered the trees that led to the forest. He glanced behind us furtively, took out a charm that was carved to resemble a wolf's nose, and arced it around us. "No one followed us, at least not in human form."

"Good." I continued walking. I was used to the occasional odd precaution on his part. Although really, none of the other apprentices had mastered animal form. Was he worried Mage Wolfson or Mage Quintal would bother to spy on us?

In a couple of strides, Ronan caught up to me, the basket in his arms held close like it was a child. "Are you ready to receive a wizard's mark?"

I halted so fast that my skirt swished about my shoes. "Yes!

Of course, yes." Yes, a hundred times to owning any sort of magic.

"Good. Because otherwise, you would've been very disappointed in the contents of our picnic." He tapped the side of the basket. "These are mostly things for the incantation."

"Truly, you can do this?" I bounced up and down on the balls of my feet, no longer able to stay still. My question wasn't about his ability, but his intentions. I believed in his skill completely.

He handed me the picnic basket. "Hold this."

I peeked under the lid. He hadn't been jesting about the contents. Only a couple of rolls and chunks of cheese were inside. The rest of the space was taken up by vials with unknown liquid, candles, strips of cloth, a sharpened spoon, two twigs, and a few other odd trinkets.

He slipped his wolf-nose charm into the basket with the other things. "I'll transform into a horse and carry you to a cottage by the seashore. That way I can be certain no one from the castle comes upon us. Take care not to spill anything."

Before I'd shut the lid, a white stallion stood in front of me, patiently waiting for me to climb on his back.

I took hold of his mane gingerly. "You might have thought to bring a saddle." Although I supposed that would've raised suspicions.

He eyed me, expectant. I pulled myself onto his back. Almost immediately, he began trotting, and when he decided I wouldn't fall off, cantering. I clung to his mane, the basket wedged between me and his neck. At first, he stayed on a path, but after half an hour, he slowed and made his way through the trees.

I wondered how he knew what lay so far away from the castle. He must have flown this way as a bird. He could change into a peregrine falcon.

The trees gave way to a rocky coastline and we came upon a squat wooden building, more shack than cottage. It was weathered and windowless, probably built for fishermen to stay in between trips. No fire came from the chimney, and the place appeared altogether abandoned.

The horse paused in front of its door, waiting for me to dismount. I slid from his back and watched Ronan, curious what he would look like when he was not quite a horse and not quite a man. The horse reared up on two legs, the way fighting stallions do, and then Ronan stood in front of me, completely calm. He brushed bits of dirt from his sleeves and took the basket from me.

"Here we are, then." He noted the sun's position in the sky and used an unlocking charm on the door. "We need to finish before sunset."

"The spell uses sunlight?" It was a common power source for such a rare spell.

"Among other things. I feel it's fitting that giving a mark be done in sunlight."

He felt? "Hasn't this spell been performed before?" I'd assumed he'd discovered it like some of the other ancient ones he ferreted from yellowing, forgotten scrolls in the back of Docendum's trove of magic texts.

He motioned me to follow him inside. "Not that I know of, but no need to fret. Incantations are like math equations. I've checked and rechecked this one to make sure it's sound." Ronan excelled at math in the same way he excelled at magic.

Inside the shack, a blackened fireplace took up most of the back wall. A bed with a sagging mattress was pushed up against one side of the room. Rickety chairs and a weathered table sat near the other wall. The place smelled of fish, salt air, and forgotten things.

Ronan left the door open for light.

I took slow steps across the floor and fiddled with the side of my skirt.

"Are you nervous?" he asked.

"A bit."

He placed the basket on the table, returned to me, and squeezed my hand. "Do you trust me?"

"Of course."

He dropped a kiss on my lips. Our kisses weren't frequent, but when they happened, they were no longer tentative. They were as familiar and sweet as sunshine that sneaks through the cracks in shuttered windows. They weren't supposed to be there, and yet they couldn't help but be bright anyway.

While he arranged things on the table, I sat on the bed, hands tucked under my skirt. He placed the vials in a row and put the candles behind them. They were made from some substance I didn't recognize. Not tallow. Not beeswax. More items came out.

Ronan pulled a dagger from the basket. I leaned forward on the bed. "What's that for?"

"You said you trusted me."

"I do," I said less certainly. I didn't think he would purposely hurt me. Never that. I just worried because the spell was untried. "What if something goes wrong? I won't find myself turned into a rabbit or something, will I?"

"Of course not. A rabbit hopping around the shack would be too distracting."

I bit my lip and didn't ask more questions. He mixed vials, carefully measuring their ingredients. My gaze kept drifting to the open door and the sunlight outside. The sky was a cloudless blue. Gulls occasionally flew by, calling one another. I couldn't see the ocean but I heard the rhythm of the waves breaking against the shore, a roar as relentless as fate itself.

He took the dagger, pricked his finger, and squeezed three drops of blood into one of the vials. "I need your blood as well."

I held out my hand. "You needn't have brought such a large dagger for such a little amount of blood."

He paused and his eyes tentatively went to mine.

I gulped. "That is all the dagger is for, isn't it?"

"Don't you trust me?"

"I would trust you more if you didn't have to keep repeating that question." The prick stung and the pain didn't stop, even after Ronan had gone back to the table. My finger burned where the blade touched it.

He set the vial with our blood aside, picked up another, and swept back over to me. "You'll need to drink this."

I swallowed, hoping it would blot out the pain in my finger. The potion tasted the way a rock might. I handed the empty vial back to him. "What was that?"

"Something to keep you alive."

I cocked my head. "Is it too late to revise my answer about whether I trust you?"

He smiled. He knew I wasn't serious. I trusted him in a way I hadn't trusted anyone since my parents died. I trusted him to love me. I'd even started to believe he would find a way to take me with him when he left Docendum.

He began to speak an incantation, his words lulling and low. The waves hitting the rocks sounded far away now. A chill crept through me. The pain in my finger bloomed across my hand, spread up my arm, and worked its way toward my heart. I tried to shake my arm but a stiffness traveled with the pain, making it hard to move.

"Ronan," I started, but didn't finish. The fingers of my injured hand were growing long and spindly. The skin on my arm cracked and darkened, becoming bark. I gasped at the horror of it. "You've turned me into a tree!"

Instead of joining in my panic and more importantly, doing something to fix this mistake, he nodded. "I said I wouldn't turn you into a rabbit. I never said anything about trees."

This wasn't a mistake. He'd done this on purpose without any warning.

My gaze flew to his face. He was intent on his vials, unconcerned with my state. I wanted to protest, to tell him to stop, but I could no longer form words. My eyes alone still worked. He stepped out of my sight of vision. All I could see was the door. Outside, the sunlight dimmed and seemed to drain away. Then I saw nothing.

When I became sensible of my surroundings once more, I was lying on the bed, human again. The shack was lit only by the candles. The outside was completely black.

I sat up, immediately feeling dizzy. "That didn't go well. You drained the sun."

Ronan laughed. My eyes traced the source of his laughter to the floor near the bed. He lay there, one hand across his stomach. "I didn't quite drain the sun. It's nighttime."

I swung my feet off the bed, a motion that reminded me that not all of my pain and stiffness had gone. "How long have we been here?"

"Several hours," he said. "Longer than I planned."

If the wizards knew we were missing, we'd both be in trouble. I more than Ronan. He was the most accomplished apprentice Docendum had seen in decades. I was a servant. My reputation, any claim to virtue, was probably already ruined. I didn't hurry off the bed, though. I needed time to regain my strength. "You could've warned me you were turning me into a tree."

Ronan pulled himself into a sitting position. "It would've only worried you. Very few wizards can manage to transform people into plants." He gave me a crooked smile. "I've joined their ranks."

My jaw went slack. "You tried an incantation on me not knowing whether you could do it?"

"Of course, I knew I could do it. I had to turn myself into a tree as well. I made sure I'd mastered that before I attempted it on you."

Then I remembered the point of the whole venture. "Did it work?" My hand went to my neck, checking for a wizard's mark. Foolishness on my part. I had run my fingers along Ronan's mark often enough to know it left no impression on the skin.

"I didn't put the mark on your neck," he said.

I smiled, all crossness gone. "It worked?"

"Yes."

I slipped off the bed and practically threw myself at him for a hug. "I have magic?"

He wrapped an arm lightly around me. His heartbeat pulsed through his tunic, strong and steady. "You have a little piece of mine. Hopefully, it's enough for you to perform a few spells to protect yourself. I'll teach you how to do invisibility, levitation, and extra strength. You mustn't ever use them in front of other people unless you're in danger." Ronan rested his cheek against my head. "Don't touch any of the magic books as those will still burn your hands. Don't try to learn more spells. To do anything else would put us both at risk. You understand?"

Back when the idea of giving me a mark had first occurred to Ronan, I'd assured him of as much. I nodded readily. "Yes."

In my defense, Ronan should have known when it came to learning, I was a liar. I'd already read half the books in Mage Wolfson's guest library.

The rest of Ronan's assertion finally registered in my mind. I pulled away from him and sat on the floor next to him. "Wait, where did you put my mark?"

His lips twitched into a smirk. "I had to conceal it, Sella. That left me little choice."

I lifted my skirt to check my calves. Not there. I didn't dare lift my skirt higher for modesty's sake. But Ronan apparently had.

His smile grew into a chuckle. "Don't look at me like I'm a rogue. We wouldn't want people accidentally catching sight of it."

"Where is it?" I repeated.

"Under your bodice."

I blushed and crossed my arms over my chest. "Did you... was I naked?"

"Yes," he said solemnly. "But you were a tree." Another smirk. "I bet you're glad now that I turned you into a Hawthorn. You had lovely white flowers, by the way."

"Is that why you turned me into a tree? For decorum's sake?"

He casually stroked a lock of my hair. "The mark can't be transferred from person to person, but trees have the fortunate ability to be grafted. To make the spell work, I turned a good portion of my body into a tree as well and enchanted objects to perform precise surgery, then when that was through, I cast a spell to make sure the graft took quickly and another to speed its healing. I admit I'm still rather weak from it all." He lowered his hand to his side. "I can't transform myself into a horse right now to carry you back."

I should've noticed before that he wasn't moving much. My gaze went over him. "Are you unwell?"

"I'll be fine. But we better not leave until morning." He said the words apologetically, breaking them to me as a piece of bad news that I might not have considered. "I need to rest, and you can't wander in the dark by yourself."

I nodded. "I suppose there's no way to beat the gossip home." It had undoubtedly started already. "We'll stay here until you're well."

He put his hand over mine. "We'll tell everyone we were climbing the cliffs, and you fell and broke both legs. Mending them took so much of my strength that I couldn't make the trip back."

"And I was too worried to leave you."

"Of course, they won't believe us." He looked at me sadly and pushed another strand of hair away from my cheek. "I'm sorry, Sella. I didn't mean to ruin your reputation."

I couldn't help but smile. "Yes, you've made that more than

clear." When we kissed, he usually pulled away first. I'd no need to set boundaries with him because he imposed them so strictly on himself.

I leaned against the wall. "I will attest to the other serving girls, as I always do, that if you hadn't been a wizard, you would've certainly become a monk."

He raised an eyebrow. "You tell people that?"

"Constantly." He should have realized by now that the castle staff spoke in knowing whispers about the time I spent in his room.

He laid his hand over mine. "They might not believe you now."

He was right. This was different.

I shrugged, although I could already feel the servants' disapproving gazes aimed in my direction. "You gave me magic," I said. "That's fair compensation."

* * *

THE NEXT MORNING while Ronan and I rode through the forest back to Docendum, a white-tailed eagle circled overhead. When it spotted us, it let out a cry and swooped downward, passing only inches above my head. Its beady eyes glared at me, then it flew off over the treetops and didn't return.

It didn't seem like a good omen.

I carried the basket, now empty of anything that would hint at the purpose of our trip. Still, I worried that the wizards would examine it and know what we'd done. Finally, we emerged from the forest and headed toward the castle grounds. Ronan transformed back into himself, hardly panting from the run.

"Did you see the bird?" I asked.

He gave a huff of laughter that held no humor. "How could I not?"

"Was it Wolfson out searching for us?"

"Mage Quintal. He takes the form of an eagle when he wants."

That was nearly as bad. Mage Quintal was the junior wizard at Docendum. He had little patience for the apprentices and none for the servants.

"Will you be in much trouble?" I asked.

"I suppose we'll see."

Ronan must have noted my worry because he reached out and squeezed my hand. "What's the worst that could happen? They'll expel me from the school? I already know more magic than most of the apprentices who graduate. Besides, Wolfson won't want to banish me." Ronan lowered his voice, perhaps to keep his words from the ears of listening eagles. "He brags too often of the things he's taught me to send me away in disgrace."

Ronan had grown more confident as he talked. I'd grown less so. It was true Mage Wolfson wouldn't send Ronan away due to our infraction, but that didn't mean he wouldn't send me away. Apparently, that outcome hadn't occurred to Ronan.

I wanted to tell him that I loved him, but how could I when he wasn't even worrying about our separation? But then, he accepted our separation as inevitable. That was the reason he'd given me magic. So, I held my tongue and promised myself that on the day we said our farewells, I would tell him. I would confess everything. I would take his hands in mine and bravely declare, "You are my world, and I, the sun that arises each day, whose only wish is to give you light and warmth, then sink with you into the night."

Perhaps it wasn't the best analogy of love. The earth and the sun were forever destined to be apart, but at least he'd know the depth of my feelings.

I half expected Mage Quintal to be sitting in a chair in the courtyard, waiting to confront us. He wasn't there. None of the teachers were. We hurried inside the castle and went our separate ways to tell our fabricated excuse; I to the head housekeeper and master cook and he to his teachers.

The housekeeper listened to my story without expression and only said, "You really must be more careful, Marcella. Such recklessness can only hurt you. Ronan will not always be around to put things right."

I understood her warning.

The kitchen servants simply gawked at me in disbelief as I told of my misadventures, but Cook Lindon pulled me into an embrace. This sort of affection wasn't normal for her. "When you didn't come back… I thought you were dead." She held me at arm's length and shook her head. "Have you no sense, child? What will become of you?"

What, indeed. Fortunately, the head cook issued no punishment for my misdeeds. The wizards didn't even speak to me about it, let alone threaten to send me away. Still, I hadn't quite escaped unscathed.

Later on, as I was collecting dishes from the apprentices' rooms, I heard a group of maids talking about me. "They ain't even hiding it now," one said. "Just goes to show why you shouldn't flaunt your prettiness. What's all her beauty got her? Decent men will want naught of her after he leaves."

The pronouncement stung. I stayed, unmoving, behind the apprentice's doorway until they left.

CHAPTER 7

The wizards didn't discipline Ronan, unless one considered a strict lecture about his priorities—which should be his studies—discipline. I marveled again that Mage Wolfson was so lenient, so willing to offer favors to his star pupil. My friendship was allowed to him like the tray of sweets the kitchen sent up each day.

Over the next week, Ronan worked on teaching me. Matter and energy were the same thing, he told me, and if one had a wizarding mark, the two could be manipulated in certain ways. All spells needed to be fueled by the magic within a wizard, but many required an extra spark to ignite the spell. He taught me how to draw that spark from the sunlight, moonlight, and fire.

I understood why Ronan said he'd given me only a little of his magic. The crescent-shaped mark above my heart was a tiny thing, not even a quarter of the size of the one on his neck. But Ronan assured me it was magic enough, and with practice, I could work the spells. Learning them required me to memorize words that had sounded like nonsensical babble before. Now my ear heard new sounds and inflections. The words had meaning, a sense to them like a language.

No one noticed the dimming of the sunshine as I practiced. The apprentices performed magic on such a continual basis that even on the brightest day, the castle courtyard often seemed to be in perpetual shade.

Instructing me to tap into energy within myself was problematic. "It's easier to do if you're angry," Ronan said. "Think of something upsetting."

At the time, I was attempting to lift his heavy wooden desk, one-handed. If the desk could have yawned at my efforts, it would have.

"When I'm with you," I said by way of explanation, "I'm too happy to be angry." The housekeeper's cold indifference toward me and the other girls' wagging tongues were so completely bearable when Ronan was around.

I thought of him leaving. That made me sad. What little strength I'd mustered drained away. I stepped away from the desk and rubbed the palm of my hand. It was red and protesting the way I'd pitted it against the desk.

"You'll improve with practice." Ronan sat on his chair, undisturbed by my failure. "If mastering incantations only took a few days, apprentices wouldn't have to stay here for years. You're actually doing quite well. Better than I expected." High praise considering how quick he was to criticize the other apprentices for their feeble abilities.

By the end of the month, I'd mastered invisibility. I still struggled with extra strength, but I'd learned levitation well enough to amuse myself by floating my chessmen around the board.

Ronan batted at my pieces when they went astray. "You're horrible at keeping secrets, and we'll both likely end up dead."

He was wrong about that. I was successfully keeping one very important secret from him. The crescent-shaped mark on my skin had grown larger as the days passed. Perhaps the same way that a branch, once grafted, also grows. I now not only had the ability to touch magical texts but to read them as well.

When I was picking up dishes from the apprentices' rooms and noticed their spell books lying open, how could I not pause to read them? Curiosity was one of my foremost faults.

I daydreamed of what I might accomplish with the use of more magic. Wizards sold their services, and I couldn't do that, but certainly, I could find ways to be useful, to make something of my life.

I discovered one other thing about my magic. Even though I'd only read an incantation once, I could recall it perfectly any time I thought about it. When Ronan had grafted his mark into me, he'd grafted that ability with it. I wasn't about to tell him. I was afraid if he realized he'd given me much more than he'd planned, he might take the mark away from me. Having magic, in a small way, made me his equal. And I couldn't bear to lose that.

It felt wrong to keep such an important secret from him, so I told myself that I would tell him on our wedding day. And if he never proposed, well, that would be his fault, not mine. Magic was a fair compensation for heartbreak as well.

Three months after I learned magic, Mage Wolfson once more requested my presence. This time not in his chambers, but at the top of the west tower room. Only Mage Wolfson ever went there. Not even the housekeeper traversed those stairs unless specifically bidden. No explanation was given to me for the summons.

Something was very wrong. I'd been discovered, caught, and could only hope it was for some small infraction such as reading the books in the guest library. Not for performing magic—not that.

I climbed the stairs as tremulously as if they were the gallows. Slow, heavy steps. My hands grew clammy and I wiped them against my skirt. By the time I knocked on the tower door,

I was ready to throw myself at the wizard's feet and beg for mercy. He must have some mercy, this man who had allowed a serving girl to befriend one of his apprentices.

I wasn't certain what Mage Wolfson knew, though, so when he bade me to come in, I slipped inside, head lowered, and held my tongue.

He sat at a desk, writing a letter. The room was larger than his receiving room in the main castle, although not so intricately decorated. The fireplace was plain stone, the chairs near them less ornate. A simple canopied bed stood by the fireplace. Two windows looked out onto opposite sides of the grounds, both surrounded by long, maroon curtains. Good windows for spying on what went on in the courtyard.

My gaze fell on what I'd first assumed to be a dark trunk behind the desk. It was the largest wolf I'd ever seen—twice the size it should have been. It lifted its head to survey me with suspicious eyes.

I froze. The animal may have been a normal wolf once, but it had been turned into something else altogether. Its jaws were wider with rows of sharp teeth, some of which protruded in spikes from the side of its mouth. Its eyes had the strange red glow of an albino even though its coat was black, save for a few gray streaks at its throat.

The beast wore a collar and was tied to a hook in the corner of the room. I was out of reach of the teeth for now.

"Sir?" I managed.

The wizard glanced up at me. I'd expected to see anger or at least censure. His expression was as cold and disinterested as ever. He gestured to a chair at the far end of the room. "Sit."

He said no more. It wasn't my place to ask why he'd summoned me. I trod softly across the room and sat on the chair. As soon as I did, I couldn't move. It was as though I was glued there. When I tried to ask why he'd done this, I couldn't open my mouth. Only an alarmed humming escaped my throat.

"Remain quiet until you're spoken to." It was an instruction the housekeeper gave us when we dealt with the highborn, and the wizard spoke it as chastisement.

I sat quietly waiting for a command or a question or verdict.

He flicked his wrist and one set of the long maroon curtains moved away from the window, slid across the room, and reconfigured themselves in front of me, completely concealing my presence.

This was bad. Was he keeping me immobile so that he could remove the mark? Perhaps he intended to extract my energy for some spell. Ronan had told me once that wizards could take the health of other wizards to lengthen their own life span. Such magic was forbidden, but Ronan performed an incantation every morning to protect himself from that sort of pilfering anyway. Wizarding law was a fluid thing at best, often ignored by the powerful and used to punish less influential wizards.

I couldn't recall any incantations to help me escape from whatever magic bound me to the chair. I began sifting through spells filed away in my memory for any bit of help they might offer.

I was so intently reading, I didn't know Ronan had come into the room until he spoke. "What is it you require, my lord?"

My breath caught. Mage Wolfson must know what Ronan had done or he wouldn't have summoned us both. He would question Ronan and when he lied, Mage Wolfson would let the curtains fall and reveal me as evidence.

A wave of nausea ran through me. What would the wizard do to him, to me?

"Ronan Clarke," Mage Wolfson's tone was unruffled, "you've reached the highest levels of magic quickly and completely. Brilliantly, I would say." A pause, "However, you've failed to master a few lessons, and I would be remiss if I didn't teach them to you."

"I'm sorry to have disappointed you." Surprise tinged

Ronan's voice but also confidence. I could picture him standing in front of Mage Wolfson's desk, shoulders back, head held high. "Which lessons have I failed? I will remedy the situation immediately."

I shut my eyes. Mage Wolfson's next words would be: Don't give magic to serving girls.

Instead, he said, "When you work for nobility, they will at times give you assignments you don't approve of. I told the class this morning that the village of Colsbury was harboring renegade leaders. Your solution to handle the insurrection involved dispatching a few spies to the village."

"Yes," Ronan said. "Spies could not only ferret out the leaders, they could also learn information about the organization."

What did any of this have to do with me?

Mage Wolfson huffed his disagreement. "Your solution wouldn't send a message to those who would ally themselves against the king. And as he's given me permission to deal with the situation however I see fit, I'm assigning you and Charles to go on horseback to an outlook above Colsbury. When you arrive, you're to burn down the village. Between the two of you, you should have enough fire to encompass the homes and prevent the escape of the renegades and those who harbored them."

I heard the words and yet a part of me couldn't believe Mage Wolfson had spoken them. The wizard wouldn't ask Ronan to do such a thing. Innocent people lived in that village—women and children who ought to be protected by the king, not slaughtered by his wizards.

"You were right," Ronan said slowly. "This is a lesson I will fail. I cannot carry out that request."

"Is this how you would answer your lord?" Mage Wolfson's calm tone turned sharp. "Let me remind you that wizards can't create gold or food. We work for nobles because they are wealthy enough to pay us handsomely. Would you refuse your lord his services in war as well?"

"I would help his troops fight to the best of their ability."

"And what if his troops burned down the village?"

"Then the act would trouble their souls, not mine."

The sound of a chair pushing away from the desk told me that Mage Wolfson had stood. "The first lesson you've failed to learn is that a conscience is a burden you can ill afford. It will keep you from doing the things you must."

"I apologize for my shortcomings." Ronan's voice was politely deferential. "Again, I must fail."

"Do you think you have a choice in the matter? If I've not disillusioned you from that notion, I will do so now." The curtain slid back toward the wall like a snake returning to its home.

Ronan caught sight of me, and his eyes widened with shock. He understood and now so did I. I wasn't here because the wizard had discovered our secrets. I was here as leverage.

Mage Wolfson snapped his fingers, and I lifted out of the chair and floated upward until I hung a few feet from the ceiling. As soon as I left the chair, feeling rushed into my limbs. I was no longer frozen, but I was still powerless, suspended like a hovering moth.

Ronan stepped toward me, completely pale. "Let her go."

Mage Wolfson flipped me onto my stomach, and I traveled, floating helplessly across the room. I didn't scream. I intended to be braver than that. Instead, I thrashed in an attempt to escape the wizard's grip. Levitating things was more difficult when they moved. As I passed the curtains, I grabbed hold of them. They ripped from the wall.

"None of that." With another snap of the wizard's fingers, the curtain ties lifted from the ground and wound around my body, pinning my arms to my side.

"Let her go," Ronan said again, pleading this time.

"Her fate is entirely in your hands."

It wasn't. It was in the wizard's, and I hated him for doing this. I glided toward the wolfhound, something the animal noticed at once. His fur bristled and he growled. I drifted closer. He sprang to his feet and lunged at me, barking furiously. He couldn't reach me. Not yet. He strained at his leash, claws scraping the floor, like knives being sharpened.

I bit my lip to keep from screaming.

"Please." Ronan lifted his hands to Mage Wolfson in desperation. "Please, don't do this. You've made your point."

"Her fate is your decision," the wizard repeated calmly. His calmness added to his cruelty. How could he so coolly threaten my life?

Tears gathered in my eyes. Frightened tears, not only for myself but for the people of Colsbury.

When I was directly above the beast, my progress halted. I was face down and could see every detail of the wolf yanking against his leash, his red eyes on me. My breaths came out in short gasps.

I should've yelled to Ronan to keep refusing, to stand firm with his conscience. Fear closed my lips completely. My noble sentiments of protecting the innocent villagers abandoned me. I thought only of myself and the snarling beast below me. Spittle flew from his mouth. His teeth could've broken my bones into pieces, and his claws were as sharp as daggers.

But I didn't beg for my life. I didn't look at Ronan lest my eyes plead my case.

And perhaps that gave Ronan the strength not to acquiesce. "A man as great as yourself wouldn't wish fire on children. There must be another solution."

"Obedience is the solution. That is lesson two."

I dropped a foot in the air, close enough that the wolf launched himself at me. His teeth didn't reach me, but his claws swiped across my face. Pain sliced me from eyebrow to chin, deep, searing. I screamed and couldn't stop even when the wizard jerked me upward.

"I'll do it!" Ronan yelled. "Let her go! I'll do it."

My screams subsided to gasps. I gazed at Ronan in appreciation, all the villagers momentarily forgotten.

His eyes were shocked, horrified. I wasn't sure if his horror was for the fate of the villagers we'd both so easily sacrificed or for my ruined face. Blood dripped onto the floor below me like red rain. It filled one of my eyes and I had to blink it away with my tears. It seeped into my mouth.

The wizard smiled in triumph, and it occurred to me that this was the first time I'd seen a true smile from him. *This* had made him smile. My face burned from anger as much as pain. I wished a thousand deaths on him.

He waved his hand. I flipped over and floated down onto his bed, leaving a red trail in my wake. The cord wound around my arms fell away. I tentatively touched my face and felt a flap of loose skin. When I pulled my hand away, blood covered it.

Ronan rushed to the side of the bed and took my hand. Perhaps for support, perhaps to keep me from touching my face again. His own hand trembled. "We need to heal her wounds. She's bound to get blood fever otherwise."

The wizard appeared next to him. He held a bottle of ointment in one hand and strips of linen cloth in the other. I knew wounds were difficult to heal, but certainly, someone of Mage Wolfson's abilities could do it. My mind clung to that idea.

He didn't hurry despite the stains I was leaving on his blankets. "You've learned your first two lessons well enough, but the third still escapes you." He uncorked the bottle and poured its contents over the bandages. "Did you think I sent this girl to you all those years ago because I cared about your childish loneliness?"

Ronan's hand was tight on mine. "I thought you sent her to help me study."

Mage Wolfson slipped the empty bottle into his pocket, pulled a strip of cloth from the pile in his hand, and draped it across my chin. I expected it to sting. Instead, it felt cool and soothing. "I sent her because you were a willful boy, and even then I knew you'd require this lesson."

What lesson? What could this attack have possibly taught Ronan except that Mage Wolfson was evil?

I wasn't foolish enough to ask this question.

He placed a strip over my upper lip. The pain there immediately diminished. "Lesson number three: attachments to women leave you vulnerable. Vulnerability is weakness. With only a bit of hesitation, you betrayed your principles and the lives of an entire village. She's made you weak."

I hoped the wizard would add that he didn't really mean to send Ronan to burn Colsbury, that this had all been a horrible, horrible test. But Mage Wolfson, too, seemed to have forgotten about the villagers. His eyes were on Ronan, a sneer growing on his lips. "Do you still think me a lonely, miserable, old man with no family, friends, or greedy children to gobble up my time?" Another strip of cloth. "I chose a solitary life, and it was the correct choice. If you're wise, you'll follow in my footsteps. If not, you'll be as vulnerable and weak as you are right now."

Ronan clenched his jaw. A muscle pulsed in his cheek. His eyes left mine and went to our hands, clasped together and both bloody now. I felt him let go a little. I grasped his hand to keep him from taking it out of mine. I would not let him pretend, even for Mage Wolfson's sake, that attachments to people were a weakness.

No one spoke again until Mage Wolfson finished coating my face with bandages. He straightened and his voice returned to that of a teacher. "The ointment I just applied was made of yarrow, goldenrod, and a drop of Monoceros. What will I find when I remove these bandages?"

Ronan's expression fell. He looked at the headboard behind

me instead of at my eyes. "The healing process has been sped to its completion."

"Yes. Her skin has already knit back together. The only proof of today will be the scars she bears. But that's for the best. When you see them, they'll remind you of the lessons you learned here."

I would be scarred. I wanted to ask how badly. Some scars were faint. Some faded away.

The wizard began plucking the bandages off. "You'll need to gather your provisions. On the morrow, you and Charles will leave for Colsbury."

The villagers, it turned out, were not forgotten after all.

CHAPTER 8

When I left the tower, I didn't return to the kitchen. I couldn't face anyone there, and I didn't have my own room to retreat to like the apprentices. Every night, I slept on a straw mattress in the kitchen, sharing the area with other servants. I fled to Ronan's room to cry privately. I assumed he'd join me soon. Mage Wolfson wouldn't keep him long.

A looking glass stood on Ronan's shelf; the fine sort needed for various spells. I took it down, almost afraid to peer into it.

Three deep welts snaked across my face from my eyebrow to my chin, pink, puckered, and horrible. I gasped and the mirror fell from my hands.

Disfigured. That was the only description for me now.

I will never marry, I thought. No man would want a wife with such a face. Not even Ronan would. I stopped myself before I let that thought take hold. The one person who wouldn't judge me for my scars was Ronan, but then, he was going to leave Docendum.

I would stay and people would turn away from me, avert their eyes. They'd tell tales and give warnings to children lest they anger the wizard and meet my fate. And yet I hadn't done anything to deserve this punishment. I'd only ever been a pawn, someone Mage Wolfson could use when it came time to force Ronan into doing his will. He'd given me to Ronan to entrap him.

I stood for some time, a hand pressed to my scars, crying. Then I noticed the pieces of glass at my feet. The mirror had broken when I'd dropped it. I stared at it, fixated on the jagged edges of its ruin, and was overcome with a need to repair it.

Ronan had given up so much to save my life. I didn't want him to think I'd been careless with his tools. Wizards had spells for fixing objects. I could repair it before he knew what had happened. I put the pieces on his desk, forming them together. With shaking hands, I took a magic book from his shelf and sat down on the floor, my back pressed against his door. I would levitate it back to his shelf as soon as he approached.

I read page after page without finding anything useful. It didn't matter. As long as I was reading, I wasn't thinking about my ruined face, even if my scars—which felt both itchy and taut —were determined to remind me. I hoped to find a spell to remove scars, but it was a narrow hope. Ronan had already told me wounds were hard to heal and some couldn't be healed at all. Even mending bones was difficult for a wizard, and given enough time, a person could accomplish the same results with a splint.

Could a beauty potion help? My face was probably beyond the realm of such enchantments.

I flipped pages, kept reading, kept searching. I found spells for mending horseshoes, coach wheels, roof beams, and tapestries. None for repairing glass. One would've thought the nobility never shattered anything.

An hour went by. My neck and dress were smeared with dry blood but I made no move to clean them. I finished the book and started on another. Every few minutes, my fingers found their way to my cheek and the ridges that had this morning been smooth flesh.

At last, I heard footsteps coming toward the room. I levitated the book onto the desk and stood just as the door opened. Ronan trudged inside, ashen and weary. His normally bright eyes seemed pinched, haunted almost. I threw my arms around him and a new set of sobs rose in my throat.

He wrapped his arm across my back and rested his forehead against my shoulder. "I'm so sorry. I'm so sorry." He repeated the phrase several more times.

"It isn't your fault. It's Wolfson's."

Ronan shook his head. "I should've known. I should've seen it years ago." He took a step away from me and raked his hand through his hair like he wanted to pull some out. "When I was fourteen, I wanted to go home. He wouldn't let me write to my family and ask that they come fetch me, so I told him he was a lonely, miserable, old man. I used those words. He said I was young and stupid, and I'd understand when I was older."

Ronan's hand dropped from his hair. "The next week he made you my study partner. I should've realized what he was doing." His gaze turned to me, fell upon my scars, and he winced.

Guilt caused that wince, I told myself, not revulsion.

"You need to go," he said, "and you mustn't come back to my room. Don't speak to me in the hallways or elsewhere. Otherwise, he'll use you to manipulate me again."

My heart stuttered and plummeted in my chest like a downed bird. Ronan might as well have asked me to give up eating. "But how will we talk to each other?"

His gaze couldn't rest on my face. It flitted around the room. "We won't. We can't anymore. You must see that."

I took a stumbling step backward, his words ringing through my head like a slap. I wanted to say, "But you need me." How foolish. He obviously didn't. It was only I who needed him, and now he was telling me to leave. I stood there for a moment, breathing hard. I nearly pointed out that the other servants had already ostracized me, and now, disfigured, my misery would be tenfold.

I was a servant, though. I had no claim on him.

And besides, I couldn't argue him into loving me.

A third time his gaze traveled to me and just as quickly fled to the wall behind me. It was too painful for him to even look at my face now.

"I'm sorry," he whispered again. "I'm sorry it must be this way. I'll do what I can for you." He turned and paced to his window, keeping his back to me. That was all. He'd dismissed me and was waiting for me to go.

I glared at his back, at his hands gripping the windowsill. Every muscle in him was rigid.

"Are you going to burn down the village?" I asked.

He didn't answer.

I put my hand on the door handle. "You might as well tell Mage Wolfson you won't do it. Let him kill me. It won't be more painful than this."

"You don't mean that," Ronan said.

I did mean it.

I left the room and slammed the door behind me, a thing no servant was allowed to do.

I don't remember the walk to the kitchen. I only remember thinking I might as well face the other servants now because my heart had already been torn from my chest, and I'd hardly notice more scorn.

When they saw me, they gasped and shrunk away as though I was a wraith. Cook Lindon took hold of my shoulders, gaped at my face, and demanded to know what had happened. I told them. I didn't even spare Ronan the detail of his agreeing to burn down the village. I should've been vague about the particulars of what the wizard commanded him to do, but my mind wasn't working clearly. I wasn't even aware I'd started crying again until I felt the tears falling on my hands. I stared at the drops on my skin like they were foreign things.

Cook Lindon washed the dried blood off me as best she could, gave me a sleeping draught, and sent me to the sick room to rest. I was too shaken to do anything but comply.

The next morning, the housekeeper told me I was no longer to take food or retrieve dishes from Ronan's room. At his request, another serving girl had been assigned the task.

I might have marched out of the castle and kept going until I cast myself into the sea. Only one thought saved me from complete despair. Ronan had been upset when he banished me from his life. He'd been angry with himself for not being able to protect me. He would think better of his edict soon. He would arrange a way to meet with me in secret. If no one saw us, Mage Wolfson wouldn't know Ronan still cared for me. We'd both climbed Docendum's walls enough times we could sneak out of the grounds without detection.

Ronan left that day with Charles, the other apprentice whom Wolfson had commanded to take part in the burning. Charles had never shown signs of a conscience, which didn't bode well for the people of Colsbury.

I wanted to warn the villagers, but Colsbury was a two-day ride—and in which direction, I knew not. Still, as I fed the pigs, I repeated the words of the incantation Ronan used to turn himself into a falcon. If I soared around the area, I might spot Charles and Ronan on the road. If I knew which way they were headed, perhaps I could fly ahead and find the village.

Only the most powerful wizards could transform into animals, but my magic was a graft of Ronan's, and he'd managed the transformation during his first few weeks at Docendum.

Nothing happened, no matter how many times I said the words. Although my mark had continued to grow, my magic was still too small or I was too unlearned for such a feat. I trudged back to the kitchen feeling ill.

No one expected the two apprentices back for four days. If I'd been in Ronan's place, I would've left Charles after the first night, alerted the villagers, and struck out on my own. If Ronan refused to carry out Mage Wolfson's orders, he'd have to come back to fetch me. Otherwise, the wizard would kill me in retribution.

We could leave for a new life together.

A wishful fantasy, perhaps, but I slept by the door each night, boots on, lest he come for me.

After four days, Ronan and Charles returned to Docendum. While I cleaned the hen house, they rode through the gates and took their horses to the stables. Ronan's face betrayed no emotion. It was carefully masked in indifference. Ashy dust covered the bottom of his cloak. He must have walked through the village of Colsbury after they'd burned it.

I felt like I would choke. One moment, I wanted to yell at him for such heartlessness, the next I was positive he hadn't complied with the wizard's order. Certainly, when the time came, Ronan had refused to set the fires—had tried to stop them —and Charles had carried out the deed.

Perhaps Ronan's cloak had swept through ashes as he'd frantically searched for survivors to help. Perhaps he'd found a way to spare some. Or perhaps he'd forever be tormented by the smell of the smoke and the villagers' screams.

I waited for Ronan to send word to me.

He didn't.

Over the next few days, when I saw him crossing the courtyard, he purposely stared elsewhere. Mage Wolfson was right, my scars were a reminder, and Ronan couldn't bear to see them. I just wasn't sure what my scars reminded him of: his failure to help me or the villagers. Maybe he simply felt guilty he'd stopped loving me when ugliness replaced my beauty.

I became reckless. At night while the others slept, I murmured the invisibility incantation and snuck downstairs to Docendum's library of magic books. The wizards had set wards around the room to keep those without magic out. Those failed to deter me. I took book after book from the shelves. I read to spite Ronan, to spite Mage Wolfson.

I gravitated to those books that dealt with spells to incapacitate one's enemies. I never wanted to be at anyone's mercy again, especially Wolfson's. I found no spell that could erase scars, though I searched. One of the books contained a beauty potion, but I didn't have access to any of the ingredients it required—a ground pearl being one of that list, a columbine grown in the snow another.

As the weeks went by, I still held out hope, faint though it was growing, that Ronan would contact me. We'd been each other's dearest friends for years, and more than friends the last year. He must miss me. Eventually, he would relent.

Three months after the tower room, when I was helping to serve the apprentices supper in the dining hall, Mage Wolfson took notice of me. Ronan sat on his left side and the wizard checked to see if his eyes were following me. They weren't, of course. They never did now.

Mage Wolfson picked up a slice of cheese. "I've been thinking of selling some servants to Lord Haddock." He bit into a slice, chewing while he considered. "Which of the serving girls do you think I should let him have?"

Ronan's gaze flicked to mine, letting me know that even though he never acknowledged my presence, he still knew where I was. His eyes left mine just as quickly. He dipped his bread in the porridge as though the topic wasn't bothersome. "You should sell Marcella." He offered me up without hesitation. He said no other words and gave no explanation.

I nearly spilled the drink I was pouring. My throat felt tight.

Breathing was hard. This was my home, and Cook Lindon was the closest thing I had to a mother. Ronan knew that.

The wizard chuckled. "You've learned your third lesson well."

Ronan took a calm bite of his bread. "I'm a quick learner."

I glanced at him. I had to see his expression. It was the same cold blank mask he'd worn for three months.

Mage Wolfson nodded. "On the morrow, I'm sending crates of wizards' orbs and medicine to Carendale Castle. She'll go in the wagon with them."

So soon. Ronan didn't take his attention from his plate. No flash of pain went across his face. If anything, he looked relieved to be rid of me.

This was to be our farewell. No goodbyes. No declarations. I would not tell him that he was my world, and I was the sun meant to warm him.

Even though I wasn't done filling glasses, I spun on my heel and stalked off to the kitchen. I set my pitcher down on the carving table and, without a word of excuse, stormed out the back door. I ran toward the orchards at the far end of the castle grounds. Once I was hidden among the trees, I repeated a transformation incantation, attempting to turn myself into a falcon. I would fly into the air, wing away, go far from here. I wouldn't be sold alongside crates of wizards' orbs and fever tinctures as though my value was not much more than either of those things.

My mark was nearly the size of Ronan's now. Surely I had sufficient power. More than one text said the way to access one's internal reserve was with firm, concentrated desire. If that was the key, my desperation should sprout wings from my back.

My plans were already expanding, options ticking away in my mind. After I flew away, I'd live as a hermit in the forest, or find some family well off enough to pay for a tutor, or better yet, go to a nunnery and spend the rest of my life repenting for ever loving Ronan.

I pressed my eyes closed and repeated the incantation, concentrating on the image of a falcon. My arms tingled. I felt them grow and stretch. I lifted them, expecting to see feathers. Instead, greyish-brown bark scaled along my skin like cracking mud. I'd pictured a falcon. Why was I turning into a tree? My feet gripped the ground and burrowed into the dirt. Twigs pushed through my arms and leaves unfurled like tiny flags. Small leaves with five points. A hawthorn tree.

In my panic, I forgot what the reverse incantation was, and when I did have the presence of mind to retrieve it from my memory, I could no longer speak. My lips were sealed together underneath the layer of bark.

Would I be stuck here forever?

I could still see the courtyard, though I didn't know how without my human eyes. Either trees had senses unknown to me, or magic preserved a wizard's sight even during these sorts of transformations.

I thought the words of the reverse incantation, shouting them in my mind.

The bark disintegrated from my body. My arms shrunk. Roots became toes once more. I ran my fingers along my face and neck to make sure I was completely human. I was, thank the saints. One of them must be the protector of girls who made rash decisions.

I recalled each word of the incantation, trying to discover my mistake. I'd pictured a falcon, said the name for a falcon, and turned into a tree. Perhaps the problem was I'd reached into my reserve using sorrow. Perhaps sorrow was forever connected to Ronan, and the hawthorn tree had become the symbol of that pain.

I tried the incantation again, feeling anger this time. Anger for Wolfson who'd nearly fed me to his beast and had forced

Ronan to kill villagers. Anger at Ronan for obeying him and abandoning me. Anger that scars would always mar my face.

Heat radiated through my body and pulsed through my blood. A stirring roiled deep inside me; some animal thing growing, reaching, snapping its teeth. Dark fur bristled on my arms. Whatever this animal was, it had no wings, and I didn't know how to control its wildness. My anger, apparently, couldn't transform itself into the shape of a falcon either.

My fingers curled into claws and my teeth sharpened—A wolf, I realized. If I finished transforming, I'd be in danger. The men at arms would spear me on sight.

I stopped repeating the incantation and the heat in my body drained away. The spell hadn't been completed, so it unraveled like knitting when the yarn was pulled. Fur faded. Claws disappeared.

I sank to the ground, exhausted, and wrapped my arms around my legs. My plan to escape had been a foolish one anyway. Where would I go, a scarred, penniless servant? How would I feed and clothe myself? The morrow would come, and with it, my sale. My fate was beyond my control. All I could hope was that since Ronan knew where I was going, he would one day come for me.

I stayed in the orchard for several more minutes, head down, defeated. Finally, I trudged back inside and told Cook Lindon of my sale. She was the only one who would miss me.

She held me enfolded in her thick arms and wept.

"Perhaps I'll be allowed to write to you," I said.

"Where would you get the parchment?" She immediately added, "Don't even think of stealing any from your new master. You've no one to look out for you at Carendale."

I knew a spell for turning onion skins into parchment. "Perhaps I can retrieve scraps from the rubbish."

She pulled away from me and shook her head, bits of brown hair coming loose from her cap. "Even if you managed to find someone to carry a letter back here, who would read it to me?"

She had a point. None of the kitchen staff could read, and the steward would think such a task beneath him. I nearly told her that Ronan would do it, but I wasn't sure he would. I wasn't sure of anything about him anymore. Besides, I didn't want him to read about my dreary life at Carendale or the menial tasks I performed there.

"If I can't write," I said, "then you'll just have to know that every wagon that comes from Carendale will carry some of my love back to you."

She forced a smile and ran her hand across my forehead, pushing away the hair I let fall over my face—my attempt to hide as much of it as possible. Her fingers brushed against the ridges on my cheek. "Perhaps it's not a bad thing, your scars. Might keep you safe from the wandering eyes of the men at Carendale."

A small blessing. Not one I considered worth the price.

CHAPTER 9

That night as I lay on my pallet, waiting to make sure the other servants were truly asleep so I could have one last visit to the library, the door to the room softly swayed open. Dimly glowing wizards' orbs hung from the hallway ceiling in case anyone needed to traverse the castle after dark, but no silhouette appeared in the doorway. No one seemed to be there at all.

Just as softly as the door had opened, it shut.

I saw no one enter, which meant the intruder was using an invisibility spell. Probably not one of the wizards. Neither would have felt the need to cloak themselves. None of the apprentices had ever come here before, but one might have come to make mischief. A serving girl who was being sold in the morning was fair game.

I shut my eyes and listened. Next to the fireplace, the master cook snored like an angry boar. Someone turned in their sleep and their straw crunched. I could barely make out the sound of careful footsteps winding around sleeping forms.

I hoped Ronan was coming to say goodbye but didn't let myself dwell on that hope. I was tired of disappointment.

Perhaps my forays into the magic library had been discovered, and someone was waiting to follow me there and entrap me.

Instinctively, I moved my hands in front of my heart, covering my mark. The footsteps came nearer. I kept very still, reminding myself to breathe like one asleep. The footsteps stopped at the side of my pallet.

Breathe in, breathe out.

Ronan's voice softly murmured words above me. Not words I was meant to hear. He was repeating some unfamiliar incantation. I could tell from the position of the sound that he'd gone from standing to kneeling.

My first thought was that he meant to remove my mark. I had to counteract his incantation. I searched through my memory and the needed spell appeared. The pages floated in my mind, preserved exactly as they'd been written.

I'd already known I could recall any spell I'd read, but until this moment, I didn't realize my memory also contained spells Ronan had learned. Because the spell I saw wasn't from a book. It was four incantations cobbled together, scrawled in his handwriting on a scrap of parchment.

I didn't have time to contemplate the implications—the vast number of spells I had at my disposal. None of it mattered unless I protected my mark.

He gently laid his hand on my cheek. That wasn't part of the spell. The touch was so light it had clearly meant to go undetected. I couldn't decide whether I should pretend to wake up or keep feigning sleep. What was he doing?

Hand still on my cheek, he let out a sharp intake of breath. That decided the matter. My eyes flew open. "Who's there?" I hissed.

He moved his hand but didn't answer. He made no sound at all.

I pulled myself up on my elbows and glared in his direction. "Ronan, I know it's you. Why are you here?"

No answer. Whatever incantation he'd done, he wasn't about to admit it.

"Come to say goodbye?" I couldn't keep the bitterness from my voice.

I knew he would give me some unsatisfactory excuse for sending me away. He'd tell me I was safer away from Wolfson. I, in return, would point out I was safe enough now that Ronan had scorned me, and I'd be even safer when he left Docendum. None of the other apprentices would care if Wolfson dangled me in front of his beast. No one cared about a scarred serving girl.

I waited for an explanation. None came.

I sat completely up. The door hadn't reopened, so I knew he was still inside. Most likely still beside me.

"Once I'm at Carendale Castle," I whispered, "will I ever see you again?"

"I don't know," he replied, still close to my pallet. "It would be best if you forgot me."

"You know I can't." I narrowed my eyes, fruitlessly scanning the area for some sign of him. "One doesn't forget about the things one loves or hates. I'll let you ponder which category you fall into."

A low sigh. I wished I could see his expression to see how my words affected him. His voice went soft. "I never should've taken you from the kitchen. All I did was harm you. If you hate me, hate me for that."

To wish our friendship away, to wish away my education—it was too much. Almost without thinking I reached out and slapped him. "You're as arrogant as the rest of them."

He took hold of my wrist, perhaps to keep me from striking him again. "I am sorry, Sella. So very sorry. I've left a few coins underneath your pillow. I wish it were more, but it's all I have." The wizards didn't allow the apprentices to have any money while they stayed at Docendum. I didn't know where he'd gotten any coins. Then I remembered the incantation. Had he found a spell to produce them? Such a thing was supposed to be impossible.

"I don't want your money," I said. "I don't want anything from you."

"I know. That's why I was trying to give you my gift without waking you." He let go of my hand.

"Did you burn down Colsbury?" I threw the words at him.

He sighed again. "What do you think?"

"I think you're a wizard."

"Yes, I am."

What did that mean? Had he done it or not? He wasn't denying it and that couldn't bode well. A moment later, I heard his footsteps heading to the door. I wanted to yell something at his retreating back but didn't know what: *I hate you! I love you! I will curse every wizard I see from now on.* All were true. Yelling any of them into the darkness would do nothing but awaken the kitchen staff. So, I lay down again, fuming, and wished I'd pretended not to wake up at all.

I considered sneaking off to the library, then realized Ronan had read all the important books there. I shut my eyes and flipped through incantations in my mind, trying to find one that produced denarites. Such a spell could prove enormously useful. If I performed it enough times and found a plausible explanation for having the money, I could buy my freedom.

As I thought of coins, incantations flashed through my mind. They involved coins by using the metal as part of the spell. Quite the opposite of what I wanted to do.

Or perhaps the spell Ronan used was one of thievery. I began searching those. While reading a spell on ways to attract your neighbor's livestock to your property, I drifted off to sleep.

The next morning, I awoke to the sound of Cook Lindon telling me the wagon was nearly packed. The rest of the staff had already gone to the kitchen without bidding me goodbye.

Cook Lindon's red eyes attested that she, at least, would miss me. Her lips trembled with emotion. So very unlike her. She carried a cloth sack that smelled of food. "Put on your boots and fetch your cloak, child. It's a cold day."

I sat up and ran my hand under my pillow. Ten gold denarites were there, enough to pay for five years of my servant's debt to my new master. I could find no comfort in the gift. It felt like Ronan considered this an ample wage for my friendship, the price to clear his conscience of my abandonment.

I stood and handed the coins to Cook Lindon. I planned to tell her to return them to Ronan, a prideful notion that would've brought me pleasure anyway, but when she gasped, I realized she thought I meant to give them to her. And really, that was a better use for the coins. I might be too proud to benefit from Ronan's largesse, but that didn't mean she shouldn't have her debt paid.

She was still staring at me with a slack jaw so I said, "I didn't steal them. Ronan will vouch for that if Mage Wolfson questions you. They're yours."

But she wasn't staring at the coins. She was gawking at my face.

"The scars," she exclaimed. "They're gone." She took my chin in her calloused hand and turned my face one way and another. "Not a trace of 'em."

My fingers flew to my cheek and the ridges that had puckered my face for months. Only smooth, continuous skin met my touch.

Ronan hadn't conjured up the coins last night. He'd performed an incantation to erase my scars. A wave of gratitude nearly made me sink to my knees. I wouldn't have to go through life disfigured. I wouldn't be stared at and pitied. I'd hunted relentlessly in the library for a healing spell and hadn't discovered one. But somehow he'd managed that feat.

"Ronan…" I said by way of explanation. "He came in last night."

Her eyes lit up with understanding. "He must'a waited to fix your scars until Wolfson wouldn't see what he'd done." She nodded at the notion. "Master Ronan's not the bad sort, after all. I reckon that's why he got you sent away. He couldn't do nothing for you here under the wizard's eye."

Her chin kept wagging, absolving Ronan even though she'd never trusted him before. "That takes some of the sting out yer going, don't it? Just look at you, all lovely again. At Carendale, you'll have no trouble at all finding a respectable lad to marry you." She lowered her voice despite the fact we were alone in the room. "No one need know about what you and Ronan did here."

"We did nothing."

"That's right. Deny any gossip that follows you, and I'll pray that Carendale has a handsome unmarried blacksmith for you. Those are always wealthy. You'll live a good life yet, you will."

I hugged her goodbye before she could plan my nuptial feast. I wasn't sure if her assertions about Ronan's reasons for sending me away were correct. Wouldn't he have said as much last night? But why else would he have suggested to Wolfson that I go if not to protect me?

Ronan had waited to cure my scars so Wolfson wouldn't know he still cared about me. Otherwise, the wizard might have kept me around to use for leverage again.

I put on my cloak and hood to shadow my face, then made my way outside and across the courtyard. I looked for Ronan, searching unabashedly for some sign of him. No one stood in the shadows of the doorways. At the sound of a box being flung into the wagon, a flock of ravens took flight from a tree and scattered into the air. They circled the yard before finding perches on a different tree. No peregrine falcon.

Perhaps Ronan was invisible, lurking somewhere in silent

mourning. I wanted to believe he'd come to see me off even though it was much more probable he was in the castle, proving to Wolfson he had no interest in my affairs.

During the three-day wagon trip to Carendale, I took stock of all the magic spells that resided in my mind. I could sort through them by thinking of a topic or I could picture a particular magic book and turn the pages to see what each held.

I never came across the spell Ronan had used to heal my scar, which meant I only had access to the spells from Ronan's memory before he gave me my mark. He had no need of finding that spell until afterward. He'd grafted his magic into me like a limb from a tree. We grew separately from then on.

I imagined him searching through hidden texts in Wolfson's and Quintal's private collections in order to help me. Or—and this scenario was more likely—studying the healing spells he already knew and stitching together this part and that to come up with a spell to erase scars.

And thus continued the back-and-forth swing of my heart like a pendulum set in motion between love and resentment. On one day, I was certain he was still the person I'd always known —good and kind and innocent of fires. His parting gift meant he still cared for me. He would send me word.

But after months at Carendale, after so many days weighed down by their utter wordlessness, I was convinced his parting spell had only been a gift of atonement. He didn't want to feel indebted to me. That was all.

When pendulums stop swinging, they do not always land in the middle. Mine stayed firmly on resentment.

I finally saw my situation at Docendum Castle with clarity: I was a lowborn servant who had loved an apprentice with all my heart. He had only enjoyed my companionship as a distraction from studying with those he found intolerable. And when my friendship turned out to be a liability, he cast me off without any consideration for my feelings.

Wizards were power-hungry and selfish, corrupted. One way or another, they were all stained with ashes. If I were to give my life for the renegades' cause, dying while disarming wizards wasn't a bad way to do it.

So what was there to do but agree with Alaric and let Madame Sutton and Master Grey place me in their chess game to depose the king?

Chess doesn't have pieces to represent wizards, but it really ought to.

CHAPTER 10

*A*fter that night with Madame Sutton and Master Grey, Alaric and I returned to Paxworth to ready ourselves for the mission. My life was invaded by a series of dressmakers and cobblers. I had to have new gowns and shoes, as the clothes I wore around Paxworth were barely nicer than the servants'.

I had no delusions I would be at court for the full two weeks of celebration. I would either achieve my goal, and the feasting would abruptly end, or I would be discovered and have no need of gowns. I was dressing for either my death or the king's. But my trunks would be searched upon entrance to Valistowe, and the king's men would expect my clothing to be like the other noblewomen's.

Madame Sutton came to Paxworth to deliver sketched plans of Valistowe Castle and the surrounding grounds. The wizards' rooms were located on the fourth floor near the king's chambers. They used magic spells as well as locks to prevent trespassing in their chambers, and they changed the spells every few weeks, depending on their whims.

This meant I'd have no way of knowing what sort of magic I would face until I reached Valistowe. The sketches indicated the wizards' chambers had windows but not whether they were big enough that I could scale the side of the castle to circumvent the spells.

Lady Edith and I would arrive the day before the wedding, and I'd have that day to do reconnaissance. After the wedding, the guests would be drinking heavily, toasting the royal couple and such. That night while everyone slept in various degrees of drunken stupor, I'd break into each of the wizards' chambers and perform incantations to destroy their marks.

When the king no longer had the protection of his wizards' magic, I'd send a signal to my lady's maid assassin that the way was clear for her to use one of the secret entrances to the king's chamber.

I needed items for all of these incantations as well as for a camouflage cloak I was enchanting for my maid. She wouldn't be invisible, but as long as she moved slowly, the material would change colors, helping her blend into the background and making her harder to spot.

Gathering the ingredients for the spells took the better part of two months and that was with Madame Sutton and Master Gray's help. I hated to think of the expense and effort the renegades undertook to fulfill my requests. Every time I contemplated abandoning my role in the upcoming treason, I remembered that expense and effort. Someone had caught and milked a wild boar for one incantation, and someone—hopefully not the same person —had climbed a mountain cliff to fetch henbane that grew there.

Madam Sutton stayed for a week to teach me royal etiquette and ensure I practiced it. She was apparently worried that such things weren't properly taught at Lady Edith's table.

Lady Edith didn't know the details of the mission, nor did she want to know. "Whatever mischief you're about," she told me, "it is your business and should stay such."

However, she did make the most of my upcoming assignment by insisting on not only gowns for herself but a new carriage as well. She claimed hers wasn't fit to be seen even by the king's servants. The renegades paid for those things and a pair of gilded inkwells as a wedding present for the royal couple.

During my many preparations, I couldn't help but wonder if Ronan would attend the king's wedding feast. In rational moments, I dismissed the idea. What were the chances that Ronan, just four years out of training, had a lord who thought him important enough to take? Most likely, he would remain at his lord's castle overseeing its safety.

Yet, part of me wished I could see him in the regal halls of Valistowe. I imagined my triumphal entry into court as a member of the highborn and Ronan's stunned surprise at seeing me. In my fantasy, Ronan looked wan and sickly and regretted spurning me. His lord, on the other hand, had a handsome son who was instantly smitten with me.

Of course, even if Ronan were at court, none of the highborn men were apt to take enough note of me to cause him jealousy. My dress would be plain next to the wealthy heiresses' voluminous silks and my jewels unimpressive. And even if I could've been assured of that smitten nobleman's son, I wouldn't wish for Ronan's presence. He was the only person in the kingdom who might suspect me of magical crimes.

Ten days before we were to leave, my assassin lady's maid came to Paxworth to practice her part. Gwenyth was a tall woman of twenty-three years with straw-colored hair, wide cheeks, and a cheerful countenance that one didn't associate with danger. She had callused palms from practicing with weaponry that one wouldn't find in a real servant whose most arduous task was dressing and undressing her mistress.

I found the sudden constant presence of a lady's maid disconcerting. I was used to dressing myself and only going to

Joanne, Lady Edith's maid, for help with my lacings. Gwenyth made me feel I was being watched or at least chaperoned.

She peppered me with questions while she dressed me. I supposed a servant would be expected to know details of my past, such as my time spent at Docendum and Carendale, but Madame Sutton and Master Gray had decided our mission was more likely to be successful if Gwenyth knew I had magical abilities, and she asked about those as well. I always felt somehow ungrateful for refusing to give her information on that subject.

On the day of our departure, as she tied sleeves to my gown, she asked, "When did you realize you could do magic?"

"I've already told you. I can't talk of such things."

"Won't, not can't," she said grudgingly. "I'm your ally, you know. Your bodyguard. If I know naught of your powers, how will I know when you need rescuing and when you don't?"

"I never need rescuing."

She huffed, clearly not believing me. "I didn't ask how any of the spells were done. Although I'd pay a pretty penny for that knowledge. I just asked when you knew."

Perhaps I was overly worried, but I didn't want to give details about magic lest I unwittingly revealed too much and allowed someone to piece together how I'd gotten a mark.

"I learned magic while at Docendum Castle." I'd already told Madame Sutton and Master Grey this, so it wasn't new information. "Docendum Castle is coincidentally also where I learned to hate wizards."

Gwenyth laughed at that. "I've heard a constant gloom hangs over Docendum, a result of all the magic performed there."

"True."

"I've heard the apprentices think nothing of turning the servants into ducks for their own amusement."

"Not true, but only because most of the apprentices can't manage that sort of magic." I couldn't. I'd tried to transform myself into various creatures. I only ever managed to become a hawthorn tree and a wolf.

I was practiced enough now, that I could take on either shape quickly and without summoning the emotions that had first accompanied them, but changing form was only valuable during a mission if I was pursued by dogs following my scent or if a wizard was after me. A disclosing spell cast by a wizard would erase my invisibility enchantment, but it wouldn't turn me human again if I were in the form of a tree or wolf. A reverse transformation spell was needed, and most didn't suspect a tree of being anything but a tree.

Gwenyth finished with my sleeves, and I sat by my looking glass so she could fix my hair. She took a section and began plaiting it. "What's the most exciting thing you've done with your magic?"

"You realize lady's maids aren't supposed to ask impertinent questions."

"And I won't when there're ears that might overhear. I just want a good story. I've never talked to a real wizard before."

A real wizard. I didn't consider myself that. I was only a girl who'd stolen magic. "It's all exciting until I run into someone who wants to hack me into little pieces. Fortunately, I'm good at dodging."

Gwenyth pinned up the plait and went to work on the second. "When are you going to tell me how Alaric and I are to get daggers? You said you'd let me know before we left."

Sneaking weapons into the Valistowe was no small task, as upon arrival, guests were required to turn all arms over to the marshal's men. Each carriage and guest would be thoroughly examined by one of the king's wizards, and wizards had finding spells to uncover weapons.

Only the king's knights were allowed to be armed, and they carried their swords on them except while sleeping. Stealing one of those would set off an immediate search. Pinching kitchen knives would be no better as the undercooks counted the silverware daily and missing knives would also set off a search. I'd considered burying daggers on the road to Valistowe and sneaking out of the castle the first night to retrieve them. Unfortunately, not only did a deep moat surround the place, the king's wizards had created flesh-eating fish to ensure no one swam across it.

I smiled at her. "You didn't notice the daggers when we packed our things?"

Gwenyth wrinkled her nose. "You hid them in your trunks? What of the wizard's finding spell?"

"The wizard won't discover them because they won't be weapons when I enter Valistowe." Finding spells had their limitations. Only a whole object would be detected, not the individual parts.

I stood and crossed the room to the chest that held my wardrobe for the trip. On top of folded kirtles, chemises, and gowns, was a box. I pulled the top off with a flourish.

It contained a headdress I'd redesigned. The silver cauls that would cover the plaits of hair on the sides of my head were the same type that many of the highborn women wore, although lacking the pearls or jewels of the truly wealthy. However, the bands that spanned my forehead and the back of my head were dagger blades I'd magicked to bend to the right shape. I'd glued garnets across them to help disguise their true form.

"Do you see any weapons?" I asked.

"No." She reached out to take the headdress.

"Careful. It has sharp edges."

Her gaze snapped to the blades' sides and her eyes widened with understanding. "Ah. That's what I call cutting fashion."

"Hopefully not too sharp. I'm going to have to wear this when we ride into the castle. Otherwise, when the soldiers paw through my trunk, they'll slice their fingers."

Gwenyth turned the headdress one way and then another. "Where's the rest of it?"

The bottom half of the daggers had been disassembled into three parts. I took out a yellow brocade gown and shook it out. The brass hand guard sat in the middle of the bodice as though it were a very long brooch. "If you noticed nothing amiss when you packed it, certainly the guards won't either." Alaric and I had purposely not told Gwenyth about this deception in order to see if it was as good as we thought.

She gave a short braying laugh, not at all upset at being duped.

I held up a jewelry box with four thick wooden legs. "The dagger handles are the front two legs."

I opened up the jewelry box and took out the bottom of a dagger's handle, a round brass pommel with a chain threaded through it. An arrangement of garnets decorated the orb, but it still made a large, ugly pendant. Its twin lay in the box, decorated with amethysts. "If I'm caught, it will be because no one will believe a woman of breeding would wear such tawdry things."

"I did wonder about those, but I was too polite to question your taste."

I returned the necklace to the box. "We'll need to remove the jewels before you use a dagger." I was counting on the fact that once the daggers were reassembled, no one would connect the pommels to the ugly pendants a few guards saw when they searched through the guests' luggage.

Gwenyth surveyed the headdress again, touching a caul that hid the tip of one blade and the tang of the other. "I won't be able to reassemble them, curved as the blades are."

I took the headdress from Gwenyth and gingerly placed it back in its box. "On our first night at Valistowe, I'll straighten the blades and deliver one to Alaric." He'd insisted on being

Gwenyth's backup, and I wanted him to be armed should we all have to leave Valistowe suddenly.

When I delivered the knife to Alaric, he would give me some of the tools I needed for my incantations. Should climbing the wall be an option to reach the wizards' rooms, he'd provide me with one of his tunics and a pair of breeches as well. I would see little else of Alaric during the mission. Highborn ladies didn't speak with their groomsmen.

"Most likely Alaric won't need a dagger," Gwenyth said, either to reassure me or to boast. "I'm more than capable of doing the job by myself." She picked up the headdress I was to wear today, a blue bourrelet made to match my gown. Instead of placing it on my head, she squinted at my hair. "I think your left plait is a little lower than the right. Sit down and I'll redo it."

"It's fine." I took the bourrelet from her and put it on. "I want to walk the grounds."

"Now? When we're nearly set to leave?"

"I have to sit in a cramped carriage all day. I'll fare better if I stretch my legs first." I headed toward the door without inviting her to join me. Privacy was another thing I would be short of today.

Lady Edith said I had a restless spirit which wasn't becoming of the highborn. A proper lady took enjoyment in sedentary arts such as embroidery, knitting, lace-making, and music. I'd little patience for most of those things.

"You'd best be fast," Gwenyth called after me, "or you'll miss breakfast."

I hadn't much of an appetite. I craved the rustling of leaves more.

I wandered outside, past rows of herbs, and through the orchard. The rose gardens at the far end of the property had grown into a thorny jumble and the hedges were wild with neglect. It was a messy, rambling place that I loved. This morning, I couldn't help but wonder if I would ever see it again.

Stealing objects for the renegades had its risks, but what I stole was sold to buy the freedom of others. Thoughts of mothers and fathers, with children held tight in their arms, had made my trips shimmying up castle walls feel like a noble endeavor. I wanted this excursion to feel the same way, but an assassination, well, just didn't.

I must've spent too long rambling around because Alaric came to fetch me.

He appeared in the hedgerow in front of me, holding my cloak draped over one arm. His gaze slid over me, taking in my new blue gown and bourrelet. "You'll have a hard time at court doing anything in secret. The eyes of every man will be on you."

I nodded at him with the practiced poise of a highborn lady. "An exaggeration, but a charming one."

"Not as much of an exaggeration as you suppose. Although if you want a swain who seeks only to praise you, I can play that part as well."

"You play many parts. What's one more?"

Alaric flirted at times, but nothing ever came of his words, which was fine with me. Mage Wolfson had not taught Ronan alone that love came with dangerous liabilities.

Alaric handed me my cloak. His eyes traveled over me again, and he clucked his tongue. "I pity the noblemen already. Their attempts to capture your attention will be sadly ill-received."

"Perhaps not." I draped the cloak over my shoulders. "Maybe my plans will go so flawlessly, I'll have time to catch a husband before I depose the monarch."

He cocked his head, one eyebrow raised. "You've always said you wanted no husband."

I had said that on more than one occasion. A friend of Alaric's showed interest in me once, and I'd refused him outright, declaring I would never marry.

"Have you changed your mind?" He looked at me solemnly, the teasing in his brown eyes gone.

Perhaps our uncertain future loosened my tongue, or perhaps I felt Alaric deserved more of an explanation. "I can't marry." I shrugged as though such a statement didn't matter. "If I married, my husband would discover I have magic. He might kill me for that sort of deception." A wedding night would reveal my mark.

"Or your husband might rejoice," Alaric pointed out.

Or use me for my magic the way the renegades were, the way Alaric was. Not for the first time, it irked me that I couldn't know what he would've thought of me if I hadn't been so very useful to his cause.

I headed toward the courtyard and the carriage waiting there.

Alaric reached out and grasped my hand, halting me. His voice went soft. "I realize you have magic. I would never kill you."

I restrained the urge to pull my hand away. I didn't want him standing this close and gazing at me with such affection.

"Yes," I kept my tone light, "but you would make a horrible husband as you may not live through the end of the month."

"I've managed to stay alive twenty-four years without incident."

"I'm sure you've had plenty of incidents." I gently pulled my hand away and continued strolling toward the courtyard.

In a couple of steps, Alaric had caught up with me. "What if I told you that after this trip, I would retire to less dangerous work?"

"I wouldn't believe you."

He took hold of my hand again, turning me to him. "I wonder, do you object to marriage altogether or only to marriage at the present time?"

Did he have a personal interest in the matter? The thought that he might ask for my hand made breathing difficult. Our friendship was enough. I didn't want to change things.

I forced a smile, still light. "Perhaps my objections are because I know I would make an insufficient wife. I'm not likely to live through the end of the month."

Alaric studied me so intently that I gulped under the pressure of his gaze. I expected him to argue the issue, but he released my hand. "I suppose there's no point in pursuing the subject until we return from court. However, I wanted you to know, in case we don't return, that—"

Impulsively, I put my fingers to his lips to stop his words. "You mustn't say such things. It's tempting fate."

He captured my hand, kept it held to his lips, and kissed my fingers. "Heaven forbid I tempt fate. Especially not after your prediction that neither of us will live through the month." His tone had returned to joking again. That was comfortable. Normal. I could breathe once more.

With a genteel bow, he offered me his arm, the way a nobleman might escort a lady. I slipped my hand through his arm, and we made our way toward the courtyard. The birds chased one another around the treetops, chirping and trilling as though it were any other day. The sky was such a pretty, oblivious blue.

After a few steps in silence, Alaric said, "Sometimes I believe you see ghosts."

"Ghosts?" I hadn't expected that accusation. "It's not in a wizard's power to speak to spirits who've passed from this life."

"Not those sorts of ghosts. Ghosts of your own making. Ghosts of the past."

Oh. Ronan. Yes, I suppose he had a way of haunting me. "We're all creations of our past."

"You can be a creation of your future instead. I've seen you playing with the tenants' children."

Tenant was a polite term for the peasants who worked Lady Edith's fields. All of them were paid, not owned, and since they were paid per acre, wives often came to help their husbands plant and harvest. A few of them worked with babies on their backs and younger children toddling around behind them.

I'd been known to hold a baby or feed the young waifs some food from the manor. "One can't always embroider," I said.

"You deserve more than the life of a thief. If I can't give that to you, I hope someone can."

"I've been adopted into the highborn class," I reminded him. "You've already given me more than I expected."

"That's not what I mean."

I knew what he meant but knowing didn't change anything. Love would always be a vulnerability I couldn't afford.

CHAPTER 11

*T*he trip to the king's castle took an entire week and would've taken longer if I hadn't cast spells beforehand to strengthen the horses and ensure the carriage wheels didn't fall apart. Occasionally, when I thought the men at arms who rode with us wouldn't notice, I also magicked the road ahead to make it smoother. This was a common task for wizards, and the men assumed some other highborn retinue had journeyed the way before us.

By the third day, I took to riding horseback because I couldn't stand to be so tightly confined in the carriage with Gwenyth, Lady Edith, and Joanne, her lady's maid. Especially since I had to listen to Lady Edith's many complaints about running a manor house: the tenants were ungrateful and slow to pay their rents. Most of those who worked for her were slothful unless constantly watched. And how could she keep up with expenses when each year the rent she collected bought less and less at the market, while at the same time, the manor house required more repairs? Her late husband, Lord Eustace, had promised the tenants he wouldn't raise their rents, and she wanted to honor his word, heaven knew that, but where would it leave her?

Apparently, it left her working for the renegades for extra coin.

Lady Edith didn't protest my switch in mode of riding, most likely because she enjoyed the added room in the carriage my absence afforded. I wished I could ride next to Alaric and pass the time talking with him, but he rode with the men guarding our retinue, and they would've thought such attention odd.

On the fourth day, Gwenyth joined me in horseback riding. She was clearly a restless spirit as well. Or at least weary of nodding to Lady Edith's complaints.

On the last night of our travels, we stayed at an inn not far from Valistowe so we could arrive at the castle in the morning, rested, bathed, and dressed in our finery. When I awoke the next day, nerves rattled my hands, and my mind seemed washed clean of everything I knew about the mission. I was certain I would forget some important detail.

The road from the village to Valistowe was as smooth as polished silver. Instead of enjoying a ride free of jarring, the steady, unbroken noise of the wheels felt ominous.

Even from a distance, I could tell Valistowe Castle, perched on the top of a vast hill, was larger and grander than any I'd visited. The gray stone walls stretched on and on, interrupted by five towers in the crenelated walls. There was something about seeing King Leofric's red flags dotted with gold stars waving from the battlements that made the place imposing, as though a waiting knight stood behind each of those flags, sword drawn, and watching.

Joanne set about nervously wiping bits of dust from Lady Edith's sleeves until Lady Edith waved her back to her seat. Joanne was a large, middle-aged woman who was as silent as Lady Edith was talkative.

Lady Edith folded her hands across her lap and gave me last-minute instructions. "Smile coyly, flirt excessively, and you'll blend in with the other girls who've come to court. However, don't speak too much or too long to any gentleman. You mustn't encourage them."

Alarm pinged around my chest, making my laces feel even tighter. Gwenyth had done them up with vigor this morning. "What if someone proposes to me?"

"Oh, they won't." Lady Edith reached over the distance between us and patted my knee reassuringly. "Not when they find you've no dowry." Her patting stopped and she pointed a finger at me. "Although that doesn't mean they won't try to deprive you of your maidenly virtue." She raised her eyebrows. "You do still have your maidenly virtue?"

A real mother wouldn't ask those sorts of questions in front of others, especially while she was taking me to court to commit treason.

"Virtue fairly seeps from me, I have so much of it."

"Good." She leaned back into her seat. "You're wise to keep your distance from the wrong sort of men."

I was half-tempted to ask who the wrong sort were—thieves and assassins, perhaps? Instead, I peered outside and ruminated about the king's wizards. My magic had its limits and taking five wizard marks in one night might overtax it. But if I didn't manage to take them all in the same night, the remaining ones would be on guard. Who knew what type of protective charms they would then employ?

I fiddled with my skirt, twisting the material. "What if none but the king's wizards are at court for the wedding?"

I needed visiting mages to deflect suspicion from me. If I gave any of the king's men a reason to suspect me of having magic, they could discover my secret simply by searching me for a mark. I shrank from that thought, from the idea of soldiers ripping my clothes away.

"A few are sure to come," Gwenyth reassured me.

Lady Edith snorted. "A few? A royal wedding doesn't happen every day. All the mages in the land will have begged their lords to let them attend so as not to miss the feasting and a chance to impress the king with their devotion. I'll be surprised if we see less than twenty."

Twenty? I'd been hoping for half a dozen. With a total of forty-six wizards in Aerador, if twenty came, my chances of seeing Ronan were close to fifty percent.

I wanted to point out, shrilly, that someone should have informed me of these odds beforehand. Ronan's presence at the castle could endanger the mission, but of course, none of the renegades knew about him or that he'd given me a mark.

Lady Edith smoothed out a wrinkle from her gown. "What need have you for a wizard?" Her eyes swerved to mine. She must have seen my worry, because she shook her head, making tsking sounds. "Never mind. It's best I not know of such things." She turned firmly to Joanne and began speaking to her.

To Gwenyth, I said, "Sixteen apprentices went through Docendum while I lived there." Granted, some of those had been there when I was seven years old. They wouldn't recall me. But others… "Some might recognize me. That type of attention…"

Gwenyth coughed out a laugh. "None of the apprentices will recognize you. They don't see servants, let alone remember them. And dressed as you are in highborn finery…" She waved her hand over me. "Well, I'd bet you your new silk stockings that not a one of them recognizes you."

Ronan would. At least he would if he got a close look at me. I might be able to keep my distance from him. The crowd would be large enough that we might never come in proximity of each other. The cathedral would be full for the wedding, and even if we were seated nearby, he'd likely only see the back of my head or I his. I could be on my way home before he chanced to spy me. And he might not even be there. Chances were, after all, greater that he would not be.

"What do I get if I win the bet?" I asked.

"My new silk stockings." She hadn't been given a wardrobe for our mission and had complained bitterly about this as we'd packed.

Another sickening thought occurred to me. "Will Wolfson be there?" I'd barely said his name in two years, and the word felt treacherous on my tongue. What would he do if he saw me?

It was all I could do to remind myself that I was a highborn lady now, someone of social standing. Even if Mage Wolfson recognized me, he couldn't grab me and threaten me with a vicious death. I was a person of consequence. And more importantly, I had knowledge of counterspells. He wouldn't be expecting that. I'd be able to protect myself.

"Who?" Lady Edith asked, returning to our conversation.

"Mage Wolfson. The one who teaches the apprentices." I'd told her more than once that I'd lived at Docendum Castle before I was sold to Carendale Castle, but she was perpetually forgetting this fact. When asked about my background, she often told people I was raised with Lord Haddock at Carendale.

She nodded, remembering now. "I imagine Wolfson will be there. He always was a social climber at heart."

She knew that sort of information about him?

Lady Edith leaned toward me. It was her habit to lower her voice when speaking ill of others as though a hushed tone made gossip less of a sin. "From what I've heard, when he was a young man, he used to brag to King Theobald about his magical aptitude to the point that everyone considered him a bore. He thought his boasts would convince the king to appoint him to his wizard council. Instead, the king made him teach the new apprentices. Not nearly the glamour of court life he'd hoped for. And that is why one should measure one's boasting carefully."

I'd known Wolfson to be bad-tempered and evil-hearted,

someone who was as integral to the gloom surrounding Docendum Castle as the dark stones and dimmed skies. This detail—that he was a disappointed social climber—was odd to consider. He'd wanted to be surrounded by courtiers, not pupils.

The carriage neared the drawbridge. Lady Edith fussed with her headdress to make sure it was properly fastened. "You shouldn't fret about encountering Wolfson. He's no longer your master and must treat you with the respect of a lady. However, if you fear he may bring up the vulgarity of your past, you should avoid him."

Oh, I definitely planned on avoiding him.

Several knights and men at arms stood in front of the draw-bridge to check incoming carriages. An elegant one ahead of us was being inspected. It was painted yellow and trimmed in brass, with carved coats of arms on the doors. The carriage made ours, still smelling of cut wood, look shabby and provincial in comparison.

I should probably get used to that feeling.

While the soldiers examined the inside of the yellow carriage, a middle-aged woman and her daughter waited outside, chatting. Their traveling gowns had voluminous sleeves and I'd never seen headdresses so wide. They must have to take care when they turned their heads not to knock things over.

The party had an escort of half a dozen men who'd dismounted from their horses already. The lord of the group, dressed in fine clothing, sat atop one of the horses. He wore an expression of tired patience, as though this inspection was an insult to his pride, but one he would endure with equanimity befitting his station.

A gray-haired man in black robes prowled around the carriage, tapping it with his wand to check for weapons. One of the king's wizards. I'd been told only sparse details about the king's wizards beyond their names and didn't know which one this was: Redboot, Zephyr, Telarian, Sciatheric, or Warison.

Lady Edith pushed the curtain away from her window and leaned out for a better view. "Lord Somerton and his family are ahead of us. By the look of that carriage, his lands must be prospering." She let the curtain fall back, and her voice dropped to a gossipy murmur. "His wife, Lady Somerton, is one of the most conceited people you're likely to meet. If her daughter is anything like her, she'll have a hard time finding a husband. Only royalty will be worthy of her notice."

I peeked out the window to get another glimpse at the young woman in question. She was near my age, blonde and pretty, with large blue eyes and the sort of pale skin that looked as though it had never endured a moment of sun.

The search of Lord Somerton's carriage continued, and with every minute of thoroughness, bits of foreboding bloomed in my chest. Wearing a dagger across my forehead had been a mistake. It marked me as an assassin. The king's men would guess my plan.

I fidgeted with the knitting needle in my pocket, trying to calm my nerves with the reassurance that I had a wand.

By the time the Somertons' carriage and entourage disappeared over the drawbridge, I was forcing myself not to ball my hands into fists. Gwenyth showed no anxiety whatsoever. The whole time we waited, she peered out the window and murmured things about the castle. "I hadn't expected it to be so very large. How many rooms do you think it has? An entire village could fit on one floor."

Lady Edith nodded. "Running a castle as grand as Valistowe requires an entire village of servants."

And they could easily fit in the massive structure. It was four stories high, with small windows on the second floor and beautiful arched ones on the third and fourth. Above them all, turrets with black spires pierced the sky.

Gwenyth craned her head farther out the window. "I can't even imagine how many fireplaces they need to warm such a place. It must burn a forest of trees every year. Or do you think the wizards enchant the castle's temperature? With five of them, they've got to do something to earn their keep." She brightened. "Perhaps they heat the bathwater as well."

Joanne grunted at the idea, letting us know it was a ridiculous notion.

"I suppose you're right about that," Gwenyth said. "I doubt you could find a wizard who'd lift a finger to help the servants with their work. It'll be the scullery maids heating water and hauling it to our baths."

Gwenyth probably didn't mean her words to be an indictment of me, but I still felt their sting.

Footsteps approached our carriage and the door opened. One of the soldiers—a mountain of a man—greeted us holding a list of guests. He wore a red tunic, black chausses, and his helmet sported a single red feather. The black-robed wizard stood next to him, smiling genially. My eyes automatically slid to his neck and the crescent-shaped moon there.

When I'd seen the wizard circling the Somerton's carriage, I'd assumed he was middle-aged. Now that he was closer, I noted the wrinkles that lined his face and deepened the corners of his mouth. His hairline had receded so completely that it was of indeterminant location underneath his hat. He must be quite old, and yet he moved with the vigor of a younger man.

"Welcome to the castle, Lady…" The wizard waited for someone to supply him with a name.

That was the disadvantage of not having the time or money to carve your heraldry on your carriage doors. One had to stoop to introductions.

"Lady Edith of Paxworth," she said with an air of importance.

The soldier scanned his list, nodded to the wizard, and wrote something on the parchment.

"Welcome, Lady Edith," the wizard said. "I'm Mage Redboot, head of the wizard council. We're happy for your safe arrival. Have you any weapons on you?"

"Only the ones our men carried to protect us." Lady Edith believed what she said to be the truth.

The wizard gestured to a knight standing not far off. "Instruct your men to give them to Sir Lawrence. They'll be returned upon your departure." He offered his hand to Lady Edith to help her out. "Your party may wait outside while we inspect your carriage."

I couldn't fault Mage Redboot for his decorum. He issued orders as though they were privileged invitations.

After Lady Edith descended from the carriage, Mage Redboot held out his hand to me. His skin was a pale yellow, mottled with age spots, but his grip was firm. I took his hand and stepped from the carriage. His eyes lingered on mine. A moment passed, then another. His gaze didn't leave my face.

Had the sun glinted off the dagger blade, drawing attention to it?

Mage Redboot turned from me without comment to help Joanne and Gwenyth out.

So perhaps not. I took several deep breaths.

The king's men pulled our trunks from the carriage and dropped them, none too gently, onto the ground. Lady Edith marched over and unlocked the trunks, sending scolding looks in their direction. "One must take care when handling a lady's things."

Alaric dismounted, as did the other men that Lady Edith hired to ride with us, and they handed over their weapons to the king's men. Alaric saw me and gave me a slight smile before turning away. Even that smile was more than he should have ventured. It wasn't proper for groomsmen to show familiarity with those of rank.

"Do be careful with those!" Lady Edith snapped at the man who was rummaging through her gowns. "My clothing is folded in a specific manner to avoid wrinkles. I'll have to dress for supper in that."

The only effect of her words was that the men went through her things more slowly, either to demonstrate they were being careful or to annoy her with their power to paw through her wardrobe as thoroughly as they liked.

The wizard tapped his wand against our carriage with the same flourish he used on the Somerton's. He waved his hands up and down as though trying to draw out some unseen force from the depths of the woodwork. I assumed this act was for our benefit as it was completely unnecessary in working a finding incantation.

When the men opened my trunk, I bit the side of my cheek to remind myself not to stare at them like I feared they'd find anything of interest. Better just to turn my attention to the wizard.

Done exorcising the demons from our carriage, Mage Redboot swaggered over to our group. "You'll excuse our intrusion into your privacy. It's an unfortunate part of our duties."

Another command uttered like an apology.

"Yes, yes." Lady Edith fluttered a hand in his direction, absolving his men of the mistreatment of our underthings.

Redboot nodded to her, then his gaze ran over me. Again, a little too long. I looked away, adopting an air of nonchalance.

"I must now try your patience further," he said, "by directing my wand over each of you." Mage Redboot stepped over to Joanne and swished his wand in a circular motion around her. A few moments later, he moved to Gwenyth and did the same thing.

She blinked her blue eyes at him like a child encountering some wonder. "I've never seen a real wand so closely before. Does it do other things besides find cutthroats?"

"Many things," Mage Redboot said with a chuckle.

True. Most wizards put a myriad of charms on their wands. Even if I'd held his wand in my hand, I wouldn't be able to tell what spells resided within it. Unless a wizard had specifically enchanted an object to work for someone else, it only worked for the original owner.

Gwenyth was still prattling on about the marvels of magic. Probably in an attempt to distract him. No one would have thought her more than an empty-headed maiden who was too uncultured to know she should hold her tongue in the presence of a wizard.

He answered her questions politely yet curtly and moved on to Lady Edith.

My hands smoothed the front of my gown. They needed something to do.

Far too soon, Mage Redboot stood before me. He smelled of the incense smoke that wizards sometimes used in spells—a sweet, sickly smell, like honey put to a flame. He swept his wand in a slow silhouette around me, never taking his eyes from my face. They were a muted gray, like something that had once been bright but had grown dingy with time.

He was staring at me more intently than he had at the others. I dropped my gaze.

"Is this your first time to court?" His voice was smooth, lulling almost.

"Yes, sir." I forced my eyes to meet his. Those who were highborn weren't required to avert their eyes when speaking to a wizard. I hoped he counted my mistake as maidenly bashfulness.

"Why have we not had the pleasure of seeing you before?"

"Our estate is quite far away, and my aunt doesn't like to travel." He probably knew I was lying. Most noblewomen, especially widowed ones, would make the effort to come to court with an eye to procuring a match for her ward. I could only hope the wizard suspected the least dangerous reason for my untruth. Lady Edith wouldn't normally have had the funds for such a trip, and anyway, she would be hard-pressed to find a man at court willing to overlook my lack of dowry and questionable parental lineage.

A smile tugged at his weathered lips. "By staying away, you've deprived the court of one of its finest blossoms."

"You're too kind." And too thorough. He'd spent enough time tracing my body with his wand that he must surely be done now. Finding charms didn't take this long to work.

He gave me another smile, this one a little oily. "I trust you'll no longer make us live with such deprivation."

Oh. He hadn't spent more time searching me because he suspected me. He was just the type of man who liked standing close to young women and flirting with them. Saints in heaven. He was old enough to be my grandfather. Was this what court was like?

I smiled back at him in relief. I wasn't about to be taken in for questioning at sword point. I hadn't just doomed all those in our party to a painful death.

He nodded at me, ever the gentleman. "You've my leave to go."

I floated back to the carriage. Once inside, I nearly giggled with Gwenyth at the ease of our entrance. Until tonight when I had to do reconnaissance, I could pretend to be like every other visitor to the castle. I could enjoy being a lady in the finest castle in the land.

Gwenyth was already venturing guesses as to what the royal cook would serve for our first meal. "Swan," she said. "Cooked and fully re-feathered. I've heard that's how they serve them to King Leofric's guests."

The front courtyard of the castle had such beautifully maintained hedges and rows of flowers that I wondered whether magic was involved in their upkeep or just exceptionally good gardeners. A large pond sat in the middle of a grassy area, most likely well-stocked with fish. A fountain burbled and sprayed at its center.

I scanned the place for the stables and saw two long buildings. One for the king's horses and one for his guests'. There must be nearly as many horses here as there were people. Lords and ladies strolled the grounds. The coach ahead of us dropped off its visitors by the front entrance and rolled off toward the coach house.

Our carriage pulled into the courtyard. "Heavens," Gwenyth said louder than a genteel woman would, "take a gander at the fountain."

I wasn't looking at the fountain. I was watching the Somertons. The mother and daughter were off to one side near the castle entrance, talking to a wizard there. A tall man with smooth black hair tied at the nape of his neck. He was angled so I couldn't see his face.

But still, my heart stuttered.

It isn't Ronan, I told myself. I was only noting the resemblance because I was worried about seeing him here. Mathematically speaking, what were the chances the first man I saw inside the castle grounds would be Ronan?

Probability was completely against it.

Mathematics, it turns out, can lie. We climbed from our carriage and made our way toward the large castle doors and the footman waiting there to greet us. As we walked closer to the Somertons, the man turned slightly, and I could tell that yes, he was most definitely Ronan.

I may have cursed.

He was older, his shoulders broader, and his jaw a bit wider. Nothing else had changed about him. He was just as handsome as my memory had painted him.

Ronan turned his head, casually taking us in, and just as casually returned his attention to the Somertons.

He didn't recognize me. A surprised breath pushed past my lips. I wasn't sure whether to be hurt or relieved.

Then his head swung back in my direction, his eyes wide, holding mine.

My pulse skittered and my footsteps felt precarious.

I expected him to detach himself from the Somertons and come say something to me. My presence here, dressed as a highborn woman, would intrigue him enough to question me. Or, at the very least, our past friendship merited a greeting.

My heart pounded in anticipation. He didn't take a step toward me. Instead, he turned back to the Somertons as though nothing out of the ordinary had just transpired.

That stung as sharp as a slap. He'd professed to severing relations between us for my safety. With Wolfson no longer my master or his, such reasons held no sway. I mattered so little to him that even satisfying his curiosity as to the nature of my rise in station wasn't worth the effort of speaking to me. My cheeks flushed hot with humiliation, and I was glad he was no longer looking at me.

Unfortunately, Lady Edith swept directly over to Lady Somerton, and I had no choice but to follow.

"Lady Winifred," Lady Edith said, all gracious cordiality. "How good to see you again. You haven't changed one bit in ten years."

Lady Winifred returned the greeting. I hardly heard what was said. Ronan had turned to me. The intensity in his eyes and the coloring at his neck revealed he wasn't as unaffected by our meeting as I'd supposed. He seemed not to know what to say or if he should say anything at all.

Lady Edith said my name, and I realized she was introducing me to the Somertons. The daughter, Floris, eyed me coolly. My throat felt too tight to allow speech, but I managed to smile and mumble, "I'm happy to make your acquaintance."

Lady Winifred returned my smile and continued to speak to Lady Edith. "I don't recall you having a daughter."

"She's my sister's child," Lady Edith clarified, relaying the story the renegades had concocted. "A sister who, alas, became estranged from my family and fell on hard times before her and her husband's unfortunate deaths. I was quite unaware of Marcella's existence. Once I learned of her, I immediately brought her to Paxworth."

I felt Ronan's gaze on me but wouldn't meet his eyes. He'd never heard me mention highborn relatives. I didn't want to see his eyebrows raised in disbelief.

"How fortunate for you both." A slight tone of disapproval laced Lady Winifred's voice. I was unsure if the disapproval was directed at me for having disreputable parents or at Lady Edith for admitting our relation.

Ronan cleared his throat. "It's a pleasure to meet you."

So, he wasn't going to reveal he knew me. My eyes went to his. Was he protecting my story, or did he just not want to admit to a relationship with someone who'd been a servant? Even though Lady Edith never disclosed the nature of my circumstances before she located me, Lord and Lady Haddock of Carendale might remember me, as well as any number of wizards from Docendum.

Ronan's expression gave away nothing. His earlier discomfort had vanished, replaced by confidence. "I hope you enjoy your time at court."

Lady Edith thanked him, said her goodbyes to Lady Winifred, and we made our way to the castle doors.

The footmen let us inside. I hardly noticed the castle's grand entrance, high ceilings, or the tapestries hanging from the walls.

My mind was dissecting Ronan's first reaction to seeing me and every look and word since. Perhaps he was ashamed of ever associating with a servant and wanted distance. Or worse, perhaps he thought I'd somehow come here to pursue him.

Well, if that was his fear, he would soon be at ease. I had no intention of even speaking to him again.

CHAPTER 12

hile we waited for our trunks to be taken to our room, a dignified woman—some branch of the housekeeping staff—showed us around the pertinent parts of the first floor. The dining hall was a huge room with an arching roof and so many wizards' orbs dangling there, they looked like an army of moons hovering against a night sky. Rows of tables and benches crowded the room, all finely made and polished. A dais stood in the front of the room, away from and above the lesser tables. The king's chair presided there, with ornately carved lions on each side. Carvings of white blossoms, a symbol of Odeway, wound around the queen-to-be's chair.

Most lords used their dining halls for ballrooms when the need arose. Valistowe had a separate ballroom, just as grand, with an inlaid floor of light and dark wood which made it like an enormous chessboard.

Eight sitting rooms were located on the first floor, all with large stone fireplaces, shelves full of books, comfortable chairs, and tables for games. Our guide took us outside and pointed out the extensive gardens, complete with walking paths, ponds, bowers, and a hedgerow maze. If we didn't find those diverting enough, a menagerie of exotic animals was kept in cages on one side of the castle.

The dining hall and ballroom had been impressive, but the beauty of the gardens made me want to weep. I'd never seen such a profusion of flowers, all placed picturesquely between trees and bushes as though by some artist's hand.

As soon as I saw the draping bowers, a part of me, some deep, foolish, unthinking part, began to devise ways I could stay at the castle. I could live here quite happily as a gardener.

But of course, that was a ridiculous notion. I couldn't stay at the royal palace, and I shouldn't even want to. Still, I tried to memorize the way the gardens were laid out so I could attempt to replicate some little piece of them on Lady Edith's estate.

After the woman finished showing us around, she took us back to the castle. We climbed the stairs to the third floor and went down ever-diminishing hallways, each one less adorned than the last, until we reached our rooms. One for Lady Edith and Joanne, an adjoining one for Gwenyth and me.

Before going inside, I turned to our guide. "Can you show my lady's maid to the kitchen?" I had kept an eye out for the number of sentries and where they were located during our tour. I wanted Gwenyth to check the servants' areas as well.

"My lady?" the woman said as though she hadn't heard me right.

"In case Gwenyth needs to fetch me something. When I can't sleep, eating soothes my nerves."

"No need," the woman said. "Servants are stationed in the hallways. You may make your requests to them."

I waved the notion away as if her solution was insufficient. That was the benefit of being a noble. I could be completely unreasonable without seeming at all out of the ordinary. "I'm particular about my food, and my lady's maid knows my tastes precisely. You can show her the way now, as I'll be resting for a bit and don't want the noise of her unpacking."

The woman smiled tolerantly, deemed it best not to argue with me, and motioned for Gwenyth to follow her.

While Gwenyth was gone, I set about retrieving the different parts of the daggers. I straightened the blades and put them and the pommels into a water basin so the jewels would soak off. I was trying to busy myself in an attempt to ignore the overriding thought that ran through my mind: Ronan was here.

This fact complicated so many others. He knew I could do magic. Granted, he thought my powers to be small and my knowledge of magic limited to three spells. When the king's wizards lost their marks, he wouldn't suspect me. Although if the other wizards all had alibis, he would have to consider me as a possibility. Would he reveal my secret to anyone?

Doing so would force him to confess he was the one who gave me my mark. He wouldn't endanger himself that way… unless he was very loyal to the king and willing to sacrifice himself to bring me to justice.

Surely, he wasn't *that* noble. Wizards protected themselves. Hadn't I already learned that?

I unpacked my gowns and hung them in the wardrobe. Despite our care in folding them, they were wrinkled, including the one I was to wear tonight. Gwenyth would have to iron it. I left it sprawled over my bed, looking like it had just fainted.

I snipped the threads holding the dagger handles to the gowns. On one, the material was unmarred, but the other had two small holes that dotted the fabric. Clearly, something had been removed from the gown, and I didn't want anyone to wonder what. Besides, a lady couldn't wear anything but her finest here. Holes wouldn't do.

When Gwenyth came back to the room, I was slumped on the bed with the dress in my lap, near tears, as I embroidered flowers over the area where the holes had been.

Gwenyth gawked at the disarray of the room and my attempt to blink away my emotions. "Whatever is the matter?"

"One of the wizards I knew at Docendum is here." I didn't think that anyone could hear me through the walls, but still, I kept my voice to a whisper.

"That handsome one we met?"

"Ronan, yes. He knows I can do magic. He believes me capable of only three spells, but if the other wizards have alibis during the night, he may suspect me."

She sat down on the bed beside me, keeping her words as hushed as mine. "You needn't worry. What alibis will the wizards have in the middle of the night?"

"Some of them must be friends and will steal off together after the nobles are asleep to renew acquaintances." That's what the servants of the visiting nobles always did when they visited Docendum or Carendale Castle.

Gwenyth scoffed. "Do you expect the wizards to break out a bottle and exchange their spells the way women exchange recipes? Bah, they hoard their secrets."

"Perhaps they'll stay up playing cards or dice." This had been a pastime of the apprentices at Docendum Castle. Ronan complained more than once about the way the other apprentices cheated.

Gwenyth surveyed my embroidery. Pitiful little flowers. "You're fretting over nothing, the same way you're fretting over that gown."

"It had holes from the weight of the handle."

"Tiny ones, I reckon."

My needle flashed in and out of the fabric. "Even tiny holes can cause problems."

She gathered one of the gowns I'd left draped over the trunk. "It's fear you have, not caution. You're searching for an excuse not to act at all." Her words were spoken well above a whisper.

I sent her a severe look.

She smirked at me and in an even louder voice added, "One can never be certain when choosing a husband, but if you keep rejecting the men Lady Edith puts before you, you'll die an old maid."

Anyone who'd heard her earlier comments would think she was simply advising a reluctant charge. I rolled my eyes. "I can't help preferring my judgment to that of others."

She gingerly plucked a blade from the basin. The gems slid off. "Are you going to take this to supper? You might not have time to come back here afterward."

"Why wouldn't I have time to return to my room?" The feasting and celebrations wouldn't start in earnest until the morrow when the wedding took place. No official activities were planned for the guests who arrived today.

Gwenyth assembled one of the daggers with practiced ease. "Because some of the court ladies are bound to invite you into their society so you can join in gossiping about the gentlemen here. You're likely to be occupied right up until bedtime with that task." She lowered her voice again. "And if you can't make it back from the stables in time, the castle doors will be locked, and you'll have to shimmy up the wall to our window. Might prove difficult in a gown."

My first choice in this string of treason: did I risk being caught with a dagger tucked into my dress or risk being detained after supper and locked out of the castle? "I can't imagine any of the court ladies seeking out my company."

"You're a newcomer. They'll want to know your prospects and judge what sort of competition you are."

That, I could imagine. Although I didn't enjoy the thought of a bunch of falsely friendly women prying me for details about how much silver Lady Edith's estate brought in each year.

"Fine," I said. "I'll take it."

I finished with my embroidery and gave the dress to Gwenyth. We still had time to spare before dinner. Instead of strolling around the gardens as so many of the nobles were doing, I used the invisibility enchantment to explore the castle.

One could only glean so much information from sketches of the place.

Most of the servants and soldiers slept on the second floor in wings of windowless rooms with only small fireplaces, if any. I'd seen worse quarters. I'd been in castles where the servants slept in damp, leaky basements.

All the king's guests had rooms on the third floor, as did the steward, an assortment of other senior staff, and several knights. The more important guests slept closer to the main staircase in large rooms with beautifully carved beds. I imagined, with a bit of indignant pique, that the mattresses were softer than those in the more distant rooms as well. Meaning, mine.

I located the servants' staircases, although I had to take care using them. The stairways were so narrow that I had to shadow in the wake of a servant in order not to jostle other people as they passed.

Guards were posted at the entrances to the fourth floor, even on the servants' staircase. Silent sentinels that stood as erectly as the feathers in their helmets. Fortunately, so many servants carried things to the fourth floor, it was easy to follow after them, undetected.

A trail of servants led to Princess Marita's chambers, the woman who would tomorrow become queen. She had a receiving room to meet with guests, a lavish bed chamber—I'd seen peasant huts smaller than her bed—and a dressing room large enough for a choir. Her attendants were in a frenzy, making alterations to her wedding dress, a gown of rich blue satin trimmed in white fur. They were presenting things to her —candles, silver bowls, flowers—for her approval.

She had the blonde hair her country was known for and a ruddy complexion I'd noticed on her father's portrait, one of many that hung in the castle's sitting rooms. It had been the only portrait besides King Leofric's that our guide pointed out to us.

Princess Marita had also inherited a prominent chin from her father but had a pleasant enough figure, straight teeth, and eyes the murky blue color of the sea. She stood in front of the largest looking glass I'd ever seen, draping different necklaces around her throat. She was nineteen years old, a year younger than me, and I'd expected her to be wistful and uncertain about her upcoming arranged marriage, perhaps even tearful at being sent to a foreign country to marry a stranger. She showed only agitation as she snapped out orders in her native tongue.

But then perhaps agitation was also a valid response.

I'd heard she spoke our language, but if that was true, she wasn't using it for the benefit of the palace servants who watched her in bewilderment and waited for her lady's maid to translate her commands.

The castle sketch had told me that one of the doorways of the king's secret passageways was a panel in her dressing room. I saw no sign of it but supposed I would have no need of it. The wizards wouldn't be in here, and they were my quarry.

I left the future queen to terrorize her attendants and went to explore the rest of the floor. I couldn't enter the king's chambers. Two guards stood without, so even invisible, I dared not open the door myself.

Two hallways flanked the king's chambers, each with three doorways. No guards were stationed in these hallways. No one took note of me softly opening the first door. It was a library of sorts. A buzz of magic hummed over the doorway, the same sharp magic that had protected Mage Wolfson's library of spell books.

I itched to go inside and see the books there, but I was here to find and assess the wizards' chambers, not browse through their tomes and perhaps inadvertently alert the wizards that someone of magical abilities had trespassed in their wing.

I shut the door and wandered down the hallway to the next room.

A large brass serpent sat coiled within the doorway, a viper that must be three times the length of my arm. Even if my memory hadn't immediately recalled a spell to explain its presence, I would've known that the snake could instantaneously transform and strike intruders. A warning saying as much was posted on the door.

A person could knock without harm, but anyone who touched the door handle would be bitten unless the wizard first called out, "Enter."

My invisibility would be of limited use against a snake. They hunted by hearing as much as by sight, and their tongues let them taste the smell of humans. The creature would know my location by that skill alone.

The boots I wore during missions would protect me from a serpent's fangs—I'd added a charm that made the leather all but impenetrable, but the rest of my body would be vulnerable.

Unless the wizards had unprotected windows, I would need to steal a shield, a falconry glove to protect my hand, and say a spell to thin and lengthen the dagger by several inches so I could cut off the snake's head.

I went to the next room in the hallway. A second brass serpent guarded its door. It was just as large as the first, coiled with its head raised half a foot above its body. Oddly, its head and eyes seemed to follow me as I walked past it. I knew of no magic that could account for this sort of effect—one that made a metal statue's eyes move. I bent down for a better look at the creature. The snake's face was concave, although why that made his eyes and face appear to follow me, I couldn't tell. Must be some bit of trickery.

At any rate, I'd found two of the wizards' chambers. I retreated down the corridor and went to the hallway flanking the other side of the king's quarters. Three doors stood there with three serpents guarding them. All were the normal sort, like the first I'd seen.

The wizards' rooms were foolishly close together. But then, they weren't worried anyone would attack them. They stayed close to the king to be at his beck and call.

I leaned closer to one of the doors and wondered if snakes were the extent of the wizard's protection or whether more metal beasts waited inside. Judging from the distance between the doors, the chambers were large enough to contain rhinoceroses.

Once I entered them, I'd need to be prepared for anything. Even if some beast charged me, my first priority would be to cast a stunning spell at the sleeping wizard so he couldn't grab his wand and fight me.

I crept toward the front of the castle and realized my snooping had taken me longer than I'd anticipated. It was nearly time to dress for supper. I would have to check the windows after the meal to see if climbing through them was an option.

I returned to my room, changed into another gown, applied powder and lip rouge, and made Gwenyth redo my hair.

As she finished with my headdress, she said, "That wizard you know, Rowan, he was more than just an acquaintance, wasn't he?"

"Ronan," I corrected and didn't comment on the rest.

She tsked in disappointment. "You shouldn't set your cap for a wizard. You know what they're like. There's not enough heart in the lot of them to pump three drops of blood."

I didn't argue with her, or perhaps more disappointing for her, supply more information. Her gaze traveled over me, surveying me. "You look fair enough to make him regret jilting you."

"Who says he jilted me?"

"If he were only someone who'd caught your fancy, you'd be happy while you readied yourself for supper because you're a lady and thus worthy of his notice now. But you're preening in revenge. Don't deny it. I know anger when I see it."

Really, Gwenyth was too perceptive. I took several deep breaths. "You're right to counsel me to control my countenance. I need to appear confident and relaxed." I would smile through supper if it killed me.

CHAPTER 13

*G*wenyth and I joined Lady Edith and Joanne for the walk downstairs. Our lady's maids would eat in a smaller adjacent dining room with other less noble guests while we ate in the main hall.

When we entered, servants washed our hands with warm rose water and showed us to a table. A harpist perched at the front of the room, playing for our enjoyment. King Leofric and Princess Marita weren't present for supper. All the chairs on the dais sat empty.

Lady Edith informed me that we weren't to see the happy couple until the wedding ceremony. I wasn't disappointed about this as it meant I didn't have to worry about royal decorum while I ate tonight. It was custom to only eat when the king ate, and at all other times sit with eyes fixed on him, lest he speak.

Supper at Paxworth was always a plain affair and over before sunset. The same was not true here. Servants filled our table with platters of cheese, venison, cooked pears, fine white bread, quail eggs, and baked chicken.

Lady Edith and I sat at one of the tables at the very back of the room, near the door where the servants streamed in and out, bringing food and drink. Our close proximity to them didn't mean they served us first. That honor was reserved for the nobles closest to the dais. From what I could gather, Lady Edith and I were seated among the less affluent highborn and the merchants who were so successful they merited invitations to the king's nuptials. Their brocades, silks, and jeweled head-dresses rivaled those at the upper tables. But alas, wealth alone wasn't enough to warrant a seat near royalty.

Master Godfrey, a local merchant, along with his wife and family, had to resign themselves to our company. Their children, Bernard and Agnes Godfrey, were about my age. Agnes wore a green brocade gown with outlandishly long sleeves trimmed in lace. Bernard wore a golden brooch. Both had obviously been well-fed and Bernard's thick cheeks made his face look childlike.

I wondered if the seating arrangement was an insult to the lesser nobles or simply a matchmaking technique, as affluent merchants often married their children to poverty-stricken nobles. With such a union, the merchants received a title for their descendants and the nobility received the fortune they needed to continue running their estates.

A Lord Percy of Gadalleigh sat to my side, and judging from his simple silk tunic, his financial standing was much like mine. He was tall, with a pleasantly handsome face and a quick smile. There was something endearing about the brown curls that fell in disarray around his face.

He flirted and complimented me as well as Agnes so that I was unsure whether he was interested in me or her or simply the sort who liked to garner the regard of women. I suspected the latter, but I smiled freely at him because I was all too aware of Ronan sitting with the Somertons and another lavishly dressed family at one of the upper tables. If Ronan ever cast his attention toward the back section of the room, I wanted to show him I'd earned an admirer.

I glanced at his table a time or two, or perhaps ten, and always found him intently engaged in conversation. Each smile he bestowed on one of his companions felt ridiculously like a tiny stab of betrayal. At Docendum Castle, I'd grown used to being the sole recipient of his smiles.

A memory flashed unbidden into my mind: I'd been helping Ronan learn the ancient language of Kemet, a land far in the east, so he could better study their magic. He'd begun calling me EnteAmari during these sessions, the name of one of their long-dead queens.

"Is that supposed to be a compliment?" I asked. I was drawing pictographs on his wax tablet to test him and was cross because this meant I couldn't sit near the fireplace lest the wax melt. It was a cold, dreary day.

Ronan was stretched out on a chair by the fire, throwing a ball up in the air and catching it. "She was the revered wife of Desher the Great. Why wouldn't you take that title as a compliment?"

"She was one wife among fifty. We would feel sorry for a woman in those circumstances today. Imagine such faithlessness."

He shrugged. "She had statues made in her honor, servants, and wealth."

"I'd rather have a husband who loved me." I held up the tablet. I'd written a phrase that meant: by the power of the king.

His gaze flicked in my direction. "She for whom the sun rises."

"Not even close." I kept the tablet raised.

"That's what EnteAmari means," he explained. "She for whom the sun rises." He smiled at me, one of his warm, familiar smiles. "Some days you're the only bit of sunshine in this place."

I'd tucked that compliment inside my heart, taking it out to admire every once in a while, like a woman admiring heirloom jewels.

I'd suffered when Ronan sent me away, yes, but part of that suffering had been knowing that Ronan would sink into the gloom of his sunless world. Apparently, his gloom had not been long-lasting.

A good friend would be happy for that fact. I was not, it turned out, a good friend.

Bernard Godfrey, the merchant's son, sat near me and occasionally asked me questions, trying to engage me in conversation. He had all the fine manners of the nobility but not their ego, which I counted as a point in his favor. He stammered and blushed when he spoke to me. I could see this vexed his mother. She knew that one in my financial state couldn't afford to put on airs or spurn a man of means. I wanted to tell him that I especially didn't merit his nervousness and any number of women seated at the lower tables would be vying for his attention by tomorrow.

When my gaze strayed from our table, it was mostly to check on the number of mages in the room. Recognizing them was easily done. An assortment of pockets marked their voluminous dark robes. The robes had to be voluminous because wizards carried so many objects in their pockets and hanging from their belts. Once, when some important wizard had visited Docendum, Wolfson had worn the skull of some unfortunate bird tied to his waist for two weeks.

I counted eighteen mages here. None of them Wolfson, although more might arrive before the wedding. All of them wore silk and brocade robes which were completely impractical for most of the work a wizard was required to do. I doubted any of them carried tallow candles, vials of oil, or clay pots nestled in their fine pockets.

With the exception of Redboot, who'd inspected our carriage, I couldn't tell which of the wizards worked for the king and which were here as guests. But the morrow would give me faces for Telarian, Zephyr, Sciatheric, and Warison. The king's wizards would sit at the high table during the feast.

I wondered what the five would do once they realized they'd lost their magic. Would any of the other wizards take pity on them and research methods to restore their marks? Ronan knew of a way, but even if he'd wanted to give them each a new mark, he wouldn't have the supplies let alone the energy, at least not in time to save the king's life. As with most things in life, much more energy was required to create something magical than to destroy it.

After supper, a jester stepped onto the dais to entertain the guests who wished to linger in the dining hall enjoying their wine. I told my companions I craved a bit of fresh air before turning in, and I pushed my chair away from the table. Despite Gwenyth's prediction about ladies seeking out my company after dinner, Agnes seemed not at all interested in furthering our acquaintance.

Lord Percy, however, reached out and put his hand on mine. "Nay. You must stay. Night air is bad for the lungs. Whereas a jester is good for the spirit."

I gently pulled my hand away. "I'm frequently outdoors at night. My constitution is used to it."

Lord Percy turned in his chair, laughing in a way that showed more reproach than humor. "What cause do you have to go out after dark? I say, your servants must be slothful if you've need to be outdoors at such hours. I've half a mind to come to Paxworth and give them a severe reprimand on your behalf."

Lady Edith sat straighter, slightly offended. "Our servants are quite attentive."

My admission to being outside at night had been a mistake and although I doubted Lord Percy was on the search for renegade operatives, I chided myself for my carelessness. "I assure you, my forays aren't far enough or long enough to merit worry on anyone's part. I simply like to stargaze at times. The sky is so lovely on a clear night."

Bernard Godfrey nodded. "I'm also familiar with the constellations. As long as the night is warm, as it is tonight, one needn't trouble about ill vapors."

"You see," I said to Lord Percy, "Master Godfrey is quite healthy. You've no cause for concern."

Bernard Godfrey stood. "I would be happy to accompany you outside." His words didn't have the easy cadence of Lord Percy's banter which made his request seem even more fraught with intent than Lord Percy's declaration that he would travel to Paxworth to scold my servants. I couldn't have someone trailing me around, especially tonight.

"No," I said, perhaps too quickly. "Now that I think on it, I should retire to bed. The journey here was taxing and I didn't sleep well."

"A proper idea." Lady Edith finally came to my aid. "You mustn't be so drowsy on the morrow that you fall asleep during the wedding ceremony."

Neither Bernard nor Lord Percy looked pleased to see me leave but couldn't contradict Lady Edith's edict. I headed toward the door, reminding myself not to move out of the servants' way. They'd been trained to move out of mine. Little details like that would reveal my lowborn beginnings.

Other guests were leaving the room as well. Some were elderly and probably retiring to their rooms, some were no doubt going to find other enjoyments—games or trysts.

By the time I reached the courtyard, I was afraid it would be strewn with people out taking advantage of the evening. Torches, enchanted to glow red and white, lined the castle wall and gave off enough light that one could ramble around a good portion of the courtyard without fear of tripping in the darkness. I only saw one couple outside, though, and they disappeared into the obscurity of the hedge maze.

It was better not to let anyone see me staring up at the wizards' windows. I dare not speak the invisibility chant in view of the castle door, lest someone saunter out and spy me vanishing. I ducked behind a tree and made the change there. Invisibility was such freedom, like shedding one's finery at the end of the night.

I strolled back to the courtyard, enjoying the breeze and pausing to look at the stars. I rarely paid attention to them, but since I'd claimed to enjoy stargazing, I took note of them, crowded together in the heavens.

Ronan had told me once that no one knew where falling stars came from. All the stars were still in the heavens, accounted for, their constellations unchanged. Just as puzzling, no one ever found where the stars landed. Stars were mysterious—there and not there, continuously out of reach. When I was invisible, I felt nearly as illusive. There and not there.

I hadn't taken many steps across the courtyard when I spotted Ronan standing by a half wall that separated a sunken garden on his other side. I stopped mid-step, worried he would see me.

Of course, he wouldn't. Wizards couldn't detect those who were invisible unless they cast a disclosing spell on that person. Ronan had no reason to suspect I was in the courtyard.

Unless, that was, he'd walked out as I'd gone behind the tree and noticed I hadn't reappeared.

Well, no matter. Even if he'd seen me stroll outside and disappear, he didn't know where I was now or where I was going. I'd traipse right by him on my way to the wizards' wing, and he, the one who'd given me the power of invisibility and silent footsteps, would be none the wiser. There was a sort of fitting justice about that.

I strode toward him, unafraid.

As I got close, he said, "Marcella?"

I halted a few feet away. Had my dress made a swishing

noise? No, I was certain it hadn't. How had he known I was near?

His eyes swept the area but didn't stop on me. Perhaps he'd only been guessing when he spoke my name.

I took a couple of slow steps.

"Marcella." The word was said with a slightly chiding tone. "It's no use pretending you're not here. I can tell, you know."

Could he? Without a disclosing spell? That was ill news, indeed. I'd better find out how.

I ensured we were still alone, then murmured the counter incantation. "How did you know?" I tried to keep my voice light, as though it didn't matter. But it most definitely mattered.

He smiled the sort of sly, enigmatic smile I remembered from our time spent holding hands. "Your perfume. I noted it when I first saw you."

I hadn't thought the scent was that strong. I'd have to wash off all traces before I went into the wizards' wing again.

Ronan cocked his head. "Why are you flitting about the courtyard, trying to remain undetected?"

Yes, that. I needed a believable excuse. "I was avoiding the company of a certain gentleman." I looked back at the doorway as though searching for said gentleman. "When I excused myself to get some fresh air, he volunteered to join me. Although I declined his company, I worried he might come after me anyway."

Ronan's eyes followed mine to the empty doorway. "Are you referring to the womanizing Lord Percy or the social climbing Bernard Godfrey?"

I blinked, surprised. I hadn't seen Ronan so much as glance in my table's direction. "You're acquainted with those gentlemen?"

"I've done business with Godfrey and know of Lord Percy. Most people at court are aware of his dalliances."

"Oh." I wasn't sure if Ronan was implying my ignorance proved I was an outsider or if he was warning me off.

Ronan's gaze traveled over me, taking in my gown and headdress. "Fortune has smiled on you. A long-lost aunt adopted you into the nobility?"

It was clear he wanted more details. I wasn't about to satisfy his curiosity. "Fortune has indeed been kind."

He nodded, coming to his own conclusions. "I suppose everyone needs an heir, and a beautiful girl who can attract money isn't a bad heir to have. Surely your goal of catching a nobleman's son isn't far away." There was censure in his voice, a bite to the words.

"What did you expect? I tried love once, but it ended badly. Through no fault of my own, the man refused to speak to me and sold me away."

Ronan, annoyingly, seemed pleased by this declaration. "You loved me?"

I wasn't answering that question, wasn't even going to honor it with a pause. "Your abandonment wasn't a complete tragedy. I learned three important lessons at Docendum Castle: Love is a liability, and I can't rely on wizards to take care of me."

"That's only two lessons."

"Yes. I'm not revealing the third." Let him wonder what it was. I wasn't telling him about my additional magic abilities.

He laughed and shook his head, amused instead of irritated. "I've missed you." A smile lingered on his lips, lighting up his expression.

This bit of cheer irked me. Happiness, it seemed, came easily to him now while it had evaded me like a hunted hare. He'd probably not thought of me a day since I left. "If I marry well enough, I'll have a wizard of my own to order around. Wouldn't that be fitting? Tell me, Ronan, are you for sale these days? What is your price?"

He bowed his head in deference, the way he would to a

woman of means. "As much as I would enjoy your company again, I don't think King Leofric would part with me."

"King Leofric?" I repeated. I didn't understand or at least didn't want to understand.

"I'm one of his council wizards. My name here is Mage Warison."

The words rushed through my ears like they were carried away on a stream. My stomach painfully twisted. I had to reach out and take hold of the wall to steady myself.

"But…" that's so unsafe, I wanted to say. Instead, I stammered, "But you're so young."

"And yet so talented. You do remember that about me?"

I didn't answer. I was staring at him, trying not to look stunned. I would have to take Ronan's mark from him. How could I do that when he'd given me my magic? And would taking his mark destroy mine as well?

"You haven't agreed about the nature of my talent." Ronan scratched the back of his neck in mock offense. "You do remember I changed into an animal my first year?" He lowered his voice. "I also changed you into a tree. That's very high-level wizardry."

"Ronan," I murmured. "You changed me into much more than a tree."

He raised his eyebrows.

"Why would you take a new name?" I wouldn't have come to Valistowe if I'd known Ronan was on the king's wizard council.

"Warison doesn't mean war," he said, guessing at the cause of my displeasure. "It's an ancient term for garrison."

"What was wrong with the name Ronan?" He'd discarded every bit of the boy I'd known. Even I, who had every reason to change my name, had kept Marcella.

"Wizards receive new names when they finish their apprenticeship. It's a step of the graduation ritual."

"You never told me you'd have a new name." Perhaps it was a

childish complaint, but it was one more piece of proof that even when we were friends, he'd not considered me part of his future.

"Didn't I?" He seemed genuinely surprised. "I'll remedy that now." He clasped his hands together the way Mage Quintal had done while lecturing. "When an apprentice graduates, his teachers present him with five possible names. Two represent his charitable qualities, two his cunning ones, and one name is a nonsense word thrown into the mix to see if apprentices have studied their terminology well.

"Unfortunately, some don't, which is how Mage Picamar ended up with a name that meant: bitter oily liquid obtained from tar." Ronan grinned, the same conspiratorial grin he'd given me back at Docendum when he'd shared stories with me. I'd eaten those stories like they were made of honey.

I wasn't that girl anymore, couldn't be, and spending time with him would only make what I had to do later harder.

I pulled away from the wall, steady again. "I should let you return to your royal duties while I go hunt up some eligible bachelors. It's no use talking with you. We both know you don't make attachments with women."

He tilted his chin down. "Is that what we both know?"

I paused, halted by the thought that Ronan might have ignored Wolfson's advice and found a highborn, influential wife. I knew nothing of Mage Warison. "Are you attached to someone?" My breath lodged into my throat as I waited for the answer.

"Well, no." He thrust his hands into his pockets. "But that's not to say that I *can't* make attachments."

"Clearly." I pushed past him, ready to glide back to the castle in a flourish of indifference.

He took hold of my arm, ruining the elegance of my exit, and propelled me back to face him. "You know I sent you to Carendale Castle for your own good. You weren't safe at Docendum."

I knew he believed this. But he was lying to himself, and I wouldn't let him lie to me as well. "Is that why you didn't speak to me before I left or afterward? Is that why you never sent word or visited, not even after you left Docendum? Somehow that kept me safer?"

"What makes you think I never visited?"

Because I never saw a peregrine falcon on the grounds of Carendale. I searched for that bird every time I went outside. I found myself watching the sky for peregrines still. "I assume if you'd come for a visit, you would have spoken to me."

Ronan's blue eyes looked black in the low light, brooding at my accusation. He pressed his lips together and remained silent. He didn't answer because he couldn't. He hadn't come.

"Goodnight, Mage Warison." By his own admission, he was no longer Ronan. I needed to remember that.

I turned and strode back to the castle. This time he didn't stop me.

CHAPTER 14

*O*nce in my room, I washed my neck and wrists with trembling hands, washed everywhere I'd dabbed perfume that morning. Ronan was Warison. I felt sick. His identity shouldn't have mattered. I owed Ronan nothing.

No, that wasn't right. He'd given me a wizard's mark. He'd saved me from Wolfson's beast. He'd removed my scars. I owed him everything.

I moaned and scrubbed my skin harder. I couldn't let old loyalties prevent me from carrying out my mission. Someone had to fight for the servant class. The renegades were depending on me. Ronan and I were on opposite sides of a revolution. That was all. Wizards were my enemies. I'd known this from the moment Wolfson nearly fed me to his beast. This was the way things had to be.

If I believed taking Ronan's mark would destroy mine, I'd be justified in abandoning the mission, but I doubted this was the case. Ronan had grafted his mark into me the way one grafted branches from one tree to another. A branch once transplanted wasn't affected by the health of the original tree. The felling of one tree would have no effect on the other.

With red, raw marks stinging my wrists, I uttered the incantation for invisibility and went outside again. I still had tasks to complete, and the night was getting late. I strode around the castle's side until I located the wizards' wing. A lattice of metal bars covered the glass windows there. No entrance could be had that way.

I trudged back around the castle toward the guest stables. Tomorrow night would be filled with slashing at snakes who tried to strike me. The wizards must keep an antidote for the venom in their rooms, but if I were bitten, I'd have a hard time explaining why I was attempting to sneak into their chambers during the middle of the night.

The stables were sprawling buildings. Their beautifully arched stone doors were probably more expensive than Paxworth's entire manor house. Inside the guest stable, the floors were clean and the stalls roomy. The smells were the same, though. Hay and horses.

I'd hoped to find Alaric alone. He knew I was coming tonight, but being a groomsman had its tasks, and he couldn't do anything to draw suspicion to himself, like stand about outside, waiting for me. I'd told him to go about his business, and I would let him know when I arrived.

Instead of being anywhere of convenience, Alaric stood at the far end of the stalls with two other men. One was about his age, the other a score older. The men were talking and drinking from chipped wooden cups. Alaric held one as well, but I knew he wasn't drinking anything tonight, not when he needed to stay alert.

I made my silent way across the stables. A couple of horses looked in my direction. Even with scrubbed hands and neck, they could smell a human passing by. I padded over and stood behind Alaric. Either I'd gotten all the perfume off, or he wasn't nearly as observant as Ronan. He gave no indication he suspected anyone was around. I blew a puff of breath across his neck. That should let him know I was nearby.

He did nothing.

I waited, then leaned closer and blew another puff.

He slapped his neck in irritation. "Blasted flies. Don't they ever sleep?"

We really should have devised a signal of some sort for this meeting. I ran a finger across the back of the nape of his neck.

He startled and spun around. Not subtle. His eyes scanned the darkness, then went still. He understood.

"What's wrong?" the older man asked.

"Just searching for that fly." He made a swatting motion. "You can catch them if you're fast enough."

The younger man snorted. "How can a groomsman be so bothered by flies?"

The two men went on to speculate, in a vulgar manner, what kind of manure the horses at Paxworth produced.

I headed away from them even before Alaric excused himself to use the outhouse. When he emerged from the stables, I took his elbow to point him in the direction of the grazing pasture. Going to the outhouse might have been a better location should anyone look for him, but I couldn't abide the smell or the flies.

Alaric rubbed his neck where I'd run my finger along it. "You shouldn't have touched me like that. It was like having someone walk over your grave."

"I may have already done that too." I let go of his elbow and kept pace beside him. "Who knows where you'll be buried."

"Such cheery thoughts. You've the dagger with you?"

"Do you want me to place it in your hand?"

"Will it be invisible still?"

"No. Once I relinquish the dagger, it will appear."

He checked behind us to make sure we were still alone, then reached into his boots and pulled a chisel from one and a hammer from the other.

I took them and placed the dagger in his still outstretched hand. He tucked it into his boot. "Do you need my clothes to wear?"

"No. The windows are impassible."

He smirked. "Some other time, then."

I didn't know how to answer that.

He laughed at my silence. "I'll keep watch for a swarm of fireflies tomorrow night."

That was the sign we'd arranged should Alaric's help be needed when it came time to dispatch the king. Gwenyth and I both carried what looked to be a hardboiled egg in our pockets. In reality, they were filled with magical fireflies enchanted to find Alaric.

"Hopefully Gwenyth can accomplish her task without any assistance." I'd told myself I was helping with this mission because I wanted to spare the thousands who would die in battles, should renegades decide to fight the king's troops. But in truth, I didn't want to lose Alaric. I'd done my best to convince him not to come on this mission at all.

He stopped by the fence. We were sufficiently far enough from the stables that we couldn't be heard, but he still kept his voice low. "Everything else is going well?"

"There's been a complication. A wizard I knew…" No, that wasn't an accurate description. "A wizard I was friends with at Docendum—he's Warison."

"You were friends with a wizard?" Alaric's expression was such that I might have said I was friends with a demon.

"He isn't as bad as the rest. Or at least he wasn't at first." I thought of the villagers at Colsbury. "I don't know what he's like now."

"He's a wizard. They're all bad."

"Technically, I'm a wizard."

"You're not the same as the others." Alaric's statement curled at the end, almost becoming a question. He wanted reassurance.

"Of course, I'm not like them. My clothes aren't as fine, and my manners are better."

He didn't smile, so I added, "Wizards work for their own benefit. I work to free others. Is that enough of a difference?"

Alaric relaxed a bit. In the dim light, his eyes seemed darker than the sky above him. Warm and earnest. The moonlight caressed his cheekbones and brushed against his nose and lips. If I'd been visible, the two of us would look like lovers at a secret tryst. But I couldn't let myself think of Alaric that way.

It was perhaps ironic that Wolfson had set out to teach Ronan that love was a liability, and I was the one who had learned the lesson so thoroughly. If Ronan's ease of conversation with Floris Somerton was any indication, the tutorial hadn't been seared into his heart like it had mine. He at least had no fear of flirting. Just the thought of taking advantage of the moonlight with Alaric made me want to edge away from him.

"I don't want to take Ronan's…Warison's mark from him. He saved my life once and helped me considerably in other ways. I'm indebted to him for that. Can we accomplish the same means of helping the servants in another way?"

Alaric stared out at the field for a long time before he answered. He was deliberating on my words, but I didn't know to what end. He might have been contemplating alternatives or he might just be questioning the depth of my resolve.

"We need to go someplace more private," he said at last. "A place where we can speak face to face." Meaning a place where I would be visible. He reached out his hand, hovering it in the air like an offering. It took me a moment to realize he wanted to hold my hand.

I hesitated, then wrapped my fingers around his. If Ronan could flirt with Floris Somerton, I could hold Alaric's hand. "Why must we have privacy?"

"I need to see you while we have this conversation. I need to look into your eyes."

What, I wondered, did he suppose he'd find in my eyes? I ambled with him along the fence line, farther away from the stables. After a couple of minutes, we climbed over the fence and went behind a large shade tree in the pasture. I became visible, though, in the darkness, I was barely just that.

I pulled my shell charm from around my neck, made it glow so Alaric could see my face, and blinked dramatically. "My eyes are as loyal as ever, true?" More blinking. "Are you reassured now?"

His gaze slid over me. "No. You look pale."

"Pale is a compliment to highborn women. We powder our faces to look pale."

"Is the tension in your brows a noble affectation too?"

My hand went to my eyebrow to see if I was scowling without realizing it. Perhaps I was. "I can't help but feel tense. I've got to kill enchanted snakes before I enter any of the wizards' rooms. And Warison…"

Alaric's eyes narrowed. "Tell me more about Warison and you."

I worried my bottom lip while I considered how much to reveal. "I helped Ronan with his studies. We were friends." The word *friends* felt like a lie. But I couldn't bring myself to admit how deeply I'd cared for Ronan and how little I'd meant to him in the end.

With halting words, I told Alaric of the day my face was slashed by Wolfson's beast, how Ronan agreed to burn Colsbury to save my life, and how afterward, he refused to speak to me again.

Alaric muttered something under his breath. Probably a curse. "Sounds like the logic of wizards. And you want to spare Warison—after he burned innocent villagers?"

Ronan had gone to the village with Charles only to save me.

I wondered, with growing offense, if Alaric would've seen me slain with far fewer qualms.

"The night before I was sent to Haddock Castle, Ronan sneaked into my room and healed my scars. I can't imagine my life if he hadn't done that. I owe him something."

Alaric scoffed. "And what do you owe the villagers who died at his hand?"

My gaze sank to the ground. Those villagers had always weighed on my conscience. None of them deserved that fate, least of all the children.

"If you hadn't been his friend," Alaric went on, "you wouldn't have gotten the scars in the first place." He took my hands in his, gently holding them. "Wizards are like lions. You can befriend a wandering cub and not get hurt, but eventually, it will grow into a lion. It will kill and destroy anyone who gets in its way, including you. Warison is a lion now who works to keep a bad king in power. We must cut his claws."

My throat grew tight with emotion. I couldn't disagree with Alaric. I'd seen the ashes on Ronan's robes after he'd gone to that village. I swallowed and nodded. Perhaps Alaric saw me as a lion too. Perhaps I was one. My gaze still felt too heavy to lift from the ground.

Alaric gently squeezed my hands. "If Warison isn't as bad as the others, living without magic will prove a benefit for him. Once he's a man instead of a lion, he'll find his soul."

I nodded again, although I knew Ronan would never see the loss of his magic as a benefit. He would see it as the worst sort of betrayal.

Alaric let go of one of my hands in order to tilt my chin up. His eyes fixed on mine, checking, I supposed, for assurances. "We're in agreement about what needs to be done?"

"Yes." The word came out with more steadiness than I felt.

"Good." He smiled and his eyes lingered on me.

We were standing close, our hands twined together. With a

jolt, it occurred to me he might try to kiss me. I stepped back from him so quickly, I nearly stumbled. "I should go. I still have unfinished tasks."

I extinguished the light. No one ought to catch sight of it as we walked back. Although mostly I snuffed the light because I didn't want to see Alaric's expression, to witness his reaction to my quick retreat. Was he hurt? Amused? Resigned? Maybe I'd completely misread his intentions.

"Be careful," he told me.

He didn't need to remind me of that. I was always careful. For example, right now I was being quite careful to avoid the wrong sort of attachment to him. "I will be."

With the utterance of the invisibility enchantment, I turned and nearly fled back toward the castle.

* * *

AFTER I LEFT ALARIC, I went to the falconry and pilfered a pair of thick leather gloves. To ensure they'd deter a snake bite, I put a strengthening charm on them. I also took a leather strap. I'd seen a heraldry shield hanging above the mantle in one of the sitting rooms on the first floor. It was wooden, a decoration to be sure, but with a strap fastened to its back, it would work well enough to fend off fangs.

I'd have to wait until tomorrow night to steal the shield. A missing pair of gloves wouldn't raise suspicions but the same wasn't true for one of the king's wall hangings.

With my ill-gotten gain secure, I returned to my room and tried to sleep. Mostly I curled in my bed and thought of Ronan.

He was a formidable wizard, and he knew I had magic. That would make my attempts to overpower him all the more diffi-cult and dangerous. But we'd also been friends. He would grant me access to his company in ways the other wizards wouldn't. Perhaps I didn't have to fight the serpent at his door. Perhaps all

I needed to gain access to his chamber was to knock and murmur my name.

I entertained that scenario. I imagined him looking at me in question and wondering about the purpose of my midnight visit. Perhaps I would kiss him, wrap my arms around his neck, and enjoy the shock in his eyes as I pointed my wand at him and uttered the words of the stunning enchantment.

It was a tempting scenario.

I could assure him if he kept my secret, I would try to return his mark after the new king's installment. Ronan might agree to such a bargain rather than handing me over to the guards. If people knew how I'd received my magic, he'd be punished. And he'd want his magic restored more than he'd want vengeance against me. But then, a bargain of that sort wouldn't preclude him from taking revenge later on. Perhaps his first action after I returned his magic would be to destroy me.

That would be a very wizardly act.

So I couldn't risk any agreement with him. I must retain my anonymity when I attacked. He couldn't know I had anything to do with the renegades.

CHAPTER 15

*M*orning came and sunlight slithered its way past the drapes. I would've gladly slept in and missed breakfast, but Gwenyth insisted on rousing me when the morning bells chimed. She reminded me I should draw no untoward attention to myself and missing an opportunity to fraternize with eligible gentlemen might cause some to wonder about my purpose at court. So, I let her dress me in my yellow gown and weave ribbons into my hair.

At breakfast, Lady Edith and I sat at the same table with Lord Percy and the Godfreys. Neither the king nor the future queen was in attendance. Perhaps they were already at the town's cathedral rehearsing their nuptial speeches. I pretended an appetite and ate lemon-glazed salmon and apples cooked with cinnamon. I had no enthusiasm for the food. It all tasted of dread. Besides, I was afraid of spilling something on my gown and having to sit through the wedding with stains marring my dignity.

Madame Godfrey and her daughter ate with practiced gusto. They were beside themselves with eagerness for the day's event and went to great lengths to predict the details of Queen Marita's wedding gown.

While Lord Percy and the men escaped into a conversation about hunting wild boars, Madame Godfrey informed me that whatever the queen donned would set the style for the upcoming year. Madame Godfrey rather lorded her knowledge of slitted sleeves, brocade patterns, and pearl buttons over the rest of us. Agnes hoped fervently the new queen would follow the styles of the Illanté nobility. They had such fine fashion there. She and her family traveled to that country frequently to avoid the winter chill of our own kingdom.

Perhaps it was childish of me, but after half an hour of this, I said, "I think a blue gown, perhaps trimmed in fur, would make a lovely wedding dress."

"Fur in the summer?" Madame Godfrey wrinkled her nose as though I'd suggested something sinful. "No, it must be lace."

"And the gown must be purple," Agnes insisted, "or in the very least red. What backward ideas about fashion you have in Paxworth."

Lady Edith glanced at me, checking to make sure I'd seen the gown, then she smiled patronizingly at the women. "It's true that noblewomen do have different taste in gowns than others. Part of our breeding, you know. I think a gown of blue trimmed in fur would befit the queen quite well."

Madame Godfrey harumphed in indignation. "Perhaps her ladyship's taste in fashion would change if she traveled more."

Impertinent. If I'd been hunting for a husband, I would reject the younger Master Godfrey on her account alone. What a wretched mother-in-law she would be.

This morning, Ronan and the other four wizards of the king's council were easy to spot eating at the important nobles' tables. They dressed in red velvet robes with gold embroidered stars over white and blue striped tunics, symbolizing the union of the two countries. I couldn't help but notice how much younger and taller Ronan was than the others. He was more handsome too, with his square jaw and his forget-me-not blue eyes. He shone like a knight from some legend while the rest of them, for all their proud airs, seemed like faded old men.

I asked Lord Percy who the men in the red robes were, and he told me each's name. Telarian was squat with a protruding stomach and arms as thick as a blacksmith. Perhaps it was the weight of his jowls, but his mouth appeared to permanently frown. Sciatheric was taller, with small, shifting eyes and a bushy black beard that rested against his chest. Mage Zephyr was a spindly man with a large nose and thinning brown hair that peeked out of his hat. Redboot was there as well, eating his food with gusto. I could now put names to my quarries' faces.

They might do very well as regular folk. They all looked capable enough of finding some sort of gainful employment.

"If you have need of a wizard's assistance," Lord Percy said, "Mage Redboot is always eager to help the young women at court." He leaned toward me and lowered his voice "Perhaps at times too eager."

"I shall do my best to avoid him."

"I'd avoid Sciatheric as well."

The wizard council, it seemed, had more than its share of knaves. "What else do you know of them?"

Lord Percy shrugged. "Only what is commonly known. Mage Zephyr considers himself the wisest, though the others dispute that claim. Sciatheric is the wealthiest, or at least the showiest. He wears ruby and emerald rings and is never without his diamond-studded moon pendant. When the king isn't present, Mage Sciatheric and Mage Telarian can't say a civil word to each other, and the older mages fault Warison for being so much younger than they." Lord Percy winked at me. "I only fault him for being handsome enough to steal women's attention away from me. Tell me you haven't fallen under his spell as well."

"I assure you I have not." And to prove it, I wouldn't let myself look at him for the rest of the meal.

Once we'd all eaten, it was time to make the exodus to the town's cathedral so we could be in our places for the royal wedding. We of the lower tables were called to our carriages first. I was surprised at this preference until we got to the cathedral, and I realized it was our lot to stand at the back and wait—captive spectators—while the more important nobles arrived. They paraded down the aisle in their finery and took their spots in front of us.

No chairs or benches lined the nave. We would all be required to stand for the ceremony, and those of us with lesser rank at court would stand the longest. Lady Edith and I ended up situated close to the side wall next to graves and statues of past cathedral patrons. I could barely see anything save the stone columns and arches stretching above us—and of course, the elaborate headdresses of the women in front of us.

I no longer wondered why Lady Edith didn't make the effort to come to court more often. Why come here to be snubbed when she could stay in Paxworth and be treated with respect by all the villagers?

The choir sang, their voices echoing through the cathedral, resolute and achingly beautiful. That was lovely, at least.

By the time King Leofric and Princess Marita arrived, my feet were tired. All of us bowed and curtsied. The rustle of fabric seemed as loud as the ocean. We had to hold this bent position for so long while they strolled to the altar, I feared I would topple into the people in front of me.

I caught only a glimpse of the royal couple as they passed our row—a flash of fine robes, his red and hers blue with white fur trim.

Finally, we were able to stand again. A hush descended on the cathedral and the bishop, somewhere in front of the crowd, began the ceremony. His booming voice spoke of loyalty, peace, and the prosperity the union would bring to our country. He also declared that the king would trample his enemies under his feet and the jaws of hell would open to receive any who opposed him. I winced at that. The bishop was referring to me. I wished Alaric and Gwenyth stood with me for support, but servants weren't allowed inside. Only I heard the pronouncement of our doom.

When the king and queen had spoken their vows, they turned to glide down the aisle and out of the cathedral. Again we bowed, bending like colorful stalks of wheat in a strong wind.

This time, I saw the king's face as he passed. He was tall with smooth brown hair tucked under his crown and a neatly trimmed beard. He had a pleasant, fatherly face that closely resembled his portraits. The exactness surprised me. Most nobles paid their artists to paint them younger and fairer than they really were. The only difference I noticed in King Leofric was that he looked wearier than the man whose face graced portraits all over the castle.

By leaning forward more than propriety probably deemed acceptable, I also caught sight of the king's sister and brother-in-law. Lord Clement was a barrel-chested man with light brown hair to his shoulders, jowls, and a thick neck. I'd imagined Lord Clement would somehow look more saintly than King Leofric. Surely, he must be a better person to want to exact so many fewer years from his servants than King Leofric did, yet I recognized in him the same haughtiness that was common among all the powerful nobles.

The only one in the wedding party who looked truly happy was the king's sister, Lord Clement's wife. Princess Beatrice was perhaps in her thirties, bright-eyed, pretty, and plump with pregnancy. She smiled as she spoke with her husband, clearly pleased that her brother had remarried. A governess carried two-year-old Princess Alfreda. The child was clutching the woman as though afraid one of the bystanders would reach out and snatch her.

I shouldn't have felt sorry for the child. She would grow up to be as conceited and greedy as the rest of the nobility. And yet how could I not pity her? Princess Alfreda had already lost her mother and was about to lose her father as well.

The king's wizards followed the royal family. As Ronan neared my row, his head turned in my direction. I averted my gaze so he wouldn't catch me staring, but not quickly enough. For a passing moment, his eyes locked onto mine. In the future, I would have to remember not to watch him. I didn't want to give him the satisfaction of thinking I had any interest in him.

The more worthy nobles in the front of the cathedral filed out next. We in the back waited for them to parade by us again —and they strolled out slowly, enjoying their importance.

I knew bringing the carriages to the cathedral and loading them with passengers took time, but I would've much rather waited out in the sunshine. To my side, the grave of a baronet and the carved effigies of those mourning him seemed to be edging closer to me, whispering that after tonight, I'd join them in the underworld.

Five wizards. All powerful. Perhaps the most powerful in the land. True, I'd inherited Ronan's power and it was considerable. I knew numerous spells, but the other wizards had practiced so much more than I.

Finally, the wedding guests consigned in the back rows of the cathedral had our turn to leave. We shuffled out with far less aplomb as no one remained to view our exit.

When we at last reached the sunlight, Lady Edith paused at the top of the steps, craning her neck left and right. "Do you see our carriage?"

"No." All the ones waiting in front of the cathedral were finer than ours, with matching horses. Apparently, having identical colored horses to pull one's carriage was expected in noble circles. The spell that was filed away in my mind for changing a horse's color suddenly made sense.

I scanned the grounds, searching for Gwenyth or Joanne among the crowds of servants milling near the road. No sign of them. They wouldn't have come up here to fetch us, would they?

My attention was drawn to the figure of a man a few feet away. For a moment I didn't recognize him, out of place as he was and dressed in formal green robes. His dark hair, mustache, and beard had been trimmed. His hooked nose looked a little less red, and his bushy eyebrows were not quite as thick. But the man was definitely Mage Wolfson.

My feet froze in shock, caught between fear and indignation. His presence here wasn't unexpected and yet all the same felt like an affront.

My sudden halting drew both Lady Edith's notice and the wizard's. His eyes traveled over me and flew open in astonishment. I should've felt some satisfaction in that. The last he'd seen me, I was a servant with a scarred face. Powerless. Damaged. Sold. Now I was noble and beautiful.

This man who stood here calmly on the cathedral steps had murdered innocent villagers and had nearly murdered me. I expected him to slink away, head averted to hide his shame. But no. He sauntered over to us, his gaze bouncing between Lady Edith and me in curiosity.

Lady Edith smiled at him politely, which was more than he deserved. I wanted to slap him.

He bowed in Lady Edith's direction, practically flowing with courtly charm. "Have we had the pleasure of meeting, my lady?"

"I don't believe we have," Lady Edith replied demurely. "I'm Lady Edith of Paxworth and this is my niece, Marcella."

He turned to me, still gracious. "Yes, we've met before. One does not easily forget such beauty."

"I suppose not," I said, "since you did your best to ruin it." To my credit, my voice didn't tremble at all. "Lady Edith, this is Mage Wolfson. He nearly killed me."

She put her hand to her chest, and her lips drew together in distaste. "Oh, dear." My real mother would have lunged at him and attempted to claw his eyes out, so perhaps I should've been glad for Lady Edith's limited maternal feelings.

Mage Wolfson's mouth curled, almost sneering until he pressed them into a controlled line again. "You must be mistaken. I'd never lift a finger against a highborn woman. You are a highborn woman, are you not?"

A not-so-subtle threat that if I publicly criticized him, if I embarrassed him at court, he would expose me as his former servant. At another time, I would have laughed at his attempt to intimidate me with my past. Almost feeding one of your servants to a beast seemed a much worse crime than being that servant.

But I couldn't afford to laugh now. A young woman at court who was presumably searching for a husband would be desperate to conceal her lowborn status. If I scoffed at Wolfson now, if I crossed him, I'd draw unwanted attention to myself. After the king's death, I didn't want anyone wondering if my lowborn beginnings had made me a candidate for the renegades.

Lady Edith drew herself up with the indignation that the nobility achieved so effortlessly. "Marcella is my niece. Are you implying otherwise?"

"Of course not." Mage Wolfson shot me a triumphant look. He knew my silence now meant I would hold my tongue.

He glanced toward the road and gave us a curt bow. "My carriage is ready. I must take my leave of you." He spun, sweeping his robes around him in an unnecessary flourish, and marched down the stairs.

Abominable man.

I watched him go, hands clenched at my side, and resolved to find out the location of his quarters. If I had any energy left after taking the other wizards' marks, I'd take his as well.

And for the first time, I looked forward to my task tonight.

CHAPTER 16

$\mathcal{K}$ing Leofric and Queen Marita presided at dinner, an elaborate meal with seven courses, including cooked stuffed piglets, cranes, and peacocks redressed in their feathers. We were served cakes of cheese, sugared fruits, and marzipan shaped like Valistowe castle. I ate more than a lady ought. It might be my last meal, and besides, propriety aside, I had a hard night's work ahead of me and needed all the strength I could get.

Every nobleman present made a toast to the couple, each trying to outdo the rest in flowery speech and sycophantary. It went on and on. Never had anyone's virtues been so sure or extolled.

No wonder the royals all became arrogant and insufferable. They were fed a constant diet of flattery.

Lord Clement and Princess Beatrice sat next to the newly-weds on the dais. I couldn't help but study them, looking for some indication they would be good leaders. Lord Clement wore a jeweled collar filled with gems on his green silk robes. His matching shoes had such long points they might have been used for daggers. He ate heartily and drank freely.

Princess Beatrice talked with her new sister-in-law in an open, friendly manner. When Queen Marita spoke to King Leofric, she did so shyly. She hardly seemed the same woman who'd been ordering about her servants yesterday.

As a servant, I'd studied people to judge their temper, ill or otherwise, by every detail of their bodies. The incline of their head, the tapping of their foot, the quickness of their speech.

Lord Clement smiled and laughed but his eyes were watchful, every so often glancing around at the crowd. I wondered what he was watching for. Trouble? Renegades?

I only took a few sips of the wine the serving girls freely supplied the guests. Those with secrets couldn't afford loose tongues, and I didn't want slow reactions tonight. The wizards, from what I could observe, weren't taking similar precautions. They toasted and drank to the royal couple repeatedly.

The Godfreys said nothing about the queen's wedding dress, but Lady Edith brought it up enough times to ensure they didn't forget we had the same taste in gowns as the new queen. Bernard made an occasional stumbling comment to draw me into conversation, and Lord Percy heaped compliments on Agnes. He flirted with her excessively—I was guessing he'd learned the extent of her fortune and the lack of mine—but when no one else looked, he sent me regretful smiles. Shameless of him, really.

After the meal was over and we'd had time to refresh ourselves from the feasting, we moved to the great hall for dancing. Bernard Godfrey asked for my hand during the first dance, but after that, his mother whisked him away. She'd found other, more powerful nobles with daughters in need of the Godfrey fortune. I didn't mind. Plenty of men—even ones from the more elite families—were pleased to make my acquaintance and lead me around the floor. I was apparently pretty enough to dance with, even if I wasn't wealthy enough to marry.

Ronan and several other wizards roamed the periphery of the hall, drinking and talking to those who were either resting from dancing, had come only to enjoy the music or—such as in the Godfreys' case—had come to ensure their children socialized with the right sort.

I hadn't expected Ronan to dance. Most wizards thought themselves too dignified for twirling about to the music. However, Floris Somerton and a few others persuaded him to take the floor on occasion. He danced well. Of course, he did. He'd not only been bestowed with intelligence, wit, and magic but grace as well.

His gaze frequently strayed to me, and he made no attempt to look away when I caught him staring. He always seemed cross and disapproving while he watched me. His ill will only made me smile more at my partners. Let Ronan see that other men considered me worthy of their attention. I wished all sorts of jealousies upon him. In reality, he was probably only scowling at the proof that men from powerful families were so easily being duped by a lowborn woman.

Mage Redboot, the wizard who'd checked our carriage, sidled up to me and enquired how I was enjoying my stay at court. I answered him politely and was glad when Lord Percy noticed my unease and asked me to dance.

After that dance, Mage Sciatheric—the other wizard Lord Percy had warned me about—sought me out. He held two glasses of wine and handed me one. "My lady looks parched." His teeth barely appeared through his dark, heavy beard in the form of a smile. "The women of the court must suffer no deprivations while Mage Sciatheric can prevent it."

I accepted the glass. What else could I do? "Thank you for your kindness, sir." I didn't want to take even one sip of the wine. A wizard could put all sorts of spells into a drink. If I kept busy talking, I wouldn't have to drink. My eyes went to a pendant around his neck, the diamond-studded silver crescent moon. "What a lovely pendant." I blinked at it as though deeply impressed. "Is it magic?"

"It is." He waggled his thick eyebrows. "It makes me irresistible to women. Is it working?"

I laughed politely. "I'm sure you need no spell for that." Love spells were unreliable at best and never strong enough to have much effect.

He took a sip of his wine, flashing rings on nearly every finger. "You're new to court?"

"Yes, I'm Lady Edith Thornton's niece."

"Yet you know some of us already," he said as if we were sharing an inside secret.

Did he mean Mage Wolfson? Had the man said something about me that was making its rounds? I didn't know whether to agree or protest. I simply stared back at the wizard, my mouth half-open.

Mage Sciatheric gestured sideways with a tilt of his head. "You must know young Warison. I've seen the two of you exchanging glances throughout the evening."

Ronan. He was talking about Ronan. And yet I still was unsure how to answer. Was he fishing for information? "We've met," I allowed.

"Have you only met?" Mage Sciatheric asked, amused. "Young Warison gives no heed to the ladies at court, but you've caught his eye easily enough. And lo," he said, still amused, "the man in question approaches. I wonder whether he wants to talk to me, his colleague, or to you, a near stranger?"

Sure enough, Ronan was striding up to us. He nodded stiffly at Mage Sciatheric and held his hand out to me. "Lady Marcella, I believe I promised you a dance. Will you oblige me with the next one?"

No such conversation had happened, but I murmured, "Of

course," and handed my glass back to Mage Sciatheric. "Thank you again for your thoughtfulness."

"Interesting," was all he said before Ronan led me away.

As we walked toward the other couples, Ronan leaned close to my ear. "I would stay away from that wizard."

"What sound advice as it can be applied to all mages."

Ronan chuckled at the barb. "Perhaps, but that one especially." His eyes went to mine with an intensity, a warning. "He has a habit of gathering information about people and threatening to reveal it unless they do as he asks. You can guess what he asks of beautiful young women. I'd hate to see you in that situation."

Ah. A blackmailer. A fine servant for a king. "And what information do you think I want hidden badly enough I might compromise myself for its sake?" A foolish question. The answer was evident and the fact I'd asked simply showed I wasn't as concerned with finding a husband as I was supposed to be.

Ronan shrugged. "I'd assumed your past wasn't well known."

"It isn't. But I wouldn't compromise myself with Mage Sciatheric for its sake." I paused and smiled. "A blackmailer must be more attractive than that to tempt me to commit sin. I do have my standards."

Ronan laughed and some of the tension drained from him. "Well, I'm glad it's only the handsome scoundrels I have to protect you from."

Protect me? He must be using the term loosely. He meant to warn me, nothing more. I didn't want him to think of himself as my protector when I was doing quite the opposite of protecting him.

We'd taken our place at the end of the line of couples and so said little more. I knew the dances of court and had practiced them many times, yet standing so close to Ronan, I had a hard time remembering where my feet should be. His arms, when on me, were strong, and I had a habit of focusing on them and forgetting all else. He smelled of cinnamon. He must've used the spice in some incense for a spell or perhaps spilled some on his robe during dinner.

When the dance finished, he returned me to a spot on the side of the ballroom, quite far from Mage Sciatheric. I regretted Ronan's parting. And despite knowing that Mage Sciatheric had taken note of my interest in Ronan, I still found my eyes wandering to him.

Finally, the festivities ended and the guests retired to their rooms for the night. Gwenyth was able to nap, but I could barely sit still as I waited for both guests and wizards to go to sleep so that the hallways would be clear.

After a couple of hours, I changed into one of Gwenyth's simple dresses—it was easier to maneuver in and less expensive should I have to burn the thing to get rid of any incriminating stains. I put on my enchanted boots, slipped the egg that held the fireflies into my pocket, and strapped a knapsack of supplies onto my back. With an uttered incantation, I vanished.

I eased from the room into the quiet of the castle hall. A servant boy was asleep on a mat down the passageway, awaiting any requests from nobles. He didn't stir as I went by. I glided silently through the hallway and down to the first floor to retrieve the heraldry shield to use as a protection against snake bites.

One would think that my many criminal expeditions into various castles would make me immune to nerves, but my stomach clenched with worry. A plot to kill the king was so much worse than stealing someone's jewels.

Once I had the shield, I said an incantation to attach the leather strap to the back. With it in hand, I made my way back up the steps and past the guards who stood at attention on the fourth floor.

Which of the wizards' rooms should I break into first? I

didn't know which chamber was Ronan's and yet I did. His was the one with the serpent whose concave face created the illusion that the snake's eyes followed anyone who looked at it. He'd designed the thing to show he was cleverer than the other wizards. I would take his mark last. That way if my attempts failed and one of the other wizards killed me, Ronan would retain his mark. I would grant him that favor for all he'd done for me.

I padded down the hallway with three rooms, choosing the door closest to the hallway first. If things went badly, it would be the easiest one to escape from. I stood in front of the brass snake for far too long, mentally repeating the reasons why my actions were necessary. Servants deserved more freedom. The renegade leaders were certain Lord Clement would give it to them.

With the shield and dagger poised in hand, I touched my elbow to the door handle. Before I could blink, metal vanished and a large tan snake appeared in front of me.

The viper reared up, hissing menacingly. Even without seeing me, it knew where I stood. It lunged forward and would've bitten my thigh had it not been for the shield. As the snake pulled back to strike from a different angle, I slashed my dagger at his head.

Even lengthened, the blade was too short. It whistled by the creature without any damage. The serpent lunged again, this time sinking his fangs into the falconer's glove. I'd been right to strengthen the leather. My skin wasn't even grazed. Better yet, the snake's fangs stuck so firmly into the glove that the serpent couldn't move away fast enough to avoid my blade.

I sliced off its head. The body fell to the floor where it writhed as though struggling for breath. I'd always been squeamish when it came to killing things. Unlike most of the kitchen servants in Docendum, I'd never broken a chicken's neck. I was excused from plucking their feathers after I threw up on one. Even watching others do the chore made my insides lurch.

Somehow, I'd imagined killing the snakes would be akin to slaying dragons, something that would make me feel like a knight. Not so. This act was plucking chickens all over again. Gagging, I used the tip of my blade to pry the snake's head off my glove. In my haste, the thing flew across the hallway and smacked the tapestry on the adjacent wall. Somewhere in its flight, the head returned to its metal form, and the noise was like a rock pelting into the fabric.

I waited, breath held. The wall was part of the king's chambers. Had he heard the noise? Would he call someone to investigate?

No sound indicated that the king's door had opened. Either he was asleep, far away, or busy with his new bride.

I pushed the snake's body against the door, hoping that, should a guard stroll by, it would be less noticeably decapitated there. With quick uttered words, my horse charm changed into a key. I pulled my knitting needle from my pocket and carefully opened the door. It let out a low creak of complaint.

A whiff of stale incense drifted from the room. No noise. I braced for a sign of some dangerous enchanted beast about to charge. Nothing was there.

I stepped inside. I had other magic fireflies besides the ones in the signal egg. Some were loose in my pocket, little bits of metal, charmed for the purpose of giving light in a dark space. That way if the wizard awoke and saw a glow in the room, he would fling spells in the firefly's direction instead of mine. The bug, however, was unnecessary. An unnatural purple flame churned in the fireplace, heating and lighting the room sufficiently that I could see an ornately carved canopy bed.

Black curtains were drawn around it, hiding its occupant. My wand's stunning spell would need to hit skin in order to work, and I was wary of crossing the room to move that curtain. Another protective spell might be nearby.

It was then I noticed an iron statue of the dog sitting by the wall not two feet away. It was a large thing, a mastiff of sorts. No doubt, it would transform the instant I passed it.

So like a wizard. Keeping an actual dog in the room wouldn't have been hard, and a living dog would've barked as soon as I opened the door. But the wizard couldn't be bothered by an animal that required daily attention. Better to keep an iron statue instead.

Magic was needed to defeat the dog, and that would tax some of my strength. Still, I didn't see another way. Even if I managed to kill the animal quickly, its barking would alert both the wizard and the guards.

I'd a spell in my repertoire for turning scraps of iron into plowshares. I pointed my wand at the animal and whispered the words. Its form melted, shimmering like a giant raindrop, and settled into the triangular shape of a plowshare. As I passed, it remained silent and inert.

I approached the bed cautiously, wand ready. The wizard might have woken. I edged closer. No worried hand emerged from the curtains. No trembling fingers grappled with a wand.

I slowly pulled back the curtains at the head of the bed.

Mage Telarian lay there, mouth open, jowls slack, deep in sleep. Without his robes and finery, he might have been just another stout villager of nearly three score years. He looked conquerable. And drunk. I pointed my wand at his face and whispered the incantation.

At my first word, his eyes fluttered open and he squinted in confusion. The wine had dulled his senses. He moved to sit up, but I finished before he did. His eyes went blank, and he fell back into his pillows.

I had forty minutes until he regained consciousness. Hopefully removing his mark would take no more than twenty minutes. If I completed the work and left before the wizard's stupor wore off, he should drift back to sleep like one who was only slightly awakened after a dream.

The incantation to turn the wizard into a tree wasn't complicated, at least not since Ronan's skill had shown me how it could be done. Magic, Ronan insisted, was like math, and most wizards were content to use already established equations. He scoffed at these lesser mages because coming up with their own equations seemed not to occur to them.

In the lesser wizards' defense, without Ronan's talent, they might create a spell that ended up hurting themselves, or just as bad, one that didn't work and therefore made them look incompetent in front of their employers. I didn't veer away much from the tested equations myself.

I turned Telarian into a tree and chiseled out his mark. Trees could lose small pieces from their trunk without causing severe damage. After I removed the mark, I swept up the bits of bark and tossed them in the fire, so as not to leave clues as to what I'd done. Then I placed my hand upon the tree's chiseled hole and used the spell to speed a wound's healing. That way Telarian wouldn't bleed to death when I changed him back to his human form.

Everything went smoothly enough, although the energy the process extracted from me was more than I expected. The wizard's magic resisted being forced into another shape. To preserve my strength, I'd dropped my invisibility while I worked. Still, I was slow.

I'd have a hard time performing five such spells in one night. And yet if I didn't complete them tonight, they would be so much harder to complete at all. Once the wizards realized some of their kind had been attacked, they wouldn't drink as they did tonight. They would add more protections to their rooms. I had to push myself.

After I returned Mage Telarian to his human form, I became

invisible again and went to the next door. Shield raised, I touched the door handle to awaken the snake. The serpent drew itself up and hissed so loudly that the noise seemed to echo in the empty hallway.

This snake stood taller than the first and swayed back and forth, beady eyes hunting for me. Almost quicker than sight, it lunged toward my middle and hit the shield.

I swung the dagger. I wanted to trap the creature's neck between my blade and the wood, but it dodged away. My blade missed the viper altogether and smacked the shield with a loud thunk. The sound could have been a knock on the door. One that might wake a sleeping wizard.

The snake struck again, low this time. Its fangs hit my boot. I pivoted and stepped on its body to keep it in place. The viper nearly tripped me, thrashing as it did. Its head whirled toward me, baring fangs and searching for a vulnerable spot. Before it could succeed, my blade severed the creature in two.

The head fell to the floor, mouth open and fangs bared, and it reverted to its metal form. So very gruesome. I tucked my blade back into my boot and was pulling out my unlocking charm when the door swung open.

Mage Sciatheric stood in rumpled night clothes, his dark hair in disarray. The gaudy moon pendant still hung around his throat. The man actually slept with the thing. He scowled, angry at being awakened. While he peered down the hallway, searching for whoever had knocked on his door, I pointed my wand at him and whispered the stunning spell.

His eyes went wide, and he reached for the wand pocket of his robes, which did little good as he wasn't wearing them. Ronan had told me once that a wise wizard slept with his wand near his pillow. If Sciatheric did, he'd neglected to bring it with him to answer the door. One would've really expected more from a wizard on the king's council.

He collapsed, and although I rushed forward to grab hold of

him, I couldn't completely keep him from hitting the ground. I could only minimize the loud thud he made as he did. This night was proving to be noisier than I'd wished.

Sciatheric was a tall man and heavy. With a suppressed grunt, I half-dragged, half-rolled him into the room and shut the door.

The same strange purple light I'd seen in Telarian's chamber flickered in Sciatheric's fireplace, sending out a glow of illumination. I noted a wild boar statue not far away, but since Sciatheric had kindly come to the door, I didn't have to concern myself with it.

Removing Telarian's mark had taken perhaps twenty-five minutes, but this time, I had to peel off all of Sciatheric's jewelry before changing him into a hawthorn tree. Metal didn't change into bark the way clothing did and would've bit into the tree's flesh in an injurious manner.

I was also wearier. Each step of the spell took longer.

After I finished chiseling out Sciatheric's mark, I leaned back on my knees and contemplated whether the time and energy to perform the healing spell was really necessary. I wasn't positive that turning Sciatheric back into a man with the wound still fresh on his neck would prove fatal. Perhaps the injury would be more of a scrape than a cut.

My speed and energy were more important than the man's safety. And besides, maybe leaving the wizard wounded would keep him from fighting me, should he awaken before I finished.

Even as these justifications entered my mind, I knew that carrying the weight of the king's death on my conscious would be burden enough. I couldn't chance that my actions would kill this man as well. He didn't deserve that, even if he was a wizard and a blackmailer.

I completed the healing spell and returned Sciatheric to his human form, unsure of how much time had passed. When I picked up the shield, it felt heavier than it had before. I uttered the words of the invisibility enchantment and opened the door.

From the floor, Sciatheric yelled, "Who's there?" He lifted his head and blinked at his surroundings in confusion. "What mischief is this?"

Curse my slowness. His voice had been loud enough to awaken both Telarian and whichever wizard was in the room on his other side.

CHAPTER 17

I hesitated in the doorway, caught by indecision. Should I do something to silence Sciatheric— another stunning spell? His yelling had ruined my chances of taking another wizard's mark tonight. Guards from the floor would be on their way to see why he had called out. The wizard at the end of the hallway had likely awakened, and if he wasn't on his way to the hallway to offer assistance, he would at least be on alert for danger, his wand in his hand.

I had to consider how to best improve my odds of taking the rest of the marks tomorrow night. I needed to throw the wizards off my trail.

My gaze landed on Sciatheric's moon pendant lying on the floor. In my hurry, I'd forgotten to put it back on his neck. It would do nicely as a false clue. I stepped back into the room and picked it up, making it vanish into my grasp.

Sciatheric knew what this meant. An invisible wizard was in his room. He lurched to his feet and hurled himself across the room at his bed. A moment later, he held his wand in front of him and furiously recited the words to a disclosing spell. It had no effect on me. He'd lost his magic.

I slipped out the door, shut it behind me, and hurried to Telarian's doorway. By that time, Sciatheric had marched into the hallway, wand clutched in his hand. He arced it across the hallway, muttering a spell.

I opened Telarian's door, paused for enough time that someone could have gone inside, then dropped the pendant in the room and closed the door again.

Sciatheric's nostrils flared like a bull's. "Telarian, you spider!" He stomped down the hallway. "What do you mean by sneaking into my room?"

A few moments later, Telarian's door swung open and he stepped out, jabbing his wand in the air. "What game are you playing? It's you who's been in my room. Don't deny it. I heard you leave just now. You knew I caught you and so now you're putting on a show for the guards."

I pressed against the wall to avoid any approaching soldiers and edged toward the stairwell. One guard strode over from the direction of the king's chambers. A clatter from the stairs meant more men were on their way up.

I couldn't go down the stairs while guards rushed up, especially not while carrying a bulky shield. I stayed flattened against the wall near the entrance to the hall, biting my lip and waiting for the men to pass by me.

Telarian held up the moon pendant, waving it like a flag before a battle. "This proves you trespassed in my room. You dropped it on the way out. The king will know of this."

Sciatheric stormed over and yanked the necklace from his hand. "More webs you spin. What this proves is your thievery!" Sciatheric stepped away, lifted his wand dramatically, and boomed out an incantation of attack, one that called fire down upon an enemy.

Before Sciatheric finished speaking, Telarian uttered the counter incantation, a spell to deflect the fire toward the speaker.

Nothing happened, of course. Telarian screeched in indignation. "You wish to kill me? You make accusations to justify my murder!" Lord Percy hadn't been jesting when he said the two men disliked each other.

Two guards from the stairs reached the hallway entrance, but instead of striding by me, they kept their distance from the wizards, standing in a spot that made it impossible for me to move past them. "Mage Sciatheric, Mage Telarian," one of the guards ventured. "Please calm yourselves."

The wizards ignored him. Telarian uttered an incantation I didn't recognize. Probably something equally dark as bolts of fire.

The guards took a few wary steps backward. They were not about to get between fighting wizards.

At this point, the wizards must have realized their phrases had no effect. I thought their astonishment would douse their anger, but somehow it only increased.

Sciatheric went red with rage. The veins in his neck stood out like bright blue rivers traversing his face. "What have you done?" He lunged at Telarian, grabbing him by the throat.

I watched, horrified. When I'd thrown Sciatheric's pendant into Telarian's room, I'd expected a diversion, not this.

Telarian didn't claw at Sciatheric's grip. He moved his hand across his wand, as though coaxing out more magic. The wand grew—which shouldn't have happened—and the new length fell to the floor, leaving the rest a short, bright silver. I didn't comprehend what I was seeing until Telarian plunged his wand into Sciatheric's chest.

All along, Telarian's wand had been a blade, a long, thin one sheathed to hide its secondary purpose.

Sciatheric gasped in pain and lurched backward, his hands clutching at the wand. Blood bloomed through his nightshirt. The wound was close to his heart.

"Fetch the physician," a guard yelled.

Sciatheric shook his head at Telarian in a reproachful manner, calmer than I'd expected for a man with a blade protruding from his chest. He staggered toward Telarian, blocking his escape. He looked like he would lean in and whisper something. Instead, he yanked the blade from his chest, and in one quick motion, he swiped it across Telarian's neck.

Someone shouted, "Fetch a wizard!"

I needed to leave. I'd seen too much already. The blood on Sciatheric's hand—had it come from his chest or Telarian's neck? The noise, the gurgling scream, I wanted to block it out. I took a stumbling step backward, nearly dropping the shield. My stomach heaved and threatened to retch on the floor. A bad response since someone was bound to notice a pile of vomit suddenly appearing.

If the guards hadn't been distracted by the two dying men in the hallway, they might have felt me fumbling with the shield as I passed by. I knocked into one of them. But they were rushing forward, finally prodded into action.

I ran down the stairs, not stopping at the third or second floor. When I arrived at the main floor, I ran, already breathless, toward the sitting room. My hands shook. I wanted to rid myself of the shield. Every moment that passed, I feared someone would come into that room and notice it missing. They would wonder. They would question. They would find me.

My panic wasn't logical, but it burrowed into me. I reached the sitting room and rehung the shield. Sciatheric and Telarian. Dying in front of me. I took deep breaths. It didn't help.

I should've headed to my room, but I didn't want to face Gwenyth. She'd be more upset by my failure to take all the marks than she'd be that I'd just caused the deaths of two men.

I wanted to see Alaric. Sneaking out of the castle for such a whim was foolish. I shouldn't bother him, and yet, I found myself—almost without thought or reason—going back up the stairs, tying up my skirts, and crawling out a garderobe window to see him.

Alaric would be awake, watching for fireflies. With that reasoning in mind, going to him now was a service. He'd be able to sleep after my update, or if so inclined, lie on his pallet and ruminate over my weaknesses as an operative. And in return, he'd do his best to extract the guilt that was hitching my breaths together.

I shimmied sideways and down the wall, hardly feeling the rocks scrape my palms, then ran to the stables. Alaric was outside, leaning against the wall near the door. He looked expectant standing there, noble. Ready to sacrifice his life if needed.

Even before I whispered his name, he probably heard my panting. His eyes darted around, and he checked over his shoulder to see that no one else was nearby. The doorway was quite empty, still, he headed toward a tree behind the stable anyway. As he walked, he asked, "Is it done?"

I shook my head, then remembered he couldn't see me. "No. There was a problem." The phrase sounded so trite, like I'd run into a small inconvenient thing.

"What went wrong?"

We reached the cover of a tree. I became visible and told him everything, including the bloody end of the wizards. I couldn't erase the sight of it from my mind. "I pitted them against each other. But I didn't think…" My hand, still trembling, went to my mouth. "It's my fault they're dead."

Alaric grunted. "Good riddance. I wish they were all so easily dispatched."

He didn't understand. He wasn't even trying. "I said I wouldn't become an assassin, but that's what I've become. Those men would be alive if not for—"

Alaric took hold of my shoulders and leaned forward so that his face was close to mine. "It's no one's fault but their own. If they hadn't been so venomous, they would've listened to one another instead of acting like rabid dogs. Normal folk wouldn't have acted so. Their deaths are their own making, not yours."

He was right, or at least I hoped he was. Still, guilt clung to me. My head sank and my vision swam. I felt like a cloth dunked in water and wrung out hard.

Alaric pulled me into a hug. He'd hugged me before, during the excitement of a mission accomplished, but not like this, in gentle, soothing comfort. His chin rested on my hair. His arms were warm and sturdy. "Perhaps things worked out well enough. As you said, you didn't have the strength to complete all five tonight. With Telarian and Sciatheric both dead, people might not even notice their marks were taken. Perhaps the other wizards won't realize what's happening yet."

That was an optimistic hope, but I didn't contradict him. I just kept leaning against Alaric. He smelled of hay. Bits of it clung to his tunic.

"You mustn't lose courage now," he murmured into my hair. "You'll be able to take the other three marks tomorrow night. You're right talented with magic. I can't believe you know a spell for changing iron into plowshares off the top of your head."

I hadn't told him how I knew so many spells. Accepting the unearned praise felt like falsehood. I pulled away from him and flicked hay from my clothes. During our hug, several pieces had switched loyalties from Alaric to me. "What if I can't accomplish the task tomorrow? I'm not a real wizard." As if to offer proof, I added, "I don't even have a wizarding name."

"Isn't Marcella a fine enough name?"

"When apprentices graduate, their teachers give them a new name, one that describes them."

Alaric's eyebrows dipped together. "Redboot…" He rolled the word over on his tongue, considering it. "Perhaps his boots were red from wading through blood."

Alaric might be right. Why else would Redboot have chosen that name? The moniker wasn't about fashion.

Alaric tucked his hands behind his back, imitating a stance wizards frequently took. "I can name you easily enough. I christen you Silver Blade, our secret weapon, the one that will bring us salvation." He held up a hand, fingers pointing to the sky. "You might think, and rightly so, that your title should be Red Blade, but no, you're not a pair of boots that retains a stain. You won't be tarnished by your doings." He smiled, took my hand, and kissed it like I was a lady. "You'll remain pure."

I smiled weakly back at him. He was trying to make me feel better. But the name Silver Blade reminded me of the wand thrust into Sciatheric. It wasn't a title I wanted. "I ought to return to my room. Gwenyth will be waiting for me."

He nodded. "Goodnight, Silver Blade."

I sighed. I would have to tell him later that I hated the name.

CHAPTER 18

*T*he next morning at breakfast everyone was abuzz with news about Mage Sciatheric's and Mage Telarian's deaths.

"It's shocking," Madame Godfrey said in a thrilled whisper. "Two of the king's wizarding council, murdering each other while we slept one floor below."

Lord Percy popped a piece of cheese into his mouth with an unimpressed air. "They had a long-standing feud. They were bound to come to blows sooner or later."

That *had* been a stroke of fortune. It would behoove me to know more about the wizards, such as who was likely to join forces to defeat an intruder. "Which of the king's wizards are friends?" I asked.

Lord Percy nodded at me. "Touché, my lady."

Which meant, apparently none of them.

Lady Edith cut through a piece of meat pie and gave me a sideways reproving look. "It was an unfortunate event to happen on the first night of the new queen's reign. A bad omen, I'm sure." She suspected I was involved but hopefully wouldn't interrogate me on the subject later.

Agnes was making her way through a bowl of candied plums. "I heard their marks were gone. Vanished from their necks."

"How very puzzling." I took a bite of my meat pie so I wouldn't have to comment further.

"You must be wrong," the elder Master Godfrey said. It was one of the rare times he'd joined the conversation. "A mark can't be stolen like some unguarded jewelry. Several wizards have to combine powers in order to remove one."

Madame Godfrey scanned the room surreptitiously. "There are enough wizards here to accomplish such a deed."

Lord Percy bestowed a confident grin on us. "But then why would Mage Sciatheric and Mage Telarian kill one another?"

I stiffened, fork grasped awkwardly in my hand. I didn't like the way Lord Percy asked the question, as though he already knew the answer.

When none of us replied, he added, "I have it from those who've spoken to the king's advisers that one of the two mages performed a spell to take the other's mark. A rogue spell, you understand, one that wasn't tested properly. It rebounded and took both wizards' marks. And thus, helpless and enraged, the two fought to the death." He ended his explanation with a flourishing wave of his knife.

Agnes leaned so far over the table toward Lord Percy that she nearly draped her sleeves through a sauce bowl. "But which was the victim and which the aggressor?"

Lord Percy shrugged. "I dare say we shall never know."

Agnes straightened and sighed. "How vexing."

How wondrous. Alaric's optimism had been verified. Since the two wizards were enemies, the king wasn't even looking for others to blame, and better still, the remaining wizards didn't suspect they were in danger.

Lady Edith dabbed a napkin against her lips. "When will the king choose new wizards to replace them?"

I hadn't even considered this possibility, that I might have to overcome two additional wizards tonight.

Madame Godfrey gazed around at the other tables. "I'm sure every mage here would fancy one of those positions."

"Yes," Lord Percy agreed, "but the wizards on the council need to approve of the king's choice. The new man's loyalty must be unquestionable. Such appointments take time. I doubt he'll announce replacements until the wedding feasting is over."

I fervently hoped he was right, but by midday Lady Ainsworth, one of the wealthier nobles, was heard to complain to several people that the king had called her wizard, Mage Saxeus, to his council. She proudly bemoaned that although the king had compensated the family for their loss, finding another wizard worthy of their family would be *so* very difficult.

This meant I needed to know where Mage Saxeus slept tonight. I went to Gwenyth at once and instructed her to ask among the servants to see if she could ferret out the information. I'd have searched about the castle myself, but following the mid-day meal, the queen invited several young noblewomen to join her in her chambers, including me.

"It's a great honor," Lady Edith told me when a messenger came with the news. "It means she's considering you for an attendant. She needs a few native ladies-in-waiting, you know, so she doesn't appear to favor the ones she brought from Odeway. Makes her more of an Aeradoran."

I very much doubted she'd choose me. Ladies-in-waiting were generally taken from the most elite noble families. Still, despite my slim chances of being selected, to decline an invitation to meet with the queen would be unthinkably rude, so I found myself reluctantly heading to the queen's chambers.

* * *

I'D NOT GIVEN a lot of notice to the fineries of the Queen Marita's receiving room when I'd glanced into it the first time. As I was ushered in with five other noblemen's daughters, I spent more time admiring the high ceiling, the bright red and yellow tapestries that hung on the walls, and the ornately carved chairs surrounding the fireplace.

Queen Marita was ensconced in a chair with a little white dog in her lap. Princess Beatrice sat by her side, and two lady's maids watched us with prim, expectant eyes.

Floris Somerton filed in alongside me, and we all sat in chairs forming a semi-circle around the queen. The other young women had been pleasant enough to me while we waited outside in the hallway. At least until Floris raked a disdainful gaze across my gown and said, "You really should have had something new made for the royal wedding. Didn't you have adequate time to prepare? Was your invitation a very last-minute affair?"

There was no way to answer that question without making myself look either poor or undeserving, and yet it galled me to let the snub go unanswered. "Don't you like it?" I asked sweetly. "I assure you it's gotten compliments from gentlemen and wizards alike. But then, some of us need fewer adornments to garner notice."

She sniffed and turned sharply to whisper things—undoubt-edly about me—to the woman next to her. The entire group looked scandalized by my impertinence. Evidently, Floris wasn't used to having her opinions challenged.

Once we were seated, a servant brought around wine in elaborately carved goblets, and the small talk began. Pleasant questions from Queen Marita. All very formal.

I wondered if the queen had already made her choice of lady's maids and these meetings were only for show. She asked us, in her thick accent, "Where do your estates lie, and what are they like?"

This gave the other women in the party a chance to boast about the beauty of their lands and invite the queen to come for a visit any time she desired.

I answered in kind, even though I knew the suggestion of a royal visit would give Lady Edith fits of worry. We didn't have the food or servants to provide for a royal entourage. So, after my invitation, I added, "Although I'm sure Your Majesty would find our estate quite lacking after being at Valistowe Castle. Everything here is so grand."

The queen didn't comment on my assessment. Perhaps she already knew a trip to Paxworth was beneath her. Or perhaps she was just asking polite questions and didn't care about our answers. The other women in the group looked as smug as cats at my admission. Which probably meant I shouldn't have disparaged my estate, but well, none of this really mattered. I wasn't vying for a place at court. If I did my job tonight, court would change completely at daybreak. According to Aeradoran law, a queen without an heir couldn't rule. Marita would soon be on her way back home with only some dreadful memories of her time here.

A harsh thought. I didn't like feeling like the villain.

Queen Marita's next question was, "How are you enjoying the wedding celebration?"

This was an opportunity for each woman to gush about the splendor of the palace, the food, the gardens, and the royal couple. After an impressive amount of flattery on these topics, Floris added, "Even the wizards here are more handsome."

Her statement caused an uncomfortable silence. Floris, it seemed, had momentarily forgotten that two of the king's wizards were dead. She cleared her throat awkwardly and took a drink from her goblet.

Perhaps to break the silence, Princess Beatrice said, "I assume you're referring to Mage Warison. He's quite young and handsome. I understand he's a favorite with the ladies at court."

"Yes," Floris said quickly. "I've always found him to be a perfect gentleman." Perhaps emboldened by the attention, she added, "I've heard in some countries, kings encourage their mages to marry because if they do, their children have a greater chance of bearing a wizarding mark."

I'd heard this theory myself, and some of the apprentices at Docendum had mages for relatives, so it could be true.

Queen Marita gave Floris a knowing smile. "You speak as one with an interest in the subject."

Floris blushed. "I'm only thinking of the welfare of the country."

Not likely. I shouldn't have felt satisfied that Ronan wasn't encouraging Floris's flirting. She could blame his aloofness on his court duties, but if he'd wanted a wife, he would've married. He was either waiting until he found the daughter of a more powerful family, or he'd adopted Mage Wolfson's views on the vulnerabilities of relationships.

Queen Marita took a sip from her cup and smiled at us. "We shall do our best to convince the eligible men at court of the virtues of marriage."

The noblewomen tittered at this pronouncement, and wanting to join in the sentiment, I raised my cup as though giving a toast. "Long live the queen."

As soon as I spoke, I worried I'd been too familiar, but Her Majesty laughed and turned to me. "Have you your eye upon someone at court?"

I froze. To say yes would be to draw unwanted attention to myself but to say no might make me appear haughty. "It isn't my place to eye the bachelors. My aunt has made it clear that choosing a husband is her domain."

The queen's eyebrows rose in amusement. "Is she choosing for you or for herself?"

"Well, many of the men I've met I would gladly leave to her."

"Indeed," Queen Marita said. She turned to her sister-in-law and gestured in my direction. "This one is clever."

Princess Beatrice smiled placidly and wrote something on a piece of parchment in her lap. I hadn't realized Princess Beatrice was taking notes and was suddenly worried about what she'd written. Was being clever good or bad? I bit the inside of my cheek, determined to say as little as possible from here on.

Queen Marita's words had the opposite effect on the other women in the room. I could have hardly spoken again if I'd wanted because the rest of them all tried to outdo each other's cleverness. It was a harder task for some than for others. For all her beauty, Floris, alas, did not excel in this venture.

After about an hour of trying to amuse the queen with witty and astute observations, Floris, in a return to flattery—her forte —told everyone that the view of the surrounding valleys from the top of the castle walls was the most breathtaking in the land. She asked if Queen Marita had taken a stroll there yet and volunteered herself as a companion.

The queen declined, but not wishing to deny the rest of us of that pleasure, she sent a message to the steward asking that he send someone to take us there after we finished with our drinks. And so, I was forced into another activity.

The walk along the castle walls took longer than was necessary, as the queen also sent for Mage Zephyr and told him to ensure the parapets were spotless before our tour so that we didn't sully the hems of our gowns.

When he reached the room and heard her request, he blinked at her, a picture of offended pride. "You want me to use my magic to clean?"

To Queen Marita's credit, she didn't modify or even repeat her request. She simply stared at him, waiting to be obeyed. She expected it as her due. Ah, to be a woman of that much power.

After a brief hesitation, the wizard bowed stiffly. "I'll gladly do whatever I can to make your guests more comfortable, Your Majesty."

At that moment, I adored the queen and could have happily contemplated a future that consisted of her ordering around wizards as though they were glorified washing women. But no. I had to hope for other things.

Once the lot of us traipsed outside, Mage Zephyr made us wait at the base of the walls for an exceedingly long time while a small funnel of rain traversed the walkway on the top of the walls. After the area was sufficiently soaked, several blasts of wind chased each other over the area.

The man had obviously never cleaned anything in his life. Rain didn't come with soap suds. Wind didn't carry scrub brushes.

At last, he finished with his lengthy and largely ineffective efforts, and one of the steward's assistants took us up the stairs. He led us around while we hefted our skirts up to keep them from dragging along the stones.

The fact that Mage Zephyr didn't check the parapets before we ascended was a sign he thought little of the queen's authority over him. Or perhaps he just knew that none in our party would be so impolite to report his inefficiencies to Her Majesty. The steward's attendant, on the other hand, overflowed with eagerness to please us. He pointed out landmarks and told us stories of the siege forty years before when Heideland invaded the country. He also spoke of the time thirteen years past when King Leofric shut the castle gates for six months to avoid the pestilence ravaging the land.

That plague had taken my parents. The peasants hadn't the luxury of locking themselves away for half a year.

After we had spanned the wall and sufficiently declared that the surrounding land was indeed the most beautiful in the country, we returned to the castle to freshen up before supper.

Despite my attempts to keep my gown clean, I'd managed to

get dirt on my hem. As I made my way down the hallway to my room, I considered the blemish crossly and wondered if the stain would come out with soap and water. I knew a spell for removing stains. It had proved to be one of the more useful bits of magic I'd learned. But I needed to conserve my strength.

I looked up to see that one of the king's guards stood waiting outside my door. This was likely not good news.

CHAPTER 19

My footsteps stuttered. Had something gone wrong? Had I been caught?

No, I couldn't allow such thoughts. I couldn't show any guilt or stare unnecessarily at the guard's sword, sheathed and hanging at his hip. I swept up to my door as though the man was there to offer me favors. He was tall, perhaps in his thirties, with heavy brows and a serious countenance. "Lady Marcella?"

"Yes?"

"Come with me, please." He didn't wait for questions but instead began marching down the hall, expecting me to join him.

I didn't move. "What's this about?"

He turned back toward me impatiently. "Mage Saxeus wishes to speak with you."

The king's new wizard. The one whose chambers Gwenyth had been enquiring about. Something *had* gone wrong, but I wasn't sure whether he'd discovered something about me or her. I needed to find out more information. "If Mage Saxeus wishes to speak to me, tell him I'm amenable to receiving visitors if my aunt is present."

The guard's expression showed only more impatience. "He bids you to come to him. I was sent to bring you."

The guard wasn't going to tell me more. A pity since I didn't know whether I should be fleeing or thinking of some explanation to spin. I reached for the doorknob. "One moment. I should tell my lady's maid of my whereabouts."

"She isn't there," the guard said.

"Where is she?"

"Mage Saxeus will explain it to you."

So the trouble involved Gwenyth. I'd no other choice but to follow after the guard, taking quick steps to keep up with his long legs. We went down the hallway, past the main stairway, and to a room only four doors away. Close enough to the stairs that it belonged to someone important.

The guard rapped on the door. "Lady Marcella to see you."

"Enter," a stern voice replied. An unhappy voice.

The guard opened the door wide and waited for me to go inside.

I straightened my shoulders and sashayed into the room. Mage Saxeus sat at his desk, writing some sort of letter. He wore red silk robes rimmed in black brocade that proclaimed his status. He had a neatly trimmed beard, small eyes, and overall, a pinched look to him as though everything displeased him.

The guard followed me inside and shut the door. Mage Saxeus set his quill back into the ink pot and turned in his chair to give me his full attention. "*That* is how one properly enters a wizard's room. One waits to be invited in. To do otherwise is foolish."

Did he know I'd been in Telarian's and Sciatheric's rooms? I tilted my head and blinked, showing no recognition of what his words might mean. "As you say, sir." I forced a smile. "I don't believe we've had the pleasure of meeting."

He stood and stalked toward me, folding his arms haughtily. "No, we've not. Although I've had the displeasure of meeting your lady's maid." His eyes were narrow and full of suspicion. "What did she mean by coming into my room?"

I didn't have to hide my surprise. Gwenyth wasn't supposed to go into his room, only find out where it was located. I'd told her about the traps set in the other wizard's rooms. Granted, Mage Saxeus was a guest here so one wouldn't expect him to endanger the lives of the servants with snares, but still, she should've known better.

"Surely, you're mistaken, sir. What would my maid be doing in your quarters?"

He gave me an exasperated huff. "That is precisely what I'm asking you. She was either acting on your orders or she was breaking castle law by entering my chamber."

My gaze circled the room. "Where is she? I'll question her."

"Then you acknowledge she wasn't acting on your orders and should be punished for attempted theft?"

"Certainly not." If I admitted she'd acted on her own, I'd be sentencing her to the king's punishment, and who knew what that would be? I had no idea how to extricate both of us from this mess.

Gwenyth would've told me to deny any knowledge of what she'd done so I could remain unhindered to complete my mission, but I couldn't abandon her. "Where is she? Let me speak with her." I fought to keep panic from creeping into my voice. A lady, even in this situation, would be more angered than worried. "I've no proof she was in your room."

His lips came together in a thin line of contempt. "I assure you the guards who carried her out can attest she was indeed in my room."

Carried her out? The words struck me like a blow. My hand flew to my throat. "What have you done to her?"

"I've done nothing to her, your ladyship. She sneaked uninvited into my room, triggered a spell, and encountered a shower of scorpions." He waved a hand behind him. "The silly girl ran straight into my desk, knocked over my candle, and set my letters on fire. She could've burned down the whole room if a passing maid hadn't heard her screams and alerted me to the intrusion."

Scorpions. How many stings did it take to kill a person? "Where is she now? Is she alive?"

One sting was usually painful but not dangerous. Multiple stings, though… Had I killed her with my errand?

Mage Saxeus frowned as though he found my outburst annoying. He was too close and still surveying me. "She's being treated in the housekeeper's room."

I spun to leave but the guard stepped staunchly in my path. Mage Saxeus grabbed my arm and turned me back to face him. "You may see her when we've discovered the nature of her crime."

I yanked my arm out of his grasp. "In normal circles, walking into a room isn't a crime." I was stalling again.

He leaned toward me, his cold brown eyes baring down on me. "Did you send her here or not? And if so, why?"

What innocent reason could I have for sending my maid to a wizard's room? If I'd sent Gwenyth to request a spell of some sort, she would've knocked and left when he didn't answer.

I swallowed, took a breath, and composed myself. "She must have misunderstood my instructions. I asked her to deliver a message, but I didn't mean for her to take it to you. I told her to take my message to the quarters of the king's newest wizard, meaning Mage Warison. I'm not sure what compelled her to come to your room."

"Oh." Saxeus drew out the word in understanding. Much of the suspicion drained from his eyes and his posture relaxed. "Well, that *is* an unfortunate misunderstanding. It seems your maid knew what you didn't: The king appointed me to replace Mage Telarian this morning." To prove this point, he gestured to his wizard's mark. The crescent shape was red now as though the skin underneath it had turned to blood. Apparently, this was a byproduct of being inducted into the wizard council, although not a permanent one since the other wizards' marks were normal.

"I'm sorry for your maid's accident," Saxeus went on, "although she showed great impropriety as well as foolishness to walk into a wizard's room, whether it be Warison's or mine."

"I imagine she just intended to leave my message and go. One doesn't expect to be attacked by other guests at the king's court."

Saxeus' eyes narrowed again. A bit of his suspicion had returned. "I found no message anywhere in the room or on her."

"She must have dropped it when she bumped into your desk, and it burned along with your letters."

He paced across the room, arms behind his back, unmollified by this answer. "If you're acquainted with Mage Warison, why did you neglect to tell your maid where his room is?"

I drew myself up, the pose of affronted dignity. "Sir, you grievously misjudge me to imply I've been to his bed chamber. I assure you I have not. I tasked my maid with finding out those details."

Mage Saxeus stopped pacing for long enough to give me a polite and insincere bow. "My apologies. I meant no such implications." He glanced at his desk. I noticed a black charred spot and places where wax had spilled on the floor. "What message did you have for my colleague? I can write it up and deliver it to him."

"It's of a personal nature." Fortunately, Ronan was so handsome, that I was probably not the first woman to send him a personal message. Mage Saxeus could count me with the other young and silly noblewomen smitten by him.

Mage Saxeus smirked. His gaze went over me, curiosity warring with skepticism. "He knows you, does he? He can vouch that you would have reasons to send him messages of a personal nature?"

"Yes. Now if you'll excuse me, I need to go to the housekeeper's room." I snapped my fingers at the guard to draw his attention. "You'll escort me there, as I don't know where that room is either." I gave the wizard one last withering glare. "If my maid dies, rest assured the king will hear of your treachery."

Mage Saxeus waved my words away like he found my complaint a trifling one. "If she dies, I'll buy you a new lady's maid."

I shouldn't have given the man cause to distrust me more than he already did, but my tongue spoke of its own accord. "People aren't interchangeable. She's my friend."

He laughed and shook his head. "My lady, you've spent too much time with your servants. I wish you luck finding a wealthy husband so your taste in friends might improve."

I stormed out the door. I didn't trust myself to respond to that.

* * *

THE HOUSEKEEPER'S room was located on the second floor of the castle. Despite its large size and fine furniture, the lack of windows made it seem closed and dreary. A lit fireplace in the back of the room and a wizards' orb sitting on a table could only do so much to dispel the darkness.

A woman lay on a pallet several feet from the fireplace. It took me a moment to realize she was Gwenyth. Her face was red and swollen, her tongue lolling out of her mouth. Sweat glistened on her skin as slick and shiny as fish scales. Her body jerked and trembled, making her disheveled hair flail around her shoulders. A seizure. The housekeeper sat beside her and dabbed her face with a wet cloth.

The castle physician knelt on her other side, ripping an old tablecloth into strips.

I hurried across the room. "How is she?" Before anyone had time to answer, I added, "Will she recover?"

"From the scorpion stings, probably." The physician's voice was the low calm I'd heard from every castle physician. No amount of illness or dismemberment rattled them. "Mage Saxeus gave us a treatment to put on those, and her fits are becoming milder, but we've also her burns to worry about."

The bottom of Gwenyth's dress was charred completely away in parts, revealing bright red welts running along her calves and up her thighs. Her thrashing might be from pain. Her eyes darted back and forth, unseeing. Gwenyth, a woman who'd this morning been lively and capable, had been reduced to this. I'd thought I'd understood the danger of this mission before, and yet I hadn't.

I lowered myself to the floor at Gwenyth's shoulder. "I'm here. I'll make sure they take care of you."

A bowl of grease sat next to the physician. Coating damaged skin with grease was the standard treatment for small burns. It seemed like little help now. She needed more. She needed magic, and I could do nothing that would reveal my abilities.

The guard had already left the housekeeper's room. I got up, dashed into the hallway, and ran after him. "Wait!" I called. "Bring Mage Saxeus here."

Instead of moving in the direction of Mage Saxeus' room, the guard turned and stared at me in disbelief. He thought I was asking for things beyond my station.

"At once," I added. "He's responsible for this." I didn't have the time to argue with him about the propriety of my order. I took an angry step toward him, my hands planted on my hips. "I'm a guest of the king and queen. If Mage Saxeus can send you to fetch me, then I can return the favor. Bring him here immediately. In fact, run to his room." This was the benefit of being a noblewoman. No demand seemed too outrageous.

The guard lifted his eyebrows. "He may be on his way to the dining hall already."

"Then run quickly."

I spun on my heel and marched back to the housekeeper's room. Once there, I knelt by Gwenyth again. Another fit was starting. I dipped a rag in the bowl of ointment and helped the housekeeper dab Gwenyth's stings, all the while silently going over my stock of incantations in search of pain-relieving spells that could be administered in secret.

Most required items I didn't have. But there was one, a less potent spell, that took its energy from fire. A fine one was burning in the hearth nearby.

I took Gwenyth's hand in mine. "You'll recover." I leaned over her as though whispering more reassurances and said the words of the incantation slowly, so as not to dim the firelight all at once.

At first, the flames diminished only a bit, then, despite my care, they nearly flickered out. My foolish, foolish desire to help. The physician and housekeeper would grow suspicious. They'd know what such a dip in firelight meant.

The physician did look up, but instead of glancing around to see if a wizard had come into the room, he snapped, "Put another log on the fire. I need light to see."

Blessed mercy. They didn't suspect. I'd forgotten there were other reasons for fires to dim.

I was saying the last word of the spell, and prolonged the syllable 'lor', holding onto it so the fire wouldn't blaze back to its normal height.

The housekeeper jumped up and went to the hearth. My "ooo" felt like a song note. I was running out of breath.

She noticed the log in the hearth was not half burned yet, and took the poker to it, adjusting its position. I ended the last word of the incantation and the flames grew and crackled, spreading upward.

At first, I wondered if the pain spell had worked at all. Gwenyth still shuddered as though some unseen foe stood over her, shaking her. But this time when her quaking ended, she lay limply on the pallet, taking long, gasping breaths.

"Good," the physician said, "the ointment has finally overcome the scorpion venom. Her fits should stop now." He motioned to the housekeeper to help him apply grease to Gwenyth's legs.

Gwenyth gazed around. Her tired eyes stopped on mine. "Sorry," she rasped out.

"This isn't your fault. I shouldn't have sent you." Despite the physician's pronouncement that Saxeus' ointment had done its job, I kept dousing her skin with it.

Gwenyth winced at the physician's touch, evidence my spell hadn't taken all the pain. Her voice dropped to a low whisper. "The maid told me it was one of two rooms. I thought the family would have the one closest to the stairs. I opened the door to check, but I couldn't tell. I didn't think—"

"Don't worry yourself over it further." I feared she was a bit delirious and might say too much.

Her swollen lips lifted in a hint of a smile. "At least now I can tell you with assurance which room it is."

"Yes. I already explained to Mage Saxeus that I meant for you to deliver a message to Mage Warison." I went on in my apology, reciting for her what I'd told the wizard. I hoped she had her faculties about her sufficiently to understand she needed to remember this version of what had transpired.

"Mage Warison," she murmured. "I warned you not to let him distract you. You should put his fine eyes behind you."

I surprised myself by laughing. "Yes, if they're behind me, they'll see how lovely I look from that angle." I ran my cloth along her forehead. "Don't worry, I intend to forgo all socialization tonight and stay here to nurse you."

She shook her head. She knew what I was really saying. "You mustn't change your plans. The future...*your* future," she amended, "is too essential to sacrifice on my account. You have men of importance to meet."

If the physician and housekeeper were listening to this conversation, and they could hardly help but do so as our voices had returned to their normal volume, they would assume Gwenyth was talking about potential suitors.

I silently stroked her hair, fighting back the protests that lined up behind my lips. If Gwenyth could urge me, while laying so badly burned on the floor, to fulfill my duty, how could I refuse her? I needed to honor her sacrifice. When I took Mage Saxeus' mark tonight, I would think of her.

The door from the hallway swung forcefully open, letting in a draft from the hallway. I turned, hoping to see Mage Saxeus. It wasn't him. Of course, it wasn't.

But the appearance of the red-robed wizard striding into the room was even more astonishing. Ronan had come.

CHAPTER 20

*R*onan's formal robes trailed behind him as he joined us. His gaze was on Gwenyth, his brow furrowed in concentration. "What's her condition?"

He'd come to help her. I wanted to cry in relief. Ronan had cured my scars even though I'd never found an incantation for such a thing. Surely, he could help her.

While the physician gave his report, Ronan kneeled by Gwenyth's head and examined the sting marks on her skin. "The venom does seem to be subsiding." He picked up Mage Saxeus' ointment and sniffed the bowl. Whatever it contained earned a nod of approval. "Here…" He slipped an arm behind Gwenyth's back and lifted her to a sitting position. "You're well enough to drink some. That will help hasten the cure's work."

She looked like a doll in his arms, my formerly assassin-strong lady's maid.

He put the bowl to her lips. She took a gulp, and some of the liquid spilled from her lips and dribbled onto her dress. She wiped her mouth. "Thank you, sir."

Ronan gently laid her down and moved to the physician's side to check the wounds on her legs.

I scooted closer to him. "You can do something to hurry along her healing?" I was telling him the spell I thought he should use.

His attention was on her burns, not me. He'd barely glanced at me since he came into the room. "That depends on the extent of her injuries." He motioned to the bandages already wound around her calves. "Are her burns there as severe?"

The physician paused slathering grease on her thighs. "Worse, I'm afraid."

Ronan swore and shook his head. His eyes finally met mine. I recognized the look I saw there. It was the same frustration of defeat I'd seen when we were children and he'd been unable to bend a spell to his purposes.

No. I wouldn't accept defeat now. "You *can* do something for her and you *must*. I don't care if you have to dip into the king's store of bat claws or shark teeth or whatever you need to do it."

His gaze shot to Gwenyth's eyes then went back to mine. He stood and offered me his hand to help me up. "Let's speak privately of our options." That meant her condition was so poor, he didn't like talking about it in front of her.

His hand around mine—one would've thought such an action, having already occurred a thousand times, wouldn't have occasioned new sensations in me. And yet I felt the pressure of his hand gripping mine with all sorts of connotations that weren't there. He was simply helping me up. The gesture meant nothing more.

Once on my feet, I dropped his hand and followed him out the door into the hallway. I barely waited for him to finish shutting the door, before blurting out, "Why can't you use the spell to speed healing?"

His words were soft, consoling. "It only works on wounds that would naturally heal. She has burns on a quarter of her body, and I'm afraid they're deep. Her case is too severe."

I would've realized this already if I'd brought the incantation to the forefront of my mind and read it, but I hadn't. I'd simply depended on the fact that magic could help her. Alarm made my breaths come quicker. "There must be some other spell you can use."

His eyes turned pitying. "Burns are difficult. They can't be knit together like other wounds."

He was right. I'd used magic before to sew torn flesh like a seamstress mending fabric. With burns, one had little to sew together. Still, I couldn't believe Ronan knew of nothing that could avail her. "You're the king's wizard. Certainly, you can save her."

"Magic has rules even king's wizards can't break. Spells aren't wishes set to words."

As if I didn't know that already. "Then turn her into some creature who can survive without all of its skin and let her heal in that form."

He raised an eyebrow, surprised at my suggestion. I expected him to protest that such a spell would take too much energy. A wizard, even a powerful one, couldn't force another human into an unnatural form for weeks. Those transformations usually lasted no longer than a few hours. But if the king's other wizards helped…which, granted, was asking much…

Instead, he said, "What creature can survive without a quarter of its skin?"

My mind ran through possibilities. Nothing that was a mammal, bird, or fish. Scales, though not skin, would transform as such. Even trees would die if stripped of too much bark. "I've heard lizards can lose their tails and live."

"And if she was suffering from a lost tail, changing her to a lizard would be a fine solution."

He wasn't even trying to be helpful. "With all your learning, you must know of some creature who can regrow skin."

His blue eyes didn't leave mine. "Sadly, that was never an area of study."

My hands slapped against my sides in irritation. "How do you know her burns are too severe for help?"

His voice turned consoling again. He'd become one forced to deliver unfortunate news. "Her burns are so deep she's no longer feeling pain. Your maid would be writhing in agony otherwise."

I stared at him, uncertain how to respond. My spell was responsible for her relief. I couldn't let him give up on her because of something I'd done. "She had wine. A lot of it. That may be the cause of her apparent calmness."

He eyed me skeptically but didn't outright call me a liar. No wine bottles were in the room. "Marcella…"

"Don't you dare say she's just a servant." The words came out harsher than I'd intended, an accusation thrown at him. I'd so counted on magic being able to help that its insufficiencies felt like a betrayal. My eyes stung and tears spilled onto my cheeks. They coursed, unchecked, down my face. "Please, Ronan. Try."

He sighed and ran his hand against the back of his neck. "I'll perform a spell to increase her body's healing power."

That was a spell unknown to me. He must have learned it after giving me my mark.

"It will cure the minor damage," he said. "Perhaps with a less extensive area of burns, her chances of recovery will improve. Perhaps it will give us time to think of something else."

Hope, at last. My mind grabbed onto the words and pressed them to my heart. Without thinking, I took one of his hands in both of mine. "Thank you."

I was mistaken in my earlier opinion that holding his hand no longer felt familiar. This felt very familiar.

His fingers curled around mine. His eyes were soft. I could tell he didn't want me to hope too much. "It's only a chance, Marcella. If the wounds fester…"

"We'll address festering wounds later. Do what you can for her now." I towed him back into the room.

We knelt beside Gwenyth, Ronan by her head, and I at her side. "Mage Warison is going to increase your body's healing power," I said brightly.

Ronan placed his hands on the top of Gwenyth's forehead and performed the spell. The fire grew dimmer with each word, but it happened so subtly that perhaps only I noticed. That, I supposed, was proof of the control Ronan possessed.

I did my best to memorize the words of the incantation for future use. It was similar to the spell to speed natural healing with a few variations. I couldn't see the burns under her bandages, but the angry crimson welts on her thighs shrunk, like waves retreating back to the sea. The blisters subsided, and some of the redness turned to a less vibrant pink. She wasn't cured, but it was something.

When Ronan finished and the fire had once again returned to a normal blaze, he examined her skin. His blue eyes were intent, so lost in his work he seemed unaware of anything else. At this point, other wizards would have been posing and posturing.

He spoke to Gwenyth casually, as though she shouldn't be embarrassed he was scrutinizing her thighs. "You responded better than I expected. Magic must fancy you."

"I hope so." She swallowed, perhaps uncomfortable at accepting a wizard's help. "Thank you, sir."

Ronan turned his attention to the physician. "I'll send you more salve. See that someone administers it on her wounds thrice daily. For the next few days, she should do nothing but sleep and drink broth."

"I'll run out of sleep draught," the physician said.

"I'll send more of that." To the housekeeper, Ronan said, "You'll see to her needs?"

The housekeeper nodded. She was a heavy-set woman of middle age, with a stern, serious countenance. A woman who emanated the proper sort of breeding for a position of importance in a castle. "I'll have a maid attend to her."

Ronan went through the physician's things and came back with a spoon and a green bottle. "I'm going to put you to sleep," he told Gwenyth. "Hopefully you'll rest well all night so you can continue healing." He poured a little of the potion onto the spoon and held it to her lips.

Gwenyth's eyes flashed to me. "You'll tell Alaric?"

"Yes." Until this moment, I hadn't considered all the implications of Gwenyth's wounds. The job of assassin would fall to Alaric.

No one asked who he was. Gwenyth had known they wouldn't. I suppose it didn't occur to them to be curious about a servant's connections.

Gwenyth swallowed the sleeping draught and lay back down, her eyes already growing heavy.

Ronan stood and held out his hand to me. "I'll escort Lady Marcella to supper."

I hesitated to leave Gwenyth.

"You can do nothing more for her," Ronan said, "and the king and queen expect you to attend the celebration of their union. You wouldn't wish to insult them."

I doubted they would notice my absence, but he was right about the rest. And I needed my strength for tonight, especially after expending energy on the spell to ease her pain.

I took his hand. As we made our way to the door, he offered me his arm and I took that as well. Declining such a gesture would've been rude and yet this felt like an intimacy I should avoid. All intimacies with Ronan would make my task tonight harder. How could I take his mark when he'd just helped Gwenyth? And if his magic could save her life, shouldn't I wait until that was accomplished before I proceeded? It was a muddle in my mind that needed sorting.

We ambled down the hallway, side by side. We'd never walked like this while I lived at Docendum, although we'd strolled hand in hand often enough while out on the forest trails. This was formal, a recognition I was a lady now. He'd probably escorted more highborn ladies around the castle than he could count. And yet his nearness felt like a magnet.

When we were a little way down the hall, I asked, "What are her chances of a full recovery?"

"Her burns cover perhaps fifteen percent of her body instead of twenty-five."

Of course, he'd replied with math. It was his second language. "And?" I coaxed.

"It's more of an improvement than I hoped for. However, it's still too early for conjecture. I've seen men with smaller wounds die and ones with greater live."

"Now that she's improved, will you be able to perform the spell to speed healing?"

He shook his head. "One precludes the other."

I'd feared that. When a spell closely resembled another, usually only one would work. Ronan had explained the phenomena by likening it to a match set to kindling. A match would burn the kindling but a second match set to the ashes would do nothing at all.

Postponing the mission might increase Gwenyth's chances of recovery if Ronan was able to find a way in which a different spell could help her.

It was a small, miserly hope. In wealthy households, wizards were called to tend wounds as frequently as physicians and knew the limitations of their power. If Ronan could have done more, he would've said as much from the beginning.

Gwenyth didn't want a postponement on her behalf. She'd made that clear already, and if I waited, Saxeus might change rooms or even worse, change the enchantment that guarded his chamber. Then her sacrifice would be for nothing.

And yet to go forward now…well, perhaps I was just looking for an excuse to postpone what I dreaded doing.

"Thank you for helping her," I said again. Healing wounds took no small amount of energy. He wouldn't recover his strength until tomorrow. Of course, tomorrow his magical energy wouldn't matter.

I felt horrible.

Ronan's eyes went to mine. "I wouldn't have told you she was just a servant. I'm not as heartless as that."

This didn't make me feel any better about my task. "Mage Saxeus already said as much. He told me if she died, he would buy me a new lady's maid."

"Mage Saxeus is an insufferable sard." Ronan stopped himself. "Pardon me. I shouldn't use vulgar language in front of a lady. What I meant to say was that if Mage Saxeus' skills matched his arrogance, the king would be well served. As that is far from the case, I won't enjoy working with him."

I laughed. I shouldn't have, but the strain of the last hour had been too great. "Is that the worst part of your job? Working with arrogant wizards?" The job certainly must have more harrowing drawbacks. A memory flitted through my mind. The gray dust of ashes on the bottom of Ronan's cloak.

He cocked his head, unsure why I'd laughed. "No. It's just one unpleasantness."

"What's the worst part then?"

"I haven't categorized them all."

Killing people should be high on that particular litany. Although I couldn't say such things after he'd helped Gwenyth. "How did you know to come to the housekeeper's room?"

"I was speaking to Mage Saxeus when your messenger found him and requested his help. Mage Saxeus told me I should be the one to answer your summons as your maid had been injured trying to deliver a message to me." Ronan's pace slowed. "Mage Saxeus was quite curious as to why you'd sent me a message."

Oh, yes. The pretended message. My mind had been so preoccupied with Gwenyth that I hadn't thought of a possible explanation for writing to him.

Best to stall. "Mage Saxeus found it hard to believe you would have business dealings with someone such as me. I'm assuming that's because you're a confirmed bachelor who gives no consideration to the women at court and not because I'm of too low a status to warrant your attention."

"Your lack of status wasn't an issue when we lived at Docendum. Why should it be now?"

I huffed. "It was very much an issue at Docendum." As it was now. My gown—the best in my wardrobe—was not only plain compared to the rest of the women's at court, after the last hour it was rumpled and spotted with ointment.

Ronan looked upward, affecting contemplation. "I don't recall kissing anyone of higher status while at Docendum."

"As Lady Edith has told me, there's a difference between the sort of woman a man kisses and the sort he introduces to his friends."

"You can't be upset that I didn't introduce you to my friends at Docendum. Everyone already knew who you were. Besides, the other apprentices weren't really friends. A better categorization would be rivals, bullies, and annoyances."

He was skirting the real issue. I wouldn't let him brush off my complaint. "You kissed me, but you never saw a future for us together. Lady Edith calls gentleman of that nature cads."

Ronan made a coughing sound in the back of his throat. "The issue wasn't your low station. The issue was that I was to become a wizard." He stopped walking altogether and turned to me, causing our arms to unlink. "Wolfson was a swine, but he was also right that to have a wife or family is to put them in danger. I didn't want to do that to you anymore. You'd endured enough at his hands."

Ronan made the decision sound so straightforward and

sensible. A noble gesture. He'd broken my heart and counted it as a virtue. I planted my hands on my hips. "Shouldn't you have given me some say in that matter? You wouldn't even speak to me."

"I didn't give you a say in the matter because I knew you wouldn't act with any degree of self-preservation. Just as I knew that once we parted, you'd form other attachments quickly enough. Your beauty and wit would see to that." He swept a hand in my direction, offering me as proof of his statement. "I was right about that, wasn't I?"

"You weren't." Mage Saxeus thought servants were inter-changeable. Ronan apparently thought the same of love. I lowered my voice to a whisper, suddenly worried someone might overhear. "How could I form other attachments when I no longer trusted men? If I'd so misjudged the one who'd been my closest companion, how could I ever have confidence in a man whom I know to a lesser degree? I no longer want attach-ments." Somewhere in that sentence I'd stopped talking about myself in the past and admitted I still couldn't trust men. I turned and continued down the hallway, stomping as I walked rather than gliding like a highborn lady.

Ronan caught up to me but didn't offer his arm. "If you've given up on men, why did you go to the trouble to come to court?"

He had me there. I couldn't tell the truth about my reasons. All I could do was shrug. "Lady Edith wanted to come."

"Surely she wouldn't force you into a marriage you didn't approve of?"

Another shrug. "Love and marriage are different matters."

He shook his head at me. "You who were so idealistic—have you really become so callous?"

The accusation was too much. "A strange criticism from a wizard."

"What do you mean by that?"

"One has to be callous to be a wizard. Callous and many other things."

His lips twitched in annoyance. "I won't ask for that list as I'm sure I wouldn't find it flattering." We were nearly to the dining room. The smell of savory meat drifted out into the hallway. Ronan's pace slowed again. "What was the message your maid meant to deliver to me?"

The message. I still hadn't thought of anything plausible. I'd been too distracted by Ronan's presence.

He watched me, waiting for a reply. I had to give him an answer or he'd suspect my story was a lie.

I gazed behind him at a tapestry that hung on the wall—a hunting scene with men on horseback and a fox woven into the trees, forever just out of their reach. Ronan used to be able to read me so well, I worried if he peered into my eyes, he'd at once see through my excuse. "I wished for a private audience with you."

"Like the one you've just had?" he asked with confusion. I'd made no request of him during our walk, brought up no subject that wasn't natural to the conversation. "What did you wish to say to me?"

The subject needed more stalling. I looked around for servants. Down the hallway, a maid was carrying a tray to the dining room. I nodded toward her. "A corridor isn't the privacy I'd imagined for our conversation."

He gave a slight bow of deference. "Very well." He took hold of my arm and steered me away from the dining hall. "We can go to one of the gardens."

I glanced over my shoulder at the door. If we went in to supper, I'd have more time to think of a reason for a private meeting. My feet slowed. "I don't wish for you to go hungry. It's nothing so urgent."

"I'll have a servant bring something to my room later."

"I thought you said missing supper would be a dishonor to His Majesty."

Ronan continued to guide me down the hallway toward the door to the courtyard. "If a private meeting was important enough that your lady's maid risked her life to deliver your message, I would be doing a disservice to make you wait any further. His Majesty will have to understand."

Was he teasing me? Did he know I was lying? I couldn't let him suspect Gwenyth had carried no letter.

We went outside and meandered through one of the gardens with hedges and bowers. Ronan wasn't pressing me for details yet, but I only had a short time until we reached some hidden corner. My mind whirred, snatching at any plausible reason I might need to speak privately with Ronan. Could Lady Edith have required some sort of magical help? Something too discreet to ask for in public? No. If she had, she'd have sent the message, not me. And besides, Ronan might insist on speaking with her before I had a chance to explain the situation to her.

The reason for the meeting had to lay squarely with me. But I could think of no clandestine magical favors I might ask of a high-ranking wizard, especially after the cold reception I'd given him when he'd spoken to me during my reconnaissance.

We reached a bench tucked under a bower by the boxwood hedges. Ronan held out his hand, gesturing for me to sit. Once I'd settled myself, he sat beside me and turned so his knees touched mine. "I'm at your service, my lady. What did you wish to discuss?"

I shifted uncomfortably on the bench. "I wanted to...well..." I could think of only one believable reason for the letter. "I wanted to apologize for the unkind reception I gave you when we first met in the garden. I shouldn't have said such unpleasant things to you."

His eyebrows lifted, but I couldn't tell whether he was

perplexed or amused by my explanation. "You wanted to apologize for things you said two nights ago?"

"Yes…" My head lowered in a contrite manner. "I owe you a debt for saving me from Wolfson's beast and erasing my scars. My gratitude was woefully absent at that meeting."

He folded his arms and leaned back, surveying me. "I see. And when are you planning to apologize for the unpleasant things you said to me a few minutes ago?"

He was right, of course, but I could think of no other reason for requesting a meeting. Best to continue with this one. I smoothed out wrinkles on my gown to give me something to do besides hold his gaze. "It was thoughtless of me to criticize your profession in the hallway. I'm not very good at apologies."

"Apparently not. You also called me callous, accused me of abandoning you, and blamed me for your distrust of men."

"Again, I'm sorry." The wrinkles would not be smoothed. The sooner I ended this conversation the better. "I'll save any other maids from the danger of delivering you messages by apologizing for everything else I've said and may say later." I scooted forward on the bench with a forced sigh of happiness. "Cook Lindon was right. It does feel better to get that off my chest."

As I began to stand, Ronan took hold of my arm to keep me seated. "What did you really want to say to me, Marcella?"

I blinked at him in what I hoped was a guileless fashion. "That *is* what I wanted to say. We meant far too much to each other in the past to quarrel here at court. I must forgive you for deserting me, mercilessly, and leaving me in a state of utter despondency, and you must forgive me for my unkind tone two nights ago. And also the bit from a few minutes ago."

"So you're saying you want reconciliation in between berating me?"

"I think you've perfectly summed up what every woman wants, yes."

I moved to stand. Ronan kept a firm hold of my arm. "What do you really want?" His eyes narrowed in suspicion.

Suspicion wasn't a place I wanted him to linger. He hadn't relinquished his hold on my arm and didn't appear likely to do so until he'd received an answer to his satisfaction. What now? I could think of only one way to convince him my desire for reconciliation was sincere. I leaned over and gently placed my hand on his cheek. My eyes refrained from meeting his. I didn't want to see displeasure or surprise at my touch. My gaze stayed on his lips, on the rise and fall of the slopes of his upper lip and the smooth sweep of the bottom of his mouth.

I leaned closer. I expected him to move away. He didn't. Perhaps he didn't think I would follow through on this show of affection. Nothing to do but prove him wrong. I pressed my lips to his. My mouth moved softly, lightly against his. Even though this was a ruse, my heart beat faster.

He didn't return my kiss. His grip on my arm tightened as though he would push me away.

Well, all was not lost. He would simply think me an emotional storm of contradictions. Granted, his rejection would leave a lasting sting, one I already dreaded. Perhaps I sighed at what could never be. Maybe it was more of a moan of longing.

His lips relented then, softened, and answered mine. He pulled me closer, welcoming me to him. I hadn't known I'd missed the feel of his chest, strong and firm, against mine. But I felt both the comfort of his arms around me and the lack of them for so long.

More than three years had passed since I'd kissed him, and no other man had held me this way. Part of me feared I'd forgotten how to kiss, that the ease I'd once had with Ronan was forever gone. Not so. The taste of his mouth, the smell of wizards' smoke that permeated his clothes, his breath warming my skin, it was all as it had been. With my eyes shut and his arms around me, I felt as though I'd been transported back to our days at Docendum. Time and location and heartache were erased and the two of us were just ourselves again, innocent and untroubled.

And yet it wasn't so. Kissing him now was dangerous. I couldn't forget that.

I'd sufficiently made my point: that I'd requested a private meeting to do more than just apologize, but despite my resolve to do otherwise, I didn't stop kissing him. In the lonely hours at Carendale, I'd longed for this embrace, craved it. I was as one deprived of air finally getting to breathe.

His hand traveled up my arm and across my shoulder until it found a place at the nape of my neck. His fingers wound into my hair there.

Ah, that. How had I forgotten the feel of his hand caressing my neck? I was sure I would never forget it again. With his arms around me, I couldn't have moved if I wanted to. The kiss was growing deeper, more insistent. I felt dizzy with it.

We couldn't continue this way. Tonight, I would have to take Ronan's power from him, the thing he valued above all else. The thing he'd already shown he valued more than me.

Ironic. If he'd valued me more than his magic, we wouldn't be in this situation. He would've come for me when he left Docendum, and I would've never been involved in a mission to take his power. Instead, I would be his downfall.

With that thought turning the kiss bitter, I pulled away from him. I couldn't meet his eyes. My cheeks warmed, although I was unsure whether from embarrassment for being so forward or shame for what I had to do later. My headdress had tilted and I did my best to put it straight.

Ronan sat back against the bench with a smile. "That apology was quite a bit better than your first."

My cheeks heated even more. My headdress was taking effort to straighten.

He cocked his head, still grinning. "Was this penance only

for the things you said to me previously or did it cover the things you said today as well? Because if you want to do penance for all the times your tongue has been too sharp—and you really should—I'd like to remind you of the many days at Docendum when you were less than agreeable."

That brought my gaze to his. "I believe you were the one who was disagreeable during our last days together."

He nodded, unperturbed by this accusation. "You're right. I should apologize to you." He moved toward me, playfully reaching for my waist to pull me back to him. I evaded his hands and stood up. "I don't want to be the sort of lady you kiss but don't introduce to your friends."

His grin turned into a laugh. "Have you given up on noblemen's sons and decided to use your lures on me, Marcella?"

"Your teachers warned you I would. Perhaps you should've listened to them."

He seemed to find this all very amusing. "As you said, I'm a confirmed bachelor. But that doesn't mean you shouldn't try to convince me otherwise." Another slow smile spread across his lips. "In truth, you can be quite convincing."

If I'd really written to Ronan in order to revive our old romance, I would be pressing for some token of commitment. I lifted my chin in challenge. "Are you going to introduce me to your friends?"

"Well, you've already met Mage Saxeus."

I blanched at the name. "One would hope you've friends who are more pleasant."

"I wouldn't think of introducing you around court as someone who was dear to me. Too dangerous. When powerful wizards form attachments, they keep their women as secret as possible and hide their families away where no one can find them."

"What a very convenient excuse for avoiding commitment."

He leaned back on his hands in an overly confident manner.

"You should try and convince me to embrace matrimony. Doing so will keep you away from every other scoundrel in court, so I'm quite willing to encourage you."

"You're too kind." *Rogue.* "Lady Edith will wonder what's become of me. I should go to her." I started back to the castle without waiting to see if he followed.

CHAPTER 21

*A*fter supper, I sent Joanne to Alaric with the camouflage cloak wrapped in a bundle and a note relating Gwenyth's condition. Should anyone look at the note, I added that depending on how Gwenyth fared, I may need someone to fetch her relations to help nurse her. I hoped he could find someone else to perform this task since Lady Edith still needed his services. I knew he would understand my true message. Despite the fact he'd volunteered to be Gwenyth's backup, I wanted him to find another renegade to kill the king. Surely the organization must have another member at Valistowe.

Perhaps I should've snuck out and delivered the message in person to emphasize this point. But after kissing Ronan the way I had, completely brazenly, I couldn't face Alaric. I feared he would somehow know what I'd done. I'd kissed the enemy and enjoyed it.

My mind kept returning to those moments in the garden. Ronan had said he wouldn't introduce me in court as someone dear to him. I'd given little attention to the sentence at the time, supposing him to be speaking in general. Now I wondered if he was in fact professing that I was dear to him. Had kissing me been more than a whim for him?

He'd encouraged me to try and convince him to give up bachelorhood. The challenge evoked all sorts of possibilities of another encounter. His lips on mine again. His arms holding me. And Ronan speaking to me in that teasing, intimate way that made us equals.

Each time these thoughts came to me, I had to remind myself that if I was successful tonight, everything would be different on the morrow.

What would Ronan do when he found himself without magic?

I could offer him a place at Paxworth. He had pride though, perhaps too much pride to accept charity from me. And even if I could restore his mark—and performing such a complicated spell was most likely beyond my current abilities—I couldn't do it without revealing the extent of my magic. Once he knew about that, he'd figure out the rest and hate me.

The festivities around the castle didn't last quite so long that night. At midnight, I became invisible and crept to Mage Saxeus' room. No serpent sat guarding his door.

Gwenyth had already discovered his trespassing spell involved scorpions falling from the ceiling. No doubt they, like the snakes, were metal until an intruder came uninvited to his room.

I was prepared for them. I'd taken a wooden washing bucket from the laundry, filled it with a few inches of water, and cast a spell to heat the water to boiling. I'd also stolen some sleeping draught from the housekeeper's room. After last night's events, I couldn't trust that once the stunning spell wore off, Mage Saxeus would simply drift into the arms of sleep.

With the bucket on my head, I unlocked the room and slipped inside. I took one step. Two.

A hissing sounded above me. The repulsive noise of falling

scorpions. Three large ones missed the bucket and dropped in front of me. My boots would protect my feet and calves from their sting, but still, only willpower kept my feet planted on the floor. I couldn't stomp on them, or I'd splash boiling water onto myself.

The water sizzled, letting me know the majority of the creatures had landed there. The three on the ground lifted their pincers and scuttled toward me. I set the bucket down firmly on them, then turned and stepped on two that were coming at me from behind.

Though I tried to be quiet, the noise was loud enough to rouse the wizard. The bed creaked with his shifting weight.

I knelt and put one hand on the bucket to turn it invisible again. My other hand gripped my wand. To cast the stunning spell, I needed a target, and the wizard was still behind his curtains. If he called out, the guards at the stairs would hear him and come.

Should I take my chances and lunge at the bed or keep still and hope Mage Saxeus would roll over and go back to sleep?

As soon as the question formed, I knew the answer. A powerful wizard, one who'd just been appointed to the king's council, wouldn't call for guards simply because he'd been wakened by a sound. He had too much vanity to tell guards he'd been frightened by a noise in the dark. Right now he was assuring himself he could take care of whatever had caused the noise.

A bony hand pushed aside the bed curtains a few inches and, wand raised, Mage Saxeus poked his face out. He squinted, searching the room.

Ah, the downfall of vanity. I hit him with the stunning spell.

His body went limp, and his wand clattered onto the floor and rolled underneath the bed.

Without wasting any time, I went to the bed and turned him into a tree. He was thick of trunk with reaching branches that were nearly bare. Perhaps a person's tree reflected his personality, and I was seeing the craggy nature of Mage Saxeus' soul. I chiseled out his mark with swift angry strokes and considered leaving him to his wounds, the way he'd left Gwenyth.

Instead, I begrudgingly performed the spell to speed healing and poured some sleeping draught down his throat. Mage Saxeus wouldn't stir until morning.

To hide my method of killing the scorpions, I deposited the contents of the bucket down the garderobe. Let the little metal beasts sink to the bottom of the moat where they'd never be found.

Instead of going downstairs to retrieve the wooden shield, I decided to save time and use the washing tub to fend off any serpent strikes. My arm slid through the handle well enough to hold it in front of me.

I reached the wizards' wings and hurried to the chamber that adjoined Mage Telarian's and Mage Sciatheric's empty rooms. This wizard would be the safest of the lot to attack because if he made noises before I stunned him, there was less chance of anyone hearing.

I dispatched the snake easily, but when I opened the door, I found the room cold and dark. Not even the bones of a fire glowed in the hearth.

Was the wizard absent or was the darkness some sort of trap, a way to keep intruders blind? I stepped inside and shut the door. Darkness. Silence.

I tossed a charmed firefly in the direction of the bed. If the wizard uttered a spell to strike at the light, I'd know where he was and send a stunning spell that way.

The bug flickered about, lighting one small piece of the room and then another. No sign of a wizard. The man was either hiding in the room, or he'd chosen a different place to sleep.

Judging by the chilly temperature, I guessed the latter, but to be certain I changed into my canine form. Without moving further into the room, I could smell that it was empty of humans.

Becoming a wolf had other advantages. In that form, I could tell by scent that the room belonged to Redboot. With any luck, I'd be able to find where he'd taken himself off to. I couldn't take the washing tub with me, so I placed it in the servant's stairwell, knowing someone would find and return it to its proper place.

Then I roamed the fourth floor, this time as an invisible wolf. The double spell was harder to maintain, one layered on the other, but it was necessary to get by the guards. I prowled the hallway, nose to the stones, sifting through the smells of everyone who'd recently walked by.

Ronan's scent, strong and sweet like the incense of saffron, was somewhere in the king's chambers. He would be my last stop of the night.

I trotted down the hallway on the other side. I went to the room that must belong to Mage Zephyr. With my muzzle pressed near the crack underneath the door, I could tell the room was cold. No fresh scent. Mage Zephyr hadn't been there for most of the day.

I had two hidden men to find, and this when I needed to preserve my strength. Working double spells to be both a wolf and invisible might prove too draining. I'd have to improvise.

I maintained the invisibility spell until I passed the guards, then searched the third floor visible as the wolf. No one should be walking around the hallways at this time of night who might see me. Even the servants who waited in the hallways, lest any guest have need of something during the night, were fast asleep on their mats.

I made my way through the third-floor hallways, hunting for the scent of either Mage Redboot or Zephyr. Each door brought me more frustration. The men weren't here. I trotted down the stairs to the second floor and roamed those hallways, growing more anxious with each door. The wizards had disappeared.

The servants had their own chapel on the second floor. Although it was dark and deserted, I checked it as well … and detected Mage Redboot's scent by the wall near the entrance.

A tapestry hung there and warm air drifted from the bottom. Something was hidden behind it: a secret room or passageway. I surveyed the area, this time seeking for whiffs of incense, smoke, or metal, some smell indicating the presence of traps. Nothing seemed amiss.

I returned to my human form and lifted the edges of the tapestry. A small door waited there. I unlocked it and ever so slowly pushed it open a crack. The room—more of a closet, really —was heated not with a hearth, but by a bit of purple magical fire in a cauldron in the corner. Its glow revealed Redboot sleeping on a thick down mattress that took up most of the space. A blanket lay in tangles at his feet, and his clothes and hat hung on hooks on the back wall. In nothing but his nightshirt, he reminded me of a plucked chicken. Pale, wrinkly, and scrawny.

A string of bells lay beside him, although for what reason I couldn't tell. At least, I couldn't tell until I lifted my wand. They began traitorously ringing.

Redboot's eyes flew open, and he reached for his wand. By the time he was halfway through an incantation to call down fire, I'd finished uttering the stunning spell.

He collapsed onto his mattress with a thud. I slipped inside the cramped little room and knelt beside him. I needed to hurry. I'd already spent too much time ferreting out his hiding spot, and I still had to find Mage Zephyr.

With quick words, I performed the incantation that changed him into a tree. He was a gnarled and twisted thing with leafless branches that looked like claws. In the small space, they grabbed at me and caught on my sleeves and hair. I avoided them the best I could and took the chisel to his mark. Removing the others had taken a quarter of an hour, but Redboot's tree was softer. The mark came out as easily as wood that had rotted away.

The ease of the task ended when I tried to heal the wound. He responded so slowly and took so much effort, I decided I had no choice but to leave him with a small injury. I didn't have time to completely speed his healing.

I uttered the spell to return him to human form, my eyes fixed upon his neck. If he bled too badly, I'd turn him into a tree again and try the healing spell again.

At first, the wound was raised and red with only a bit of blood seeping in the middle. Well enough. He would live. I gathered my things to leave.

Then the wound grew and peeled back on itself. Larger, I was sure, than the area I'd chiseled out. This was wrong. I stared, unable to understand what was happening. Time was already short—and now this.

I placed my hand on his chest where his nightshirt hung open and began uttering my spell. As I spoke, the skin beneath my fingers rippled. Something warm and slick met my hands. My eyes flew open. Redboot's face was melting as though made of hot candle wax. I jerked away from him, the rest of the words forgotten. Sinews withered away and Redboot's skull appeared like an egg emerging in a bloody nest.

I screamed and leaped to my feet, horrified. Even as the sound left my throat, I knew screaming was a grave mistake, but the cry had a will of its own.

What had I done? What had gone so gruesomely wrong? My hands were wet with blood.

The flesh on Redboot's head had completely dissolved and his skull gaped at me with hollow eyes. I bent to wipe my hands on the mattress—getting blood on my clothes would raise suspicions—but even the blood on my skin vanished like dew in the sun.

None of this made sense. I needed to get out of this room before I started shrieking again. I grabbed my tools, every moment expecting his skeleton fingers to reach out and clasp my hair the way his branches had.

As I bolted to the door to escape, I cast one last look at Redboot. He was nothing but a skeleton in night clothes, his jaw slack in a chilling grin. I rushed from the room, leaving the door ajar and the tapestry swinging like an executioner's ax.

I had the presence of mind to utter the invisibility enchantment and ran out of the chapel, taking startled, gasping breaths. In one of the rooms down the hallway, a dog barked. I heard the noise of people stirring. Someone called, "Who's there? Who screamed?"

A man opened his door and peered outside. Then another.

I kept running, afraid the lot of them would pour into the hallway and block my way, trapping me there. I'd been so stupid. My scream had woken people and soon guards would be searching the halls. Why had Redboot dissolved that way?

The mission was over for tonight. Perhaps for good. Even if Mage Zephyr slept through the commotion, roaming the hallways as a wolf to find him was out of the question. I'd failed—and this time because of my utter stupidity. Of all the ways I might possibly be caught, of all the obstacles that might have prevented me from carrying out my task—I'd screamed. The whole awful business could've been over tonight, but instead, something had gone amiss with the spell, and I'd let my nerves get the best of me.

What had I done wrong? I couldn't have forgotten any of the phrases. My perfect memory allowed me to read them word for word from the page. I'd performed the same spell on three other wizards, with no awful surprises.

By the time I reached the staircase, guards were thundering down them.

I stayed at the bottom of the second-floor landing, pressed to the wall, waiting for the way to clear.

After the guards passed by, I started up the steps. I was halfway to the third floor when I heard voices, two people coming down.

"Most likely one of the maids had a nightmare," a man said, "and she's too embarrassed to admit she yelled loud enough to wake half the wing, but none of the servants will rest well until we check the floor. Otherwise, they'll believe some poor maid's been stabbed, and the murderer is loose among them."

I couldn't let them find me. I turned and began down the stairs to wait again. When I heard Ronan's voice answer the first man, I nearly stumbled.

"I wasn't faulting your diligence," Ronan said. "Of course, we must reassure the servants, but as I was the wizard stationed in the king's chambers tonight, you should've contacted another mage."

"We tried but not a one of them opened their door."

"Not even Mage Saxeus? He was assigned to handle any magical needs that arise tonight."

"Not even Mage Saxeus. If you don't mind me saying so, not a good start on his first day as a council wizard."

I was nearly to the second floor. If Ronan swept the area with a disclosing spell, I'd be caught. How would I explain that I was lurking about in the middle of the night cloaked in invisibility? Was it better to drop my invisibility and pretend I'd been unable to sleep and had come downstairs to check on Gwenyth?

I glanced over my shoulder. Ronan was a dozen steps away, speaking to an older guard whose uniform emblems announced his high rank. Ronan held his wand loosely, not the grip of one who was performing any spells. He seemed to believe the problem on the second floor didn't require magical intervention.

I was safe for the moment. All I had to do was wait for them to pass by. I pressed myself to the wall near the landing and took slow measured breaths.

Ronan walked with an air of easy confidence. "Perhaps Mage Saxeus didn't understand the nature of his duties. Redboot will give him a tongue-lashing for his negligence."

The guard grunted in reply. "Mages Redboot and Zephyr also didn't open their doors. Did they celebrate to the point of drunkenness?"

Ronan and the guard were now so close, I could've reached out and touched Ronan's robe. As he passed, his gaze swung in my direction.

I froze, a breath lodging in my throat. Somehow, he knew I was there.

But then his gaze returned to the guard, and I realized he'd just been surveying the area. "Mages Redboot and Zephyr," he said dryly, "are so spooked by the events of last night their caution drove them into mouse holes."

"Such men of power, afraid?"

I couldn't tell whether the guard was indeed incredulous or mocking them. Maybe both.

"I assume," Ronan said, "their paranoia comes from having too many enemies."

I didn't hear more of the conversation. I crept up the stairs to the third floor and dashed down the hallway to my room. I had no way to tell Alaric I'd failed. Again. But he would learn of the disaster soon enough. My head pounded with worry. What had I done by killing one of the king's wizards—and the senior wizard at that? What would happen on the morrow when the wizards realized someone was hunting them?

A rhetorical question. I knew what would happen. They would begin hunting me.

CHAPTER 22

I woke late the next morning, a product of being out in the night and then lying in bed, concocting horrible scenarios to fret over. I finally decided I would need to be alert for whatever awaited me the next day and took a drop of the sleeping draught. It was more potent than I expected. I slept through the morning bells and would've entirely missed breakfast if one of the castle maids hadn't knocked on my door.

She was a pert girl with freckles and red hair. "Mage Warison sent me," she explained. "He said your lady's maid is unwell, and you required someone's help to dress."

Thoughtful of him to remember me when he must have quite a bit on his mind. I nodded dumbly as though yes, this was the reason I was still in my night clothes, my hair wild and unplaited.

She set about helping me into a gown. Her name was Alice, and she had a penchant for talking. With very little encouragement on my part, she told me that the castle was in an uproar.

"Mage Redboot was murdered last night," she said in a hushed voice. "Awful like. When they found him, he was nothing but a skeleton."

The word murdered made my stomach lurch. I wasn't just someone who took magic from men who'd abused it. I'd become a murderer. "Have they any idea who did it?"

"A powerful wizard," Alice said. "Who else could strip a man down to his bones?"

I shifted uncomfortably. "Many powerful wizards are here in the castle."

"Aye, and they're getting fewer with each passing day. That's the truth. And the ones left are beginning to act peculiar-like. This morning Mage Saxeus burst from his room, raving like a madman. Kept screaming he'd been robbed. No one could calm him."

As she brushed my hair, she murmured more about the happenings in the castle—how none of the servants got more than a few hours of sleep because guards searched every room on the second floor.

Another thing to feel guilty about. When guests came to Docendum and Carendale, our workload always increased. I couldn't imagine what having so many highborn, demanding guests at the castle must be like for the servants.

After Alice made me presentable, I shuffled off to the dining hall to see how much of breakfast I'd missed. At my table, the discussion was of the night's events. Lord Percy was enjoying an undue amount of attention, as he knew details others weren't privy to. He was acquainted with the Ainsworth family whom Mage Saxeus had worked for before his elevation and had learned things from them.

"Saxeus' mark was stripped from him like linen from a bed. The bloke hasn't a lick of magic left. No one has any idea who did it."

Master Godfrey finished off a piece of goose. "Someone clearly didn't approve of the king's choice of appointment."

"I thought," Madame Godfrey said, "that only a group of

wizards could erase a mark. How did a group of them manage it without anyone knowing?"

Lord Percy shrugged. "I suppose the same way the assailants found Redboot and turned him into a skeleton."

Agnes shivered. "It's so brutal, so horrible."

"So uncivilized," Lady Edith agreed, frowning her disapproval. "Really, it was a most unbecoming murder. One wonders about people who would do such a thing."

She didn't glance at me as she said the words, but they were directed at me. She suspected I was involved and didn't approve of me skeletonizing people.

"Perhaps his death was an accident," I said, "something that went awry."

Everyone at the table stared at me.

Agnes cocked her head, considering me like I was a simpleton. "You think an accomplished wizard accidentally uttered some spell in the middle of the night that dissolved his own flesh?" She snorted in derision. "It's just as probable that a knight found with a sword sticking from his chest accidentally ran himself through."

Her family laughed at this notion with her.

Lady Edith, to her credit, came to my defense. "Magic is a good deal trickier than a sword. Although still, one would expect people to act more carefully."

Meaning she was rebuking me for being careless.

"Two attacks on wizards in one night," Bernard said. "It can't have been a coincidence. Both wizards were part of the king's council. Do you think rogue wizards are challenging the king by destroying his wizards?" He regarded a couple of wizards eating together at one of the high tables.

Lord Percy spread some butter on a roll. "Whatever the motive, I imagine the king's next appointments won't be eager to accept the position."

Master Godfrey scanned the room, taking in the mages and

their robes. "Who can King Leofric trust now that he knows some of Aerador's wizards are working against him?"

"Who indeed," Madame Godfrey said. "It makes one look at all the visiting wizards with suspicion."

And I hoped everyone's suspicions didn't wander.

Agnes made a tsking sound. "What will become of Mage Saxeus?"

Lord Percy bit into his roll, chewing without concern. "The king's steward asked Lord Ainsworth if Saxeus could retire to their estate."

"Will they take him back?" Lady Edith asked. "I would've felt quite abandoned if I went to a wedding and without any notice my wizard threw me over to work elsewhere."

"I imagine they'll take him," Lord Percy said. "The king offered to pay for a cottage on their estate, so Saxeus would have a place to live. If you ask me, that's high payment for a day's work."

"Very generous of the king," Madame Godfrey declared and everyone jumped in to agree, that King Leofric was the most generous of men, as though he might hear the conversation. He wasn't even at breakfast. Neither Ronan nor Mage Zephyr had come either.

A trumpeter at the front of the room blew a short note and all the wizards in the dining hall stood and began filing out of the room.

"Where are they going?" I asked.

"Convening with the king," Lady Edith said. "If you'd been on time this morning, you'd have heard the steward announce the meeting to them."

Agnes craned her neck to watch them go. "Do you suppose King Leofric is sending all but his own wizards away?"

"That's what I would do," Madame Godfrey said. "Send the lot packing and make his next appointments carefully. He needn't rush to choose. He still has two wizards left on his council to see to anything he needs."

The other wizards were my alibi. If they left today and Mage Zephyr and Ronan lost their marks tonight, everyone would know that an unknown wizard was among them. They would search the men for marks, and when they didn't find any, would they think to search the women? Or would Ronan save them the trouble and tell them of my mark right off?

If he admitted he'd given a woman a mark and she'd used that power in an act of rebellion, he might be put to death too. Would that be how our story ended, like some tale of tragedy meant to warn people not to give power or affection where it wasn't deserved?

"If King Leofric sends them away," Master Godfrey drew my attention back to the conversation, "he'll never discover who the guilty wizards are."

Lord Percy leaned forward and lowered his voice, taking us into his confidence. "It's my understanding the meeting was called in part to uncover the truth of the murder."

I took a drink with a mostly steady hand. "Do they have clues to the rogue wizards' identity?"

"They must have," Lord Percy said as though it was self-evident.

Anxiety crept up my back. Had I dropped any of my spell things when I'd fled Redboot's room?

"One would suppose," Lady Edith said, "that someone clever enough to take a wizard's mark would be careful not to leave clues behind."

I *had* been careful but perhaps not careful enough. If the king was about to discover the truth, I should devise a way to escape and take Alaric, Lady Edith, Joanne, and… how could I take Gwenyth with me?

Her health was already uncertain. Sitting in a carriage for days was out of the question.

Although perhaps I was worrying when it wasn't necessary. The king might have no idea as to my identity. Surely, I'd left nothing behind that could point to me.

Alaric would tell me that we should stay and complete the mission. If we failed, if nothing changed, the renegades would begin planning to go to battle again.

In order to make a sound choice, I needed to know what was transpiring in the king's meeting. Eavesdropping on a collection of wizards would be dangerous. Normally, I'd stay clear of a group of wizards who were looking for a traitor, but it was my fault the mission was in jeopardy. I should find out if the people who'd come with me to Valistowe were also in danger.

I excused myself from breakfast so I could pay a visit to the king's council room.

* * *

TEN MINUTES LATER, I'd shed my heavy gown. Dressed only in my chemise and boots, I turned invisible, went outside, and scaled the wall of the castle. I'd taken off my gown to protect it from dirt and tears as well as for ease of climbing, although doing so almost seemed to be tempting fate. This would be the time one of the wizards shot a disclosing spell in my direction—when I was hardly dressed.

Once I reached the king's council chamber window, I stood precariously perched, feet doing their best to find purchase on jutting stone blocks while my hands gripped the windowsill. Rows of iron bars prevented entrance of any sort, but I didn't want to enter, I only wanted to hear.

The king sat on an ornately carved throne with a red velvet canopy that hung over it as though it needed shade. He sat stiffly, his expression stern.

Four chairs flanked the throne. The steward, the marshal, and Ronan sat in three. The other was empty. More than two dozen smaller chairs faced the throne in less ornate supplication. The men sitting in them wore their stately robes, proof of their magic.

Mage Zephyr, now the senior wizard, paced across the front of the room addressing the group. "We must do our part to root out the treachery among us," he boomed loud enough that hearing him was quite easy. "Mage Redboot was left no more than a skeleton. What dark spell is that? I know naught of its origin. What book tells of it?"

None of the wizards answered. A few shook their heads. Former Mage Saxeus sat with the group of wizards, looking flushed and sullen. I noticed Wolfson among the group as well, sitting with an expression of firm disapproval.

Ronan's brows drew together the way they did when he considered a puzzle. "Redboot's condition may not be the result of a spell."

Mage Zephyr snorted in derision. "You are truly inexperienced if you think any other cause but magic could—"

Ronan cut him off. "I never claimed magic wasn't involved. I simply meant it might not have been the purpose of the spell. Since Telarian, Sciatheric, and Saxeus' marks were all taken, we can assume Redboot's was as well. He might have been using magic to stave off aging, and his disintegration was caused by the loss of that magic."

Meaning, Ronan believed Redboot had used dark magic to take the life of some other wizard or wizards to lengthen his own. At this accusation, a murmur went through the group.

My shoulders raised, lifted as the weight of guilt slid from them. If Ronan was right, Redboot's death wasn't my fault. Not really. He'd held death off by unlawful magic. I'd just taken away his protection.

The king tapped his fingers on his armrest. "It's a heavy thing to accuse a man of dark magic, especially one who no longer can speak in his defense. What proof do you offer?"

Ronan had his answer ready. "Redboot was at least one hundred and twenty-six. I know because he once took credit for the spell that keeps crossbow strings dry in the rain. One of the books that recorded the incantation was written one hundred and ten years ago."

The murmur that went through the crowd this time was louder and peppered with outraged exclamations.

"If you knew this about him," the king said, silencing the crowd, "why didn't you inform me?"

The question made me roll my eyes on Ronan's behalf. Did the king really expect his newest wizard to make an enemy of a senior wizard who used dark magic?

"I apologize," Ronan replied calmly. "I'd supposed Redboot was simply taking false credit for the spell, a fault of vanity, nothing else. Now I believe he told the truth. In the legend Nabaddon, that dark wizard met a similar end."

Mage Zephyr stopped his pacing for long enough to scoff at Ronan. "You're too soon out of the nursery. The legend of Nabaddon isn't a historical source. It's nothing but a bedtime tale meant to entertain children."

"And yet even when we entertain children," Ronan answered, "we don't always lie to them. Apparently, it is true that when a wizard with an unnaturally prolonged life dies, his flesh reverts to what it would have been without magic holding it together."

Exactly. I wasn't a murderer. I would continue telling myself this until the words scrubbed away the images of the man's dissolving flesh.

Zephyr didn't argue with Ronan's assertion, perhaps because the king said, "Your theory would explain many things, I suppose." Leofric's countenance darkened. He shook his head and muttered a curse. "How is it that I knew so little about my head wizard that I couldn't tell his heart was so black?"

"You're not to blame." Zephyr's voice turned soothing. "He fooled everyone. He was an expert at hiding his crimes."

Well, Zephyr had changed his opinion quickly. He was probably emphasizing Redboot's skill so that no one could blame Zephyr for not detecting Redboot's true nature earlier. "Regardless of the cause of Redboot's demise," Zephyr went on, "we must find the man guilty of last night's crimes."

"Men," Saxeus interjected.

A manifestation of Saxeus' ego. He was certain a lone wizard couldn't possibly have overpowered him.

"Or men," Zephyr amended.

"I suspect only one wizard was involved," Ronan said.

Why was he so perceptive?

Zephyr glared at him. "Enlighten us, Mage Warison. What book have you read that lists a spell where only one wizard is needed to accomplish the task of removing a wizard's mark?"

Ronan sent him a patient smile. "My assumption isn't based on any books. It comes from the size of Redboot's room. The space only allowed for one other person."

The steward and marshal both chuckled. Zephyr flushed. The king leaned across his armrest and directed his attention at Ronan. "What else have you deduced about the identity of the traitor?"

I held my breath. Even Ronan, as brilliant as he was, couldn't know my identity.

Ronan bowed his head apologetically. "I'm afraid we must wait to hear from our witnesses to discern more of the traitor's identity."

Witnesses? No witnesses had seen me.

"Currently," Ronan went on. "Our only clue is that most of Mage Saxeus' scorpions were missing from his room. He knows they were there a day earlier." Ronan gestured in Saxeus' direction. "Did you grant anyone access to your room who might have magically removed them?"

"No," Saxeus muttered. "I'm not a fool."

Perhaps not a fool, but I could think of other unpleasant titles for him.

Ronan steepled his fingers together in thought. "Then the scorpions were removed when the traitor broke in. Otherwise, more of their remains would've been found in your room."

Mages. It never occurred to them someone might kill the scorpions and dispose of them elsewhere. They were used to leaving their rubbish lying around for others to clean.

"Perhaps," Ronan continued, "the wizard carried enchanted creatures with him who could eat scorpions…" He turned to the marshal. "Did any of the guests bring metal owls to the castle? Or perhaps bats?"

"Or chickens," someone in the audience called out. "As you know, nothing strikes fear into the hearts of enemies like a wizard wielding his magic chicken."

Scattered laughter rippled through the audience. I craned my head to get a better view of the wizard who'd spoken. With the exception of Ronan, I'd always thought wizards to be a humorless bunch. The speaker was a rotund, middle-aged man with a bushy brown beard and a bulbous nose.

"I'll check the records," the marshal replied. "Although, I can assure you no guests brought metal chickens with them. I would recollect such baggage."

"Well then, Bodkin," one of the wizards called, "You've still time to make an enchanted chicken your signature magic symbol."

"And so I shall!" Bodkin called back.

A few more wizards chortled at that. Hearing wizards laugh was an odd sensation. It made the group seem less sinister and more like regular folk.

"Sire, if I may speak." A gray-haired wizard stood and bowed to the king. I recognized him. Mage Goldenthatch had visited Docendum on occasion to teach classes on herbology. "As much as I hope you catch the traitor, I believe it's in your best interest to permit, nay insist, that all wizards save Warison and Zephyr depart from Valistowe at once. Such an order would ensure not only the safety of the remaining council but every other innocent wizard as well." He lifted his hands in entreaty. "We don't know where the traitor will strike next. He may target any of us."

The marshal hardly let him finish. "Your Majesty, I counsel you not to send any of the wizards away. Doing so would give the traitor a head start evading our men." The marshal gave Goldenthatch a look that indicated his request made him a suspect. "He's probably hoping to escape that way."

Goldenthatch pursed his lips in indignation. "Our safety—"

The marshal spoke over him, "Will be guaranteed if you all sleep together in the great hall as I suggested."

"Or," Goldenthatch said, "such a sleeping arrangement will make us easier to kill as we'll be trapped in the room with the traitor. Do you think your guards will keep him from acting?"

"No," the marshal answered patiently. "I think my guards will awaken the rest of you if they see anything suspicious, and *you'll* keep the traitor from acting."

Goldenthatch huffed, disgruntled. "What if he has some spell to poison the air and means to kill us all?"

"You've clearly given our deaths thought," Bodkin called out. He gestured to the marshal. "I request the spot closest to the door. I'm going to sleep with my lips pressed to the crack."

"Sire." Goldenthatch turned to the king. "I know your intentions are honorable, but locking up wizards without their consent is unprecedented, and I—"

King Leofric slammed his hand down on this armrest. "A rogue wizard singlehandedly stripped marks from four of the most formidable wizards in the land. He likely wanted them all dead as well, but instead of leaving knives plunged into their chests which might be traced, he turned Telarian and Sciatheric against one another so that they destroyed each other for him.

The king gave me more credit than I wanted.

"The same man," King Leofric continued, "found Redboot hiding in a room that even *I* didn't know existed." He waved a hand in Saxeus' direction. "He either favored Saxeus, or—just as likely—only spared his life to draw out his suffering. He expects Saxeus to lay in bed tonight, unprotected, wondering where the missing scorpions are and who controls them now."

I'd never expected any such thing. Although now that the king brought it up, I did hope Saxeus worried a bit every time he climbed beneath his covers.

"The man is playing with us," King Leofric said. "He's not only powerful, he's also daring, intelligent, and cunning. *That* is the sort of wizard we must search for."

No one spoke for a few moments, then Mage Bodkin said, "Well, those requirements disqualify several of the wizards in the room. My innocence was proved at 'daring.'"

I'd begun to rather like Mage Bodkin.

"Are you a wizard?" someone called. "I thought you were a jester."

"No," Bodkin returned, "if I were a jester, people would listen to me more often and welcome me more warmly."

"That's enough," the king said with more exasperation than anger. I marveled at his lenience in letting his subjects speak out of turn. But then, wizards had privileges even the highborn didn't have.

A knock sounded on the door. Every head in the room turned to it. "At last," the king said, "the witnesses."

CHAPTER 23

I whispered, prayerlike, "There were no witnesses," over and over again.

One of the guards opened the door and the head housekeeper ushered two servant children inside. A boy and a girl, perhaps ten or eleven years old. Both took small reluctant steps into the room. The girl wrung her hands, trembling. The boy was as pale as milk.

Could they have been in Saxeus room somewhere, unseen and watching me? I knew it was unlikely and yet my stomach wouldn't unclench.

The two bowed to King Leofric, gawked at the wizards, and huddled closer together.

The housekeeper nudged the children toward the king. "Go on then, tell his majesty what you saw."

Neither child spoke and the housekeeper's expression grew so tightlipped I thought she would smack them.

"Thank you for your assistance," the king told her. "I'll question the children now." He motioned for them to come and smiled gently. "You aren't in any sort of trouble. Nothing you say will make us angry."

At the word, 'us,' the girl's gaze traveled around the room, taking in the wizards again.

"After you're done helping me," King Leofric drew her attention back, "Madame Hauville will take the two of you to the kitchen and let you eat as many sweets as you want. Would you like that?"

The girl nodded. The boy said, "Yes, sir. I mean, your Sireness, sir." He gulped at the mangled address. "I mean Your Majesty, sire." He bit his lip and blinked, near tears.

King Leofric smiled again. "You needn't be frightened. Simply tell me your story as you would tell it to your father."

The children edged closer to the king as though he were a safe island in a sea of uncertain consequences. The boy spoke first, his voice rushed. "People keep saying I'm making up tales. But truly, sire, last night while I slept in the hallway, right where I'm supposed to be, sire, I woke to the sound of an animal trotting by. You know, the click of claws a dog makes when it walks."

Oh. The witness had seen my wolf form. My identity was still safe.

The boy shifted anxiously from one foot to the other. "I opened my eyes and saw an enormous black wolf roaming the halls—all by itself like—going from door to door, sniffing. And it weren't none of the dogs here at the castle neither. This one had red eyes and was unnatural big. It had a neck like an ox and so many teeth it could hardly shut its mouth."

An exaggeration, but not much of one. The only animal I'd ever been able to transform into was the form of Wolfson's beast. That animal was a part of me, the manifestation of my anger.

At the pronouncement of the wolf's appearance, so many wizards began speaking that I couldn't make out what any of them said.

"An unnaturally big wolf?" Ronan asked loudly enough to silence the talking. "And it was completely black?"

The boy nodded. "Excepting some gray bits at its neck, Sir. I knew if I moved, it would rip my throat out, so I squeezed my eyes tight and didn't so much as twitch until morning bells."

The king turned to the girl. "Were you nearby when this happened? Speak up so we can hear."

"No, sire," she stammered. "I sleep in a different hall but I saw the same beast prowling by. It wasn't no normal wolf, sire. Twas as big as a lion. I ain't never seen the likes of it before."

"She may not have seen it before," a wizard near the window said, "but some of us have." I recognized the man's voice. Stewart—the apprentice whose horse had one day disappeared and never been spoken of again. "These children are describing a beast at Docendum castle. Mage Wolfson's pet."

All eyes swung to Wolfson. His face reddened, and he waved a hand in Stewart's direction, flicking away the accusation. "Nonsense." I'd heard that gruff, dismissive tone many times. A tone with a threat weaved into it. Servants and apprentices both remained silent after being subjected to it.

Wizards had no such qualms. "I too have seen Mage Wolfson's unholy creation," a man near the front proclaimed. Two more wizards joined in agreement.

Ronan narrowed his eyes at his old teacher. "I've met this wolf as well. Why would you bring it to the castle?"

Mage Wolfson crossed his arms stiffly. "I haven't. You should already know as much. Such an animal would've been discovered by Mage Redboot on my entry and refused admittance."

"Unless," Mage Zephyr said, "Mage Redboot was in league with you and allowed you to bring the beast in." He nodded knowingly. "Perhaps Mage Redboot had a change of heart about his dealings with you, and you killed him to hide your secret."

Mage Wolfson stood, bristling with offense. "Where would I keep that animal during my stay? Someone would've seen it."

"And someone has." Mage Zephyr swept a hand toward the children. "Two witnesses in different locations described your pet. This is the evidence we've been seeking."

Mage Wolfson lifted his hands, palms out to block the accusations. "Search the castle. You won't find the animal. And when you send a messenger to Docendum, you'll discover the wolf is still there."

The wizards apparently didn't believe his denial. Several drew their wands. Mage Zephyr took a protective step toward the king. Wolfson scowled at the group.

If bolts of fire began swooshing past me on their way into the room, I would have to move away from the window very quickly.

Ronan motioned for the housekeeper to take the children away and calmly addressed the group. "I imagine a search would produce no such animal. But what's to say Mage Wolfson didn't transform into the creature and hunt for Redboot that way?"

Wolfson gaped at Ronan, mouth dropping open. The sight of Wolfson's Adam's apple bobbing and sweat gathering on his forehead nearly transfixed me. It was probably wicked of me to enjoy the sight of his fear. I would have to add that failing to the list of my others.

All around the room, wizards joined in agreement with Ronan's assertion. "Of course, the black beast is one of Wolfson's forms," Stewart called out. "Who else would know to use it?"

Whatever Mage Wolfson had done to Stewart's horse, he hadn't forgotten about it.

"I made no such transformation," Mage Wolfson insisted. His voice went high with desperation. "Someone is trying to implicate me. I'm loyal to the king." He turned to King Leofric beseechingly, hands pressed together in entreaty. "You know of my loyalty, sire."

The king stared at him, unmoved, and didn't answer.

Mage Goldenthatch stood, his wand gripped in his hand. "Your loyalty is debatable, but your jealousy is well known. Your goal has always been to rise to the king's council. Is this how you plan to manage the task? You'll kill so many of the king's wizards that he's bound to eventually call you?"

Mage Wolfson's eyes darted around the room, growing wilder with each moment. "I couldn't have done it. Someone else here is the traitor."

Ronan considered him. "Why couldn't you have done it?" His voice was as cold as a knife blade, and the words were a thrust at Mage Wolfson. Ronan hadn't forgotten his grudge against his old teacher, either.

I was comforted to know I deserved as much revenge as Stewart's horse.

"What proof of your innocence do you offer?" Ronan repeated.

The room quieted. Every set of eyes fixed on Wolfson.

Wolfson's nostrils flared and his jaw moved up and down, chewing on his words before spitting them out. "I couldn't have done it." He gulped and his voice faltered. "I'm unable to trans-form into an animal shape."

I wouldn't have believed this, even though Mage Wolfson himself proclaimed it, except I saw the truth of the confession in Ronan's eyes. He'd known this secret already, and he'd demanded proof to humiliate his old teacher.

"Impossible," Saxeus exploded. "For years, you've told us of your animal exploits."

A rumble of agreement traveled around the room. Every wand was out. The group looked like they could easily turn into a mob.

The king stood and stepped toward Wolfson like he wanted to throttle him. "When I renewed your position as head of Docendum, you showed me your animal transformation. Now you expect me to believe you're incapable of such a feat?"

Wolfson stumbled past the other wizards to the front of the room and practically threw himself at the king's feet. "A trick, Your Majesty. I'd brought a trained dog that I'd turned invisible. When I told you I was going to transform, I made the dog visible and myself invisible." Wolfson clasped his hands together. "I'm guilty of one small deception, sire—merely to impress you—but nothing more."

Wolfson turned to Ronan, his eyes beseeching. "You've always suspected the truth. Tell him. It's the reason Mage Quintal always taught the transformation lessons."

Ronan's voice was as chilly as it had been before. "I learned all my important lessons from you, Mage Wolfson. You made sure I learned them well."

The king stepped away from Wolfson's groveling hands and strode back to his throne. "You've given me proof today. If not proof of your crimes against my wizard council, then proof that you're a traitor to my trust."

The king sank onto the throne, ignoring Wolfson's continued protests. "Mage Warison, take this man from here and remove his mark at once." He waved his hand in the direction of the seated wizards. "All of you will participate in the removal. Let it be a warning for any others who harbor betrayal toward my house."

At the pronouncement, Mage Wolfson reached out to the king, wailing, "No! I'm innocent!"

His words had no effect. Ronan plucked Wolfson's wand from his hand. Two other mages grabbed Wolfson's arms and dragged him out the door. The other wizards followed, most of them commenting that they'd never trusted Wolfson.

Perhaps I should've felt a little guilty that he was paying for my crime, but his fate was still better than the one he'd ordered for the villagers of Colsbury. I could muster no pity.

Mage Zephyr didn't join the other wizards. When the rest had gone and only the marshal and king remained seated, Mage

Zephyr stood, hands clasped behind his back. "Do you plan to let him live, Sire?"

The king hesitated. "If the attacks end, we'll know Wolfson was responsible and acted on his own. Then he'll stand trial for his crimes. This seems the most likely scenario. However, if the attacks continue, we'll consider his innocence."

Such a pronouncement was almost enough to tempt me to forgo removing any more marks.

"If the attacks continue," the marshal said, "it may simply mean Wolfson has a partner."

The king conceded the point with a nod. "That is a possibility as well."

"Let's hope the matter is closed." Mage Zephyr drew nearer to the throne. "Whatever the case, you need to call, without delay, at least one new wizard to the council. Preferably two."

The king rubbed his beard wearily and slumped in his throne. "It seems I was unwise in my other appointments, and now you ask for me to choose two more men?"

"Many talented wizards live in your land," Mage Zephyr insisted. "The task won't be difficult. If you take my recommendation—"

The king lifted his hand to stop him. "Your previous recommendation lasted one day. The only thing of note Saxeus accomplished during his service was to nearly burn one of my guests to death."

He meant Gwenyth. I liked King Leofric right then. He'd not only heard of her accident, he disapproved of Mage Saxeus' actions. He'd called Gwenyth his guest.

I snuffed out the thought. I was working against him.

"Although," the king went on, "perhaps Saxeus was still more worthy than the mages I chose. When they lost their marks, two killed each other and the third dissolved into a skeleton."

"My lord—"

King Leofric raised a hand. "New appointments will take some thought. I mustn't make a hasty decision."

The marshal leaned toward the king. "Your Majesty, you may not have time for lengthy deliberation. The attack on your wizards could be the first part of an attempt on your life."

"I realize that," the king said wearily. "And I'm sure every wizard worth his salt realizes that as well. They'll be hesitant to take a position on my council now. They saw how easily their peers succumbed to an enemy."

Mage Zephyr began pacing in front of the throne again. "Hopefully the matter is at an end, but if Wolfson has an accomplice..."

"All the more reason to be careful," the king said. "I must investigate each wizard thoroughly. If my daughter ends up succeeding me, I need to ensure that those who protect and advise her are not just powerful men but honorable ones as well. As I choose the next wizards, I must think of Alfreda."

He was thinking of his daughter instead of himself. I shut my eyes. How could I be part of this man's death?

I didn't stay longer to eavesdrop. I'd learned more than what I'd come for. The king didn't suspect me. He wouldn't add any other wizards to his council tonight. I should've been relieved.

Relief wasn't among my feelings, however. Ronan knew Wolfson wasn't the wizard who'd taken a wolf's form last night. He would continue to search for the traitor.

CHAPTER 24

*A*fter I left the wizards, I dressed and went to the housekeeper's room to check on Gwenyth. The door was open and the housekeeper absent. Gwenyth was alone, eyes open, staring at the ceiling.

My footsteps stuttered. *She's dead*, I thought. But then she turned her head. I shut the door so we'd have ample warning if someone entered the room and pulled a chair over to her pallet. "How are you faring?"

"Mage Warison came by this morning and gave me a spell for the pain. Fortunately, it's still working. All the physician offered was strong wine."

She didn't have to explain why she couldn't take much of that. The risk of a loose tongue was too great. "It was kind of Mage Warison to remember you."

She fluttered a hand in impatience, making it clear she didn't want to expound on Ronan's virtues. "I'm not sure when someone will return to tend to me. What happened last night? I've heard the servants whispering Redboot's name but no one will tell me what befell him."

I gave her a brief retelling of events, mentioning what I'd

overheard in the wizards' meeting. "Ronan knows Wolfson wasn't responsible."

"But he was still willing to take his old master's mark. Played like a true wizard."

I bristled in Ronan's defense. "Wolfson is a murderer, a horrible beast. Ronan was right to make sure he's defanged. And besides, he probably saved your life."

Gwenyth sent me a long, penetrating look. "Warison might be the most merciful wizard in the land, but he's still a wizard. I know he's handsome and when his fine eyes are upon you, you forget the purpose of our cause, but try and remember this: if he finds out what you've done, he'll kill you. He's loyal to the king, not you."

She was right of course. And I would have to face him as an enemy tonight. All other protestations died on my lips.

* * *

I was restless or perhaps just unsupervised, so before dinner, I headed to the stables, visible this time, under the pretense that I'd come to discuss dispatching Alaric to fetch some of Gwenyth's relatives. I pretended I was beyond myself with worry, which might explain my lack of propriety should anyone wonder why a high-born woman had traipsed out to the stables instead of sending a message.

When Alaric saw me enter the stable, his mouth went slack with surprise, and apprehension flickered in his eyes. He thought something else had gone wrong. In the span of a breath, he squashed the emotion with a mask of cool, polite servitude.

For a couple of minutes, we spoke of Gwenyth. He rationally pointed out it was late in the day. By the time he readied a horse and packed provisions, he wouldn't get past the village before having to stop for the night. He suggested waiting until first light and seeing how Gwenyth fared then.

Halfway through his protest, I waved my hand in front of my nose and insisted the smell of the stable was too overpowering for my delicate sensibilities. We moved outside to the shade tree, and I gave him the details I'd heard from the wizards' meeting with the king.

When I finished, Alaric nodded as though agreeing to some command I'd issued. "Having all the visiting wizards in one place tonight is a bit of bad luck, but I don't see that we've any choice except to continue as planned."

"The wizards will all have alibis. They'll know someone else is to blame, and they'll search for me."

Alaric shrugged. "But by that point, the king will be dead and our mission accomplished."

I don't know what I supposed Alaric would say. Of course, he would put the mission's success above my safety. That had always been the case. And yet his words seemed to sink to the ground in front of me with a heaviness that dragged my heart with it. Alaric's response made me feel small and uncared for. So very, very expendable.

"Cheer up," he said. "You'll find a way to escape. You always do."

That's because I'd never been pursued by twenty wizards and all the king's men before. "Did you find someone else to act as an assassin like I asked?"

He sighed as though he knew I was about to become unreasonable. "No."

I crossed my arms. "Are the leaders refusing to assign someone else? I need to have a word with them." I'd agreed to come to Valistowe in part to keep Alaric from needlessly dying in a battle. The least the leaders could do was keep him safe for me now.

"I didn't ask anyone. Very few renegades reside at Valistowe. I'm the best suited for the task."

Or the most willing. Perhaps I should've been comforted

that my life wasn't the only one Alaric was willing to sacrifice to the cause, but I wasn't. He'd ignored my wishes and hadn't cared what his death would do to me. "What if I can't carry through with taking Ronan's mark? What if I find loyalties to people a stronger pull than the mission's success?" Perhaps I said the words to hurt Alaric, to remind him that loyalties mattered to me.

His voice grew soft. "You know the importance of what you do. As you act, think of the many servants in the land. Think of averting a war."

If any words could spur me to action, those were the words.

Alaric's eyes didn't leave mine. "I believe in you, Marcella. Remember that. Wear my belief like a talisman, like that shell and carved horse you always keep with you."

Those. Yes. The bits of my life with Ronan that were forever with me. Those mementos and Alaric's belief would be a fine comfort for me when we were both thrown onto a pyre.

Alaric bowed his head like a servant at the end of a conversation. "I shall await your signal tonight." He turned and strode back to the stable.

I watched him go, then stalked toward the castle feeling worse than I had when I'd come.

* * *

AFTER DINNER, I went into the ballroom with the intention of keeping an eye on Mage Zephyr. I meant to follow him when he left so that no matter where he hid, I could find him.

Almost as soon as I stepped foot into the ballroom, Ronan intercepted me. He wore a light blue robe that made his eyes seem bright and piercing. How many robes did the king's wizards own? All of them were so fine and formal and completely impractical.

He offered me his arm. "Will you stroll around the grounds

with me? I don't have long before it's my turn to guard the king, and I'd prefer to spend what time I have with you."

That would put an end to my idea of following Zephyr.

"You don't want to dance?" I asked. Going outside alone with Ronan would make tongues wag, but I was a bit late to insist on a chaperone. I'd kissed him shamelessly last night.

"You wanted me to introduce you to my friends. We may encounter some on our stroll. That should make you happier than dancing."

With that insistence, there was nothing to do but take his arm and let him lead me outside.

Clouds had shuffled across the sky during the day and were congregated over the courtyard, blotting out the moon and stars. The night was cool, but I felt a flush of heat warming my cheeks. Did Ronan expect me to kiss him again? He might. I'd made my interest in him clear enough last night.

I should've found the idea distasteful, and yet my heart was traitorously beating in anticipation. I couldn't look at his handsome face. The feel of his arm linked with mine was distracting enough.

We wandered toward a fountain in the center of a garden walk. Wizards' orbs of all different colors hung from posts, gathered together like glowing flowers. Their shadows were tinted with color so that the water rippled yellow, orange, and pink, as though something from a fairy realm.

Ronan tilted his head, contemplating me. "Do you have any apologies to offer me tonight, my lady?"

"Alas. I haven't been rude to you today."

"Most likely because we've spent no time together, but I'm sure you have some commentary on my dealings of late."

"None at all." I paused. "That isn't to say I don't have commentary on your other choices."

He laughed, a sound deep and rich. "What choices of mine do you know of?"

"You became a wizard. Isn't that enough?"

His eyebrows rose. "Is it?" His question seemed sincere. As though he was unsure why I would disapprove of that action.

I didn't respond beyond a shrug. To say more might make him think I had renegade tendencies. We padded up to the fountain.

"Speaking of wizards we've both known," he said, "have you heard about Mage Wolfson?"

Best to play ignorant. I wasn't sure what was common knowledge in the court regarding Wolfson. "Do you mean Mage Saxeus? I heard about him and Mage Redboot at breakfast."

"No, Mage Wolfson. The king believes he was involved in the doings of last night and ordered his mark removed." Ronan paused, studying my reaction. "You don't look surprised."

"Should his treachery surprise me?" I dipped my hand into the fountain's water, distorting the colors. "The magic you hold in such high esteem brings quite a lot of people to ruin, doesn't it? Is it too late for you to consider a career in something else…a cobbler, perhaps? You make lovely shoes. Or at least quiet ones." I was jesting, but a note of desperation leaked into my voice. At that moment, I'd have given anything to convince Ronan to take up a different profession.

"I prefer to make spells rather than slippers. I'll try to avoid ruin."

We left the fountain and ambled further down the lane where it was more private. When we reached a bench, he took his wand from his pocket, arced it into a circle surrounding us, and said an incantation I wasn't familiar with. The air shimmered and thickened.

I sat on the bench, taking care not to wrinkle my gown. "What did you just do?"

"I issued a silencing spell." He joined me on the bench, his wand on his lap. "While we stay within two feet of each other, our words will be muffled and incomprehensible to any who pass by."

That would be a useful spell to have. "I thought we went on this stroll so you could introduce me to your friends. Is this an admittance that wizards have no friends?"

"Not ones I trust with secrets."

I leaned toward him. "Will we be discussing your secrets or mine? I do hope it's yours. I already know all of mine."

He stretched his free hand along the back of the bench, a casual gesture. "I was simply wondering how your magic has served you. You speak so ill of sorcery that you've made me wonder if anything has gone amiss."

My secrets, then. I shrugged nonchalantly. "Nothing has gone amiss. I've had little need for most of what you taught me."

In the evening light, his blue eyes looked black. Dark and penetrating. "You used the invisibility spell the other day."

"Yes," I said, as though remembering. "I only meant that on my estate, I've little need for the protections you gave me. Invisibility did come in handy to avoid Lord Percy."

"I thought you were avoiding Bernard Godfrey."

"I avoid many people. Sometimes I confuse them."

"And the boots that make no sound?"

"Pardon?"

"You wore them the other day when you were invisible. I'm surprised you took them with you to court. They're rather shabby things, aren't they? Not fit for a lady."

"Invisibility wouldn't do me much good if I clatter about."

His questions proved he was suspicious of my actions, but those suspicions couldn't run deep. He wouldn't suppose me capable of more than minor mischief. I fiddled with my sleeve and peered out across the garden to the plants that were only lumpy silhouettes in the night.

Ronan's fingers tapped against the back of the bench. "Have you learned any other spells besides the ones I taught you?"

I chuckled as though the question was ridiculous. "How would I have managed such a feat? I've told no one of my mark, and even if I had, no wizard would be so foolish as to teach me."

"Yes, only a very foolish wizard would teach you anything— or," he added with a sigh, "one who was completely smitten with you."

My gaze shot to him. "Were you smitten?" I didn't believe it. Not when he'd turned away from me so easily.

He tilted his head. "Does that surprise you?"

"Yes."

"Then you've forgotten most of our years together and only remember our last three months."

He was right, but still. "Those were the most memorable of our months."

He shook his head. "I remember them all. I remember when you used to be happy and light and witty."

I laid my hands across my knees and pursed my lips in offended dignity. "I'm still witty."

He laughed, so he couldn't deny my claim. His hand slid over mine. "But not happy? Not light?"

Not since I came to court. And perhaps not earlier either. Admitting as much bothered me. A capable woman should've been able to overcome her affections and disappointment in a matter that was years old. The vine of one's love, unwatered, should wither. Instead, seeing Ronan had sent new tendrils squeezing my heart.

I looked at the shapeless plants in the garden again. "Do you want me to be happy?"

He gently took my chin and turned it back to him. "Yes. I want nothing more." His blue eyes were on mine, searching my face with such intensity that I believed him. Here was the Ronan of old, the Ronan I'd loved. I shut my eyes and leaned toward him, lips falling open. A shameless request, perhaps, but one he obliged.

He dropped soft, adoring kisses on my mouth, my cheeks, and my closed lids. His lips returned to mine with warmth and eagerness. I wrapped my arms around his neck and sighed, completely undone. This was dangerous and wrong, kissing the enemy, and yet I melted into him like drips of wax clinging to a candle. For several minutes, only one thought occupied my mind. Ronan wanted nothing more than my happiness. He cared for me. Even as poor and unconnected as I was, he was kissing me as a suitor would.

Or perhaps as a rogue would. He was, after all, a wizard.

Still, while I kissed him, the world and all of its consequences faded and blurred. I could abandon the renegades and be the woman Ronan thought I was. That was still a possibility. Or better yet, I could convince Ronan to join our cause.

While his lips found my neck, I murmured, "Would you ever consider leaving the king's council and moving to a poor country estate?"

If he was willing to give up power for love, then perhaps I could convince him to give up his position so I didn't have to take his mark. The chances of his agreeing were as likely as a sudden frost, but I silently begged him to say yes.

Yes, yes, yes...

He lifted his head, a smile on his lips. "Or I could find you an estate close to court with a suitable chaperone."

Like a proper suitor? Foolishly, I entertained the thought of Ronan as a husband for several distracting moments. It could never be, of course. If Ronan saw that my wizard's mark was equal in size to his own, he would know me capable of more than the magic he'd given me. He would figure out the rest.

"I couldn't leave Lady Edith," I said.

His eyebrow quirked up. "If you came to court to find a husband, wasn't leaving Lady Edith part of the plan?"

Ah. Yes. I laid my head against Ronan's chest so he couldn't see my face. He was too adept at reading my expression. "I worry for your safety here. Three of the king's wizards are dead. Another was stricken of his mark."

Ronan's hand moved comfortingly along my back. "You're worried, even after I told you Wolfson was charged with the crime?"

A mistake on my part. Only Ronan and I knew Wolfson wasn't the cause. I gulped and was glad he couldn't see that action. "But certainly more than one wizard is required to take another's mark. He must have at least one partner here at court. Perhaps several."

I hadn't realized Ronan was tense until I felt him relax. He didn't know I'd heard his pronouncement to the wizards that one man alone was responsible for Redboot's death.

"I'm sure I can handle any enemies of the king."

Such overconfidence was dangerous. I straightened, pulling away from him. "Have you any idea how many enemies the king has? Have you never heard of the renegades?"

"Yes," he said with a derisive cough. "I've heard of them."

A chill went through me. No sympathy colored his response. I was almost afraid to ask the next question. "Do you track down the renegades and kill them like Wolfson did?"

"I don't do anything like Wolfson did. The man had little more understanding than his beast and less finesse."

Not a better answer. "So, you track down renegades with more finesse, people who simply want their freedom?" I'd said too much, but I couldn't take back my words.

Ronan's gaze snapped to mine. "I protect the king. I don't track down or battle anyone who hasn't already decided to fight against him." Ronan spoke like he was self-evidently in the right.

I couldn't leave it alone. I couldn't leave him smugly standing on his high ground, dismissing every belief I'd fought for. "The morality of owning people doesn't trouble you?"

A flicker of something went through his eyes, some small

discomfort. "Parents own their children to the same degree. Do you suppose that an evil as well?"

"Parents love their children and so do what's best for them. Masters have no such love."

"Bad parents and bad masters don't. Good ones do. We both grew up with a bad mage and that tainted our experience." He put his hand on mine in an encouraging manner. "But one must rise above such beginnings. Surely your time at Carendale castle wasn't so filled with deprivations. Lord Haddock is a generous man toward those in his household, treating them like family."

Well, if he was, he didn't bother to find out what went on in his kitchen. "Cook Fletcher hated me and tried to starve me. I rarely saw Lord Haddock."

Ronan winced. "I'm sorry. I didn't know." He shifted on the bench, his hand falling away from mine. "Did you manage to get food?"

"Yes, I became invisible and stole it."

He nodded, relieved. I also could read him well. He was pained at inadvertently being the cause of my hunger but could comfort himself that the magic he'd given me had been its reprieve.

He cleared his throat. "Your unfortunate experience with the cook shows that masters aren't the sole source of oppression, nor can one uproot it by doing away with the nobility. Human nature is the cause. The good will be good, and we must minimize or do away with the bad as we're able." He lifted a hand to me, offering me as proof. "I'm sure you treat your servants at Paxworth well. Better than well, I imagine. You probably feed every urchin who finds his way to the kitchen and let your tenants give you promises in lieu of rent."

I couldn't deny that. Lady Edith and I had done both on occasion. "But bad masters aren't held accountable. No one cares that their servants are overworked or underfed or are fed to beasts on their master's whim."

"A good king encourages his nobles to treat their servants fairly and kindly. And for the most part, they do."

"For the most part?" I repeated. "What do you know of a servant's lot?"

"I know King Leofric treats his servants well. That's why they're loyal to him." Ronan's expression grew solemn and his jaw tight. "Last year when the king's boat sank, several servants risked the icy waters, trying to save the queen and prince. Sadly, those servants died beside their masters. The boat's sinking wasn't an accident, as some have suggested. It was an executed attack by at least one renegade. Perhaps the whole organization."

My face flushed. I hoped in the low light, he couldn't tell. "How do you know?"

"Because the king didn't drown, but a man sitting on shore did."

Meaning the wizard's protection against assassins had been triggered and backlashed against the would-be assassin. The scenario was horrifying to consider—the queen, the prince, and their servants had all died. Pointlessly. Tragically. Was this the attempt that Master Grey and Madam Sutton had casually mentioned when they recruited me for this mission? Had they seen the king's family and servants as expendable?

"And that," Ronan said, "is why I fight the renegades."

Ronan's motives seemed so reasonable when explained his way. Perhaps he even believed the renegades to be unjustified malcontents. He made King Leofric seem like he could march up to the cathedral and take his place with the saints.

But part of King Leofric's wealth—part of this massive castle and all its fineries—came from the sweat and toil of the servants, from those who enjoyed so very few fruits of their labors. I'd been part of that class. I knew one thing for certain: owning servants for twenty years was wrong.

I needed to keep that fact firmly in my mind.

Ronan slipped his hand over mine. "I've ruined the night with talk of politics and assassins. You may duly reprimand me. One of the rules of court we learned at Docendum was to refrain from such topics."

We. As though I went to classes with him instead of learning his lessons by quizzing him.

"You were always a poor follower of rules," I said. "I'll be disappointed if that's changed." Our words were light again. Polite. Probably a bit pained on my part. I wanted to continue speaking of renegades and convince him I was right. I wanted to ask him how he could've been my friend for years and yet care so little about the plight of the serving class.

He glanced behind us at the castle. "I suppose we should head back. I'm to stay near the king later tonight, and if I'm gone too long, people will wonder if I've succumbed to my fellow wizards' fate."

His words reminded me that I could stun Ronan, take his mark, and leave him sleeping in the garden. Before he woke, I might be able to find Mage Zephyr, tell him Ronan wished to speak to him, and lead him away.

If I tried such an option, my identity would be known as soon as Ronan awoke, but Alaric's way would be clear to complete his task. Perhaps dying a martyr wouldn't be the worst fate I could face.

Even as the plan flashed through my mind, I dismissed it. Too risky and in all probability unworkable. Mage Zephyr wasn't likely to believe a message from a stranger or go off alone with me. And besides, I was determined to take Ronan's mark in a way to keep the truth of my villainy from him. This would spare not only my life but his regard. Perhaps I shouldn't have cared about the latter. But again, sentimentality was one of my failings.

We strolled arm in arm back toward the castle. "Will you be

with the king all night?" I asked. "If Gwenyth is in need of more help, will I be able to reach you?"

Ronan shook his head. "The king's safety must be my only priority tonight. Mage Zephyr will be on duty should any pressing needs arise in the castle, but I doubt you'll manage to coax him to step foot out of his chambers. Despite the precaution of having all the other wizards sleep together under guard, I imagine he'll be awake until dawn, sitting in front of his door, wand in hand."

Ronan was right, of course, which only made my task harder.

CHAPTER 25

That night as I climbed the stairs, invisible, I was still unsure how to disarm Mage Zephyr. Even if I managed to dispatch his serpent in complete silence, as soon as I opened his door, he'd shoot a disclosing spell in my direction.

Would it be better if I didn't attempt anything tonight? I could sleep and let the wizards stay up all night. However, if I waited until tomorrow, the wizards would think of more ways to protect themselves. Perhaps the king would add more wizards to his counsel. Time was not my benefactor.

I reached the wizards' hallway. The hanging orbs glowed brighter than normal, making the corridor seem like sunlight had been trapped inside.

Two guards stood on either side of Mage Zephyr's doorway, with the metal snake on the floor between them. The wizard wasn't depending on his magic alone to keep him safe tonight.

Still invisible, I changed to my wolf form and slowly, so as not to make any clicking sound with my claws, padded to the doorway.

I half expected Mage Zephyr to be gone, hidden in some far-off part of the castle. My canine senses told me he was indeed inside, despite all of the incense he was burning to try and mask his scent.

I sniffed the guards. Neither exhibited the sweat of fear. They weren't expecting an attack. Perhaps they felt sure that with Wolfson's arrest, and the other wizards accounted for, the castle was safe again.

I could hit both guards with stunning spells and hope the second man didn't call out when he saw the first toppling over. But even if I was quick enough with my wand to avoid a cry of alarm, the noise the men would make as they crashed to the floor was problematic. I couldn't catch both to ease them soundlessly to the ground.

I turned into my human form, still invisible, and stood contemplating the problem until I had a plan.

Slowly, I crept beside the guard on the left of the door. He looked the most tired of the two. Back in Docendum, the apprentices had at times used a spell that caused sneezing. They thought it hilarious to discomfort the servants, who were charged with being silent, or they used it on the other apprentices in class.

I slipped my wand from my pocket and hit the man with the spell. Once he was sneezing, I pushed him off-balance toward the door. He put out his hand to steady himself and brushed the doorknob.

Immediately, the snake sprang to life, hissing and vicious.

I jumped out of the way and fled down the hall. The guard yelled, "It bit me!"

I glanced over my shoulder. The other guard, sensibly, had drawn his sword and was backing away from the advancing serpent. "Why did you go and touch the door?" he snapped.

"I tripped," the first man sputtered.

I reached the corner of the hallway. From that vantage point, I could duck completely out of sight should the wizard storm out and cast a disclosing spell.

Mage Zephyr flung open his door, wand raised. "What's going on?"

"Call off your beast," the second guard demanded.

The first said, "I stumbled and accidentally touched the knob. Give me the antidote for the snake's venom."

The wizard's reaction would determine whether I could come out of hiding. Was he smart enough to be suspicious or was he only angry?

Mage Zephyr cursed. "Do you think I've time to spend on fools who can't keep from touching my doorknob?"

Bless his cantankerous soul. He was a firm believer in the incompetence of those around him. I slipped from my hiding place at the corner and hurried toward the wizard's door.

With a flourish, Mage Zephyr swooshed his wand at the snake. The creature slithered to its original position and reverted to metal, head raised, ready to strike again.

The wizard grumbled a few more things and gestured for the injured man to limp into his room. Before shutting his door, Mage Zephyr turned to the second guard. "I trust you can manage by yourself and won't do anything foolish until I've healed your companion." He slammed the door without waiting for an answer.

By that time, I was inside.

Mage Zephyr's chambers weren't much different from the other wizards' rooms. The fireplace's purple glow lit the room. A large canopy bed stood in one corner of the room. A cluttered desk squatted in the other. Shelves lined the walls, filled with books, bottles, boxes, and all manners of oddities.

I pressed my back against the door and waited. Mage Zephyr tromped to a shelf and rifled through bottles. "Best guards in the kingdom, my eye."

The injured man slumped on the floor not far from me, holding his thigh and gritting his teeth. He pulled off his boot. "My leg is swelling. Hurry."

The wizard plucked a stout blue bottle from the shelf and shuffled, unhurried, to the guard. "Open your mouth."

The guard did. The wizard poured a bit on the guard's tongue. "Now I need to put some on the wound." Mage Zephyr gestured to the man's leg. "Do I need to instruct you in everything? Move your breeches, man, or you'll die of your own incompetence."

The guard undid his belt and lowered his breeches. Zephyr drizzled a few drops on the two red puncture marks. "There. You'll be right as rain before you can pull your boot back on."

That wouldn't do. I needed him out of commission. I hit the man with a stunning spell. He slumped over and sprawled on the ground beside his boot. Perhaps I was too hasty. If he'd pulled his breeches up first, the view would have been less offensive.

The wizard's jaw dropped, and he hurriedly checked the blue bottle to make certain it was the right potion. I whispered the words of the stunning spell and with a flick of my wand, hit Zephyr. His head snapped back and his eyes shut. The bottle tumbled onto the floor.

I darted forward and grabbed hold of his robe, trying to prevent him from loudly smacking into the floor. He was heavier than he looked and clattered a bit on his way down. Hopefully, nothing that worried the guard outside. For all he knew, the antidote involved things that made thuds and took twenty minutes to perform.

One thing I was certain of, the guard wouldn't come in without knocking. Not with the snake outside. Still, the faster I could do this, the better. I dropped the invisibility enchantment so it wouldn't take any of my energy and set to work changing Zephyr into a tree.

His trunk was thick and bloated with spindly branches and undernourished leaves. Really, I was quite convinced the tree's form reflected the personality of the human. I was glad Ronan had told me I had lovely flowers.

I began chiseling Zephyr's mark off. Next, I would have to face Ronan.

Would the same sort of diversion with the guards work at the king's chambers—a guard injured so that Ronan needed to take the man inside his room?

Probably not. Ronan was smarter than Zephyr. And besides, if one of the guards needed help, Ronan would send someone to fetch Zephyr. I would either have to sneak into Queen Marita's chambers and use the secret tunnel there or wait outside the king's door until morning when Ronan finished his shift. He'd be tired then and more prone to make a mistake.

Once Zephyr's mark was gone, I put my hands over his wound to speed its healing. I'd just returned him to his human form when the door burst open.

No knock, no shout of a guard, no warning. The door swung wildly on its hinges, and Ronan stood framed in the hall lights, wand outstretched.

Ronan.

And there I was, a dark figure leaning over the wizard as though I'd murdered him and the guard, both.

Ronan spoke the words for a killing curse, the one that called down fire. He was done with the incantation before fully seeing me. I knew because when the flames swooshed into the room, illuminating it, I saw the instant his eyes widened in recognition.

Fortunately, I was not so easy to destroy. With a swipe of my wand, I directed the bolts into the chimney. They crashed there with such force that bits of stones crumbled and fell to the ground.

I leapt to my feet. The room darkened again. Zephyr's remaining guard pushed passed Ronan, drawing his sword. "Intruder!" he yelled and lunged at me.

From the end of my wand, I called forth a burst of wind and knocked the guard into Ronan. Both stumbled out of my way, leaving a small area of freedom in the doorway.

The next moment I was the wolf, dashing past the two. As soon as I reached the hallway, I added the invisibility enchantment. The sounds of more guards hurrying toward us echoed in the hall.

Ronan must have hit me with a disclosing spell. As I sprinted to the stairs, the six soldiers rushing up the hall were quite able to see me, or at least see the wolf. A disclosing spell stripped away invisibility but reversing a transformation was more complicated. A wizard needed to be closer and had to keep me in one place for several seconds to perform it.

"Don't kill the wolf!" Ronan yelled from somewhere behind me. "Only capture it!"

I would've liked to think he wished to spare my life, but it was equally likely he wanted to pry the names of my accomplices from me.

One of the soldiers swung his sword at my head, ignoring Ronan's command. I dodged out of the way and repeated the incantation for invisibility. It only lasted until Ronan waved his wand in my direction again, but it gave me a few seconds to plow past the men unhindered.

More soldiers joined their comrades in the hallway. They spotted me easily enough. A man threw himself at me, toppling me to the ground. His elbows jabbed painfully into my stomach. I scrabbled and bit until I escaped his grip. Then I bounded down the hallway, invisible once more.

Judging by the men's shouts and pursuit, Ronan quickly revealed me. This didn't matter. Canines were faster than men. I left them all and sprinted to the staircase, invoking invisibility again. Ronan canceled the spell again. The men had no question that I headed down the stairs and not toward the queen's chambers.

"After him!" one of the guards yelled. They assumed a wizard was a man. But Ronan would tell them soon enough whom they were chasing.

Where could I go? What would I do now that Ronan knew the truth?

The doors on the first floor would be barricaded before I reached them. If I decided to go that way, I'd have to fight past guards. I stayed visible until the moment I reached the entrance to the third floor. By the time Ronan swished his wand again, my direction was uncertain. They couldn't tell if I'd continued down the stairs or fled into one of the third-floor hallways. Ronan would need a minute to be certain which.

I tore down the passageway. The window by the garderobes was my best bet out of the castle.

"Alert the outer wall!" someone shouted.

More problems. I wouldn't be able to crawl over the outer wall unnoticed—although the moat filled with flesh-eating fish was also preventative. And now that Ronan knew who I was, Lady Edith and everyone connected with our party would be questioned, probably branded as traitors. I'd no way to warn them what had happened.

The clamor of feet continued down the stairs and shouts grew more distant. The bulk of the men had gone that way instead of pursuing me on the third floor.

Ronan wouldn't be so easy to lose. Once he didn't easily find me down below, he could transform into a dog and sniff me out. I'd have to be out of a window by then.

The doors to the guests' chambers began popping open. Men dressed in nightshirts and caps peered into the hallway to see what the clamor was about. A fortunate turn of events. These windows were closer. And if Ronan traced my scent here, he'd have to change back into a human in order to open the door and explain the situation to the occupants. Every moment counted.

Once Ronan discovered I'd gone out a window, he'd most likely think I'd transformed into a bird and suppose I escaped the castle that way. He'd change into a bird himself and soar over the grounds searching for some animal in the air. That would give me the time I needed to hide.

I slipped past one of the gaping men and into his chambers. His wife lay in the bed, gripping her covers. I ran straight to the window and transformed back into a woman. I was still invisible, but now had hands to open the shutters. The wife caught sight of the window opening and gasped in shock. I shot her with a stunning spell.

I was ready to shoot her husband as well, but he didn't notice her gasp or the limp end to it. He'd stepped outside to start a conversation with another guest.

I tied my skirts up and went out the window. Blood pounded through my ears, insisting that I flee, that I hurry. I had to force myself to climb down the wall carefully, to find a secure foothold before moving my hands. With every shift of my feet, I repeated the incantation to turn into a bird so I really could soar away. The spell didn't work. It never did.

Soldiers poured onto the castle grounds, swords drawn, their helmet feathers bobbing up and down like jumping candle flames. Men with longbows hurried to the drawbridge and outer wall. The wizards' orbs shone more brightly so that the soldiers could better search.

No sign of Ronan.

When I deemed I was close enough to the ground, I jumped. I'd been optimistic in my estimate of how close I was. The ground met me with a slap that went through my bones and stole my breath. I coaxed air back into my lungs and ran, staggering at first, toward one of the gardens.

Disappearing into the hedge mazes might be dangerous. In fact, any place that made a good hiding spot would be among the first places the soldiers and wizards checked. Sometimes hiding in the open was best.

I fled to a grouping of trees that lined the garden's entrance, stood next to them, and turned into a hawthorn. Visible now. My panting breaths and racing heartbeat were replaced with the silent steadiness of wood. The only movements that went through me were a slight swaying of my branches in the wind—branches with fine, strong leaves, I was comforted to note, in case my assessment that the trees matched our personalities was accurate. Cloaked like this, no scent of human or wolf would betray me.

Archers rushed up the stairs to the outer wall. Soldiers spread out along its base. Minutes plodded by. The marshal and a group of soldiers hurried past with hunting dogs. The animals caught my scent on the castle wall where I'd climbed down, and they shuffled, nose to the earth, over to the garden. A dead end. They circled fruitlessly, unable to trace me.

Just feet away from where I stood, the marshal swore and spat on the dirt. "Probably changed into an owl or a bat, but we'll have to finish inspecting the area anyway."

The group split up, dogs eagerly pulling on their leashes.

After that, only an occasional soldier marched by. None paid any attention to the trees. I'd feared all the wizards would be called to search the grounds, but none appeared. Perhaps Ronan had ordered the wizards to stay where they were, cooped up in a group until he ascertained who among them had helped me learn so much magic.

I would stay here until they had given up hope of finding me. I could wait. As a tree, I felt no hunger or thirst. Eventually, the king's men would have to lower the drawbridge and let people in and out.

My greatest fear was for the safety of the others in my party. I hoped they would be able to sufficiently profess their ignorance of my crimes.

Ronan strode around the castle grounds, wand gripped in his hand. He surveyed the sky, scowling, then scanned the courtyard. For a moment, his gaze landed on me. But only for a moment. He paced toward the garden, looking beyond me into the mass of hedges.

If I'd had a breath, I would have held it.

He won't discover me, I told myself. He had no reason to cast any sort of spell on this copse of trees. And yet he marched in my direction.

I expected him to stalk past me and head into the garden. Instead, he stopped directly in front of me and lifted his wand. "A hawthorn tree. You chose to hide in *that* form? Didn't you consider I'd know every hawthorn tree on the grounds? I've no choice in the matter. I think of you each time I see one."

With a muttered statement and a flick of his wand, I stood before him, human again.

CHAPTER 26

I stared at Ronan, stunned. I wouldn't fight him. Not yet. Not when he could call armed men with one shout. I had to stall while I retrieved my wand from my pocket. My arms fell to my sides. "Do you really think of me when you see hawthorns? If so, I'm surprised you didn't cut them down long ago so they didn't irritate your memory."

His expression was hard and angry. No tones of mercy softened his voice. "I cannot believe it was you, all along." He shook his head, his lips pressed together. "I should've known the truth when witnesses said they'd seen Mage Wolfson's hound. You had reason to implicate him, didn't you? You hate him."

Ronan's eyes were firmly on mine, glaring in indignation—and not watching what my hand was doing. I slid it into my pocket. "Many people hate Wolfson. I assume most of the apprentices who learned his lessons hate him."

"Most of the apprentices didn't ever see his hound. That privilege was reserved for very few."

"How fortunate that I was among the privileged." In one quick motion, I swung my wand toward Ronan and uttered a stunning spell.

As I spoke, he grabbed my arm and jerked my aim upward. The spell shot harmlessly into the sky.

I wrenched my arm, trying to free myself from his grasp. He was too strong, too determined, and not about to let me go. I kicked his leg, an action without much force due to his boots and the constraints of my dress.

When I kicked again, he pushed me to the ground and pointed his wand at me. He uttered the words of transformation —that of a mouse. It took me several seconds to recall the counterspell. By the time I began repeating it, I was falling, shrinking, unable to stop the change from happening. Before the alteration was even complete, he reached down and grabbed me, holding me tight. He loomed like a giant over me and could've easily crushed me with a squeeze of his hand.

He repeated the words of another transformation spell, this one directed at himself—a falcon. I bit his thumb. Drew blood. No release. He didn't even stutter in his incantation.

His fingers grew hard, changing into claws that gripped me just as tightly as his hands had. With a flap of striped wings, he shot into the sky. The ground fell away at a dizzying rate.

My heartbeat thrummed impossibly fast. What was he going to do? He wouldn't kill me. Not before he extracted the names of my accomplices.

Even if I could've thought of a way to change back into a human, I dare not do it now, soaring through the sky, or I'd plunge to my death.

We flew to the top of one of the castle's towers, a dark, unlit place. He sailed over the crenelations and circled the area, slowing. Shapes cluttered the floor near the walls. The place must be used as a storage area.

Ronan landed on the stone floor, the foot that grasped me, held aloft. The next moment, he was human.

I bit him again. He still didn't release me. "Stop it," he hissed. He grasped my tail and let go of my body, leaving me to dangle upside down in the air. Two fingers were all that kept me captive.

He calmly swished his wand in an arc, and a wizards' orb hanging from a post lit up, making the darkness retreat. He turned his wand on me and I fell to the floor in a heap, human again. I'd been holding my wand when he'd transformed me, and it returned in my hand until the impact of my fall jarred it loose.

I reached for it, fingers almost there.

A burst of wind from Ronan's wand knocked it away from me. It clanked and rolled across the floor.

"A knitting needle," he said, his wand still pointed at me. "I'm not sure whether to find that an insult to my profession or a brilliant stroke of subterfuge."

I sat up slowly. Any sudden movement toward my wand would bring forth some sort of retribution.

He stepped closer to me. "No one thinks anything of a woman carrying around knitting needles, do they?"

"And I've also made some very sturdy socks during this trip."

He didn't laugh. "Who taught you magic? Who are you working with?"

I resisted the urge to feel my pocket and reassure myself that the other contents were still there: a matching knitting needle and the length of yarn. The egg-shaped signal sat in my other pocket. Sending it flying into Ronan might cause him to drop his wand, but I didn't dare use it. If I did, Alaric would think the way clear to kill the king and would die trying before I could stop him.

"Who?" Ronan repeated, louder.

"I'm not keen to tell you. Once I do, you'll have no reason not to destroy me."

"Then let's start with a different question. How did you manage to take the rest of the wizards' marks?"

That was a surprise. "You don't know? I thought you

would've figured that out by now." I forced a smile. "If you'll give me my wand, I'll happily show you."

With his wand pointed at my heart, he stared at me, silent and thinking. He did that at Docendum sometimes, ponder some problem for minutes at a time.

I gestured to the sky. "Aren't you afraid I'll transform into a bird and escape?"

"You can't transform into a bird. If you could, you'd have flown away from the castle when you had the chance."

This would've been a perfect time to prove him wrong, but although I said the words of bird transformation in my mind, nothing happened.

"You can transform into a tree though," he said, "which is no easy feat. Not many wizards can manage plant life." He tilted his chin down. "Did you turn them into trees and chisel out their marks?"

"I got the idea from you," I said.

His eyes narrowed. "Who taught you? Who?"

I held up one hand, a signal I was going to stand. Slowly, I did. "Before you decide to march me in front of the king and the other wizards, remember—you're the one who gave me magic. The other mages will undoubtedly take your mark for such a crime, and considering all the trouble I've caused—perhaps slay you as well. However, if you let me take your mark now, I'll spare your life and keep your secret. You'll just be one more victim of the unknown traitor wizard."

Ronan shook his head in undisguised disgust. "Ah Marcella, you've proven Wolfson right. He said friends were a liability, and this is how you used my friendship: To kill wizards and try to assassinate the king."

The words hit me like a slap. I'd blamed Ronan for his disloyalty, and yet spoken from his tongue, my treachery seemed the blacker of the two.

My hands clenched at my sides. "I only took the wizards'

marks. They managed their own deaths without my help. And King Leofric keeps servants bound for twenty years. Did he not suppose his subjects would rather have someone else rule? Don't blame me for what his greed has caused. Blame him for our suffering."

Ronan scoffed, wand unwaveringly pointing at me. "You think killing an innocent man—your monarch—will relieve any suffering? A change of power will fill the servants' bellies? Has it ever occurred to you Lord Clement as a regent might be worse? Heaven knows he hasn't the wit or the sensibilities King Leofric has."

"Perhaps Lord Clement will be better because he'll see what happens to kings who take their subjects' labors for twenty years." My hand slid into my pocket and tightened around the yarn, hiding it in my palm.

"Is that how you justify murder—it will help you terrorize the next monarch?" Ronan gritted his teeth. "Who taught you magic? It has to be someone who's mastered plant transformation. Thanks to your work this week, only a handful of those remain. Flitterwochen? Caltrop? Rattoner? Was it Perigee? Apricus?"

I wouldn't be so easily painted a villain. "Can you speak to me of murder after what you did to the villagers of Colsbury? You didn't care about their innocence, just as you never saw me as a person entitled to rights. I was a servant to you—someone who could be bought and sold."

His mouth opened in disbelief. "You think I actually killed those people?"

"I saw the ash on your cloak."

"As did Wolfson. That was the idea. I killed no one."

"Then what happened to the villagers?"

He coughed, offended. "I had a two-day journey to convince Charles we could make some gold by warning the villagers instead. They agreed that burning the village would be for the best so that Wolfson would think they were dead and wouldn't keep pursuing them. They packed up their belongings, took their animals, and left."

While Ronan spoke, I'd worked a spell into the yarn. I finished the last utterance and tossed it onto his outstretched arm. It coiled around his wrist, wrapping so tightly that he dropped his wand and clawed at the yarn.

Retrieving my wand would take longer than it took him to break the yarn and retrieve his. I dived for his wand, not as a woman but as the black wolf. I would snap it in two if I could, eat the pieces if I had to, then go for my own.

Just as I reached his wand, a massive paw batted my head, knocking me away. The wand skittered across the floor out of reach. Ronan had transformed into a bear.

As animals, neither of us could wield our wands. We didn't dare transform back into humans, though, lest we be torn apart by a beast before we reached our wand.

Well, then. This was how we would decide the matter. I didn't want to hurt him, but he'd left me no choice.

I growled, showing my teeth. The bear stood on its hind legs, lifted powerful paws, and bellowed. His claws could slice through my fur.

I circled him. He turned, preventing me from reaching his back.

I'd have to be faster than he was. I darted toward him. He swiped a paw at me. I dodged backward, narrowly missing the blow. I dashed forward again and sank my teeth into the fur on his leg. Before I could draw blood, he swung me away, flinging me into a wall.

Pain slammed into my back. I hardly took note of it. I scrambled up and rushed at him again. If I gave him any amount of time unchallenged, he would transform into a human and grab his wand. Then I'd be finished.

Even as I charged toward him, I kept track of the position of both our wands. I would do best to push him farther away from his. I lunged for his right arm, his wand arm. With the wolf's massive jaws, if I got a good hold, I could break his bones.

He hit me in the mouth and snapped at my neck. His teeth grazed against my fur but did little damage before I pulled away and dived at him again. This went on for several minutes: the two of us trading blows.

Fighting a bear was easier than fighting Ronan. A bear was dangerous, was a beast to be defeated. And as the wolf, I could give way to my animal instincts and let them protect me.

He charged. I dodged and found myself close to his side. Before he could turn on me again, my teeth dug into his shoulder. I tasted blood. He howled, spun, and slammed me into the parapet.

My head rang and the breath pushed from my lungs. He freed himself from my grip. With a swing of his paw, he sent me flying into a group of barrels. Another flash of pain. The barrel I'd hit toppled into the others and lay tilted like a fainter caught by those behind him.

Get up, I told myself. My limbs were slow to obey. I felt like a marionette whose strings had been cut.

Ronan changed into a human and staggered toward his wand. His robe and shirt were ripped at his shoulder and blood trickled down his skin.

He was moving too slowly—a failing of the human form. I managed to get to my feet and spring at him.

It had been a mistake for him to change into a human, an overconfidence that was common in wizards. He went down under my weight and hit the floor. His head snapped back at the impact and he let out an "Ooof!"

I ought to rip his neck open before he changed into some other beast. His throat was exposed, as vulnerable as a child's.

My life was at stake. The mission could still be successful. I had no other choice.

I plunged at him, mouth open, jaw snapping, but at the last moment, I couldn't bite him. Not Ronan. I couldn't take his life even if it meant losing mine. And certainly, it would mean losing mine. Instead of his skin, my teeth sank into his robe and tunic. When I reared back, they ripped away with the ease of flower petals. His chest was bare, unprotected, still vulnerable.

And it was scarred. Three jagged pink welts ran across his heart. I recognized those scars. I'd seen them often enough. They were my scars. The ones I'd had after Wolfson's beast attacked me.

I don't remember thinking the words to transform into a human, but suddenly I was. It was as though my body knew I could no longer be a wolf. I knelt beside Ronan, touched his scarred chest, and bit back a sob.

He could've easily killed me then, either as a bear or by using some other incantation. I hadn't the power to think of any counter spells—to think of anything but what those scars meant.

Whatever incantation he'd discovered or created, it had required he take the scars onto his own body, and he'd placed them over his heart.

I ran my fingers across the familiar ridges and bumps. "You didn't cure the wound. You took it from me. I searched for that spell—one to cure wounds completely. I never found it."

Ronan put his hand over mine, not to push my hand away, but to hold it, to hold onto me. "Where did you look?" His voice still had an edge. He wanted the name of my accomplice.

Keeping quiet on the matter might preserve my life longer, might provide me with another attempt to escape, but the fight had gone out of me. I couldn't hurt Ronan further, and that meant the mission had failed. I was through with all of it. I was at his mercy.

My gaze went to his left shoulder to see how deeply it was injured. A row of puncture wounds lined each side of his shoulder, small tears that were busy bleeding. Magic would be able to knit them together. I touched one, murmured the healing incantation, and felt the wound disappear underneath my hand. Some of my strength went with it, and I'd already expended quite a bit tonight.

"Marcella, who taught you?"

My fingers, now coated red with blood, moved to the next wound. "When you named wizards who could transform into plants, you left one off the list."

"One who's kept his abilities a secret?"

"Of course not. Has a wizard ever been modest about his power?" I uttered the incantation a second time and winced as some more of my strength vanished with the wound.

Ronan pulled my hand away, keeping it tight in his grasp. "I'll tend to those later. Tell me who the wizard is." He sat up on one elbow, gritting his teeth at the pain the motion caused.

I curled my legs underneath me. "Of course, you must learn the name. Lesson number one of wizardry: A mage must know who his enemies are. Very well, the name you seek is your own. You taught me."

His grip on my hand tightened, and his expression grew hard, as though he thought I was trying to blackmail him. "Don't protect your teacher, Marcella. He could have done this infernal work himself, but instead, he sent you to face danger and die on his behalf. He's a coward. What sort of man treats a woman so?"

"You did."

He cursed and sat up straighter. "I didn't. I taught you three spells for your protection."

"And when you did, you inadvertently gave me the ability to touch and read every magic book in the castle."

Ronan drew in a long breath, then another, his eyes never leaving mine. He was weighing my words. "And you were able to read and memorize that many spells at Docendum before

Wolfson sent you to Carendale?" He clearly didn't believe me. "It takes apprentices years to learn such things with their teachers. You managed to slip in a lot of memorizations after scrubbing the dishes, did you?"

I toyed with letting him think I was a prodigy to rival himself. If the wizards were going to kill me, let them suppose they were executing the greatest genius among them. The knowledge of being bested by a woman, and a lowborn servant at that, would sour in their stomachs.

But I didn't want to lie to Ronan anymore. "You didn't think about the nature of grafts before you grafted part of your magic into me. You'd already given yourself the ability to remember every spell you read. That ability transferred as well."

His eyes widened in shock. He hadn't considered this possibility and was at last understanding. "You remember every spell you read?"

"Better. I remembered all the ones you'd read at Docendum and the ones you'd created too. You were so very knowledgeable and brilliant. I wouldn't know half as much had I been given the expertise of another wizard."

Ronan's face went white. He dropped my hand and swallowed hard, still staring at me.

I didn't know what he would do next and half expected he would summon something horrible to consume me. I had just aptly proved to be his greatest mistake.

He blinked at me. "You…you have my knowledge and my power?"

"I only know the incantations you learned before the graft and the ones I read afterward."

He scrubbed a hand over his face. He was well aware of how much he'd learned in those years and how many new spells he'd cobbled together during that time.

"I don't have all of your power," I continued. "My ability to transform is limited to two things: the wolf and the tree."

Perhaps my impending death had loosened my tongue. I knew the scholar in him would appreciate my theories on the matter. "One form I learned through loving you and the other through hating you—or hating Wolfson. I'm not sure which. But in any regard, perhaps strong emotions are needed for transformation, and I never had any stronger than those."

Ronan lay back down on the floor, dragging more deep breaths between his teeth. He pinched the bridge of his nose and shut his eyes.

I checked his bleeding shoulder. "I'm sorry I hurt you, and I'm sorry I betrayed your trust, but I've been a servant. For many, it's no better than being a slave. How could I not work to further the renegades' cause?"

He let out a grunt of bitterness. "And they were happy enough to use you. They'll promise the servants access to the sun and stars." His eyes flew open and his gaze bore into mine. "Make no mistake about it. The renegade leaders want power, and once they use your sacrifices to seize it, they'll do little to help the plight of the poor."

He sounded so certain I wondered if he'd somehow discovered who the renegade leaders were. "How can you know that?"

"I know because I've studied history. You studied it with me. How can you *not* know? This won't end with King Leofric's death."

The two of us had learned about long-ago uprisings in our country and others. Often they involved some leader who claimed power when succession wasn't clear. Usually, he promised lower taxes and a war upon an enemy country, which he assured people would restore honor and bring a bounty of treasures to the country's coffers. That seldom happened.

But this was different. This uprising was about lessening the bondage of those born or sold into it.

Still, shaking off Ronan's words wasn't easily done. What did I know of the renegade leaders' plans and designs? I didn't know who they were. Master Grey and Madame Sutton had told me King Leofric's death would usher in Lord Clement as a more lenient regent ruler. I'd no reason to suspect they didn't believe it. Alaric and Gwenyth certainly did. They were willing to give their lives for that belief.

The renegade leaders' true aim, however, might be something quite different, some grab for power. And even if it wasn't, the king's death might cause formidable lords and barons to take advantage of the situation and claim they were better suited to act as the crown princess's regents. Or perhaps an invading force would see this time of weakness as an opportunity to invade.

Why had I never considered all the ramifications before? I knew the answer as soon as I asked myself the question. I had wanted to believe the renegades could and would fix the plight of the servants, that they had wise, selfless leaders who'd thought through the implications of the assassination and determined it to be the best course of action.

Under Ronan's scornful logic, I was no longer certain. Ronan was so often right about things. Was he this time? If the situation became worse in Aerador, I'd be complicit not only in King Leofric's death but also in the ensuing chaos and bloodshed.

I sat there, paralyzed by the thought. Then I realized it didn't matter. My mission had failed. The king was safe. I wasn't. I had no idea what Ronan planned to do with me.

My stomach felt as though it was filled with sand. I wilted under his gaze. "Will you turn me over to the king for execution?"

CHAPTER 27

*R*onan placed his hand across the wounds on his shoulder and uttered the incantation of healing. The rest vanished. "How can I turn you over for execution? Your actions, in great measure, are my fault. I sent you away naive, powerful, and angry. I should've known better."

A relieved breath slipped from my lips. I wouldn't have to face death. Although that didn't mean he wouldn't lock me away in a tower.

The effort of performing the healing spell had taken its toll on Ronan. He lay back down and rested on the floor. "I should've known better," he muttered again, "but there is no fool like one in love."

"You loved me then?" I felt an unreasonable brightness at his words.

"I love you still." No tenderness colored his words, only frustration. His eyes went to mine. "I could've destroyed you while we were fighting, but I couldn't bring myself to do it."

"I thought you did a fair job of trying." My back still ached where it had hit the barrels. I was bruised all over. Despite this, I couldn't help but smile. He loved me. Warmth filled me, erasing so many scars that had, though unseen, been over my heart.

"I was trying to dissuade you," he said. "If I'd wanted to kill you, I'd be holding your broken body and murmuring tearful apologies instead of having this conversation."

"You should still give me some tearful apologies. I deserve them."

Back when we lived in Docendum, we sometimes escaped from the castle and picnicked in the woods. After eating, Ronan would lie down on our blanket, stretching out, and I would settle into the crook of his arm and stare up at the sky with him.

The old habit tugged at me. I wanted a few moments to relive those days. I lay next to him, resting my head on his right shoulder, the one not injured in our fight, in case it was still tender.

Perhaps Ronan also remembered those days. He pulled me closer so that I was pressed up against his side. "I *am* sorry, Marcella. I thought of you every day. I even flew to Carendale twice to check on you."

I turned to gape at him. "Why didn't you speak to me?"

"I knew you hated me. Besides, I saw you with Alaric, walking or huddled together, laughing as thick as thieves. Which I realize now was an apt description of your activities." Ronan's hand curved around mine possessively. "I thought you'd revised your goals for a nobleman's son. I wanted happiness for you, and you seemed to have found it, but I couldn't visit again. It was too painful to see you in love with another man."

I'd asked for tearful confessions from him, but I was the one whose eyes filled. Ronan had come to Carendale to see me. He'd cared enough to do that. And he'd stopped visiting for the same reason. My heart broke for the waste of it. Things might have been different if he'd bothered to speak to me. "There's never been anyone for me but you, Ronan. Granted, that was partially because I never trusted anyone after you, but it's also because I never wanted anyone else."

Ronan brought my hand to his lips and kissed my knuckles. "I've never stopped loving you and will never love another. Of course, that's partially because what Mage Wolfson said is true: a wizard cannot afford attachments. Look how miserably I've failed at my duty in protecting the king."

"I feel you've been rather successful on that front." I snuggled closer into his side. "How did you know Alaric's name?"

"You didn't think I would learn my rival's name? I notice you retained him when you moved to Paxworth. You're certain you never wanted anyone but me?"

"He's a friend."

"I see."

I wasn't sure what Ronan thought he saw and didn't want to discuss Alaric further or why he'd come to Valistowe with me. "How do you know I was in Mage Zephyr's chamber?"

"I heard a commotion from his guards, and knowing Zephyr to be a target, I went to the hallway to see if a problem had arisen. The remaining guard told me his companion had been bitten by the snake and Zephyr was giving him the antidote. Later, I went back to check on the situation again. When I found only one guard at the door, I knew something was wrong. Giving the antidote doesn't take long."

And I had thought it would be difficult to draw Ronan from the king's room. A commotion outside was all it took. Foolish of him to put himself at risk that way, rushing into what might have been a trap. "I should've known you'd catch me eventually. You're the king's most formidable wizard."

"Currently, I'm the king's only wizard." Saying the words seemed to remind him of his duties. He pulled himself to a sitting position, bringing me along with him. "I need to return and guard him until other wizards can be appointed."

"Guard against what?" I asked. "You've a firm hand on his attacker."

"True. Although, you aren't his only enemy. Still, I suppose the soldiers outside his room and his brother-in-law standing guard inside are sufficient to keep him safe tonight." Ronan cocked his head at me. "Were you the one chosen to assassinate him? How did you plan to do it?"

I flushed and didn't answer. Ronan had said he wouldn't turn me over to the king. He'd made no such guarantee for Gwenyth or Alaric.

Ronan shook his head, answering the question for me. "You weren't the assassin. Such things aren't in your nature. One of the others must have been tasked with it. Alaric, I imagine."

"I've done quite a few things that were not in my nature since I left Docendum. Alaric isn't an assassin." This was true. He hadn't committed that crime yet.

Ronan rolled his eyes at my protest. "When you worked in the kitchen, you couldn't even pluck a chicken, let alone break its neck. No one who knows you would trust you to carry through with a murder. You don't want to implicate Alaric. I suppose that doesn't surprise me." The way Ronan said Alaric's name implied he would happily throw him in a dungeon.

I wrapped my arms around my knees, trembling with worry. Another punishment had just occurred to me. Ronan would take my wizarding mark, and I was loath to lose it. Magic had become a part of me. "Let me and my party go unharmed, and I'll promise not to hurt the king or take the mark of another wizard."

I thought of Lady Edith and Joanne, unaware of any of this, Gwenyth recovering from her burns, and Alaric who'd believed in me even though I'd failed him in more than one regard. "Before I leave, I'll use my magic to do something helpful for the king." I was reaching for anything to bargain with. "I'm very adept at making orchards grow. Or I could fix roads or sharpen plows." Most wizards hated doing these sorts of tasks because they considered the work beneath them.

Ronan didn't speak. His gaze was firmly on my eyes, his eyebrows furrowed. Whatever he was thinking about, it wasn't fixing roads.

I hugged my knees tighter. "I didn't kill any of the king's wizards...at least not on purpose." It was perhaps a weak argument since three had still died. "If I'd taken Zephyr's mark and left him as a tree, I would've escaped before you found me, but I was trying to preserve his life. The three that died wouldn't have done so if they hadn't been bent on bloodthirsty revenge and using dark magic." I swallowed. Ronan's expression hadn't changed. "Now the king can choose more worthy wizards—assuming that such exist—and you'll be the senior wizard in his council. When one looks at it that way, the king and you are both better off for my visit."

Ronan's silence was unbearable. I knew he was weighing all the options. A judge, whose verdict was still uncertain.

"Please let us go," I begged, "or at least let the others go. Only I have cause to be punished. Lady Edith has no idea what my aim in coming here was or even that I have magic."

Finally, he said, "If I let you go, will I ever see you again?"

That was what he was concerned about? "Do you want to see me again?" He'd admitted he'd loved me, but even back at Docendum when he'd loved me, he'd made no plans for a future together. Ronan's duty was to the king, the man I'd tried to help assassinate.

"Haven't I made my intentions clear enough?" He leaned over, put his hand around my back, and pulled me closer. His free hand brushed across my cheek, then threaded through the hair at my neck. His lips came down on mine. A light kiss that grew deeper and set my pulse racing.

After all I'd done, he still wanted to kiss me? I could only wonder at him. What did this kiss mean? What sort of future could he possibly imagine for us? Then my mind became otherwise preoccupied with kissing him. One of my hands tangled into his silky hair. The other found the scars that striped his chest and stayed firmly pressed there. Each beat of his heart was a comforting thrum. He loved me still.

I leaned into his touch, lulled by the security of it, the familiarity. And yet this wasn't familiar. Back at Docendum, Ronan had never let our kisses go on for so long. He'd always showed restraint and put up boundaries. Now his lips were grazing along my neck, and he was holding me as though he had no intention of ever letting me go.

And I didn't want him to let me go. I sighed because I knew it couldn't continue forever. The world awaited us.

At the sound of my sigh, he pulled away from me, checking my expression. "I wouldn't force you to stay anywhere you didn't wish. You can return to Paxworth if that's your desire. You, Lady Edith, and your lady's maids, although I suspect yours didn't innocently mistake Mage Saxeus' room."

"You would let me go free?" That was a boon. I dared not ask about my magic yet.

"I would, but I'm asking you to stay. I don't want to lose you a second time."

"Stay where?" I gestured to the courtyard. "Didn't you tell the guards what I've done? Aren't they searching for me? I can't stay."

He shook his head. "I didn't tell them I recognized the wizard. As you pointed out, to claim you have magic implicates me. Wolfson knows of our association and would happily take revenge on me."

Ronan rubbed the back of his neck, still thinking. "I'll inform the other mages that a foreign wizard snuck onto the grounds undetected, carried out the attack on Zephyr, and was chased off. I followed him, we fought, and I destroyed him—alas, never uncovering his identity. The wizards will be so happy to be exonerated from suspicion they won't ask too many questions."

Ronan took my hand in his. "You can remain at court. Or if you'd rather, I'll buy you a home in the village and visit when I'm able." His eyes watched mine with weighted seriousness. "Whether you stay or go, you must promise to have nothing else to do with the renegades. No contact of any kind. Anything less will revoke not only your freedom but that of your entire party."

A forceful threat. One I had little leverage to argue with, and yet my heart twisted at the thought of walking away from the plight of those in servitude.

Lie, a voice in my head told me. Ronan was willing to believe me. Having gained his trust, however, I couldn't bring myself to do something to dash it. Sooner or later, he'd put me to the test. When that test came, I didn't want to fail it.

My fingers curled around his. "You might be right about the renegade leaders or you might be wrong. I've no way to know their true motives. My loyalty isn't to them but to those trapped in service for twenty years. If I'm to cut all associations with the renegades, then I ask you to promise to use your position as the king's advisor to influence him to change his laws in their favor."

Ronan's eyebrows quirked up. My request had been a bold one, especially given my lack of leverage. "The king doesn't consult wizards about laws," he said. "He has other advisors for that."

"Advise him anyway. Many of the servants are so weary of their burdens, they're willing to take up arms against his troops." I squeezed Ronan's hand, pleading. "The man who risked Wolfson's wrath to save villagers cares for the innocent. The man who fell in love with a kitchen girl must see that servants ought to have rights. You aren't an ordinary wizard. You're capable of anything."

He smiled, but it was a sad smile. "You always thought me so. There is much I'm incapable of. However, I'll give you my word that I'll try." He smiled again, and this time there was more warmth in his expression. "That is one of the reasons I love you. You always believed me to be better than I was, and so I became better in order not to disappoint you."

He would try to help the servants. It was enough. He was right about my optimism in his abilities because I had no doubt he would find a way. I threw my arms around him, nearly knocking him to the ground. "Thank you, Ronan. I'm so glad I didn't kill you!"

* * *

WE SPENT several more minutes on the tower. Mostly I was showing him with a succession of kisses how glad I was I hadn't killed him. He in turn was busy showing me the many benefits of staying with him at court. He was quite convincing.

At last, he pulled away from me regretfully. "I need to return to the king and report the traitor wizard's destruction. If I don't come soon, King Leofric will fear something ill has befallen me." His eyes ran over me. "And you need to return to your room and burn your clothes lest anyone see them and wonder what you were doing in them." He stood and helped me up.

My dress was in a horrible state. My sleeve and a piece near the middle were ripped. The front was soiled from where I'd brushed up against the castle wall while I climbed down. I wiped away bits of moss. Were those blood splatters as well?

Ronan looked down at his tunic and robe, torn so that they hung loose from his chest. Not a fitting way to present himself to the king. He took the sides of his tunic, held them together, and said a mending incantation, then did the same with his robe. Mending spells were unreliable. The robe was repaired in a haphazard manner which made it clear he'd been in some sort of a brawl. I didn't bother trying to fix my tears. He was right. I'd have to burn these clothes.

"How do we get down from this tower?" I asked.

"The trap door is underneath those." He pointed to the rows of large, heavy barrels. "This is the wizards' tower. We don't make it easy to access." He strolled off in the opposite direction, thinking out loud. "I'll tell King Leofric the foreign wizard was probably part of a plot to keep the king's marriage and the subsequent union with Odeway from progressing."

I'd have to turn invisible as soon as we left the tower. Fortunately, the castle guards would open the doors for Ronan. I could slip in at the same time.

I was so engrossed debating what to tell the others about this night that I forgot about my wand until Ronan bent and picked up his. I turned to where mine had fallen. The darkness and the irregular pattern of stone obscured any sight of my knitting needle, but as the wolf, I'd known right where it lay. I scanned that area, taking no notice of the floor by my feet until I stepped on an object. A crack sounded. I stumbled. Two dozen fireflies twirled up from the ground and zipped over the crenelations toward the courtyard.

The egg must have fallen from my pocket. I'd accidentally set the thing off—the signal that the way was clear to kill the king.

I could see the next events unroll in horrible clarity. Alaric wouldn't question my message. He'd go to Leofric's chamber with a weapon, but instead of harming the king, Alaric would inflict the fatal wound on himself.

I'd no way to tell him the message was a mistake. I'd inadvertently lured Alaric to his death.

Ronan looked across the tower where the bugs disappeared. "What was that?"

Even then, I hated to implicate Alaric, but I'd no choice. I needed Ronan's help. We had to find and stop Alaric.

I rushed toward Ronan and took hold of his hand. "Promise me you'll help me save Alaric."

"What?"

My words came out in a panicked tumble. "I accidentally stepped on the signal. That was the sign that the wizards' protection was gone. Now Alaric will try to slay the king and will be slain in his place."

I was afraid Ronan wouldn't find this news nearly as upsetting as I did and was anticipating he'd tilt his head and say, "Alaric? You mean the one you just swore wasn't an assassin?"

Instead of saying those words, Ronan cursed. "Where is he now? In the stables?"

I searched the floor for my wand but still didn't see it. "Probably. He may have already left. He's got a camouflage cloak so he'll be moving slowly. We need to find him."

A swish of Ronan's wand illuminated the area where my wand lay. I hurried to it and picked it up.

Ronan raked his hand through his hair. "You can't go hunting about the courtyard for him. A noblewoman in a torn, dirty gown roaming around in the middle of the night is bound to draw the wrong sort of attention."

"That's why I need your help." I wasn't quite thinking clearly. My mind was too busy calculating how long I had left until Alaric lay dead somewhere. "He'll use one of the secret entrances to the king's chamber. Do you know them? Which one is closest to the stables? You can go there. I'll head to the stables. Perhaps I can intercept him and explain."

"A noblewoman in a torn and dirty dress going to the stables in the middle of the night will also draw attention."

I lifted my hands in frustration. "While we stand here arguing, Alaric is heading toward the castle."

"Very well." Ronan flicked his wand.

I felt myself shrinking, changing, falling. My fingernails curled into black claws surrounded by fur. I was a mouse again.

I squeaked indignantly. I'd definitely not requested this. Did Ronan mean to keep me a prisoner somewhere while he took care of Alaric? After all, Ronan had never said he would help Alaric.

I turned to plead with Ronan.

He'd vanished.

CHAPTER 28

A falcon plucked me up in his claws. With a flap of his wings, we flew up and over the tower's crenelations. Wherever he was taking me, he wanted to go speedily there. His talons pinched the fur at my side, perhaps doing more damage to my gown. I hoped when he changed me back I would still be decent.

We swooped over the courtyard high above its trees and gardens. The wizards' orbs seemed like small glowing apples. He glided toward a third-floor garderobe window, dived through it, and just when I feared we would smack into a wall, he changed directions and winged down the hallway. He stopped short of the stairs, landed, and released me.

I sat on the floor, whiskers twitching, while he transformed back into a human. He swished his wand at me, and legs akimbo, I returned to my natural state.

He held his hand out to help me up. "Become invisible and follow me."

I winked out of sight. "Where are we going?"

"To the king's chamber." He headed past guards posted at the bottom of the stairs and took the steps two at a time, nearly running. "We don't know which passageway Alaric is taking," he whispered, supposing me close enough to hear. I was, but just barely keeping up with him. "However, we know where he'll end up. The passageways within the courtyard all converge on the same entrance. You can stand there to stop him, but first I'll have to speak to the king and explain the situation. Remain silent until I call upon you. Lord Clement is in the room with King Leofric and will need to be sent away before you reveal yourself."

I wanted to know how Ronan planned to explain the situation to King Leofric in a way that wouldn't make him send guards to apprehend Alaric or, for that matter, me. I couldn't ask. By that point, we were passing the guards posted at the top of the stairs.

The soldiers nodded at Ronan and didn't ask why he was in such a hurry. I trailed after him as closely as I could.

When he got to the king's chamber, the guards there stepped away to allow Ronan to pass. Ronan waved his wand at the door, most likely canceling a magical protection he'd put in place, and opened the door.

He paused once the door was open and turned to speak to the guards—allowing me to slip inside before him. "Be on the alert for a man with a camouflage cloak sneaking about in the hallway. If you find him, do not kill him. I want to question anyone who's acting in a suspicious manner."

"Yes, my lord," they said in unison.

The king's receiving room had a high arched ceiling painted white with red stars. So high in fact, that even the huge stone fireplace on the back wall appeared small in comparison.

King Leofric swept into the chamber from an adjoining room followed by Queen Marita and Lord Clement. The latter had his sword drawn and was fully dressed. The king and queen wore finely embroidered robes over their night clothes.

King Leofric strode toward Ronan, arms outstretched. I

didn't know what he meant by this gesture and was alarmed until the king embraced Ronan—embraced him. I would've been less surprised if the king had slapped him.

"You're safe and well?" King Leofric's gaze went to Ronan's neck, reassuring himself that the wizarding mark was still there.

Queen Marita put her hands to her chest in relief. Lord Clement, unnoticed by anyone but myself, looked less happy to see Ronan, safe and still marked.

Curious.

"I fought the attacking wizard," Ronan said. "He was a mage not from this country. I wish I could've brought you more answers, but his destruction was so complete that not even a body is left. I can give you no information about him."

Lord Clement sheathed his sword. "We know what his intentions were. He meant to destroy the king's wizards so he could kill Leofric."

"True," Ronan said. "That plan is quite spoiled, but I'm afraid, Your Majesty, you're not out of danger yet. An assassin is on the loose, one aware of the inner workings of the castle."

Why was Ronan telling the king about Alaric? He knew I wanted to stop Alaric, not have the king's men hunt him.

The king glanced around the room. His eyes were tired and worried. "How do you know of this assassin?"

"The mage revealed as much before his death." Ronan strode to the king's desk, picked up a pen and parchment, and began scrawling something. "We need to join another wizard to the circle immediately, tonight. I suggest Lord Clement take the queen back to her chamber where she'll be safe. Then he must go waken Mage Apricus or Mage Perigee—if King Leofric accepts my recommendations for the council—and bring one straightway to your chambers."

Lord Clement folded his arms across his wide chest. "Surely, the need isn't so urgent as to make a hasty selection in the middle of the night. And which of the mages would take a place on the wizarding council when three are now dead and two stripped of their power? Each night another falls." His eyes narrowed on Ronan. "You say there's no corpse of the defeated wizard. Are you sure you destroyed him?"

"Quite." Ronan's gaze left the parchment and went to the king. "Send your brother-in-law to the wizards at once. You're in grave danger until we have another in the circle."

Queen Marita wrung her hands and turned to her husband. "Why are you in danger? I thought you were protected as long as one wizard in the circle remains." She gestured to Ronan. "This one remains."

The king took her arm in a soothing gesture. "We've told those who know of the reflecting spell that it works with even one wizard remaining, but it isn't so. Two are needed for it to be effective. With Mage Zephyr gone, I'm vulnerable."

Lord Clement's jaw dropped open, then quickly snapped shut. Queen Marita gulped and scanned the room as though searching for an assailant. "Yes then, you must send for another wizard at once."

"I will," King Leofric said, still calming his wife. "Although whether one will accept is another matter. But no need to worry. I've soldiers about and a powerful mage here with me. An assassin would have a difficult time reaching me. Besides, the assassin doesn't know that one wizard isn't enough to keep the reflecting spell intact. No one does except the wizards who were on the council and me."

"And now," Ronan said tightly, "Lord Clement and the queen know as well." He wasn't happy about this revelation, perhaps because I was listening.

I was invisible, armed with magic, and standing before King Leofric. If I was willing to die for the aim of the mission, I could take King Leofric's life then and there.

Part of me, some foolish part that pictured a glorious martyr's death, urged me to do just that.

That part was perhaps more easily snuffed than it should've been. Ronan's words had an effect on me. Looking at King Leofric and Lord Clement together, I couldn't say with any certainty that Lord Clement would be a better ruler or that Leofric's death wouldn't throw the country into a chaos that made everything worse.

And besides, I'd grown so happy at the thought of being with Ronan, of finally having my love for him returned, I found myself unwilling to die for a cause. I wanted a future.

Overall, I was a very bad revolutionary.

Ronan stopped writing for long enough to wave a hand in Lord Clement's direction. "Hurry. Take the queen to her room and bring Mage Apricus or Mage Perigee. Whichever will come."

King Leofric straightened. "Does the king not decide which wizards join his council? I never officially decided on your recommendations."

Ronan let out a patient breath. "Of course, Your Majesty. Choose whomever you think is worthy of your trust." He emphasized the word trust as though it was a subject they'd talked about before.

"Fine," King Leofric said, grudgingly accepting Ronan's point. "I'll trust your judgment. Bring Mage Apricus or Mage Perigee. If neither will come, ask for Mage Furtivis or Mage Caltrop. I suppose we'll see which of our choices are the bravest and most loyal."

Lord Clement gave a brief nod. "I'll go at once." He held his arm out to Queen Marita. She took it, sniffling, and the two walked to a tapestry on the back wall. He tugged it aside, revealing what looked like a large wooden panel. He twisted a piece of wood to unlock it and pushed open a door. The two went through and the tapestry swung back across the wall.

Ronan put down his pen and turned to the king. "I've

another candidate," he said in a hushed tone. "The perfect candidate because no one knows of this mage's existence."

I froze where I stood. He was speaking of me.

"This week," Ronan went on, "a formidable wizard disarmed your circle. To make that harder to happen again, one of the wizards on the council should be a secret. Doing so will give you an extra layer of protection."

He wanted me to be part of King Leofric's circle of protection? Had I understood him correctly? What exactly would that entail?

The king shook his head. "Do you mean a mage from another land? I'd not trust a foreigner. Besides, once a new mage takes residence at court and his mark turns red, everyone will know he's part of my council."

"Not a foreigner, sire," Ronan spoke quickly. "This is someone no one would suspect because the mage's mark isn't on the neck, and therefore not visible—"

"Not visible?" King Leofric interrupted. "I've never heard of such a thing."

"Exactly my point," Ronan said.

My hands went to my throat. I didn't know if I wanted to be on the king's council. I'd no idea what duties the position required. Ronan really should have discussed it with me before offering me up.

Ronan placed his hands behind his back. "This mage is powerful, knowledgeable, and even more important, ethical and charitable. Qualities, as you know, that can be difficult to find among wizards but should be found in your councilors."

Ethical and charitable, Ronan thought me to be so. And at that moment, I wanted to live up to his description. Maybe being on the king's council wouldn't be such a bad thing. I'd have access to all of their magic books and any items I needed for spells. After all, I'd be expected to practice. I felt my heart lifting at the idea. Instead of having my magic taken from me, Ronan was offering to expand it. No wonder he didn't ask my opinion on the matter. He knew the lure that learning held for me.

King Leofric's eyebrows knit together. "And why has this mage kept himself a secret? Why didn't he go to Docendum to learn with the other apprentices? In fact, how does he know the working of any spells if he hasn't learned from another mage?"

"All of those questions have answers, Your Majesty, but I suggest you agree to put this mage on your council before I answer them. I expect an assassin to make an attempt on your life shortly. I would've already taken you through the passageways to another location, but I'm afraid we'd run into him there. I would advise we leave by the front and retire to my chambers, but I may be wrong about the assassin's route. If he can't access the passageways, he'll wait in the hallway for you to emerge.

"Our best bet is to join this mage to the circle at once. The mage came in with me when I entered your room and is willing to join the council provided that you promise to lower the number of years required to pay off the servants' price."

Ronan was brilliant. If the king agreed, we would achieve our aim without any bloodshed. Perhaps I was too hopeful and too reckless. "Abolish it," I whispered to Ronan.

"I meant abolish it," Ronan said.

King Leofric's head swiveled one way and the other, searching. "Did he just say something? I heard a noise."

"Abolish the servants' price," Ronan repeated. "All people in the land will still be subject to taxes, but not indentured servitude."

"Why would a wizard make such a demand?" the king sputtered.

"The mage is not only ethical," Ronan said, "but also has quite strong feelings about the struggles of the servant class."

I clasped my hands together. Alaric and Gwenyth would be thrilled at this outcome; all the renegades would be. The king just needed to agree so I could make myself visible. That way when Alaric came, I could tell him not to act.

"Abolish it?" the king repeated, no less pleased. "It's one thing to agree to such a thing for my own servants. But the nobles would revolt if I required the same."

Ronan spread his hands out like he was showing something to the king. "You can fear a revolt from the nobles or a revolt from the servants. Many of them are ready to take up weapons to fight for their freedom. Besides, fewer servants paying off their debts to their masters means more free villagers who earn wages and pay taxes to the king. More wealth for you and less for the nobles. That will result in more power for you."

Ronan would, of course, point out these benefits, issues I hadn't even considered.

King Leofric rubbed his temple. "If I issued such a decree, some of my barons would take up arms against me."

"An insurrection would be justification for you to defeat them and take their lands. The result will also be more wealth and power for you."

"If I win."

I couldn't stay silent any longer. "You'll win because the people will support you. If you do away with the servants' price, they'll fight for you."

The king whirled at the sound of my voice. "Who is that?"

Ronan glared in my direction. Perhaps I should've remained quiet.

The king stepped nearer, eyes squinting to try and catch sight of me. "That was a woman's voice. A *woman* is in here."

Ronan nodded, unruffled. "I told you no one will suspect this mage belongs to your circle. You must decide whether to agree to her terms. An assassin is coming and the other wizards might not accept your invitation."

King Leofric straightened, turning toward me again. "I'll lower it to seven years. The same as Marseden."

He was going to haggle like a fishwife when his life was at stake? "Be better than Marseden. Abolish it."

"Six years," he said.

"You haven't the time to bargain," I said.

He folded his arms and rocked back on his heels. "Once Clement comes back with a mage, you'll have lost the leverage of expediency."

I snorted. "You've such faith in wizards who are, by nature, utterly self-interested."

The king glanced back at Ronan. Ronan shrugged. "Her experience with mages has not led her to believe well of them, and," he shot me a warning look, "she can be unduly scornful of those she believes—unjustly at times—to be unprincipled. It's a failing she'll contain while in your employ. At court, she'll be nothing but polite."

Fine. I shouldn't have snorted while talking to the king or said the whole lot of his wizards were completely self-interested. And King Leofric was right that if Clement convinced another mage to come, I'd have little bargaining power. Still, I pressed my point. "If you abolish the servants' price, the people will love and remember you. As Mage Warison pointed out, you'll have no loss of wealth or power."

King Leofric grumbled and contemplated the matter for what seemed a long time. "Very well. It is settled. I'll have a secret mage on the council. Show yourself."

I uttered the counter incantation and stood before the king. His gaze ran over me with alarm, taking in my clothing.

"She helped me fight the wizard," Ronan said by way of explanation, "and didn't have time to make herself presentable."

The king's eyes continued to scrutinize me. "Lady Edith of Paxworth's niece. I suppose that would explain your affinity with the servants. There's talk around court that Edith plucked you from that class."

I wasn't sure if he expected me to deny it. I nodded, chin raised.

Ronan picked up the paper from the king's desk and brought it over to me. "This is the spell. Read it."

While I did, Ronan took my arm and towed me toward the window. "We must circle the king as we speak the incantation. Draw the energy from the moonlight, the fire, and yourself."

Three at once. Complicated but doable. "And afterward, I'll look for the assassin?" I asked Ronan. Performing the spell would put Alaric in danger again. I had to remind myself that the courtyard was full of soldiers. Alaric would have to move slowly to get by them to a tunnel entrance.

"Yes," Ronan agreed.

The king followed us. "If the spell is successful, you'll have no need to hunt for assassins. Let their works be their judgment."

I couldn't very well explain that I wanted to save the assassin.

Ronan went behind the king and held his hands out to me. "The circle must remain unbroken as the incantation is spoken."

I slipped the paper into my pocket, an act which caused the king to frown. "Shouldn't that be somewhere you can read?"

"I've already memorized it," I said.

"She has," Ronan assured him. "I told you she was worthy of the position."

The king relented with clear trepidation and let Ronan and I join hands.

While we recited the incantation, I tugged at the energy of the moon and fire—so heavily on the fire at first—that it nearly snuffed out. Standing in the dark wouldn't do. I reached for more moonlight, pulling it like an unspooling ribbon. The energy I still lacked filled in from my core. It was still such a great amount that its loss left me dizzy and weak. I feared the incantation would completely drain me and I would faint.

Collapsing wouldn't be an auspicious beginning as a royal mage and might make the king doubt I was as worthy as Ronan professed.

We uttered the last words and the mark on my chest burned as though a flame had touched it. Ronan released my hands and stepped away from the king. I moved more slowly, testing each step before I put my weight into it. My strength would take a few minutes to return.

"Did it work?" the king asked. "Where is her mark? We need to check."

My hands flew to my bodice. King or no, I wasn't about to let him check.

"I'm sure the incantation was successful," Ronan said. "We performed it flawlessly."

The king grunted, unmollified. "What if women can't be a part of the reflecting spell? We'd best see her mark to be certain it's changed to red."

Ronan took a protective step toward me. "It would be improper to look."

"I'll examine it," I said, "as soon as I have the privacy to do so." Almost without pause, I added, "I'll go into the secret passageway and check."

I didn't need to worry about running into Lord Clement there. If he returned with a mage, he would bring him through the main door. I was eager for any excuse to go to the passageway where I could intercept Alaric. Although hopefully, he wouldn't find me while I was undressing to see if my mark was now as reddened as it felt.

King Leofric dismissed my suggestion with a wave of his hand. "The passages are dimly lit. Just undress by the fire, and Mage Warison and I will look elsewhere until you finish." He turned his back to me, already assuming I would comply.

My gaze went to Ronan, silently asking for help.

"Check quickly." Ronan turned his back as well. "Then King

Leofric and I can go tell the mages that the traitor wizard is dead and their magic is safe."

I stifled a groan. Every moment I delayed finding Alaric put him in danger. I worked at my lacings, which fortunately were in the front of this gown. "Have you any idea how long it takes for a woman to undress?"

"No," Ronan said, "but I can help if you like."

Such gallantry.

The king turned his head to give Ronan a reproving look.

"I'm only thinking of your life, sire," Ronan said.

I glanced at the wall with the passageway. And my heart stopped. The edge of the tapestry had been pushed away from the doorway to allow a large bow and arrow to protrude. And the bow had already been drawn back.

Alaric.

"No!" I screamed, hoping he would recognize my voice.

I was still screaming when the arrow sliced across the room and struck deep into the king's back. He stumbled forward at the impact. Ronan whirled, wand raised to strike at the intruder.

The tapestry swished back over the door. Alaric must be retreating.

King Leofric straightened and the arrow spit out of his back. No blood darkened his clothing. Not even the hole remained in his robe. When he turned, his expression was unmarred of any pain. "No need to check your mark after all," he said. "The incantation worked."

I'd just caused Alaric's death. No, perhaps not his death. Alaric might not have delivered a fatal wound. Perhaps the injury was one that magic could cure. Alaric might yet get away.

I ran to the tapestry, yanked it away from the wall, and pushed open the door. The passageway was dim and dank, filled with shadows. I rushed inside anyway and nearly ran into a man who stood, one hand on the wall, not far away.

I blinked, letting my eyes adjust to the light.

He wasn't Alaric.

Lord Clement stared at me, eyes bulging in anger. He placed a heavy hand on my shoulder, blocking my way forward. He must have come back without a mage and was now wondering who I was and why I was tearing into the passageway.

I didn't have time to think of an excuse. I needed to dart around him to find Alaric.

The next moment, I realized Lord Clement wasn't trying to block my way. He'd put his hand on my shoulder to steady himself. His other hand went to his back, the same spot where King Leofric was shot. When he lifted his hand, blood darkened it.

I hadn't heard Ronan enter the passageway but he was at my side, pulling the man away from me. "You tried to kill your brother-in-law?" It was more of an exclamation of disgust than a question. Ronan shoved Lord Clement toward the door.

He stumbled forward and fell into King Leofric's chamber where he lay sprawled on the floor, his face pinched with pain.

"Here is the assassin," Ronan called.

Lord Clement moaned and flopped over on his back as though to hide the wound. His hand, however, still smeared with blood, carried the evidence. I watched him, unable to tear my gaze away. I feared that if I did, Lord Clement would somehow transform into Alaric.

King Leofric strode over to his brother-in-law, gaping. "You?" he asked, as if there was some way the man could deny involvement. "Why?"

Lord Clement only grimaced in response. Ronan knelt by him, turned him onto his stomach, and ripped through his tunic to inspect the wound. Skin could be knitted with magic, and bones set, but pierced organs were a different matter. His life depended on what the arrow had damaged.

King Leofric shook his head, bewildered. "You stayed in my

chambers to guard me and then came back to take my life like a thief?"

A steady stream of blood ran from the wound, making it impossible to see the extent of the damage. Ronan flicked his wand at the man's back to slow the flow and mopped at the blood with Clement's tunic. "He stayed in your chambers so he'd be among the first to know if I'd fallen victim to the traitor wizard. When he discovered you were vulnerable, instead of going to fetch a mage, he went for a bow and arrow. I'd already said an assassin was about. Clement wanted to make sure he did his work before you were able to find another wizard willing to join the council. Clement would then rule Aerador as the regent king until Princess Alfreda was of age—if he ever let her come of age."

Clement didn't deny or confirm the accusation, just took shallow, labored breaths.

King Leofric's hands clenched and unclenched at his side. The paleness of shock gave way to the red flush of anger. "You thought to take my kingdom by killing me? You whom I invited into my home—whom I entrusted with my daughter?" His voice dropped to a dangerous hiss. "Did my sister know of this?"

Lord Clement's eyes finally focused on King Leofric. "Of course not," he rasped out. "She's a woman incapable of such force." It was unclear whether he said the words as a compliment or indictment. He shut his eyes and coughed. His coughing turned to convulsing. Tremors that didn't cease. Blood leaked from his mouth and at last, he went still.

Ronan put his hand on the man's chest to check for breathing. He shook his head. "The damage was too extensive. Magic couldn't save him."

King Leofric seemed hardly to hear Ronan. "This was the assassin you warned me of? You knew of Clement's intentions?"

Ronan stood, wiping his hands on his robes. "I'd no notion. I worried that the attack would come from an outside enemy."

Ronan's eyes darted to the tapestry. He'd remembered Alaric was still unaccounted for. "In fact, I fear another attack could still come. I suggest leaving Marcella here to guard your room while we wake the marshal and your war advisors. We've no idea how the king of Marseden will react to the news of his grandson's death."

"A woman as a guard?" Leofric asked.

"A woman with magic," Ronan emphasized. "You saw how fearlessly she pursued Clement. She reached the passageway ahead of either of us."

King Leofric lowered his voice. "She was screaming, 'No!' the entire time."

Had I? I hadn't been aware of it.

Ronan swept his hand in my direction. "That's part of her fierce determination to protect you—the war cry. She was letting the assassin know he wouldn't escape her wrath."

King Leofric mumbled some sort of complaint I couldn't make out. "Very well," he told Ronan at last. He turned to me and spoke distinctly, as though I might have trouble understanding orders. "Other than my wife, detain anyone who comes through that passage. Do not kill them. I want to know who, if anyone else, is behind this attack."

I nodded, even though I had no intention of ever letting him know who was behind anything that had happened in the castle recently.

He paused before turning to leave. "You'll say nothing of your position or what's transpired tonight. In fact, you'll never reveal anything you see or learn while on my council. As far as everyone is concerned, you're simply another guest at court, and..." his lips twitched in disapproval, "don't use more war cries. You must act the part of a lady: genteel, mannerly, and gracious." It was clear by his tone he was unsure whether I could accomplish this feat.

I remembered my manners enough to curtsy. "Yes, Your Majesty."

"I'll send men to take Clement's body." He scowled at his brother-in-law, and for several moments, emotion overtook him and he didn't speak. He took a deep breath and forced his attention back to me. "Become invisible and stay that way until they leave. I don't want them to think I'm keeping women in my chambers, especially ones with ripped gowns."

"Yes, Your Majesty." I muttered the incantation for invisibility, glad the spell was second nature to me. My magical energy felt completely depleted.

King Leofric trudged toward the door. He brushed the sleeves of his robe as though he needed to wipe off any remnants of this night.

I waited until the king and Ronan left, then slipped behind the tapestry and became visible again.

CHAPTER 29

The passageway was cold and drafty, untouched by the fires of the king's room. A wizards' orb had hung in the passageway once but it had been smashed. Probably by Lord Clement. Other small orbs were positioned not far away where the passage broke into three corridors. I sat with my shell charm in my lap for light, my back pressed to the door. I didn't want to see the blood on the stone floor. The passageway was dim enough that one wouldn't notice it unless one knew it was there. But my eyes returned to the spots again and again.

"Marcella?"

A beautiful sound—my name whispered on Alaric's lips.

"What are you doing here?" he asked.

I straightened and looked for him in the darkness. "Thank the heavens you found me. I set off the signal accidentally. I was afraid you would die before I could stop you."

"I see." Disappointment laced his words.

"The news is good," I added quickly. "King Leofric promised to abolish the servants' price."

"What? Who did King Leofric make this promise to?"

"Ronan." I couldn't tell Alaric how it had happened or that I was on the king's council. I settled for, "Ronan forced that concession from the king in exchange for keeping him safe."

Silence. I couldn't see Alaric's face in the shadows.

"Why would Ronan do such a thing?"

"Because I asked him to. He wants me to stay at court with him."

More silence. Alaric took off his cloak and appeared before me, one hand on his hip. "You were supposed to take his mark. Instead, you let him talk you into staying at court?"

"I'm not powerful enough to overcome him and found, when it came down to it, that I didn't want to." I glanced over my shoulder at the still closed door. "It isn't safe for you to be visible."

"I have to be visible to have this conversation with you." He sat down beside me, eyes trained on mine. "You've already decided? You're going to stay for Ronan, a wizard?"

I nodded, hating the disapproval in Alaric's eyes. "The king said he would abolish the servants' price. We've more than accomplished our goal in coming here." I nearly added, "We would've all sacrificed much more to accomplish much less." He understood the mathematics of sacrifice, but I couldn't bring myself to say the words. Staying with Ronan didn't feel like a sacrifice.

Alaric frowned. "You believe King Leofric will keep his word? Why would he? Whatever sway Ronan has over Leofric will be short-lived. He'll send Ronan packing for the impertinence of telling him what to do. Lord Clement, on the other hand, has already shown his willingness to lower the servants' price. We should throw our lot in with him."

"That's not possible." Informing Alaric of what happened would break my promise of just minutes ago to King Leofric. My tongue hesitated to do so.

Alaric placed his hand on mine. "It *is* possible. We didn't tell you this before in case something went wrong and you were caught, but Lord Clement has been helping our cause. It was he who told us about the secret passageways. Should he succeed King Leofric, he's already agreed to lower the price in Aerador to five years and eventually abolish it."

A chill went through me. Words halted in my mouth. All I could think was that Ronan had been right. Lord Clement had used the renegades with the aim of seizing power.

Would he have carried through with his promises, or having achieved his goal, would he have turned on the renegades— perhaps blamed them for Leofric's death and used that excuse to hunt them down? I didn't know anything about the man except that he was capable of treachery.

"One ruler has shown his colors already," Alaric went on. "The other made promises under duress. Which do you think is more likely to keep his word?"

"Leofric," I said. "Because Clement is dead." Alaric would no doubt learn of the events tomorrow when the rest of court heard the news. Telling him now wasn't really going against my loyalty to King Leofric. I was, after all, convincing a would-be assassin to abandon his attempts. "Not half an hour since, Clement shot Leofric with an arrow from this very passage-way. It ended up embedded in his own back. I saw him die myself."

Alaric drew back in shock, then cursed and rubbed his forehead.

"King Leofric will keep his word," I said. "Ronan convinced him that abolishing the price would limit his nobles' power and increase his own."

Alaric scoffed. "A wizard *would* think of such a thing." His jaw went tight. "You're actually going to stay with him?"

"He's not like the other wizards. He asked the king to help the servants. Doesn't that tell you something of his nature?"

"It tells me he wants you," Alaric said bitterly. "And apparently you've no qualms with that."

I didn't. I wrapped my arms around myself to keep away the chill. "Ronan has a kind heart and is a good man."

Alaric's gaze went to the rip in my sleeve, then took in the general state of my dress. "What happened to you? Were you injured?"

"Oh." I pulled my sleeve up to hide the tear. "Um, it's nothing. I was just fighting with Ronan."

"A kind heart, you say?"

"I was a wolf and he was a bear."

"A good man?"

"We made up afterward."

Alaric rolled his eyes. He was determined to dislike Ronan.

I dipped my chin. "He brought me here so I could keep you from inflicting death upon yourself."

"And he's no doubt waiting with men at all the entrances of this passageway to arrest me so he can find out the whereabouts of my companions."

"He already knows the whereabouts of our entire party. He could've turned us in for treason but instead created a story about a foreign wizard being to blame for the attacks on the wizards. He agreed to let the rest of you go. You can leave in the morning, if you want. I've asked you to take word to Gwenyth's relatives of her condition so you've an excuse to go."

Alaric put his elbows on his knees and considered this. "I don't want to leave Gwenyth. I'll wait a day or two and see if she's able to travel. The sooner she leaves this place, the better. If she's not able to travel, well, I'll have to go report to Grey and Sutton that Mage Warison discovered our plans. They'll want to move me somewhere else, give me a new identity."

My heart squeezed tight. I'd saved Alaric's life but I was still losing him.

He turned to me, his brown hair shaggy, his eyes resigned. "When I leave, will I ever see you again?"

I shrugged and teared up. For the last few years, Alaric had been my dearest friend. And now he would leave, disappear. He took me in his arms and hugged me. We stayed that way for a while, embracing in the dark corridor. I tried to memorize the feel of his arms, his scent, his voice so it wouldn't be completely lost to me.

Finally, he stood to go.

"Be careful when you return to the stables," I said. "The king's men all went on alert after I took Zephyr's mark."

Alaric nodded and put the cloak back on. Then he was gone.

* * *

I slept through breakfast and might have missed the mid-day meal if Alice hadn't come in to help me dress. By that time, I'd just finished washing off the remaining smudges of dirt that had escaped my notice last night.

"Mage Warison told me not to come this morning," she said, gathering my kirtle and gown. "He said you were up late tending to Gwenyth. How does she fare?"

I wished I knew. "Better than I'd expected." This was true as she hadn't been arrested and executed for treason.

"Well, you've missed such an abundance of news this morning, such happenings, that you'll fear sleeping in again lest you wake up and find the world run by fairies and imps."

Alice dressed me, relating the attack on Zephyr—mage no more—and that Mage Warison had fought and destroyed the foreign wizard responsible for the attacks. This was indeed a heroic tale with the two grappling at one point as lions. It ended with the foreign wizard, near death, avoiding capture and interrogation by uttering a spell that dissolved him like dew on the grass.

"But we can guess right enough who sent him," Alice said as she finished lacing up my gown, "because the most shocking news of all is that last night Lord Clement tried to kill King

Leofric. Can you imagine? His own brother-in-law. He died in the attempt, although no one is saying how that happened."

She brushed my hair, continuing with more details and their accompanying outrage. She only occasionally stopped to pull bits of rubble from my tresses and asked, "La, how in the world did you get pebbles in your hair?"

That either happened when I crawled down the castle wall, knocking off rock flecks as I went, or when I wrestled Ronan on the top of the tower. "I've no idea," I said.

She was too absorbed in her gossip to consider the matter. "Poor Princess Beatrice. She's beside herself. Her husband's attack was an act of war, it was. Though I doubt there'll be any talk of such from King Leofric. He loves his sister, he does. He'll probably offer to send men to help her rule her lands, lest any interlopers see her as weak."

The nice thing about having an overly talkative lady's maid was I didn't have to say anything at all. She didn't notice my silence and probably thought I was too enthralled with her news to speak.

In truth, I didn't want to think about any of it: Lord Clement's bulging eyes or the shocked betrayal in King Leofric's voice. I wished I could see Ronan again, talk to him and have him reassure me everything would be fine. He'd said he wanted me to stay at Valistowe, and I'd agreed to that when I became part of the king's council.

Now, sitting in front of a looking glass, I'd no idea what to expect next. What would I be doing each day and where exactly would I live?

Would Ronan announce that I was staying on because he was courting me? If he wanted a respectable relationship, he would need to make his intentions public, despite his desire for secrecy. The thought of strolling with him every night through the castle gardens seemed like a prize.

Alice finished with my plaits and began tying them in place

with ribbons. "At breakfast, Wolfson insisted the attack on Zephyr proved he was innocent of taking any of the wizards' marks, but the other mages are having none of it. They said Wolfson was likely working with Lord Clement. Little good his innocence will do him at this point anyway. His magic is gone, he can't teach at Docendum, and he's been banished from court. Such a topple in fortunes. Who knows what he'll do now? Might have to learn how to push a plow. At least Zephyr will be allowed to stay on at the castle as an advisor, even though he hasn't a lick of magic anymore."

I did feel a bit sorry for Zephyr, although I hoped a humbler position might be good for his disposition. I couldn't feel sorry for Wolfson. I wondered where he'd go for work and imagined what would transpire if, unprotected as he was now, he ever happened on any of the Colsbury villagers who knew of his order to burn their village.

After Alice finished with me, I stopped by Lady Edith's chambers to accompany her to the meal. I needed to tell her that Alaric would be leaving soon.

Joanne was pinning Lady Edith's headdress in place. Lady Edith surveyed me through the looking glass with the same air of tolerant disapproval she'd frequently worn during our stay at court and made a tutting sound with her tongue. "Another night, another uproar, another wizard incapacitated."

I cleared my throat. "I hear Mage Warison defeated the foreign wizard and no other wizards are now in danger."

She arched a doubtful eyebrow at me. "And do you believe that to be true?"

"I do, ma'am."

She hmphed, still unhappy. "Lord Clement is dead. Supposedly in an assassination attempt." Her tone implied she believed I may have been wielding the implement of his death shortly beforehand.

I whispered, "I'd nothing to do with that." Perhaps in the

details, this wasn't accurate. My joining the wizard council prevented King Leofric's death and caused Clement's.

Lady Edith swiveled in her seat and lowered her voice. "When I agreed to take you to court, I assumed flirting, coquettish behavior, and a good deal of spying would transpire." Her hand fluttered upward. "Perhaps even a small theft or two. But I'd no idea blood would be rolling through the hallways. It's become positively harrowing to wake up each morning and find out who else met their demise during the night. Are the lot of you trying to see us all hanged?"

I stared guiltily at my hands. We'd involved her in far too much danger. "I'm sorry, ma'am."

"As you should be. Tell whoever is in charge of this assignment that as compensation, I expect repairs to Paxworth's kitchen to be done forthwith."

My head snapped up. "What?" That's what concerned her? Greater compensation?

"It's not too much to ask." She sniffed and turned around to face the mirror again. "I'm sure I won't have a peaceful night's rest for weeks. Such commotion. Wizards and lords keeling over left and right."

Joanne said nothing during all of this. She never had an opinion about Lady Edith's affairs unless asked to produce one.

Despite Lady Edith's complete lack of motherly affection, I would miss her. She had such firm practicality mixed with her prim propriety. "You'll have to send your request through Alaric," I said. "I appreciate all you've done for me, but I won't be returning to Paxworth with you."

She dabbed at a piece of hair that was trying to escape her headdress. "Yes, I'd heard that congratulations were in order."

"Congratulations?"

"Lady Petronia, the queen's head lady-in-waiting, came to my room earlier to tell me that her highness has chosen you to be one of her attendants."

"Oh." This must be the solution to keep me close by. I hadn't the background or breeding to be chosen on my own merits. To be a queen's attendant was an honor. I shouldn't immediately worry I'd be stuck all day with a pampered monarch, deferring to her every whim. But I'd led a life of independence for the last two years, and the thought of losing that freedom made my chest feel uncomfortably tight.

I was not one to simper. Fawning was also not my forte. The queen would expect both.

Had Ronan gotten me the position because he didn't want to let people know he loved me? Perhaps he was having second thoughts on the matter himself. We'd professed our feelings to each other after combat and with the fear of death still coloring our words. In the calm light of morning among court ladies who were swishing around their silks, brocades, and doweries, my coarseness, poverty, and life of crime must be far less appealing.

He might regret accepting the kisses I'd showered on him last night.

I wanted to go to Ronan right then and ask him what he planned for us, but I knew I wouldn't find him. If he wasn't still busy with the king's advisors or wizards, he'd be catching up on the sleep he lost last night.

"Didn't you know about your appointment?" Lady Edith asked.

I shrugged vaguely. "Mage Warison mentioned something about me staying."

"Mage Warison? When did you talk to him?"

"Last night after supper." It was true that we talked then, though that conversation seemed to have happened ages ago.

"It's peculiar that one of the king's wizards would know the queen's appointments. Although I suppose he had his reasons." She waved off Joanne's attempts to straighten her veil, stood, and swept over to me. She gave me a long, knowing look. "Wizards are men of the world. Insist on an official engagement before you so much as let him kiss you. Otherwise, you may easily find yourself ruined. You're pretty, my dear, but not wealthy enough to tempt him into marriage."

 Her expression softened with something close to care. "I wasn't born with the Thornton name, but I've become attached to it and would rather you didn't sully it. The last thing I want is for you to show up at Paxworth with your life in shambles and a reputation that's preceded you." She lifted a finger reconsidering. "Well, perhaps not the *last* thing. Don't go and get yourself hanged, either."

I nodded obediently. She hadn't said she would turn me away if my life were in shambles, which I found touching. "I'll do my utmost to uphold the honor of your name." She would be shocked to know I'd already kissed Ronan. Excessively. Still, she was right that I needed to be careful of my reputation at court.

Lady Edith glided past me. "You'd best enquire with Lady Petronia to see if there's anything the queen requires of you today."

I bade Lady Edith goodbye and made my way to the stairs to go to Queen Marita's chambers. The guard there stopped me, asked my business, and escorted me to the queen's chamberlain.

"That doesn't seem likely," the man said when the guard told him why I wanted to see Lady Petronia. "The queen hasn't chosen her new attendants yet."

"Perhaps there's been some confusion," I said. "I didn't speak to Lady Petronia. Only my aunt, Lady Edith of Paxworth, did."

The chamberlain frowned at me like I was trying to sneak uninvited into the queen's rooms, which was ironic because I'd already sneaked uninvited into the queen's rooms. I'd better methods than this.

"Paxworth?" he said as though the word tasted of dirt. "I've never heard of that holding."

I wasn't sure how he wanted me to respond to that. *Well then, you're not as knowledgeable as you suppose.* Or, *I'll try to be from a more illustrious place next time I require your attention.*

I remembered that Ronan had assured the king I could be polite and said, "Paxworth is a lovely place. If you ever travel to the western part of the country, you should visit."

He regarded me again with an unspoken sigh hovering on his lips. "I'll check with Lady Petronia." He left me there with the guard to wait for his verdict.

After twenty minutes, the chamberlain came back looking less pleased than before. "I'll show you to her."

I'd assumed he meant Lady Petronia. Instead, he took me to the queen's receiving room. Queen Marita sat on her throne, bereft of any other attendants.

I curtsied. Queen Marita stared imperiously at me until the chamberlain left. Then she slipped from her throne and stalked toward me, continuing to stare at me like I was an intruder.

"Perhaps there's been a mistake," I said. "Lady Edith told me you'd chosen me for an attendant."

Queen Marita folded her arms. Haughty. Displeased. "I didn't choose you."

Well, this had suddenly become exceedingly awkward. Still, part of me laughed at Lady Edith's sending me here to look the fool in front of the queen. It meant my adoptive mother had a keen, hereto-unknown sense of revenge. *That* would teach me to kill off too many people during her next trip to court. The queen must think me proud beyond my station to assume such an honor. I bowed my head. "I beg your pardon. There must've been a mis—"

"My *husband* chose you," Queen Marita barked, her words an indictment. "Why did he choose you?"

Even worse. Queen Marita feared I was carrying on a dalliance with her new husband. My eyes snapped to hers and my mouth dropped open. Apparently, the king was keeping my position a secret even from his wife and hadn't considered how his request would appear to her.

"I assume," I stuttered, "he chose me on Ronan's behalf. I mean, Mage Warison. We are…" I didn't know how much to say about that either. I was second-guessing Ronan's intentions, and besides, he'd said wizards kept their relationships guarded. "Mage Warison hoped I would stay longer at court." That much was safe to say, wasn't it? I felt myself blushing hotly.

"Mage Warison?" Queen Marita's scowl vanished. "The one who saved Leofric's life?"

"Yes, Your Majesty."

She smiled and clucked her tongue. "Ah. That explains why my husband was eager to grant him favors. Leofric really should have told me so." She waved a hand to stop further explanation on my part. "I understand mages in your country are coy about such matters. A strange custom. In my country, mages marry and have children like everyone else."

"They do?" I was truly surprised. "They don't worry about someone threatening to harm their families in order to manipulate them?"

"Wizards are powerful men. Only fools would hurt their families."

"Or other wizards."

She nodded. "Yes, the wizards in your country fight with each other. I've seen this. It is not so much that way in my country."

It wasn't? For perhaps the first time, it occurred to me that relations among wizards could change, that their structure wasn't carved in stone any more than the servants' was. Perhaps someday they might even come to accept having a woman among their ranks. And if not, well, now that I would have access to the king's store of magical books, who was to say I couldn't someday give a mark to another woman and create companions that way?

"Odeway sounds lovely," I said. "I wish we lived in your country."

A dimple puckered Queen Marita's cheek. "You must be very much in love with Mage Warison to wish to be somewhere besides Aerador."

I blushed again. "Either that or I've heard how stunning the mountain ranges in your country are."

She tilted her head and laughed. She looked pretty that way, laughing and relaxed. "Yes, I remember your wit. Now I'll be glad my husband chose you. I'll be glad for Mage Warison." She leaned toward me confidentially. "He is a handsome one. It would be such…how do you say… a travesty if he didn't make some woman happy."

"A travesty," I agreed.

"And you, an orphan from a poor holding…" She clasped her hands together. "It's like a story of the winged women."

Winged women? What in heavens did they do with orphans in Odeway?

The queen looked upward, thinking. "No, not winged women. How do you say? Ah, I remember. Fairy tales."

"Oh," I said. "Yes, our story is like a fairy tale." One where the hero and heroine nearly killed each other.

"You mustn't mind my fancies." She fluttered her hand. "I love to read the stories of romance and adventure. Leofric says I may have my own library here."

And yet another reason to like the queen. "I would be happy to help procure books. I know of many good ones."

She brightened. "Yes, you must do this."

I decided then that I wouldn't mind being Marita's lady-in-waiting after all.

CHAPTER 30

I went to visit Gwenyth next. She was splayed out straight like a doll, her legs wrapped in linen bandages. The doctor had just finished changing them and was standing to leave. "She's recovering nicely," he told me. "Mage Warison came by this morning with some salve to help keep infection at bay."

"Mage Warison was here?" Did the man never sleep? "I'll have to thank him."

The doctor left, and I shut the door so I could talk to Gwenyth privately.

"I imagine," Gwenyth said dryly, "that you've already thanked Mage Warison enough." Her tone made it clear she was aware of my decision to stay at Valistowe.

I pulled a chair over to her pallet, took out my knitting, and repeated the spell Ronan had used when he muffled our conversation. "What have you already heard?"

"Everything. Alaric came by earlier to see when I'll be able to travel. The doctor says not until two weeks at the earliest. Then I can go a short distance if I'm laying down and well padded. Alaric is going to procure a wagon and blankets."

"Did he tell you that King Leofric agreed to abolish the servants' price?"

"Yes, and I'll believe it's the truth when I hear those words come from his mouth and see the sweet sight of his noblemen bursting into tears."

"I'd no idea you were so peevish when you were cross."

She grunted and finally turned her gaze to mine. "When we first came to court, I worried your knowledge of magic would be insufficient to complete your task. I worried wizards might find and kill you. I never worried one would woo you to his side. Clearly, my anxiety was misplaced." She let out a long unenthusiastic sigh. "And yet I will grudgingly admit that for a wizard, Warison isn't horrible. Perhaps he's a decent fellow beneath his charm and power."

"High praise."

"I've no idea what Grey and Sutton will say of all of this."

"If it isn't 'Thank you', I don't want to know. We achieved the aim of the mission even if we didn't do it the way they imagined."

"We don't know that it's achieved," she muttered, "and now the man who championed our cause is dead." She didn't add, "All because you couldn't bring yourself to take Ronan's mark," but the implication was there.

"King Leofric will abolish the servants' price," I said, though I was growing less confident of this fact under the harsh glare of Alaric and Gwenyth's skepticism. What power did I have to hold a king to his word if he changed his mind?

Gwenyth and I talked for a bit longer. She reluctantly forgave me for being in love with Ronan and for my misplaced faith in Leofric. "I hope you're right," she said. "Hope is all the lot of us have left now."

I wished I'd pinned down King Leofric as to when he would implement his new law. What was to say he wouldn't wait for ten years?

After I left Gwenyth, I wandered around the castle in hopes I'd run into Ronan.

There was no sign of him.

Earlier when I'd talked with Queen Marita, she told me I should spend as much time with Lady Edith as I could before she returned to Paxworth, so I was back at my old table that night at supper. No one asked where I'd been all day.

Lady Edith informed them of my appointment and they gave me hearty congratulations. Madame Godfrey even smiled at me with approval and, I thought, design. Perhaps she had put me back in the running for her son's attention.

The talk turned to the events of last night and what they meant for the country's future with Marseden. Lord Percy said that King Leofric had been meeting with his advisors all day. He wasn't in the dining hall. The entire dais sat empty.

Agnes was sure King Regnault of Marseden would consider his grandson's death an act of war and invade us shortly. Her mother was equally sure we would invade Marseden as that country must be behind Lord Clement's treachery. We discussed whether Princess Beatrice would be able to retain her Marseden holdings in her child's name and if King Leofric should help her protect those lands from any attempt on King Regnault's part to strip them from her. Each person had an opinion of the response Aerador should use in the wake of the assassination attempt.

Such were the matters of importance decided at our table.

Toward the end of the meal, King Leofric, Ronan, and several of his advisors strode into the room. A mage I didn't recognize followed the group. Everyone stood and bowed, staying that way until King Leofric took his place on the dais and bade us sit. He looked as though he hadn't slept all night. Ronan appeared equally tired. He took the seat on the dais reserved for the king's senior wizard. The other mage sat next to him. The other three chairs for the wizard council sat woefully empty.

Ronan's gaze went to the back of the room and found me. I smiled. He returned the gesture but his expression was far too solemn to be encouraging.

King Leofric started a speech, reporting what had transpired the night before. I wondered if he thought anyone in the room still ignorant of the facts. He announced that Mage Apricus had joined the wizard council. Other appointments would follow. He reassured everyone that even though troubling events had plagued the castle this week, the security and prosperity of the country were assured. He went on to classify the country's many strengths and assets.

I stopped paying attention during that part. Nothing is so dull as a list of the country's virtues. My attention, however, sprang back when the king began speaking about the servants.

"I'm sure you're all aware of the other problem we have with Marseden. Many in our servant class are migrating unlawfully to Marseden as that country has a more lenient price for their indentureship. Some have suggested the answer to our labor shortage is to increase the servants' price by another year, but we've seen the results of this ill-thought-out policy. They'll leave all the faster. And should Marseden ever go to war with us, they'll have three times the foot soldiers we can muster.

"The custom of indentured servitude, therefore, puts our country in danger. We've seen this week that we're not as safe as we suppose, that outside powers dare to strike at the very heart of our country. I'm afraid I can no longer support the policy of indentureship. I'm passing a law that will take effect three months hence which abolishes the practice."

I wasn't sure what I expected the king to say about his new law. I'd known he wouldn't admit to making a bargain with an invisible mage to save his life, but still, I was impressed how he made the policy sound like he'd deliberated about it for some time and had come to the conclusion on his own.

I wished Gwenyth and Alaric could've been in the room to hear it. The nobles didn't, as Gwenyth predicted, burst into tears. Shocked expressions, yes. Exclamations of disapproval, yes. Outright glares of hostility, absolutely. But no tears. I sat smiling, glad my faith in King Leofric hadn't been in vain.

The king held out a hand to stop the ever-loudening grumbling. "I'm assuming you'd rather have paid servants than none at all because they've fled to Marseden."

Someone yelled, "Post more soldiers at the borders to keep them from leaving!"

The king glowered at the man. "You're insisting you can't do without your servants, but you expect me to do without my armies so that more can be posted at the border? Think of what you ask. Marseden would see large armies at their borders as an act of aggression. And if my armies were stretched across the border they'd be easily breached during an invasion." He shook his head. "I'll continue to meet with my advisers and hear your concerns on the issue, but I'm convinced this is the right path. I'll leave you to finish your meal."

The marshal stood and led the call, "The king has spoken! Long live the king!"

The nobles repeated the chant less enthusiastically.

I spoke loudly. On the dais, Ronan's eyes met mine and his smile seemed more genuine this time.

After the king left, people finished their meals quickly. Some nearly stormed out. Other noblemen withdrew in groups, talking in lowered voices.

I made my way toward the front of the room, weaving around clusters of people. Ronan might be too busy to talk to me now, but at least we could arrange a time to meet later.

Floris and another young noblewoman stepped into my

path, a brunette who for some reason had entirely done away with her eyebrows. Their absence caused me to stare, despite knowing it was ill-mannered.

"Lady Marcella," Floris said, all forced smiles. "A rumor is floating about, though I can't see how it could be true." She took a moment to regard my dress in a way that made it obvious she found it lacking. "A rumor that you're to be one of the queen's attendants. I keep telling people that the queen hasn't yet chosen those appointments. Have you any idea how such gossip started?"

"I try to avoid gossip," I said, "so I've no idea how any of it starts."

The brunette would've raised her eyebrows smugly if she'd had any. Floris drew herself up in satisfaction. "I knew it wasn't true."

I tried for patience. "I didn't say it wasn't true. I just said I'd no idea how the news spread."

Both women gaped at me. "The queen chose you?" the brunette sputtered. "Before she even finished interviewing all the ladies at court? She hasn't even met the most qualified women. I've yet to meet her."

I wanted to say, "Alas, eyebrows were a requirement," but for the second time that day, I remembered King Leofric's injunction to be polite. "I'm sure your time with her will come."

I didn't notice Ronan making his way toward us until Floris turned to greet him. "Mage Warison, all the castle sings your praises today." She looped her arm through his. "I've heard a dozen versions of how you bested the rogue wizard and insist on hearing the tale from your own mouth." Her gaze went to his lips and she licked her own. The tale was not all she wanted from his mouth.

I'd no idea how to react. What was the appropriate genteel response when a woman had her arm entwined with the man who—if he would admit it—was supposedly courting me?

Restraint was probably called for, discretion of some sort. I crossed my arms and glared at Floris.

The brunette noticed my reaction and shook her head pityingly.

"I must defer until another time," Ronan told Floris with all decorum. "I've matters to discuss with Lady Marcella."

"Surely, any matters with her can wait." Floris pouted, pink lips pursed. "My curiosity is most urgent."

Would it be impolite to rip her hand off Ronan? Probably.

Ronan gave Floris a slight bow. "I'm afraid I must disappoint your curiosity." He lowered his arm to remove Floris's grasp, stepped over to me, and offered his arm to me. "Lady Marcella."

I took his arm with perhaps too much self-satisfaction and let him lead me from the room. When we were down the hallway, Ronan flicked his wand and said the muffling incantation so we could speak in private, despite the presence of others coming and going.

"I refrained from turning Floris into a toad," I said. "I think I should be commended for that."

"I'd commend you if you actually had the ability to turn her into a toad."

"I'm working on animal transformations. One never knows when the capability will appear."

He headed toward the front entrance. "You're far too kind for that sort of prank. And besides, I turned none of the men who paid you attention into toads."

"I would let you turn a few into toads."

Ronan laughed and shook his head. "You trust me to resist Floris's charms, don't you?"

"I suppose."

"Good, because I've other matters to discuss with you. The king asked my opinion on whom he should appoint as the new headmaster at Docendum. Your time there with wizards has given you insights that others might not see, so I'd like your opinion as well. I've several I'm considering and—"

"Mage Bodkin." I'd liked him since I'd heard him joking with the other wizards during the king's inquest.

"Mage Bodkin?" Ronan's tone said the man wasn't on his list of possible candidates. "He's qualified, I suppose, but not among the most powerful or knowledgeable of wizards."

"And not among the most cunning or ambitious either. Let the apprentices have a man who'll teach them decency first and magic second. Let them have someone who'll make them laugh more and compete less. Perhaps then our country will be like Odeway where the wizards don't fight one another."

We walked for a bit in silence while Ronan contemplated my words. "How did you become acquainted with Mage Bodkin?"

"I'm not acquainted with him. I spied on the king's wizard meeting and found him refreshingly unlike the rest of you."

"I'll ignore the implicit insult in that assessment, as well as your confession of a crime, and add Mage Bodkin to my suggestions for the king. He's a good fellow and perhaps that's what the apprentices need."

We went out the front entrance and Ronan led me along the road that carriages took when dropping visitors off.

"Now I'm curious," Ronan said. "What would your suggestions be for new members of the wizards' council?"

"Stewart," I said.

"Stewart?" he repeated as though he had no idea who I meant. He shook his head, "I've too little sleep. What's his mage name?"

How would I know that? "He was a few years your elder at Docendum. When we were children, Wolfson did something to his horse. You recall it disappeared. Stewart must have refused to bend to whatever horrible thing Wolfson was attempting to force him to do."

"Ah, yes. Stewart goes by Mage Vincere now. I'll consider

him. He hasn't much experience, but I suppose experience can be gained more easily than character."

Instead of heading around the castle toward the gardens, Ronan guided me further along the road. "Where are we going?" I asked.

"To the stables."

I slowed my pace, suddenly wary. "Why?"

"Because I know Alaric won't speak to me without you there and I require his help."

"Why?" What sort of help could a wizard need from Alaric?

"Ah, Marcella," Ronan said, shaking his head, "did you never calculate the consequences of your revolution before you put it in motion? Next time, you should be more careful before you force a king to enact your policies."

"I...what consequences do you speak of?"

He sighed. "We must prepare for battle now."

My hand went to my throat and my mind to the conversation at dinner. "Will we have war with Marseden?"

"With Marseden? We've no way to know that yet. King Regnault may have been involved in Lord Clement's plot, and with that plan thwarted, he may take other measures to seize power in Aerador. Or he may be horrified to learn of his grandson's treachery. Time and spying will tell. Neither monarch is the type to easily or recklessly dispatch armies."

"Then why prepare for battle?" I had been trying to avoid that from the start. "And what does any of it have to do with Alaric?"

"I need Alaric's help to prevent treason."

It wasn't an answer, but we were close enough to the stables that the stable master had come out to see what we wanted. Ronan dispensed with the muffling spell and told him to have Alaric bring out two of Lady Edith's horses. "Lady Marcella is contemplating keeping one with her in Valistowe, and I want to see the condition of the animals. Have him bring them to the field behind the stables. We'll wait there."

A few minutes later, Ronan and I stood in the field, and Alaric arrived towing two mares. He eyed Ronan suspiciously. "The horses you requested, my lord."

I wanted to rush over to Alaric, grab his hands, and tell him the king's announcement, but anyone watching would find such a thing notable. I kept my place beside Ronan, chin lifted like an indifferent highborn woman, but my voice betrayed my emotion. "Have you heard the news about the servants' price?"

"I did." Alaric still eyed Ronan. "I imagine the servants' quarters will be full of celebration tonight."

Ronan nodded. "And the noblemen's chambers, full of sedition. That's why I've come to talk to you."

Alaric dropped the horses' ropes, allowing them to graze while we talked. "What have I to do with noblemen's matters, my lord?" Alaric didn't quite pull off the guise of an obedient groomsman. His gaze on Ronan was too solid, his stance too straight.

Ronan pulled his wand slowly from his pocket. "I'm casting a muffling spell so we can speak privately, nothing more." His words were low, his flick of the wand almost imperceptible.

He slid his wand back into his pocket. "I'm assuming the renegades have sympathizers in castles throughout the land, and you have methods of contacting them. King Leofric needs eyes and ears in those places. Some of his barons may band together and revolt. If King Leofric is forewarned a rebellion is brewing, he'll be able to arrest the leaders and commandeer their lands—a potent deterrent for any other barons who may consider the same course of action."

Alaric didn't respond. He was perhaps debating whether Ronan's words were a trap.

"Do you really think it will come to that?" I asked Ronan.

"Certainly, raising and outfitting an army is more expensive for the barons than paying their servants for their service."

Both men stared at me as though I'd asked if the sky was, in fact, green.

"Some men," Ronan explained, "look for any excuse to seize power."

"Some men," Alaric added, "would rather fight a war than be forced to loosen their purse strings and do a kind turn for their servants."

Ronan returned his attention to Alaric. "Marcella assured King Leofric that if he abolished indentureship, he'd have the servant class' support. Did she misspeak in that regard?"

"No," Alaric said. "It's safe to say the lowborn will support him."

"Then the renegades will help us?"

"I've no knowledge of them," Alaric said, "and can speak only for myself, my lord."

Ronan sighed. "Yes, yes, you're only a simple groomsman and have no way to reach a single renegade. I understand. On the morrow, I'll send you to Paxworth to fetch any belongings Lady Marcella requires. Speak to whomever you must during the errand and get back to me with your leaders' answer. We'll need to set up ways to relay information."

Alaric gave a curt nod. "I'll leave then, my lord." He jerked his thumb in the horses' direction. "Will Lady Marcella be keeping one of these horses at court?"

"Heavens, no," I said. "Lady Edith would skin me alive if I took any of her horses."

"That she would." Alaric gathered the horses' reins and took leave of us. I was heartened to see there wasn't quite as much dislike in his eyes for Ronan as there had been at the beginning of the conversation.

How strange it was that two people could start the week

enemies and end it as wary allies. They would end up being allies, I was sure, even if the two never liked each other.

* * *

AFTER THAT, Ronan and I wandered into the maze in the garden to speak privately. "Are you certain you wouldn't rather go inside to sleep for a bit?" I asked. I was trying to be unselfish and think of his comfort.

He took my hand and smiled. "I'm quite certain I would rather be with you."

His smile was reassuring, as was the feel of his hand around mine. He hadn't changed his mind about the two of us.

"Good," I said, "then we can discuss my place at court."

"Did you not hear you're to be one of the queen's attendants?"

I cocked my head at him. He'd known, probably discussed with King Leofric about giving me that position. "Yes, I spoke to the queen. Did it not occur to either of you what she would assume when the king specifically requested me?"

Ronan looked at me without any understanding. "Did she think you unqualified?"

"No, she thought her husband enamored with me."

Ronan drew to a stop. "Oh, no. We must set that to rights at once."

I tugged at his hand, pulling him forward again. "I already did. I told her you were the one smitten with me. If you were trying to keep your attentions a secret, we'll have to rely on her discretion."

"If I were trying to keep my attentions a secret, I've made a poor start. We've gone strolling about this evening and last. Lady Somerton will no doubt share her opinion about that with everyone she knows." His eyebrows knit together. "It's hard to unlearn some of Wolfson's lessons. All my practical sensibilities tell me it's safest for you if no one knows the extent of my feelings, and yet…" He let out a long breath. "My desire to be with you openly seems to outweigh all else." His footsteps slowed to a stop again, and he turned to better see my expression. "Would you encourage me to be practical or not?"

I shrugged and smiled. "I've never been the practical sort. Your sensibilities will get no help from that quarter."

He nodded, still debating the matter. "I also dislike the idea of any of the lords or knights supposing you unattached and trying to win your affections."

"Lord Percy is quite attentive."

"Lord Percy would make an admirable toad."

I laughed and squeezed his hand. "We'll let others know we're courting. You needn't fear anyone will threaten my safety as a way to influence you. I can defend myself."

His eyebrow quirked up. "You've not practiced as much as the other mages. You are a novice among experts."

"And yet I held my own against the best of the king's wizards."

"While they slept."

"I was talking about you."

"I must see to it that you practice more. The next wizard you battle might not be in love with you."

My heart lifted. He loved me. I would never grow weary of hearing him say those words. "I will happily practice because I don't want you to worry." And because I knew he would teach me.

"Such sacrifices you'll make for me?" He laughed, his eyes bright as a sunny day. "Good. We'll start with transformation. If you've the power to change into a tree, you've the power to manage more animal forms than a wolf."

"You want to practice right now?" I'd thought we'd come to this secluded spot for other reasons.

"I've something for you to see on top of the wizards' tower, but you'll need to transform into a bird to reach it."

"Or I could use the stairs. You did say there was a trapdoor there, didn't you?"

"The door is underneath barrels which makes it unusable unless we fly to the tower first and move them." He rubbed his hands together, ready to proceed with my first lesson. "Do you recall the enchantment to change into a falcon?"

"Yes, but it's never worked before."

"You said you needed a strong emotion to perform these sorts of spells." He put his hands on my shoulders and drew me closer. "Let that emotion be happiness. Let it give you wings."

Ah, poetry. So chivalrous. He lowered his head and kissed me, which was a mistake if he wanted me to transform into a bird. I wrapped my arms around him, glad to be human. The kiss was as familiar and tender as the ones we shared at Docendum, but better. It came with a future attached to it.

He pulled away and murmured, "Say the spell."

I did, not believing for a moment it would work. An odd sensation came over me, I was shrinking. My arms flung out at my sides as though blown that way by a gale. I cried out in surprise and the sound was a screech.

Still, I doubted I'd made the spell work. More likely, Ronan had transformed me.

With a flap of my wings, I shot upward, leaving the hedges and trees of the garden behind. Flying wasn't effortless. My arms felt the strain of each wingbeat. But it was glorious, taking to the sky. Instead of heading directly to the tower, I circled the courtyard, testing the air. Up high, I could glide, sailing on the current in larger and larger loops. The wind rushing by felt like a caress.

Another falcon tailed me, swooping to one side and then another. Ronan, of course. Probably herding me toward the tower. I wondered if he ever turned into a bird and flew just for the pure joy of it. Finally, I sailed over the crenelations and perched on the edge of one of the barrels.

Ronan glided past me. He transformed into human before landing on the ground, effortlessly transitioning to his legs.

I repeated the incantation to change back. Nothing happened. Ronan strolled over to me. "Are you trying to transform and can't or did you enjoy being a bird so much you're hoping I won't make you give it up quite yet?"

I ruffled my feathers and squawked.

"Very well," he said. "I'll help you. Transforming, like all else, takes practice."

I became myself again, now standing precariously on the barrel. I put my hands on his shoulders. He encircled my waist and set me on the floor.

"Becoming a falcon was your doing," I said, "not mine."

"That's part of practicing. But now that you know how to be a bird, you'll find it easier to become one again. I wager that soon when you say the spell, the transformation works."

He must have seen the eagerness in my eyes because he added, "Don't try it presently. I've something to show you and if you take to the sky again, who knows how long you'll be up there soaring around."

He towed me to the middle of the floor where a small table and two stools waited. Five tiny scrolls lay in the middle of the table.

"What's this?" I asked.

He swept his hand toward the closest stool. "Look at them and see."

I took my place on the stool and picked up one of the scrolls. "Is this more practice? Are these enchantments I'm to perform?" I unwrapped the scroll. The word Amaranth was written in Ronan's hand.

I stared at him in question.

"Do you know what it means?" he asked.

"No."

"Are you sure? I can't help you. That's part of the rules."

"What rules?" I was already searching books for the word. A few, very conveniently, had glossaries of terms.

"The mage rules," Ronan said.

I located the word's definition. "Amaranth is a flower that never fades."

"Correct. Read the other scrolls."

Was it a list of items needed for some spell? I'd no idea where to find an Amaranth. The glossaries didn't tell locations.

The next word was Lucerna. I knew the meaning of that one: light. I unrolled Flagrantitelum, Astrid, and Magasclades. Some checking of glossaries turned up the definition 'passionate weapon' for the first and 'beautiful and loved' for the second. I couldn't find a definition for Magasclades.

I laid the parchments in front of me and cocked my head. "My first lesson as a mage is a vocabulary test?"

"This isn't a lesson. It's the ceremony where you choose your mage name."

My eyes flew to his, remembering what he'd told me. A mage's teachers presented him with five possibilities. Two represented his charitable qualities, two his cunning ones, and one name was a nonsense word thrown in to test his knowledge of wizarding vocabulary.

I smoothed out the word Magasclades. "This must be one of my negative qualities. Does it mean 'she who holds grudges'?"

He laughed. "I can't tell you until after you choose."

It took me several long minutes to dredge through texts to find that the word meant mage toppler.

I turned it over. "That's something I'd rather forget." I flipped over Flagrantitelum. "Nor will I call myself a passionate weapon."

I regarded the other words. "Which describes my charitable qualities, and which is the nonsense word?"

"I confess I didn't throw in a nonsense word. I had too many compliments I wanted to give you. I nearly put in EnteAmari as well." He leaned forward confidentially. "If EnteAmari is your favorite, we can pretend I wrote that one instead of one of the others."

She for whom the sun rises. I beamed and returned to the parchments. "I can't imagine calling myself Mage EnteAmari. I like the meaning of Astrid best: beautiful and loved, but I like the sound of Amaranth better."

"Then be Mage Amaranth," he said, "Because you need no name to prove you are beautiful and loved. I will tell you so every day."

I left my seat, came round to his side of the table, and sat on his lap. "And I'll tell you that I love you every day as well. I'll tell you—"

Instead of letting me tell him anything more, he kissed me. But then, words weren't always necessary for such declarations. With my lips pressed to his, I made my feelings clear enough.

* * *

NOTE FROM JANETTE

I hope you enjoyed the book! Is it too soon to ~~beg~~ ask you for a review? Yes? No? (I don't want to be one of those needy authors.) But I would really appreciate two sentences on Amazon (or more if you're one of those people who always went above and beyond in your English classes.) Authors love you. Consider it your good deed for the day.

REVIEW THE WIZARD'S Mark here Pretty please leave a review. This link should take you there. (No promises. Technology hates me.)

And if you want to be in the know about all my new releases, sales, and occasionally weigh in on my cover choices, sign up for my newsletter. You'll get a free copy of my novel *Fame, Glory, and Other Things On My To-do List.*

CLICK HERE TO SIGN UP FOR NEWSLETTER

Also, if you enjoyed this book, check out my other titles. And if you didn't enjoy this book, um, still check out the other books because they'll probably be better...

Janette

OTHER TITLES BY JANETTE RALLISON/CJ HILL

My Unfair Godmother

My Fairly Dangerous Godmother

All's Fair in Love, War, and High School

Blue Eyes and Other Teenage Hazards

Revenge of the Cheerleaders

Fame, Glory, and Other Things on my To Do List

It's a Mall World After All

How to Take The Ex Out of Ex-boyfriend

Slayers (under pen name CJ Hill)

Slayers: Friends and Traitors (under pen name CJ Hill)

Slayers: Playing With Fire (under pen name CJ Hill)

Slayers: The Dragon Lords (under pen name CJ Hill)

Slayers: Into the Firestorm (under pen name CJ Hill)

Slayers: The Making of a Mentor: A Tor.Com Original (under pen name CJ Hill)

Erasing Time (under pen name CJ Hill)

Echo in Time (under pen name CJ Hill)

If you like audiobooks, try:

Just One Wish audiobook

My Fairly Dangerous Godmother audiobook

How I Met Your Brother audiobook

Erasing Time audiobook (under pen name CJ Hill)

Echo in Time audiobook (under pen name CJ Hill)

Masquerade audiobook

What the Doctor Ordered audiobook

My Double Life audiobook

Her Ex-crush Bodyguard audiobook

Covertly Yours audiobook (novella)

<u>An Unexpected Boyfriend for Christmas</u>

The Cowboy and the Girl Next Door

To Listen to Janette's audiobooks for free, subscribe to her audiobook channel on YouTube here:
https://www.youtube.com/channel/UCh0_trjYz3T_Hd72bM0qk_Q

Manufactured by Amazon.ca
Acheson, AB

14546250R00208